"ARE YOU REALLY FROM THE FUTURE . . ."

. . . Simon asked, "or simply some exotic land? If Jacques accidentally snatched you from the other end of the Silk Road, you can make the journey back."

"I am not from China, or Cathay, or whatever you want to call it," Diane replied. "I was born and raised in the United States, in Seattle. In the twentieth century. You don't believe me do you?"

Simon glared at her, as if this was all her fault. "But you still belong somewhere," he persisted.

"Not in China." She paused. "Maybe not back in Seattle, even if I could get there." She had changed so much since meeting Simon. Her old life meant nothing to her.

He gave her one of those faint smiles that always melted her defensiveness. "You're going to try to tell me that you belong with me."

"I don't have to tell you. You already know we belong together."

He gave her a sharp shake of his head. It simply could not be.

Books by Susan Sizemore

Published by HarperPaperbacks

The Autumn Lord

 Susan Sizemore

HarperPaperbacks
A Division of HarperCollinsPublishers

HarperPaperbacks
A Division of HarperCollins*Publishers*
10 East 53rd Street, New York, N.Y. 10022-5299

If you purchased this book without a cover, you should be aware
that this book is stolen property. It was reported as "unsold and
destroyed" to the publisher and neither the author nor the
publisher has received any payment for this "stripped book."

This is a work of fiction. The characters, incidents, and
dialogues are products of the author's imagination and are not to
be construed as real. Any resemblance to actual events or
persons, living or dead, is entirely coincidental.

Copyright © 1996 by Susan Sizemore
All rights reserved. No part of this book may be used or
reproduced in any manner whatsoever without written
permission of the publisher, except in the case of brief
quotations embodied in critical articles and reviews.
For information address HarperCollins*Publishers,*
10 East 53rd Street, New York, N.Y. 10022-5299.

ISBN 0-06-108208-2

HarperCollins®, ®, HarperPaperbacks™, and
HarperMonogram® are trademarks of HarperCollins*Publishers,* Inc.

Cover illustration by Jon Paul

First HarperPaperbacks printing: December 1996

Printed in the United States of America

Visit HarperPaperbacks on the World Wide Web at
http://www.harpercollins.com/paperbacks

❖ 10 9 8 7 6 5 4 3 2 1

This book is for Dr. Terri Johnson, her surgical team, the emergency room staff, and the nurses and technicians at Methodist Hospital who saved my life. And to all you wonderful people who visited, called, sent flowers, cards, and e-mail while I was recovering. Special thanks to my very understanding editor, Abigail Kamen Holland.

The author would like the readers to know that she does not share Diane Teal's opinion of Percy Bysshe Shelley's abilities as a poet.

Prologue

France, Poitou region, 1173
    "You're sulking again, Simon."

Simon de Argent looked up over his steepled, long-fingered hands and said, "So I am, Jacques. How clever of you to notice. Try the wine, my friend," he added. The baron's voice was deep and rich, flavored with weariness, sadness, and, perhaps, a bit too much wine.

"I think I will."

Yves, Simon's servant, hurried forward with a silver ewer to serve the old man as he took a seat by the fire opposite the Baron of Marbeau. The room was dark but for the flames burning in the fireplace. Jacques had designed the fireplace himself and oversaw its construction in Simon's personal quarters. Jacques had spent his long life coming up with such clever notions for the family he served. He was a master of many arts, arcane and mundane alike. Some called him the greatest wizard of the time, and who was he to deny such claims when they were true? He didn't feel clever now, however, as he gazed at his melancholy friend.

"I miss your smile, Simon. I miss your laughter." He gestured toward the lute resting on a nearby table. "I miss your songs."

Simon was famous in the courts of Poitou and Aquitaine for his poetry and music. The ladies had flocked around him, and not just because he had a way with the lute and a flattering turn of phrase. Many a woman had broken her heart with wanting, but not having, Simon de Argent. Music and charm had both deserted the Lord of Marbeau of late. Perhaps what he needed was someone he wanted. Jacques didn't think Simon was very good at knowing how to want anything, or knowing how to get it if he did.

"You spend too much time alone."

"I have you," Simon replied. "I keep my bed warm as well," he added before Jacques could suggest a younger and more sensual companion than himself.

"Alys," the old man scoffed. "The woman's a—"

"I know what she is. I don't care."

"You care about nothing!" Jacques knew his shouted words were a lie. Simon cared too much. A storm raged outside, and thunder punctuated the old man's angry words. "You need something new to care for, that's all."

Simon picked up his silver winecup and twirled it between his hands. He did not seem perturbed by Jacques's words. "I'm too old to care."

Jacques laughed, a dry-as-bones dusty cackle. "I've seen seventy years, lad, to your thirty-four. I'm not old." He tapped his forehead. "Not in here, where it counts. You've a sound body, and hardly any silver that shows in that lion's mane of yours. I know very well that you got those lines around your eyes from laughter, and not from hard living. Don't you dare claim age as the cause of this drawn out, petulant mood of yours."

Simon raised one offended eyebrow. "Petulant? I?" Jacques nodded. Simon put the winecup back down, and turned his gaze to watch the fire. "Petulant?" he repeated. "I suppose I am. I don't care. Go to bed, Jacques," he added. "For I don't know who's more bored with this conversation, you or I."

"I am," Jacques answered. He drained his wine, grateful for its warmth, then stood. "I," he told his friend and patron, "have better things to occupy my time than to crawl under the covers and sleep my life away. I," he said, "have work to do."

Wild work, he added to himself as he left Simon de Argent's chamber. Jacques planned magical work, a spell to be performed while the storm was still strong. For it seemed only some great act of magic would find the cure for his friend's sore heart and soul.

1

"Nice outfit, Teal. You going to a party?"

Diane hit the pause button on her VCR remote, freezing Carole Lombard in mid-quip to William Powell. She glanced out the window as a streak of lightning illuminated the darkness outside. "I'm supposed to, Ellie," she answered her roommate, who'd just come in from work. "I'd rather not. It's a wretched night and I've got movies to watch." She pointed at the pile of videotapes on the coffee table. "My editor asked for an article on feminism in 1930s screwball comedies."

"Oow, that sounds exciting." Ellie gave a wide yawn.

Diane made a face at Ellie's lack of respect for film history, but all she said in response was, "It's a living."

Ellie nodded. "What kind of party is it?"

"One my mom's giving for some singer."

Ellie's eyes lit up. She was far more impressed by Diane Teal's mother being an A&R rep for a record company than Diane was. "If you don't go, can I borrow your clothes and go in your place?"

The outfit in question consisted of a long, ivory silk broomstraw skirt, and a matching long-sleeved silk tunic. Diane had twisted her heavy black hair into a knot at the back of her head, held in place by jade-tipped hairsticks.

She hadn't yet decided whether to accessorize this simple outfit with the teal-green shawl embroidered with silver Chinese dragons she had on the couch beside her. She thought a raincoat would probably be more practical considering the weather outside.

"September in Seattle," she said, "isn't supposed to be the rainy season. You wouldn't like him," she added to Ellie.

Ellie blinked innocently. "Who?"

"The singer. The guy Mom's giving the party for. He's some French folk singer. Does medieval ballads or something."

"Boring."

"My assessment, exactly. Richer than Pearl Jam, though," she added with a wry smile. "Mom wants me to meet him."

"Why?"

"He's single. Mom says he's gorgeous and charming and intelligent and that I could do worse. She expects me at eight." Diane did not want to go, even though she'd gone through the motions of dressing for a formal reception. She hated to disappoint her mother, but music was not her thing. Matchmaking was definitely not her thing. Movies were her thing. "I think I'll stay home and watch TV."

Ellie stretched. "I'm going to take a shower. Let me know if I can borrow the outfit," she added as she walked down the short hall toward the bathroom.

Diane sat back on the couch and pressed the button to start the tape once more. She sighed contentedly, happy to be alone with the films that were far more interesting to her than any people she'd ever met.

Her contentment was rattled a moment later by a loud clap of thunder that shook the whole building. The sound was so startling that she jumped to her feet in alarm.

"What the—"

She took a step toward the window. She hadn't seen any lightning flash, there had been no loud crackle of energy as the lightning bolt grounded itself nearby. There had only been the roar of the thunder. Maybe it wasn't thunder, she thought and went to the window.

"Maybe it was an explosion of some sort," she said as she peered into the darkness through the rain-obscured glass. "Maybe it was a car wre—"

The lightning bolt that came after the thunder hit her before she had a chance to finish.

"Not tonight, Alys," Simon said to the pretty girl who'd come in a few minutes after the old wizard left. She wore a heavy cloak, but he doubted she wore much beneath it. For all that he'd claimed to Jacques that he kept his bed well-warmed, he had no interest in tupping tonight. He might not have been averse to a bit of cuddling beneath warm furs on this stormy night, but Lady Alys was not the cuddling sort. She liked to do the deed and get on about her own business. Normally, Simon was more than agreeable to send her on her way, with perhaps a small present clutched in her greedy little hands.

She pouted at his words. Her full lips were made for such an expression. "You sent for me."

He hadn't, but he didn't bother to argue as Alys poured herself a cup of wine. Perhaps his steward had seen fit to instruct his mistress to attend him. Or, more likely, she was lying. She thought herself irresistible, with her green eyes, masses of red curls, and lush body. Simon took release from her often enough, but he was quite capable of resisting any woman's allure. He was no raw boy, after all.

He let a disapproving silence grow between them while she finished her wine. When she approached his chair and would have taken his hand, he stood. "No."

She let her cloak fall. As he'd guessed, she wore only

her linen chemise beneath it. "I've seen it all before," he told her as she leaned against him. He put his hands on her shoulders. "Why aren't you content to take no for an answer tonight, my dear?"

She looked up at him, false tears gleaming in her lovely eyes. "You've grown tired of me, haven't you?"

He smiled, and ran a finger along the line of her jaw. "What makes you say that?"

She fluttered her lashes at him. A tear slid prettily down her cheek. He had to struggle against a cynical laugh at her obviousness. "You haven't sent for me all week," she told him. "I've missed your loving, my lord."

"I'm old," he said. "My needs are waning."

"You have the appetite of a bull, my lord," she protested. "A ram."

Her words were meant to flatter, but they left him wondering if his loveplay seemed like no more than the rutting of a mindless animal to the woman. He set her gently aside. "Not tonight," he said. "I'm tired." He picked up her cloak and settled it around her shoulders. "Go on, now."

She glared at him, her body stiff with sudden rage. "You are tired of me!" When he didn't answer, she threw a goblet at him. "There's someone else!"

He stepped out of the goblet's path. "No."

"Who is she? I'll kill the bitch!"

Alys would have thrown something else, but Simon grabbed her around the waist before she could snatch up another weapon. She screamed at him in fury, but within moments he had her securely wrapped in her heavy cloak. Then he scooped her up and deposited her unceremoniously on the landing outside his door.

"Calm down," he told her as she stared up at him in the light thrown by a wall sconce. "We'll talk tomorrow," he added, before he stepped back and slammed the thick door behind him.

Once he was alone he wasn't sure whether to sigh wearily or to laugh faintly at Alys's little scene. All he did know was that his reaction to both of their behavior was not a strong one. Pity. He almost missed the time when he was capable of feeling things deeply. Almost. He had learned that indifference was a better way to deal with the world than to rage against its inevitable injustice.

He decided on a faint laugh at his and the woman's farcical behavior, and went to settle in his chair. He considered drinking more wine, but ended up staring into the fire, conjuring up fanciful images in the dancing light.

It was peaceful. Restful. Until the explosion shattered the night.

Simon lifted his head in alarm as the sound roared through the castle. It left him stunned, shaken to his bones.

"Jacques!" he said as he stumbled to his feet, unable to hear the sound of his voice for the ringing in his ears.

Fear raced through him. So certain was he that his wizard friend was in danger, that he shed his indifference, grabbed a sword, and raced out of his quarters. Guards and servants were already gathered outside his door. He pushed his way through the press of bodies and raced up the stairs that led to Jacques's tower workroom.

"What hit me?"

"I'm afraid I did. Are you hurt?"

The voice was masculine, cracked with age. Diane had never heard it before. She didn't want to open her eyes. She was afraid of what she'd find when she did. She was lying down, and she hurt all over. And the man had said he'd hit her.

"Actually, I didn't hit you." He almost sounded like he'd read her mind. "It was the spell I sent to fetch you that might have injured you."

Spell. Magical spell? Right.

She opened her eyes and got unsteadily to her feet. The bearded old guy on the other side of the room looked more like George Carlin than he did Merlin. The room had stone walls. The stone room was round, like a tower. It was lit by torches stuck into metal brackets. The floor seemed to be covered in straw. There was no glass in the narrow window, and the howling roar of the storm was blowing in along with the rain. The room was full of tables and chests, all of them piled high with mysterious beakers and pots, leatherbound books, parchment scrolls, bunches of dried herbs, and unrecognizable lumps of stuff.

Diane closed her eyes again. Spell. Fetch. Injured. This was crazy. She refused to be calm about it. She looked at the old guy. "Who are you? Where am I?"

"Jacques of Pelliel. And you are?"

He sounded remarkably calm and polite. Diane was feeling less calm by the moment, and she hadn't been too calm to begin with. "Diane Teal," she told Jacques. "Where am I?" she repeated.

"I've never seen anyone like you before."

"I've never seen anyone like you, either. What is this place?"

"My workroom, of course."

It looked like the set of a medieval movie. "What happened to my apartment? How did I get here?"

"I told you. I brought you here. With magic. You have very pretty eyes."

He acted as though he'd never seen anyone with Asian features. "Yeah, sure. What's really going on? What am I doing here?" Her voice rose with growing hysteria. "Where is here? What happened? What—"

The wizard pointed at her and mumbled something. The words froze in her throat a moment before the man with the sword burst into the room.

The tip of the sword was pressed to her throat before

she could draw another breath. It was cold against her skin, cold and sharp, but so was the expression in the swordsman's eyes. She wanted to scream, but no sound would come out. Even if she'd been able to make a sound, she thought the look in the man's eyes might have terrified her into silence. He was a tall man, broad-shouldered, with an arrogant, angular, hawk-nosed face, set in hard, angry lines.

"Are you all right, Jacques?" Simon asked.

"Of course, my friend," the old man answered. "Put your sword up, man. You're frightening the girl."

Girl? Was that what this stranger was? He flicked his gaze over her form. The creature had a woman's body, all right, outlined enticingly by the softly clinging pale fabric of her dress. A female, then, but many a demon had a woman's form. Simon backed the strange woman against the wall, directly beneath one of the torches, so he could study her in the light.

She stared back at him with dark, almond-shaped eyes. Her hair was thick and heavy, blacker than night. The shape of her face was wrong, the cheekbones too high, the color of her skin pale, but tinted with gold rather than a healthy rose. She was not like anyone he'd ever seen. He didn't know whether to be repelled, frightened, or intrigued. For, despite her strangeness, she wasn't exactly ugly. But, he reminded himself forcefully, the devil could show a pleasant face.

He kept the point of his sword poised against her long, slender throat as he asked, "What sort of creature is this? Did a demon come to you out of the storm?"

"No, I don't think so," Jacques answered in his inevitably calm way. "Her name's Diane."

"Did she cause the noise?"

"No, I did that."

"Where did she come from?"

"Excellent question."

"Jacques!"

Simon was more than a little annoyed to have rushed to his friend's rescue only to find that Jacques seemed to be perfectly all right. He might have rounded on the old man and demanded a full explanation, but he didn't dare turn from the creature he held at bay. For all that she looked soft and female and terrified, he was still warrior enough not to take any chances.

Jacques crossed the room and put a hand on Simon's shoulder. "She's harmless. Leave her alone. Go to bed. I'll explain all about her in the morning."

"Explain now."

The old man hesitated, then sighed. "She's a great storyteller. The finest storyteller ever born, this I swear," Jacques answered smoothly. "I sent for her from— Brittany. To entertain you. She arrived earlier today. She's exhausted, so I let her sleep in my quarters."

Simon had no doubt that the old man was lying, but he also knew that this tale was all he'd get until Jacques felt good and ready to speak the truth. "She doesn't look like she's from Brittany." Unless, of course, she had sprung out of one of the circles of fairy stones said to litter the landscape there.

"I never said she was Breton. I said she came from there." Jacques moved his hand from Simon's shoulder to press down on his sword arm. "Don't harm her. Stop frightening her. Go away."

Simon finally took his gaze off the girl and looked at his friend. He slowly lowered the sword. Out of the corner of his eye he saw the girl slump to her knees on the rushes. She was shaking with fear. He stepped back, not liking the sensation of having a woman cower at his feet.

He glanced down at her as he moved away, and noticed the design on the bluish-green cloth that had slipped down around her shoulders. Despite her fear, she looked at him with angry eyes when he snatched the cloth from her. He put his sword down on one of Jacques's littered tables, then shook out the length of heavy silk. He held it up near the torch to study the exquisitely worked design repeated three-across and three-down on the square cloth. The shape of the heraldic beast stitched in metallic thread was of a more elongated shape than he was used to, but familiar and recognizable nonetheless.

"The silver dragons of Marbeau."

Jacques squinted over his shoulder at the embroidery work. "And a finer working of your device I've never seen."

"Nor I," Simon conceded. He glared down at the girl. She was glaring back. "What is the meaning of this?"

"I commissioned it," Jacques answered, in the usual smooth-as-honey tone he used when he lied. "Diane brings you a new banner for your house."

"From Brittany?"

Jacques ignored his skepticism as he nodded. "From Brittany."

"Of course."

From Hong Kong, Diane thought. *It's from Hong Kong!*

But the words wouldn't come out of her mouth. No sound would come out, though she longed to tell these strange men that the scarf had been sent to her by her grandmother. That she distinctly remembered leaving it on the couch when she went to look out the window. That it was her property, and that she wanted it back. She also wanted to get out of there, but was shaking too hard to climb to her feet and run for it. She hated being a coward, but the situation, and the blond man with the sword, had her too shaken up to react in any other way.

The worst part was that she suddenly couldn't talk. They were talking about her, but she couldn't respond. She couldn't speak up for herself, couldn't refute a word the old man said, couldn't make the swordsman acknowledge her as a person rather than treat her like a thing he might decide to dispose of at any moment. She hated that. She hated him. She just couldn't tell him so.

Simon looked down at the woman once more as he folded the banner over his arm. "Thank you for the gift, then, Diane of Brittany." Her eyes flashed hatred at him for all that she was still trembling with fear. He wasn't sure what to do about either emotion, or why he should even want to do anything. Jacques had made it clear that the woman was not his concern. Good. He didn't want anything to be his concern.

So he retrieved his sword and walked to the door. The hour grew late. The storm still raged. Jacques was being enigmatic. He'd already had to deal with Alys. The excitement of coming to an unnecessary rescue was wearing off. Jacques would explain when he chose to. Besides, if the old man wanted to keep an unusual looking woman in his room, what business was it of his, just because he was master of the castle?

When Simon reached the doorway he said, "Since you're so eager for privacy I'll leave you alone to have your way with the creature." He slammed the door hard behind him as he left.

2

"Oh, dear."

Diane wanted to ask the old man what he meant, but words still wouldn't come. She kept trying to speak, but she couldn't make a sound. She couldn't even scream. If there was one thing she really wanted to do, it was scream. Instead, she banged her fist on the arm of a thick wooden chair, hoping to get the distracted wizard's attention.

Jacques had helped her to a chair before he began looking though a pile of books. She'd sat and watched him with her hands held to her throat as minutes dragged slowly by. She was more afraid of having lost her voice than of having been wounded by the swordsman. She knew she hadn't been wounded. The sword had lain cold and heavy against her throat, but the man who threatened her hadn't let the delicately poised tip cut her skin the whole time he'd discussed her with the old man.

She tried not to think about the swordsman, but she couldn't help wondering who he was. She wondered why he'd threatened her. Why he'd insulted her. Why he'd stolen her shawl. She had questions. She had many concerns. Why was she mute? Where was she? How had she gotten here—wherever here was? Jacques said he'd brought her here by magic. Odd as it seemed, she believed that he was a wizard. She wanted to ask about what sort of magical world this was. Most importantly, she wanted to ask when was she going to be allowed to go home? She couldn't ask. All she could do was wait.

Patience was not one of her virtues, but getting up and kicking Jacques to get his attention probably wouldn't do her any good. It might bring the swordsman back, and she wasn't ready to face him again.

When Jacques finally looked at her, he said, "I'm afraid I've put a curse on you." He closed the book, its ancient leather binding creaking loudly as he did so. The silence in the room drowned out the dying storm outside. All Diane could do was wait. He combed his gnarled fingers thoughtfully through his long beard for a while, then went on. "Not exactly a curse, a *geis*, actually."

Diane didn't know the difference, and she couldn't ask. She made a questioning gesture, instead.

"Ah, well, the difference is subtle, I'll admit," he told her. "But a curse is harder to break than a *geis*. All you have to do is perform the necessary act that fulfills the *geis* and you'll be free of it." He smiled as though he'd just been awarded the Nobel Prize for Magic. "Simple."

She crossed her arms and glared.

He rubbed his chin. "I suppose you want to know what the *geis* is and how to fulfill it?"

She nodded.

"The *geis* is my fault, I'm afraid. I thought it would be safer for you if I did all the talking when Simon came rushing in. So, I put a silence spell on you. Only it wasn't the spell I intended. I'm getting on a bit, you know."

The look she gave him was not sympathetic.

He tugged on his beard. "I suppose you feel you have a right to be angry with me." He waved a finger at her. "But I'm sure this is for your own good as well as Simon's. Simon," he explained, "is the handsome fellow who came rushing to my defense earlier."

The guy who'd threatened to stab her, in other words.

"He's very protective," the old wizard went on. "You'll come to appreciate that about him. Now, as to how to break the *geis*— oh, I should explain the limits it's put on your behavior first."

Diane touched her throat. She tried to speak, but, of course, no words came out. She would have screamed in frustration if she'd been able. Since she couldn't, she resorted to standing up and stomping her foot.

Jacques just gave an amiable nod at her behavior. "You're very communicative even without a voice. Now, there are many men who would think having a mute woman about the house a distinct advantage. Don't worry, Simon is not such a man."

She didn't care what sort of man Simon was. She wanted her voice back. Maybe more importantly, she wanted to escape from this musty, drafty, weird room and the crazy old man who occupied it. She thought of running, but Simon and his sword might be lurking outside the door.

No, it wasn't Simon's being on the other side of the door that frightened her, it was the fear that she'd gone mad. Or maybe she was dead and this was some sort of afterlife. Maybe being hit by lightning had put her in a coma and her imagination had conjured up this place. If it had, she wondered how her imagination had dreamed up a medieval setting with people as incomprehensible as Jacques and his big, sword-wielding buddy.

Before she could go on with any more tangled, fearful thoughts, Jacques continued. "The point of my original spell was to find someone with the ability to draw my friend out of his current despondency. He hasn't been himself since—well, for some time now. I thought to bring him cheer, to restore a smile to his dark countenance. He's a man who once loved song and dance and story-telling. When I performed the spell that conjured you from—" He waved his hands dramatically. "From wherever it is you appeared from."

Seattle, she wanted to tell him. *I'm from Seattle*. She also wanted to know just where she was now. Was this Middle Earth? Narnia? The Enchanted Castle at Disneyworld, maybe?

"The spell was to find the right troubadour. I planned to send a messenger to bring this minstrel to Castle Marbeau once I'd seen him in my glass." He held up a small mirror. "I saw you, and you're distinctly not a him, are you? I'm sure that's for the best, for I have sworn never to do ill with my magic. Still, I didn't exactly plan to conjure you away from your own land. But my power seems to be strong tonight—it comes and goes, my age, you know—and so I accidentally called you here. Actually, it's more convenient than sending a messenger, don't you think?"

Accident? The man had accidentally used some sort of powerful magic on her? Nonsense. There was no such thing as magic. Special effects, yes. Physics, yes. Electricity and nuclear reactions, magnetism, and genetic engineering, yes. Magic, no, even if she couldn't stop herself from believing in it just now.

"Of course you don't think any of this is convenient. The *geis* certainly isn't." Jacques took off the odd-shaped hat he wore—more like a baby bonnet, Diane thought, than a wizard's pointy hat—long enough to scratch his bald head. Then he plopped the hat back on and explained, "The rules of the *geis* are these: You have been rendered mute, but since I have claimed that you are a storyteller, you may speak only when you have a tale to tell. Go ahead," he urged, "tell me a story."

Diane just stared at him for a few moments. This was completely ridiculous. How could she be mute, and able to talk for a specific function? Was the man trying to tell her he'd turned her into an entertainment center?

Something that could be switched on and off for this Simon person's pleasure? She practically boiled with anger at this outrageous notion. It wasn't just anger, but humiliation that scalded her. Impossible. Ridiculous.

She tried to speak, to shout out her fury.

Nothing. Silence.

She closed her eyes for a long time and battled the blinding rage. When she had fought through her wild emotions to a bit of calm she looked once more at the patiently waiting Jacques.

"Try," he coaxed. "You have the gift of storytelling on the tip of your tongue. All you have to do is use it."

She thoroughly hated him, and herself for giving in to his urging, but she swallowed hard and said, "Once upon a time"?

He clapped his hands with pleasure. "There? You see? I told you. Go on."

She couldn't. She had quite a few things she wanted to say to him. She tried to speak, but no other words came out. Why was it she could say "once upon a time"?

She put her hand over her mouth as she finished speaking. Tears began to roll down her cheeks, obscuring her view of the wizard.

Within moments she was silently sobbing, every bit of control she'd been exercising over her emotions dissolved in the unstoppable tears. She didn't know where she was. She didn't know what was the matter with her! A bad, nasty man had tried to kill her! She wanted to go home! She got to her feet, blind with tears, shaking with hysteria. She tried to run, but the most she could do was start to fall as the world began to go black around her.

Jacques moved swiftly despite his age. He caught her in his strong, gnarled hands. "Poor lamb," he said. "You've had enough for one night." He guided her across the room, helped her lie down in a feather-soft bed, pulled a cover up over her. He stroked her hair, and said, "It's going to be all right, sweeting. My magic always turns out for the best. You'll see. You'll even break the *geis* and get your voice back soon. You sleep now."

She had to obey him. She even wanted to. Closing her eyes and burrowing into the covers seemed the most natural thing in the world to do. The safest. She sighed and curled around herself, the tears and terror fading as peaceful darkness eased closer. She just barely heard him say one last thing before sleep cradled her completely.

"To break the *geis* all you have to do is fall in love."

Diane tried not to be frightened as she looked around the wizard's room. She hated the way she'd reacted last night, and was determined not to repeat the experience. When she'd woken up she'd hoped that the whole thing had been a nightmare. Hope fled when she opened her eyes. Or maybe she just wasn't awake yet, she thought, as she threw off the covers and got to her feet.

The room was dim except for the golden light thrown by a stand of candles next to the table where Jacques worked on something. There was very little light coming in the narrow window, but the window did let in a cool breeze. Without the protection of the blankets, Diane shivered. Her silk skirt and tunic were no protection against the damp chill of the place, and the hay spread on the floor was scratchy against her cold feet. She found her shoes placed neatly next to the bed and hurried to put them on before she approached the old wizard.

Jacques hummed as he mixed what looked like dried herbs in a black stone mortar. The scent thrown up by the crushed plants was both sharp and sweet at once. Diane breathed deeply of the fragrance as she stood across the table waiting to get the old man's attention. She tried to

speak, of course, but the whatever it was he called it—
goose? No, gaze.

"*Geis*," he said as he turned his benign smile on her.
"You must accept, my dear, that the only way you may
speak is by telling stories. I have named you a Breton, and
the Bretons are famous for their lays of heroes, and lovers,
and wild adventures. Speak of these things, and your
voice is yours to use."

Diane couldn't take the man's sympathetic expression.
Or maybe it was pity. So she turned away, with her arms
cradled protectively over her stomach. She didn't want
pity, and she wouldn't let the fear overwhelm her again.
She took a few deep breaths and tried to think.

Stories. He wanted her to tell stories. If that was the
only way she could communicate, fine. She'd do anything
to get her voice back. Only she wasn't a storyteller. She
wasn't even that much of a reader. Even the fantasy
worlds that resembled this place, she mainly knew about
from the film versions of the novels. If she'd been a
reader, she'd be able to remember book plots to recite. All
she really knew about were films. She watched them,
studied them, wrote about them. Film was a visual art.

But what was a movie without a script?

Scripts. Of course. Plots. She knew thousands of movie
plots.

What was the last thing she'd been watching?

She turned back to Jacques. "Once upon a time there
was a rich man who a silly young woman mistook for a—a
servant. And, uh—" She faltered, and stared helplessly at
the wizard, unsure of how to explain the plot of *My Man
Godfrey* to someone who lived in what looked like the set
for *The Sword and the Stone*.

Jacques put away his mortar and pestle and came to
take her hands. "You see, you *are* a troubadour." He led
her to a chair, pulled over another one and sat down
beside her. "Shall I help you with the right words while

you provide the tale?" Diane nodded eagerly to his suggestion. "Very well," he said. "Now, tell me more about this rich man and the silly girl."

She did, stumbling and stuttering to a silent, frustrated halt frequently, but with Jacques's help she began to learn the art of storytelling.

3

"You'll do fine."

Diane wasn't so sure she believed Jacques's reassurance. So she tried to keep her mind off her nervousness by concentrating on keeping her balance in high heels as she followed the old man down the uneven, slab-like steps. They were on their way to someplace he called the great hall. She wasn't sure she wanted to go. She'd gotten used to Jacques and his odd quarters. She really wasn't in any hurry to explore the rest of her surroundings, but he'd insisted that she show up and be the dinner speaker in the hall. After a day of learning how to use her voice she'd finally grown hungry enough to venture outside the wizard's quarters with him.

She wasn't happy to learn that the rest of the place was as primitive as his stone-walled tower room. All the walls were stone, as were the pitted, treacherous steps. At least the stairs weren't covered in straw like the wooden floor in Jacques's room, that would have made negotiating them in the smoky torchlight even more difficult. She noticed that there were no hallways in the tower, just landings with narrow doorways on either side. She wondered what was behind the metal-studded doors, but she couldn't ask. Besides, Jacques hurried her downstairs too quickly for her to find a diversion from her premiere performance. The closer they got to the noisy hall, the more nervous she became, but she supposed there was no getting out of it now.

Jacques would have preferred to lead Diane to Simon's chamber where she could entertain the baron in private. But he thought both the girl and his friend might object to such an obvious ploy. So, after spending the day helping her to gain some confidence in her craft, he'd insisted that she make her debut in the great hall. He would rather have kept her from the curious and callous stares of Simon's soldiers and servants, but he hoped they'd appreciate her entertainer's talent and ignore her strange appearance. He hoped, but he was none too certain of how Simon de Argent's retainers would react. More importantly, he wasn't sure how Simon would react to the girl's presence. In private, his friend was a reasonable man, though far too taciturn of late. In public he was still the Lord of Marbeau and wore a cold, hard, soldier's face.

Simon looked up a moment before silence descended on the hall. From his central seat on the dais he had a clear view of the tower doorway, so he was the first to see Diane of Brittany come into the room. His thoughts had turned to the strange woman several times during the day. He'd almost climbed the stairs to Jacques's quarters once or twice. In the end, he'd decided that putting a curb on his curiosity might be the wisest course. He hadn't expected the old man to bring her into the hall.

Simon should have, of course. After all, Jacques had said the Breton storyteller had come to Marbeau to amuse the lord of the castle. He didn't want to be amused, as Jacques knew very well. But he couldn't very well deny his people diversion as the long days of autumn drew down on the land. Jacques knew that as well. Damn it. So the woman would have her chance to interrupt his household and his life.

"I pray for her sake that she's talented," he muttered under his breath as he drew his gaze over the approaching storyteller.

The night before he'd thought her some strange, fey creature Jacques had drawn up from the underworld. Her extraordinary looks had no such chilling effect on him now. Rather the opposite, actually. The pale material of her clothing shimmered in the light of torches and candles, the subtle movement of the soft fabric left him wondering about the womanly shape it covered. Her hair had a blue-black sheen to it, like Damascus steel. She wore it loosely about her shoulders, like a maiden's. It enhanced the heart shape of her face and the size of her teardrop eyes.

Eyes that were full of fear as her gaze met his, then slid quickly away as Jacques took her hand and led her toward the dais. The gaping crowd parted like water before them. Silence followed them in a rippling wave.

While keeping a mask of indifference on his features, Simon carefully watched the effect this Diane of Brittany had on his household. He did not know what Jacques's game was in bringing the woman to Marbeau, but he did know he didn't need any more dissension among his people than he already had. Guest of his old friend or no, he'd cast the woman out at the first sign of trouble.

As the shock wore off, an angry murmur soon ran through the crowd gathered at the trestle tables. And, from the way heads turned, it didn't look like trouble was going to be long in coming. He saw fingers held up in the gesture of protection against the evil eye. Father Andre crossed himself hurriedly as he backed up against a wall tapestry behind the dais, then a second time while he mumbled something in Latin. Simon sighed, his chaplain obviously wasn't going to be any help in calming the populace.

Beside him, in the high-backed chair that he'd let her

appropriate, though it was meant for the lady of the castle, he heard Alys squeak in alarm. He was almost amused at his mistress's reaction as he looked between fair Alys and the dark woman Jacques had brought to the foot of the dais. He wondered which of the pair was more frightened. After a moment, he decided that it must be Diane, even though she showed no outward dismay at the hostile from the people who surrounded her. For all that she held herself proudly, the fear in her eyes gave her away. Somehow, that combination of pride used to cover apprehension called to him.

Alys pushed herself up out of the chair and pointed at the newcomer. "What is that?" Then she put her hand dramatically on his arm. "You'll protect me from it, won't you, my lord?"

Oh, for heaven's sake, Diane thought, her nervousness suddenly buried by annoyance at the woman's reaction. She crossed her arms and glared at the redhead, but the woman wouldn't meet her eyes for more than a moment. The red-haired woman looked anxiously at Simon, so Diane looked at him as well.

She'd spent most of her trip across the room concentrating on him, actually. He was the one familiar figure in a sea of strange new sights. The room was dark, and smoky from an unvented fire in a circular, stone pit. It was full of oddly dressed people who collectively smelled like a sweaty locker room and looked at her like *she* was some kind of freak. There were people with swords in the crowd, just about everybody seemed to have a knife.

Simon was the only thing that was familiar, and even though he'd held a sword at her throat the night before, she felt safer looking at him than at the hostile crowd that was now at her back. He looked calm, self-assured, in control, all the things she wasn't. When he looked at her he almost conveyed some of those emotions to her. Almost. Since, while his glance held a bit of reassurance, it also held cold warning. As though he was ready to blame her for the way his posse was behaving. And, even if Jacques hadn't told her, she had no doubt that he was the one who held tight control over this stinking rabble.

When Jacques touched her shoulder reassuringly, she jumped nervously. Simon saw her reaction, and she could tell that the gesture he made of raising a silver goblet to his lips, was to hide a smile.

Then his girlfriend repeated, stridently, "Will you protect me from the monster, my lord? See how she glowers at me!"

"She's no monster," Jacques said.

"She's a woman," Simon told his companion.

"She's hideous," the redhead answered. "Monstrous."

Simon gave a flinty smile. "Then she won't be any competition for you, will she, my dear?" Though Diane heard the sarcasm in Simon's voice, the other woman didn't seem to. While his girlfriend preened, Simon looked Diane over critically, in a way that made her go cold with anger. It also made her go hot, and flushed with embarrassment, and deeper sensations she had no intention of dwelling on.

Simon's lips quirked up, in response to her blush, Diane thought, but it was the redhead he patted on the arm. "No, my dear, there's no competition at all."

"What's the monster woman doing here?" the redhead demanded of the wizard.

Jacques ignored her. He turned and loudly addressed the crowd. "Diane of Brittany has come among us to recite tales of heroes and battles, deeds of honor, and great loves. She comes to entertain my Lord Simon and his household." He threw a stern look over his shoulder at Simon. "Has she not, my lord?"

One of Simon's fair brows angled up at a sarcastic angle at Jacques, but he stood and made an imperious gesture.

A man standing behind Simon's chair called out, "Silence," in a deep, ringing voice. Gradually, the room quieted.

Into an oppressive silence, Simon said, "Speak, woman, before our dinner grows cold."

It wasn't the most magnanimous of introductions, but Diane supposed she'd better do as he'd said. She didn't look forward to trying to entertain this rabble, but maybe if she got it over with she could go hide in Jacques's room again. Maybe she'd even get something to eat.

Jacques led his young protégé to stand on the dais, facing the high table, but visible to the entire room. "I must go," he told her. She gave him a frightened look, but he didn't relent. "You must learn to do this on your own," he whispered. "Besides I have a coded message that I must translate for Simon as soon as possible. So, I'll see you after dinner." He smiled, gave her another reassuring pat, then stepped away.

Diane's mind raced as she watched the old man disappear into the crowd. She was on her own! He'd gotten her into this and wasn't even going to stay to give her moral support!

"Well?" Simon drawled. "You can speak, can't you?"

She couldn't even explain to him that, no, she couldn't. So she just gave him an acid-bath look and thought furiously to come up with a story that would suit this weird bunch of people. Jacques had said something about heroes and battles and honor and love. Okay, she thought, the plot of *Excalibur* and all those other King Arthur movies had all that stuff.

Speaking as loudly as she could, she said, "Once upon a time there was a king named Uther Pendragon who had the hots—who lusted—after the wife of his friend—"

She gave them as much of the story as she could remember, culling the details from half a dozen movies to patch together a whole tale. She told them about Merlin, and the sword in the stone, and the knights of the Round Table, the quest for the Grail, the illicit love of Lancelot and Guinevere, and about Mordred, and battles and betrayals, and they ate it up. The crowd's reaction was more than enthusiastic, with hoots and laughter, and applause.

She was still nervous as she spoke, but after the first few minutes she got caught up in the story. Also, doing her best to get it right kept her from succumbing to stage fright. She couldn't look at Simon as she talked, though. She was afraid that his expression would be cynical, or sarcastic, or worse, bored. She didn't want to deal with that—although she didn't know why she thought his opinion was important.

Eventually, she felt compelled to look at him. It was as though his eyes were burning holes into the back of her head, as though he was daring her to face him. She told herself she was being ridiculous, but when she turned toward him the force of his furious glower was enough to nearly knock her off the dais. Frightened, she took a step back, words frozen in her throat. She did lose her balance and landed hard. Though it was only a long step down to the floor, the impact was enough for her to twist her ankle.

She would have cried out in pain if she could, but in a moment she forgot the sharp ache as Simon loomed over her. His face was a harsh mask. He grabbed her by the shoulders, his hands mercilessly hard. She remembered the sword he'd rested against her throat the night before, and found that his fury was an even more dangerous weapon. She would have pulled away if he'd let her, but instead his grip tightened. She felt small in his grasp, and very frightened.

"How dare you tell that tale in this castle?"

She had no words to answer him with, but he shook her, as though he could force an explanation out of her that way. She tried to fend him off, but he just shook harder. And there was no escaping from the pain, hurt, and anger in his amber-colored eyes.

On the dais, the redhaired woman laughed. Simon stopped shaking her and gave the woman a withering look. Abruptly, he dropped his hands from her shoulders. His face had been pale with fury, now a flush colored his cheeks, as though embarrassment were replacing his anger.

Diane shook with fear while the crowd jeered and shouted. The noise nearly deafened her. Simon pushed her away. She barely heard him when he said, "Get out."

4

The surprising thing was that it wasn't dark outside. The castle had been dark, but daylight still clung to the
world out in the open. Actually, the surprising thing was
that she was here at all, but Diane tried to cope with the
moment rather than freeze in panic at the whole, impossible
fantasy situation. The sky over the steep, narrow trackway
was lit with a rich sunset-gold. On the high cliff behind her,
the castle brooded like a stone monster with a hangover. She
refused to look back at it, and fought the illogical fear that
the crouching beast behind her was ready to pounce. It was
Simon who had pounced on her for no reason, had her
driven out of the dubious protection of his fortress. She
didn't understand any of it, and she couldn't banish the horrible look of mingled pain and fury that he'd turned on her.

What had she done?

She supposed she'd never know. She supposed she
should be grateful she was free of the strange place. Not
that the outside world was any less strange. Well, she
could comfort herself that at least the outside world didn't
have Simon, with his sword and his temper, in it.
Somehow the thought wasn't comforting. Nothing was.
So, she concentrated on the path instead, and walked with
careful slowness instead of giving in to the urge to run.

Once away from the castle, the path led through fields that looked like they were in the process of being harvested. Beyond the fields were a line of jagged hills covered in dense forest. There was no semblance of a town in sight, nothing which even vaguely resembled civilization. Diane was alone, in the middle of nowhere, and night was slowly falling.

What did I do to him? she wondered. *What did I say? What did I—*

Don't think about him, she commanded herself. She ordered herself to think about the fact that her feet hurt, or that she was hungry. No, maybe it was better not to think of those unpleasant details. Of course it was very hard not to think of them, when she was miserable, and frightened. Eventually, she took off her shoes while she stood at a fork in the path, and debated which way to go. She chose the wider track to the left, and continued on. Hobbled, really, as her flimsy pumps had raised blisters on both heels, and she'd bruised her ankle badly when she'd slipped off the dais.

Night closed in quickly as she moved into the depths of the forest. She had no idea where she was going. As long as it was away from Simon de Argent she supposed the journey was worth it. Things had to get better soon, didn't they? They had to start making sense. All she knew was that she wasn't in Seattle—hell, she wasn't even in Kansas.

Gradually, the track widened a bit. As she rounded a curve she could see a bonfire in the distance. The sounds of laughter and singing and the scent of roasting meat floated to her on the evening breeze. As she hurried forward, houses came into view, and a crowd of people. Hopefulness flooded her to know that she wasn't completely alone in the world. She hurried on, dropping her shoes in her haste to reach the village. She would have called out if she could, she would have laughed. Tears of relief did stream down her face as people turned her way.

Then the singing stopped. Hands pointed. Looks of horror appeared on dirty faces as she came into the firelight. An angry, frightened murmur began, growing in volume like the incoming tide on a small sea.

The mob closed in around her before she had a chance to turn and run.

"What do you mean you sent her packing?"

Simon de Argent was so full of fury that he scarcely heard the angry accusation in the old man's voice. He continued to pace before the fireplace in his chamber, unable to even try to assume the false calm he normally wore. "Of course I sent the vixen packing."

"Where?"

He stopped and turned on Jacques. His old friend had come into his chamber holding a report from one of his spies, but had brought up the subject of Diane before handing over the parchment. Simon wanted to study the needed information, but supposed he'd have to deal with the news that Jacques's protégé was no longer in the castle. "Where did she go? Back to Brittany, or to the devil. What do I care as long as she gets off my lands?"

Jacques eyes widened with alarm. "She's outside? Alone?"

"That's how she came to Marbeau, isn't it? On her own?"

"NO!"

Simon frowned at the old man's strangled shout. He could tell that an explanation he wasn't going to like was in the offing. "She's not a traveling player, I suppose?"

"No. She's—" Jacques's pointed dramatically toward the door. "Never mind what she is. You must go after her."

"I'll do no such thing." He paced the room, still burning with humiliation from the storyteller's thinly disguised rumor mongering. He paused before the fireplace and stared into the dancing flames for a few moments, but turned abruptly back to Jacques as the memories began to claw at him.

Words came out of him, clipped and hard as stone. "It's lucky I didn't kill her." Red rage had almost overtaken him. He almost had.

The puzzled look on Jacques face nearly made him laugh. But the laugh would have been full of madness. Madness had its appeal, but he couldn't afford to take that kind of comfort.

"What did Diane do? Was her story not to your liking?"

Simon couldn't stop the laughter this time, but he cut it off before it could get out of control. Since Jacques knew the events better than anyone, in fact had his own part in them, Simon managed to explain, "Genevieve and Berengar," he said. "Denis. Even you and Vivienne. The whole sordid tale. She only left out Felice. Which is good, since I surely would have killed her if she'd tried to amuse the household with that tale."

Jacques ran his fingers through his beard. "She did what? In detail? How could she know about—"

"Oh, she dressed the telling up in romance, with kings and quests and holy relics, changed the names, even, but with enough truth intact to scald the skin off me. I wanted to stop her as soon as I saw where the story was going, and I should have. Instead I was frozen in place, in shock at the effrontery. It was like being in hell and having the devil recite all my sins for the world to hear. I should have killed her," he added. His hand closed tightly over his sword hilt. "Perhaps I'll hunt her down and do it now."

When he would have left the room, Jacques stepped in his way. "You'll hunt her down, my friend," he said. His wizened features had grown as stiff and stern as granite.

"You'll find her, and you'll bring her back. Safe and unharmed."

"I'll do no—"

"She knows nothing of your sins. Or of the sins against you. She knows nothing of you. She was only telling a story that has nothing to do with you."

"Nothing? Indeed. And how can you say she knows nothing of me?"

"How could she? She's from the future."

Simon found himself blinking, owl-like, with confusion. Jacques had said many an odd thing to him in his time, but this was the strangest statement of all. "What?"

Jacques nodded. "From the future, I tell you. She was born many centuries from now, and comes from a land we've never heard of. I've been thinking over the spell I cast to draw her to Marbeau and that is the only feasible explanation."

"What the devil are you talking about?"

Jacques's expression remained hard with anger. "I'm talking about your selfish, foolish, behavior and what I tried to do to help you! I ripped an innocent woman out of her own time and place for your sake." He pointed to the door. "Now you're going to fetch her back and treat her with the honor she deserves!"

There had been a bit more arguing, and more explanations from Jacques about the *geis* and the storytelling. Since Jacques did not lie, Simon eventually came to believe that the old man at least believed the tale he told. Which was how Simon came to be riding along the forest trail looking for Jacques's lost lamb as dark fell on the countryside.

Despite the light of a harvest moon, Diane had been nowhere to be seen in the open countryside. He didn't know if she'd stayed to the road or taken off across the newly harvested fields. She might be on her way to Tours, or Chinon, or asleep in the warm depths of a stack of grain. He had no way of knowing. It was too dark to follow a trail, and she couldn't answer him if he called out.

"Jacques and his foolish dabbling in magic," Simon complained to his horse as he came to the edge of the forest south of the castle. What was most annoying was that the dear old man had only been trying to help him. In trying to help, Jacques had brought about more trouble than either Simon or this Diane of Brittany—who wasn't actually from Brittany—needed or deserved.

Well, perhaps he deserved the trouble, Simon conceded as the horse picked its way carefully along the rutted roadway. He had been sulking and brooding and in a foul temper—and he didn't intend to change his mood, either. He had no reason too. The world was ugly and harsh. There was no love or loyalty or friendship or honor or God that could be trusted. Yet, friendship, honor, loyalty, and submission to God were the only life he knew.

"Why bother?" he muttered darkly.

He came to a split in the road and hesitated for a moment beneath the shadowed trees. Each track led to two villages in his demesne: one of farmers who worked his fields, the other of woodsmen, woodcutters, charcoal burners, gamekeepers and the like. All of his folk would be celebrating the harvest festival tonight. Simon felt no cause for celebrating.

His only hope was that the hard-negotiated truce and Peace of God would last long enough for the earth's bounty to be taken in and safely stored, that his people would survive through one more winter. His dark thoughts were punctuated by the soft call of an owl, and then, faintly, off to the left, shouting. He spurred the horse to the left.

Apparently, Diane's storytelling didn't suit the farmers of Marbeau any better than it did their lord.

* * *

Diane silently screamed as a rock hit her in the ribs. Her throat hurt even without the sound. The sharp edge of the stone cut her on the forehead. The heat from the towering blaze behind her singed her skin. The mob surrounded her in a vicious crescent, making a game of backing her toward the bonfire. They were going to burn her to death, she knew it. They joked about it among themselves.

She was terrified, hurting, but angry as well. The tears that nearly blinded her were from anger. She hated the helplessness. She hated being the victim. She hated this place and these people.

"Demon!" someone shouted, and hit her on the shoulder with his fist.

Another rock hit her on the back. With the air knocked out of her, she fell to the ground, and very nearly under the stamping hooves of a big white horse.

The horse reared and turned aside. Diane rolled away. The crowd parted in front of the big animal as she fought her way to her knees.

"Stand back!"

The voice came from far above her, a deep, furious shout. Like the voice of God. Still gasping hard for breath, Diane looked up, and higher up, until she saw the rider on the white horse. Not God, but a warrior angel, hawk-faced, with a nimbus of gold hair for a halo. Fierce, dangerous, and furious, he was the most beautiful sight she'd ever seen.

"Go."

Simon didn't need to say another word to disperse the villagers. One word, and his angry look was enough to turn the peasants' mob frenzy into cold terror. He was their lord and they knew the best way to stay alive this night was to get out of his sight. They melted away, slinking back to their hovels, leaving him alone with their victim before the fire.

Why had they attacked her? he wondered as he got down from his horse. Because her eyes had an odd shape to them? Because her skin was a different color than theirs? How could they tell, when they were as encrusted with dirt as the earth itself?

"Fools," he muttered. "Do they think she's a demon?" Then he laughed at his own foolishness, because he'd had the same notion himself last night. This was no demon before him, but an injured, frightened woman.

He knelt beside her, careful to move slowly so as not to frighten her anymore than she already seemed. She looked at him in awe for a moment, then recognition slowly dawned in her large dark eyes. She turned her face away from him, her eyes closed as he ran his hands over her. Her silk dress was torn, tattered, and stained, but still soft to the touch. The skin beneath it was soft as well, he noted, though he kept his touch impersonal as he checked her for wounds. After a few moments, he decided it would be better to continue the examination back at the castle where he could call for bandages and salves if they proved necessary. So, he helped her up and onto the horse.

She didn't speak, of course, on the way back. Jacques and his *geis* saw to that. The silence was to be expected, and he didn't say anything either. He would have, he supposed, if she'd even once looked at him. She didn't turn her head, or acknowledge him in any way, though he could feel the heat of her body, like branding accusations, burning into his skin.

After a while it occurred to him that she was somewhat annoyed with him for tossing her out into the ugly world in the first place.

5

The room was warm. Diane hadn't realized that she was so cold until her teeth chattered when Simon carried her into the warm room. She must have been in some kind of shock, she supposed, because she didn't really *feel* cold. She must have fallen into some kind of daze during the ride, because as the warmth spread over her she became aware of being held in the arms of the man who'd rescued her. She was holding onto him, her arms slung around his neck, her head rested on his chest. It was as though she was taking comfort from his strong embrace and the deep, steady thud of his heartbeat.

She was acting like she was *grateful*. She wondered how long this had been going on. There was something comforting about being held close to his broad chest. He felt and smelled very male, and that had lulled her into feeling protected. She just didn't know when it had happened, though she vaguely remembered being carried through the darkened hall and up the stairs. Maybe she'd gone into a shock-induced stupor at some point and her body and subconscious had responded to some primitive female instinct.

It was disgusting.

Diane Teal, at heart you are a wimp, she told herself as

Simon set her down on a chair near the fireplace. The worst part was that she was actually reluctant to let him go.

"Awake at last, I see," Simon said as she snatched her hands away from him as though she'd been burned. He straightened, aware of the emptiness now that she no longer filled his arms. Oddly enough, he was not glad to be relieved of the burden. He went to the door and spoke to the manservant that waited on the landing. "Yves, have my bathing tub filled."

While waiting for hot water he brought the water jug and basin from his bedside table. He supposed he should call for Jacques, or that he should have taken her to the old man straight away. He should let Jacques see to the girl's hurts. Instead, he poured water into the basin, set it on the floor, then knelt and drew his dagger.

"Hold still."

Diane held her breath at the sight of the knife, then she closed her eyes to block out the sight of it altogether. She heard Simon chuckle, and knew he was amused at her fear. Oddly enough, his amusement was more reassuring than it was annoying. Her curiosity got the better of her when she heard the dry rasp of silk being ripped. She opened her eyes to find that Simon had slit her skirt halfway up the thigh.

She barely had the chance to wonder why before he said, "This rag will do to wash the blood off." He dipped a strip of the torn cloth in water then raised it toward her face. Their gazes met as Diane flinched as far back as she could into the chair. Simon sighed. "You know it has to be done. Just close your eyes and tell me one of your tales while I work." When she hesitated, he added, "I promise not to throw you out of the castle again whether I like your story or not. Go on," he urged gently. "It'll take your mind off the pain."

She doubted that. But he was right, she didn't want to think about it. So, she closed her eyes as he'd suggested, and called up comforting images that filled her mind in grainy black-and-white—none of these colorized classics for her, thank you, Mr. Turner. She began reciting the best movie plot she could think of.

Her voice came out as a dry croak from her earlier silent screaming, but it felt so good to be able to talk that it was easy to ignore the discomfort. At first she concentrated on the words as hard as she could, so hard that she almost didn't notice the gentle touch of the cool cloth against her bruised skin.

What she did notice was the touch of Simon's strong, sure fingers along her jaw as he moved her head from side to side as he checked her for other injuries. Soon the gentle stroking of the cloth across her abraded skin was more like a caress than washing. Then she noticed the warmth of his breath as he leaned close to her. She sensed the size of him, how it blocked out the light of the fire, but not the heat. Or maybe the heat was coming from him. Her voice faltered as she realized just how intimately close they were to each other.

He was smiling, and it transformed his hawk-featured face. She realized for the first time that the man was handsome.

"Go on," he urged, while she studied his transformed features like she'd never seen him before. "I was enjoying this tale."

Then he sat back on his heels as the door opened. Diane deliberately made herself look at anything but the man before her. She paid careful attention to the three people who came in. The servants carried a large, steaming, wooden bucket in each hand. They moved efficiently into the shadowed depths of the room, poured the water into a tub. Then two of them hurried out.

"Anything more, my lord?" the third man asked.

"Bring wine, cheese, and bread for my guest, Yves," Simon replied as he rose to his feet with leonine grace.

Diane reminded herself that she had never much liked cats. Yves answered Simon and hurried out. Leaving her alone with the lion.

At least the big cat was in a good mood, because Simon was still smiling when he held his hand out to her. "Come with me. Now," he added.

She shook her head.

His hard expression returned when she didn't instantly do his bidding. She wasn't used to unquestioning obedience. He was. He grabbed her hands and pulled her to her feet. The next thing she knew he'd also stripped the tattered remains of her skirt and tunic off her. She would have screamed in outrage, but couldn't. Not because she had no voice, but because silent laughter crowded out her indignation at the look of consternation on Simon's face. His open-mouthed stare was so unexpected that she forgot her aches in her own amused reaction.

"What the devil are you wearing under your clothes, woman?"

He stepped back, and looked her over like he'd never seen underwear before. Maybe he hadn't. At least maybe he'd never seen anything from Victoria's Secret, in this case, an ivory satin Wonderbra, a wispy bit of lace panties and sheer pantyhose that had long since become a road map of runs and tears. She vaguely wondered what had happened to her shoes, then finally grew embarrassed as Simon's look turned from consternation, to purely masculine interest.

"What is that wrapping covering your breasts?" he asked as he took a step closer to her. He reached out to touch her.

Diane shook her head wildly, stepped back, and crossed her arms over her chest.

"Ah, it's there for modesty's sake," he said. She nodded. A puzzled expression lit his gold-hazel eyes. "Then why is it covering so little? And why does it thrust your bosom forward, as though as an offering meant to be taken in a man's hands?" While she blushed in shock, and felt her nipples go hard at what had to be reaction to the creamy richness of his voice, he dropped his gaze to her panties. "And those, my dear, are an invitation to sin."

She backed away as she realized just how vulnerable she was being alone with this man. He'd saved her, and now he was gazing at her with a hungry expression she found far more dangerous than the mob's attack. It was far more frightening, because something primal inside her reacted to the look in his eyes.

When she took another step backward, her injured ankle twinged. Diane gasped as pain shot through her, waking her other aches from the mob's treatment of her. Her body forcefully reminded her that arousal was not only inappropriate, but stupid, because it *hurt*. Pain was not an aphrodisiac, but Diane was glad that she hurt because it brought her back to the strange, twisted reality of this situation.

Simon recalled his reason for undressing the girl when her face clouded with pain. The first stirrings of lust cleared, and he once again saw cuts and bruises instead of the firm young body of a beautiful woman. Beautiful? he wondered sardonically as he made himself forget his arousal. When and why had he decided this gold-skinned stranger was a beauty? Not that it mattered. What mattered was attending to her ills.

He pointed to the bath. "Go on. The hot water will help."

She didn't put up any more silent argument, and he firmly turned his face away rather than watch her hobble into the shadows where the steaming tub waited. He looked into the fire as he heard the first splash of water followed by a soft, satisfied sigh. He was glad that she could make at least enough sound to show her comfort.

He recalled how his body had tightened with sudden

desire at the sight of her in her alluring undergarments. It made him wonder what sort of sign of satisfaction this silent woman might make in the midst of passion. Such speculation, he decided, was best not to dwell on.

From the flames, his gaze was drawn up to the banner newly placed above the fireplace.

The blue-green square of silk with its nine fierce dragons was the finest piece of needlework he'd ever seen. A far more accurate representation of his coat of arms than the tapestry hanging behind the high table in the hall. These dragons seemed alive. They shimmered and danced in the play of the firelight— claws bared, fangs gaping. The girl had arrived in his castle with the emblem of his house wrapped around her shoulders like an ornament. Or wrapped up like a gift for the Lord of Marbeau, perhaps?

Oh, Jacques, he thought tiredly. *Would oblivion not be a better gift for the two of us? You still suffer from an excess of hope, old man.*

Hope was never something Simon had believed in, not even the hope of heaven. It held no reality for him. One simply did what one had to in this life. He was convinced there was nothing more, even though Jacques constantly tried to prove differently. But, then, the wizard had the power of his magic, it gave him possibilities. Simon had only his lands and a sword to hold them with, and he was very nearly tired of the game of war, which was the only life he could envision.

He reached up to touch the banner and traced the outline of one of the beasts. He wondered how Diane had known of the nine dragons of Marbeau that slept in the hills surrounding his castle. Jacques claimed it was a coincidence that she'd repeated old court scandals as a heroic *chanson.* Perhaps the design of the banner was a coincidence as well.

"And Jacques is a senile fool," he murmured under his

breath, knowing full well that his friend was neither. Just—optimistic. Simon had given up optimism along with a great many other emotions. He didn't want to be reminded of any of them now. So he turned away from the dragons that symbolized the extravagantly emotional history of his house.

Yves returned and put a laden tray on the table next to Simon's chair. Simon dismissed the man with a flick of his hand, then went to pour himself a goblet of wine. As he did, he noticed the pile of silk rags lying at his feet. He glanced from them to the magnificent banner. Should he wrap the girl in it? He wondered. Hand her back to Jacques the way he'd found her except for her clothes? No, Jacques wouldn't appreciate such provocation, nor did Diane deserve the humiliation. What did she deserve? Something to wear, for one thing, he decided. He went to the great carved wooden chest that sat at the foot of his bed.

He paused a moment before opening the lid, and almost laughed at the notion of a supposedly legendary warrior such as himself showing fear at opening a clothes chest. The room was mostly in darkness. Away from the fireplace, the tiny flame of an hour candle at the head of the bed served as all the light he wanted. The pleasant scent of dried herbs greeted him as he opened the chest. The herbs had been reverently placed among the folded clothing by some devoted serving woman when she'd put the things away for the last time. The smell was evocative of days gone by, as was the feel of the cloth as he plunged his hands blindly into the chest.

They're dead things, he told himself, dead as the wife who wore them. It's your memories that make you think this is worse than thrusting your arm into a pit of snakes. Simon knew that the past was something to be ignored, forgotten. Or, better yet, conquered. Never mind what woman had once worn this clothing. They would do for Diane for now.

He pulled out an armful of dresses and dumped them on the floor beside the shallow tub. The girl drew up her knees and wrapped her arms around them when he approached. He could make out little more than pale skin and a fall of hair darker than the shadows surrounding her. He respected her modesty and quickly looked away.

"Clothes for you," he told her. "There's food waiting as well. Jacques can see to your hurts if you like. But first," he added as his curiosity got the better of him, "sit by the fire for a while and finish telling me the tale of Rick the innkeeper and the fortress of Casablanca."

6

"*What is she doing here?*"

"We need to talk."

Simon had been enjoying himself. Which, of course, was a foolhardy and dangerous pastime. He sat with his legs stretched out before him, and a goblet of wine cradled in his hands. Though his muscles tightened with tension, he didn't change his position as Alys and Jacques entered the room, both speaking at once. He did look up at the dissimilar pair: one red-faced with fury, the other visage creased with age and concern. "Good evening," he drawled.

"Get that bitch out of here! No doubt the slut's found her way into your bed already."

Diane had stopped speaking as soon as the door opened. Now, he watched her curl up in the deep chair while Alys spit venomous accusations about her. Even though she tried to make herself look small and unnoticed, Alys wasn't about to leave the storyteller alone. Diane's shrinking was more out of embarrassment than fear, Simon thought, but he knew his mistress wouldn't see anything but a cringing peasant before her.

When Alys raised a hand to strike Diane, Simon quietly said, "No."

The angry woman spun away from her victim, as though Simon's voice had been a yank on a leash.

Diane wondered at the force of command behind one softly spoken word. Simon, she thought, really was used to being instantly obeyed. And everyone was used to obeying him, even pissed off, foul-mouthed bimbo girlfriends. Wherever this place was, it wasn't run by committee. Whoever had the biggest sword was in charge, she supposed. Which meant Simon was the most uncivilized person in the castle. She shouldn't let herself get lulled into thinking he was anything but a brute, despite his kindness during the last several hours.

Simon stood as Alys turned to him. Her face was livid with anger, but then, she knew she was lovely when she was angry. He put his hand on her arm. "Calm yourself, Alys."

Her eyes flashed green fury. It was very impressive. "I thought you'd sent the demon away and now I find her in your room. The servants say you've bathed with her."

He raised a brow. "Do they?"

She was not warned by his sarcasm. "Have you bedded her as well?"

"No." He smiled slowly, and unable to keep himself from provoking her, added, "Should I?"

Over Alys's head, he saw his silent storyteller get to her feet. Diane tilted her chin up at a proud angle, but the look she directed at him was one of alarm. Damn. He thought he'd forsworn emotion, especially emotion brought on by female involvement. Now here were two women disturbed by a reckless jest. One would have to be placated, the other reassured. He didn't know if he had the energy to deal with both of them. He certainly didn't want to deal with either of them.

He scowled at Jacques. "This is your doing." The old man merely smiled benignly.

Alys pulled away from his grasp. Diane moved closer

to the fire, away from the confrontation, he thought. Or, she tried. The firelight reflected the gold embroidery on the sleeve of her gown and the sight caught Alys's eye.

"What's she doing in Lady Genevieve's clothes?" she demanded.

Simon refused to react to either his mistress's anger, or that name on her lips. He said calmly, "Wearing them. And I haven't bedded the minstrel. Diane is my chattel. She wears what I give her. You are my lover."

Alys preened. "You've never said you loved me before."

Nor had he said it now. He didn't think Alys was fool enough to think he had, but he let it go for the sake of peace. "You are my favored companion. Would I dress you in someone else's cast-off finery?" he asked before she could point out that he'd never allowed her into the former Lady of Marbeau's clothes chest.

Diane turned her back on the room. She gazed into the fire while Simon continued to placate the woman's jealousy. Further conversation meant nothing to her. Simon had called her his chattel. Property. She held her hands out to the fire, cold with the realization that he believed he owned her.

Maybe he did. Jacques had brought her here to entertain his lord. His lord and her master? Everybody's master. Not hers, Diane thought, no matter what he claimed. She'd been threatened, insulted, beaten up, and now told she was the great Lord Simon's chattel. Well, she wasn't going to buy into it. Lord Simon might be dictator of the world, but it wasn't her world. She wasn't going to play by his rules.

She turned back to tell him so just as his girlfriend walked out of the room. Instead of confronting Simon, all Diane could do was watch Alys go, and stand there in frustrated silence. While she tried to get her voice to work she noticed that the long train of the other woman's dress swished a trail in the straw scattered on the floor. Like snail slime, she thought.

At least Alys could walk out. And speak her mind.

Diane was suddenly devastated by the knowledge that she was tired, hurt, and had absolutely nowhere she could go. She would have sunk wearily back into the chair and cried like a baby, but Jacques appropriated the seat before she could move. She looked around desperately, ready to hide herself in the nearest dim corner.

Simon caught the girl as she swayed forward. She looked at him in surprise as she came into his arms, as though she hadn't noticed that she was about to faint. He resisted the urge to cup her cheek and tell her everything was going to be all right. He did help her into his chair before he turned to Jacques.

"About time you got her to bed."

Jacques felt a glow of pleasure at Simon's words. It seemed that magic was at work between his friend and the girl from the future. He knew neither of them were aware of it yet, though their gazes and responses kept playing off each other. This magic had felt right from the beginning. He had known it would work, of course. He just hadn't expected Simon to come out of his grim shell so soon. Yet, here he was treating Diane with the sort of tenderness Jacques hadn't seen in him since Felice was a child.

Of course, Jacques had hopes that Simon would look on Diane as more than a daughter, and certainly more than that vixen Alys. What he needed was someone to love, not someone to bed. He needed someone to teach him that he was not at all the cynical, dried husk of a man he thought he was. No doubt Simon had something wonderful to teach Diane as well, or the magic would not be at work between them. Jacques wondered at what the future would bring to his friend and his newfound lady.

Ah, well, this wasn't the time to discuss it. Thinking of

Felice reminded Jacques of why he'd come to Simon's chamber in the first place.

He held up the message he'd decoded. "I'll put Diane to bed as soon as we discuss this."

Simon spared one more glance for the storyteller before he gave his attention to Jacques. He supposed it could do no harm if the girl heard his secrets. It wasn't as if she was likely to repeat anything she heard. The *geis* was a cruel trick of fate, but until, and if, it was broken, it had advantages as well. Besides, she'd probably be asleep within the next few minutes.

He stretched tired muscles. "I'm for bed soon, myself. Yet, from the worried look on your face, old friend, it's doubtful I'll find sleep easy after I've heard the latest news. So, what treachery are they up to now?"

Jacques folded his hands on his stomach. "There was nothing very new about Denis in the message I deciphered. I learned from our spy that he burned your last letter."

"I suspected he would."

"And he still follows like a puppy in the train of Henry Plantagenet."

"And young Henry and his brothers are still bent on claiming their birthrights a little too early."

"Alas, yes."

"That family will destroy both of ours, and many others before they're done."

Jacques sighed at the truth of Simon's words. "As to new developments, Vivienne is said to be trying to call up a demon to come to the rebels' aid." He gave a low laugh. "There's a bishop riding with the rebels who swears he'll burn the witch if she succeeds."

"Young Henry would prefer to have the demon and the crown, I imagine." Simon wasn't sure whether to laugh or to be concerned. "If Vivienne can call up a demon it will have the bishop for breakfast, with Henry passing it the salt for seasoning. *Can* she conjure a demon?"

"Not from any magic I taught her," Jacques answered. "But she's a clever girl."

Simon glanced at the being from a distant world Jacques had conjured to Marbeau. "If you can bring Diane here—"

"That's an entirely different spell than summoning a demon."

"I'm happy to hear it."

Far from being asleep, Diane leaned forward in her chair, big dark eyes bright with interest. She gazed back at him with a disturbing mixture of hostility and sympathy. He turned away from that look. He especially didn't want the sympathy. He wasn't sure he wanted the discerning curiosity the girl so openly displayed, either. Intelligent women were always dangerous. Even silent, unimportant ones who had a look of kindness about them.

Diane wondered if Simon knew how brittle his voice sounded. For all that he projected, a wall of cynical indifference, she had the feeling that there were some things going on here that the man was deeply disturbed about. He sounded too calm, his movements were too studied. The expression in his eyes had been guarded when he'd looked at her, but she'd seen the pain hiding in the depths.

She hadn't liked what she'd seen in those amber-colored eyes. Especially since her first impulse had been to comfort the man. As Simon and Jacques's conversation continued, she held perfectly still, and told herself she hadn't seen anything. She looked at the floor rather than at the tall, still figure of Simon de Argent. His emotions were none of her business, and she wasn't going to let herself get caught up in worrying about his problems.

It wasn't just that she had enough problems of her own. She'd never found it hard to find room to care for others, even when her own world was in turmoil. She just knew on some basic, gut level that it would be dangerous for her to let her guard down with this man. So, she concentrated on what they said rather than trying to discern the effect it had on the Lord of Marbeau. She didn't know where Marbeau was or what was going on, but any kind of information had to be of some help to her. Maybe she'd even overhear some clue on how she could get back home.

Jacques carefully watched the very subtle interplay between Simon and his young protégé. *She's good for him,* Jacques reiterated to himself. *He'll be good for her. They just don't know it yet.* He had done no harm in bringing them together. He was sure they'd work it out. Meanwhile, he had other news to deliver. "How goes the harvest?"

Simon gave him a curious look. "Well enough, I'm told. Why? Have you news of raiders?"

Jacques nodded. "That I have. All the kings and counts and princes who've spent the summer at war have decided the campaigns are done for now."

"And have released their mercenaries to fend for themselves through the season of truce," Simon finished for him. He ran a hand through his hair. "So there are hungry cutthroats roaming the countryside already."

"Bit early in the year for raiders," Jacques said. "But nothing's gone right this year."

"There's no reason to expect things to quiet down now."

"I had hopes."

"You always do, old friend. It's good to have some warning."

Jacques stood. "Spies have their uses. Gives us time for you to increase the guard patrols. I'll see if I can work out a spell to make the raiders pass us by."

Simon chuckled. "When Denis has already given them a map to our door?"

Jacques put a comforting hand on Simon's shoulder. "I doubt Denis is as wicked as that."

"Go to bed, old man," was the only reply he received.

Simon waved dismissively toward Diane. "And don't forget to take your attempt at distraction with you. And please recall that I prefer to choose my own bed partners," he added while Jacques helped Diane to stand.

Don't forget to take your attempt at distraction with you.

Oooh, the man was so infuriating. So commanding. So patronizing. Autocratic. Aristocratic. Arrogant. He had the I'm-Mr.-Go-Where-I-Say-Do-What-I-Want-Because-It's-My-God-Given-Right-to-Run-Peoples'-Lives routine down cold.

Something definitely needed to be done about that kind of attitude.

Anyway, it wasn't as if she'd actually intended to stay in the same room with the man any longer than she had to. Of course she'd gotten up and left with Jacques, without a backward glance for Lord High and Mighty Simon de Argent. Shuffled out, actually, since it had been impossible to flounce, or even stomp, with a sore foot and a heavy wool dress with a stupid long train. Anyway, she'd been happy to leave. She hadn't wanted to stay in the first place. Why should she?

She was happy to be out of his exalted presence, she told herself as she settled down on the bed in Jacques's tower chamber. The place was too dark now that Jacques had extinguished all the candles and torches. Dark and cold. She didn't like sleeping in rooms that were either. Jacques was sleeping on a pallet on the floor, which made her feel guilty since he'd obviously given up his own bed. He'd told her he was tough and stringy and used to sleeping wherever he lay his head, and obviously meant it because he was already snoring. She still hated using what the old man probably thought was a luxurious bed. She wished she had a decent pair of pajamas to sleep in. Instead she'd stripped down to the linen slip she'd had to put on earlier to keep the wool dress from scraping her skin raw. The blankets she pulled up around her ears weren't any too soft, either. And they smelled of mildew. She wished she was home.

She wished she'd never met Simon de Argent. He'd put her through more emotional trauma in less than two days than anyone else she'd ever met. Emotional and physical trauma. He played with swords. He played God.

I prefer to choose my own bed partners.

She had news for Simon de Argent: So did she. He was not among the candidates for the position. Keanu Reeves, he was not. At least Keanu was Asian-American, which made him a far more likely candidate for her fantasies than any blond, amber-eyed not-exactly-twentysomething lord of wherever this place was.

Don't think about him anymore, she told herself. She turned over several times as she tried to find a position that didn't press on some bruised spot. Just lie still and go to sleep, she thought. Maybe when she woke up the nightmare would finally be over. What if it wasn't a nightmare? It was best to pretend it was if she wanted to get to sleep, she decided.

Besides, she didn't have to be his lordship's pet—chattel—storyteller, if she didn't want to. She didn't have to do anything for Simon de Argent. She didn't owe him anything.

Except her life, she thought as she drifted off to sleep with the image of a fierce gold angel pulling her away from the fire.

7

"She said no, my lord."

Simon raised a skeptical brow at the servant. "I sincerely doubt that, Yves."

Yves blushed and shuffled his feet while the men with Simon laughed. The *geis* forcing Diane to be silent except when performing had become common knowledge. "I meant to say that she indicated that she would not attend you, my lord."

Again, Simon thought. Diane had refused every summons to his presence for the last two days. Jacques had assured him that she had taken no great harm from the peasants' attack, though she was spending her time curled up in bed while the bruises healed. Jacques said she was simply sulking for some reason. Jacques also said that she was as good at sulking as Simon himself.

Simon had reserved comment on the old man's opinion. What he ought to do was ignore the fool woman, but he found he could not. He had only called for her in the first place because he thought she'd appreciate the chance to use her voice. But she would not come. Instead of proper obedience and gratitude he had gotten repeated refusals. She didn't have a voice to make excuses with. She simply didn't come when ordered.

He was beginning to be annoyed with such queenly haughtiness.

"That's an odd entertainer your wizard presented to you, my lord," Joscelin deBroc commented. "Normally they enjoy performing. Perhaps she has some private reason for not coming down."

"You promised us a tale from the woman, my lord," Sir Thierry Turpeney reminded him. "Something to ease our spirits before we ride out with the dawn."

Thierry was not actually riding out on patrol. He was being left in charge of Marbeau while Simon took most of his force on patrols of his land. Simon didn't point out to the man that he was going to continue to enjoy hot food and a warm bed, and hence did not need his spirit eased.

Her other refusals had been delivered to the privacy of his chamber. No one had known about Diane's behavior but Jacques and Yves. He'd been displeased, but had let the matter go. This time he could not, as Yves had brought the answer to him in the great hall where he'd gathered his men together for a midday meeting. He could not allow defiance from anyone in front of his knights.

"Did you tell her I wish her to amuse not just myself but my men?"

"Yes, my lord," Yves answered.

Joscelin leaned forward in his chair. He was an easygoing lad, newly knighted, and always eager to think the best of everyone. "Perhaps the minstrel is a modest sort."

"Modest?" Thierry asked. "How could that be?"

"Well—" Joscelin rubbed his chin thoughtfully. "Perhaps she is yet a maid, and takes offense or misunderstands what Lord Simon meant when she was told to entertain his men. Perhaps she fears for her chastity, and so refuses to attend us on those grounds."

"Chaste? Maidenly? A common traveling storyteller?" Thierry gave a jeering laugh. He gestured with his winecup at the other men in the hall. "Did you hear this fool?"

Simon was thoughtful as he watched the boy's cheeks color bright red. He frowned as the hall filled with laughter and lewd comments at Joscelin's suggestion. Simon was not among those who found the notion of a maiden modest entertainer amusing. In fact, he stood and glared his men into silence.

"We'll see," he said, and strode off toward the tower stairs with one hand on his sword hilt.

How was he to know what the woman was in her own place and time? Perhaps it was as Joscelin suggested, and she misinterpreted his commands. Or perhaps she was just sulking. In any event, he would not allow her to disobey him in front of his men.

The effect when he banged open the door of Jacques chamber was all he could have wished for. Diane jumped up from the bed and whirled toward him, startled as a doe. The comb she'd been using on her thick black hair dropped from her hands. Simon walked forward, she backed away.

He retrieved the ivory comb from the rushes. "Did I startle you?" he asked as he held the comb out to her.

Diane stared at his hand while she absorbed the rich sound of his voice. Oddly enough, she'd missed hearing his voice in the last couple of days. Maybe because she had no voice of her own, or because Jacques spent more time reading than speaking when he was even in the room at all. Maybe because Simon's voice was the most beautiful thing she'd yet encountered in this horrible place.

His hand, she noticed now, was almost as beautiful as his voice, long-fingered, and elegant even though a thin scar marked the skin just below his knuckles. A barbarian's hand, she reminded herself even as he gallantly offered her the comb.

When she put out her hand to take it he let the comb

drop back to the floor and reached for her instead. She looked up at his face as he grasped her fingers and pulled her forward. "I've missed hearing your voice."

A shock went through her, from his touch, and from the echo of her thought in his words. She would have pulled away, but his hand was as strong as it was beautiful. His grip wasn't painful, but it was implacable.

He drew her a step closer. She wished she could run. She wished Jacques were here. She wished she could do anything but be trapped in his grasp, forced to meet the sardonic light in his eyes and the faintly mocking smile that transformed the normally grim set of his lips. Since no wish of hers was likely to come true she supposed all she could do was face Simon de Argent as bravely as she could. So she squared her shoulders and glared at him.

"You have a beautiful voice," he told her.

Simon did not know what had compelled those words from him, though they were nothing more than the truth. He had come in meaning to drag Diane out by the hair if he had to. Instead, he found himself willing to persuade when a command should have been enough. It had to do with the sad, lost look he'd seen on her face before surprise at his entrance drove her up off the bed. There had been that moment of fear, quickly replaced by defiance. Though he should have been angry at the defiance he found that he admired it instead.

"This would be easier if you cowered, you know."

She tilted her head to one side. The simple gesture conveyed a wealth of sarcastic bravado.

"So you refuse to fear me, do you?"

She gave an emphatic nod.

He ran a finger along her stubbornly set jaw. Her skin had the look of pearl mixed with gold, but far from being made of hard gem and metal, she was soft to the touch. His fingers wanted to turn the touch to a caress even as she sharply pulled her head away.

He denied the impulse and kept his voice light as he said, "Another man would beat you for such insolence."

The look of feigned innocence she gave him at this statement almost made him laugh.

"Don't talk to me like that," he warned, and was warmed by the startled smile that broke like sunrise over her face. "Fortunately for you, I'm too lazy to beat you. Come with me," he requested mildly. He released her hand, to let her know he would not drag her away, and to kill the temptation to draw her even closer. "Come down to the hall and tell a story. You'll enjoy using your voice."

Diane had the distinct impression that the man didn't know the word *please*, but that he was doing the best he could with his limited vocabulary. He was, in fact, being charming. She didn't like it a bit. Charm was harder to deal with than despotism. Besides, he was right. She put a hand to her throat. Her vocal chords' refusal to work was driving her crazy. She did want to talk. The ache to speak grew worse with every passing minute.

"Will you tell me a story, Diane?"

His rich voice flowed over her like honey, persuasive and pleading. His expression was full of understanding. With her hand still touching her throat she turned her back to him. She wished she could plug her ears against that seductive voice. She looked at the rough stone wall before her and tried to pretend his large, solid presence had no effect on her.

He thinks he owns you, she reminded herself. Jacques brought you here to amuse him. You're no more than an organic film projector to him. Just a VCR he plays and pauses and turns off at his whim. He wasn't trying to turn her off now, another part of her argued. He was politely asking her to do the one thing she could do. He also wasn't the person responsible for her problems, even though he was the reason she was here. Jacques's reason, not Simon's. Still, she hated being no more than a toy for the lord of Marbeau, of having been presented to Simon as a gift. He'd accepted the gift, or he wouldn't be here.

"You have a talent, a gift you can share with me and my people."

Damn the man for picking up the very words she thought and speaking them when she couldn't! She spun around, but not away from him because he put both of his hands on her shoulders. "Spit your fury on me if you must, girl," he said, voice coldly quiet, "but know that you will regret it."

She'd raised a hand to slap him, or to try to push him away, but dropped it back to her side at his words. She realized there was only so far she could go to thwart this man's wishes and after that point came deep trouble. He'd thrown her out into the ugly world beyond the castle once. The hard look on his face told her he could do it again. The faint lift of one of his eyebrows told her that he wouldn't do it if she behaved reasonably. Reasonable by his standards. Which were not her own. There were parameters she was going to have to live with, weren't there?

"You cannot survive on pride here," he told her. "You can't expect to have things your own way. You are a woman and a stranger with no feudal ties to protect you. Whatever you were in your own place, whoever you were, means nothing here. It's a pity. It should not have happened. It did. Deal with it. If you don't, Diane, you will not survive."

He squeezed her shoulders. The gesture was both comforting and a warning, because though his touch was gentle it reminded her of how much larger he was, how much stronger.

"And I'm not the only one with a sword."

She damned the man once again for his ability to read her mind. And though she resented the truth he'd spoken, she was grateful he'd put it into words as well.

"So," he said. "Will you come with me to the ladies' solar and give us a story?"

Diane considered her options. Stay in Jacques's room and sulk, or do as Simon asked. She was getting more and more frustrated with hiding out in Jacques's room. Maybe she'd think of something else eventually, but until then—

She sighed, looked away, and nodded.

He lifted her chin with his fingers and turned her head. He gave her one of his rare, faint smiles. "Good. Maybe this time you'll be able to finish the Casablanca story for me."

8

Alys looked up from the circle of women gathered around a large embroidery frame as he stepped into the room. She smiled and stood, and held her hand out, but Simon turned to a serving woman before acknowledging his mistress. "Tell my knights that their company is wanted in the solar."

Then he came fully into the room, Diane trailing reluctantly behind him, hidden in his shadow for the moment. He looked around, as reluctant as she was to be here. For this was the place where the gentlewomen of Marbeau spent their days and slept when they had no man to bed with them at night. Here, they spun and wove and sewed and cared for their babes and talked and plotted among themselves. No man was comfortable in this women's country. Particularly not a man with no wife to smile at as she glanced up from her work or children to toddle across the rush-covered floor into his waiting arms.

He did not come here often, nor did he stay very long when he did, and now here he was braving the lionesses' den at the price of a story. He glanced back in unreasonable annoyance at Diane, then took her arm and pulled her forward just as Alys approached.

"I've brought the storyteller," he said. "For you."

As expected, Alys's face clouded with fury, but she didn't shout. Not in front of the other women. She forced a smile to her lips, stepped close to him and spoke quietly. "I don't want your storyteller." She put a delicate hand on his arm as she leaned even closer. With her breasts pressed hard against his chest, she said, "I want you."

"Well, I'm not going to take you in front of a crowd," he answered.

She thrust out her lip in a pretty pout, and pressed her hips against his. "I haven't seen you in days and days. You don't send for me. You haven't come down to the hall for the evening meal. You haven't even been to Mass."

"I've been planning a campaign."

"There's always war. Have you not missed being with me?" Her tone indicated that there was going to be a battle with her if he didn't say something placating soon.

So he took Alys in his arms and said, loud enough for the avid watchers to hear, "Being absent from your presence, sweet lady, has left me parched with thirst for the sight of your beauty. To see you again refreshes me like cool water from a hidden spring."

He kissed her cheek, and heard her women snicker and giggle as he did so. From the corner of his vision he glimpsed Diane as she rolled her eyes heavenward. Clearly, she was unimpressed with his eloquence. Perhaps they did not practice the false flattery of courtiers in her land. If so, it was a lucky place for a man to live.

Alys accepted his lying devotion easily enough, especially since it was spoken in front of the other castle women. She cared no more for him than he did for her, though he knew she had missed his company for her own purposes. Curious, prying Alys hated not knowing every little detail of his plans and projects. That he was leaving the castle without her knowing when he would return or how long he would be gone or where he planned to ride must have galled her. He had no doubt that she would want to crawl into his bed tonight to bid him a fond farewell—and find out things he had no intention of telling her while they dallied.

"Come, let us listen to the storyteller."

Alys fluttered her eyelashes at him. "As you wish, my lord."

"I crave only your pleasure, my dear."

He kept his arm attentively around Alys's shoulders as he escorted her back to her seat, then he stood beside her with his hand on her shoulder. This left Diane alone in the middle of the room while a dozen knights filed in. The women eagerly made room for the men, and they were soon settled on cushions and benches and reclining at favored ladies' feet. He watched Diane react nervously to all this activity, with her arms crossed protectively under her breasts.

Diane shivered with apprehension as the crowd gathered around her. People stared at her and talked about her as though she weren't there. So, she countered by pretending they weren't there, either. All but Simon, that is. She wondered if she could ever escape his sharp scrutiny. It was like she physically felt it, as though his awareness of her seeped all the way into her bones and blood.

The problem was, that as the silence grew, her mind went blank. She couldn't think of a story. Her mind remained on Simon, and the disgusting exchange he'd had with Bimbo Alys. Did either of them really believe that the other was in love? Cynicism fairly dripped off both of them when they were together. The odd thing was, Diane somehow expected better of Simon. As if she really knew the man.

The only thing that came to her as the crowd grew restless, stirred in their seats and mumbled to each other, were the lyrics of a song from *Operation: Mindcrime*. Which was a rock opera of sorts and not a movie, but at least it had a storyline. So, since it fit the criteria of the stupid curse or spell or whatever it was, and she had to do something, she ended up keeping her attention firmly on Simon as she sang the first words of "I Don't Believe in Love," *a cappella*. Even though she didn't have the greatest voice in the world, she could at least carry a tune, and his nod of approval gave her the encouragement to go on.

So, his storyteller had a talent for song, Simon thought as she began to sing. He was pleased at first to discover that she shared his own musical gift. Though he did not know why he should care that Diane had an interest in music when he'd given it up himself.

The meaning of the song was rather hard to follow at first, though the theme that believing in love was not worth the pain of being in love soon became clear. How true, Simon thought, and how sad. He enjoyed himself as he listened, even though Diane's singing voice did not match the quality of her speaking voice. What interested him was that listening to this song was like looking at one section of a cathedral window and having to guess the parable depicted in colored glass that made up the rest. This was very different from listening to a section of the *Song of Roland*, or some other familiar *chanson de geste*.

"How intriguing," he said as the song finished. "Jacques is right in his claim that this Diane is anything but boring."

His words earned him a vicious look from Alys. So he clapped loudly to show Diane even more approval. His knights and gentlewomen had to clap along with him whether they enjoyed the performance or not. Alys wasn't happy, but the applause drew a smile from Diane. Simon thought bringing the girl a bit of joy was worth rousing the displeasure of the pampered beauty beside him.

He wondered if he should ask her to sing the rest of this song cycle, but before he could make a request, her smile

widened, she bowed to him, and began the Casablanca tale
he'd already asked for.

"Ah, good."

He took a seat beside Alys, and leaned forward, eager
to finally hear out the story of Rick, Lady Ilsaf and the
valiant Victor of Laslo.

Diane had barely reached the part where the marshal
Louis has sent his guardsmen out to round up the usual
suspects when Simon's own marshal rushed into the
room.

Simon bolted to his feet, all thought of pleasure ban-
ished. "What?"

"Lord Simon, a messenger has just brought word of
raiders attacking Domiere!"

Anger surged through Simon at the raiders daring to
attack an abbey of holy sisters. "That's not ten miles from
Marbeau. It looks like we ride now instead of waiting for
the dawn." He gathered his men with a grim look.

Diane scampered to the side as the group of men
headed for the door. She definitely wanted to stay out of
their way. She'd seen an instant change come over them
the moment they'd heard of the attack. It was like this
massive surge of testosterone had washed over every last
man in the room. Even Simon, no, especially Simon, who
she sometimes suspected of being civilized but really
wasn't. She could practically taste the urge for battle in
the air. Or, maybe, it was just an overpowering stench of
sweat as Simon's warriors hurried past her.

With war on their minds they left the womenfolk without a backward glance or a word of farewell. It worried
Diane that the women didn't seem to notice that they
were being abandoned, but then, the women carried
knives, too. Maybe they found warfare normal.

All Diane knew was that she didn't find anybody's
behavior normal, and she was once again completely dis-
oriented by this strange place. Once the men were gone,

the women gathered around Alys. They talked among themselves and ignored Diane. All except Alys, who gave her a look full of anger and calculation. Diane didn't wait for Bimbo Alys to tell her to get out. She hurried back to the relative shelter of Jacques's tower without any urging.

"Come along to the hall if you want dinner."

Diane sighed, but she followed the old man out of his chamber.

It looked like Jacques wasn't going to let her hide any more than Simon had. She decided to pretend she was brave and go along with it. She'd retreated yesterday, then she'd spent the night thinking over what Simon had said about dealing with this place. She was ashamed of her own reaction. She had to go forward, not withdraw into childish terror.

Besides, she was hungry, and dinner, such as it was, was downstairs.

The hall was just as dark and smoky as she remembered from her first excursion. Servants moved around, and there were guards standing at the main door, but with Simon and most of the soldiers gone the place was subdued. People still stared at her like she was a freak, and muttered and made signs as she passed by. Diane pretended not to notice.

She did take Jacques's hand as they made their way between tables to the platform where Lady Alys and a few men sat facing the room while they ate their dinner. The old man's skin felt dry and fragile as paper, but his grip was strong and reassuring just the same. She liked Jacques. Despite the fact that he was responsible for her being here, he was so well-meaning that it was impossible not to like him.

Not everyone liked Jacques, she decided as she saw the looks Alys and the man seated beside her gave the old wizard. Diane had noticed the man yesterday because of his red hair. Seated next to the redhaired Alys, it was obvious the two were related. Brother and sister, she guessed, from the resemblance and their ages. Both were young and attractive, though the man had a narrow scar on his left cheek.

Alys pointed at Diane. "You don't mean to seat *that* at my lord's high table, do you?"

"Of course," Jacques replied, and led Diane to one of the benches. After she was seated, Jacques turned to speak mildly to Alys. "Be a good girl and don't cause any trouble."

"Don't give me orders, old man," she countered. "Your days at Marbeau are numbered."

Jacques gave a loud laugh, then ignored Alys as he sat down beside Diane. In the suddenly quiet room, he gestured to a servant.

The man hurried forward and put large flat loaves of bread down on the table in front of them. Another servant dumped a ladle of some sort of stew thing onto the bread. Was Simon too poor to afford dishes? Diane wondered as she stared at the greasy concoction before her. She'd been eating cheese, chunks of bread and dried fruit whenever Jacques or Simon remembered to feed her at all. This was her first encounter with Marbeau's cooked cuisine and she had no idea what to do. She wanted to ask for some utensils. Since she didn't have any voice, she tugged on Jacques's sleeve instead.

Unfortunately, he was distracted by Alys's brother before she could get his attention.

"My sister does not want the foreigner at her table."

"It's not her table, Sir Thierry."

Diane quickly broke off a piece of bread on the edge of the loaf and stuffed it into her mouth. Since she couldn't get involved in any argument concerning her, she figured she might as well eat her dinner while the others talked.

Besides, if she concentrated on the food maybe she could pretend she didn't hear any of the ugly things said about her.

Jacques watched as Thierry Turpeney's eyes narrowed. The man reminded him of a fox, cunning enough, but vermin just the same. Thierry wasn't quite as given to indulging his tempestuous nature as his sister, but he had too many strong appetites and hated to be thwarted.

Jacques wished Simon hadn't left Thierry in charge of the castle's defenses, but understood his friend's reasons. It was a way of seemingly showing he trusted this pair that had once been so close to Denis. Simon said it was easy enough to trust the Turpeneys when he never planned to be more than a day's ride away from Marbeau, and Jacques himself actually remained in charge of the castle. The more trusted of the guards knew it, even if Thierry did not.

He held up a hand in a conciliatory gesture just the same. "I meant to say that Lady Alys may head Simon's household, but it is the custom for the wizard of Marbeau to offer the baron's hospitality to his personal guests—whether they be low or high born." Jacques looked toward the man seated at the far end of the table. "Is that not so, Father Andre?"

The priest looked past the rim of the large winecup he held. His voice was barely audible when he replied, "That is so, I believe. Or so I've heard. I don't recall—"

"There, you see? The priest confirms that I have a right to have Diane by my side."

"Lord Simon would approve?" Thierry questioned. "Having the foreigner at the high table is no stain on the honor of Marbeau?"

"None whatsoever."

The young knight seemed willing enough to be mollified. In fact, as he looked Diane over carefully he showed an interest Jacques did not like. The young woman was quietly eating her meal, her face turned away from the conversation. It looked to Jacques that Thierry was aware of the elegance of her high-cheekboned profile.

"What of my honor?"

"Oh, leave be, Alys. There's no harm in this."

Jacques should have been pleased when Thierry spoke to his sister, but the smirk on the man's face did not reassure him.

Alys slapped her hand on the polished wood tabletop. "I don't want her here. She's ugly and vile. The sight of her spoils my meal."

"Do you fear her, then?"

Perhaps it had been a bad idea to risk a confrontation by bringing Diane down to dinner while Simon was away, Jacques thought. Alys seemed to feel threatened by the storyteller. He wasn't about to do anything to mollify her fears. But then, she was well aware that Jacques wanted her out of Simon's bed, and someone who'd care for the man in it. Alys was no doubt quite concerned that Simon hadn't showed any interest in her since the night of Diane's arrival.

Diane tried not to listen to the conversation, but was aware of every word. As she listened she began to wonder just why she liked Jacques. The man was obviously using her as a pawn in some game he was playing with this pair. She'd like to think he was the good guy, but she didn't like being used. Especially when she didn't know what the game was.

If there had to be games, she thought, it would be nice if they'd let her play. If somebody would just explain the rules, she'd be happy to choose a side and start kicking the opposing players around. Better to play than try to stay neutral, she thought. Better to play than to be the playing piece.

The conversation went on and on while Diane methodically ate around the rim of her flat bread. Nobody bothered to even speak to her even though they felt perfectly comfortable talking about her. After awhile she stopped feeling insulted. She even stopped being annoyed. She started to get bored. When she was finished with as much of the meal as she could stand to eat, she got up from her seat and went to stand at the foot of the dais.

This time she didn't mind that the attention of everybody in the room immediately riveted on her. She was sick of a lot of the things she'd heard and felt. She was really sick of this foreign demon nonsense. She wanted to tell them that foreign devil was how her grandparents' people referred to Europeans when they first encountered them. While she wasn't sure where she was, this place had a distinctly European flavor to it. Actually, *stench* was a better word than flavor. This place made her ashamed that she'd once been so proud to be half Scottish.

Since all she could do was tell stories instead of explain what she thought and felt, she would give them a story from the Asian side of her ancestry. Actually, the story she decided on was Japanese because the world's best samurai movie was the only thing she could think of that these warrior barbarians could relate to.

"Once upon a time there was a poor village that was under constant attack by robbers. The harvest was stolen and burned. The villagers had nothing to eat. They were hungry. They had nothing. No knights to protect them. When the villagers held a meeting, someone suggested asking knights to drive off the robbers. The villagers were unsure of this plan. How could they—poor, hungry, unworthy farmers—persuade men of the proud warrior class to help them? How? Find hungry samurai—or knights—the wise village elder advised."

As she continued telling the story, she watched her audience carefully. Jacques sat back with his hands folded over his stomach and smiled encouragement at her. The plot of *The Seven Samurai* got mixed reactions from the rest of the group. Everyone seemed to like the part about the girl disguised as a boy who had a romance with the youngest samurai. They laughed when it turned out that the supposedly completely destitute villagers were able to scrape together enough supplies for a party. There was a disappointed reaction from the women and servants when Toshiro Mifune's peasant pretending to be samurai character got killed. All in all it went pretty well, but she wondered why Sir Thierry was frowning angrily at her when she was finished.

He banged a fist on the table when she was done. "How dare a peasant pretend to be a knight?" He glared at her. "I should slit your throat for the insult, girl."

"Yes," Alys suggested smoothly. "Why don't you?"

Diane had no idea what the man was angry about. She looked to Jacques for help.

"The impostor died in the end, Thierry," Jacques pointed out to the angry man. "As he deserved."

"But they buried him as a knight!"

So? Diane thought. *What's the problem?*

"The peasant dog deserved to be thrown on the dung heap!" Thierry insisted.

"It's disgraceful," Alys added. "The storyteller should be punished for such a wicked tale."

Diane decided she'd had enough of this weird place and nasty people for one evening. They didn't get it, she couldn't explain it, and she didn't care. She made a gesture at Thierry that she hoped he wouldn't interpret as a polite farewell, and turned around and left the hall.

9

Jacques closed the door quietly behind him and leaned against the thick, old wood. When Diane looked up from where she sat on the bed, he said, "I'm not sure if the evening was a success or not."

She smiled, then the smile eased into a silent laugh.

"I'm glad to see you enjoyed yourself, my dear," he told her. He came to sit beside her. "Alys insists on drama, and her brother's not much better." He patted her knee. "Everyone else enjoyed your story. You keep telling stories and soon the people of Marbeau will love you."

Her expression told him that she wasn't interested in having the people love her.

He patted her knee again. "There, there. Have they hurt you that much with their ignorant insults, my dear? Or is it just Simon you want to love you?" he asked, then cackled with laughter at her outraged reaction.

She shook her head and assumed an air of indifferent dignity. Jacques let the subject go. He crossed the room and picked up a papyrus scroll from his work table. He sat down in his chair by the lit brazier, to warm his old bones and for light to read the difficult-to-decipher Egyptian characters. It was up to Simon and Diane to find comfort with each other.

Diane watched the old man for a while. Despite the age difference, and the strange circumstances, he reminded her of her father in the way he just disappeared into whatever he was reading. The problem was, he didn't physically disappear. She had to go to the bathroom really bad, and hated having to use the wooden bucket provided for the sanitation purposes unless she was alone. She didn't like using it then, but at least it wasn't quite as humiliating in private. With Jacques present, she had to consider the alternative, which was maybe worse. It was bug-infested and stank, but at least offered privacy. This indoor outhouse called a garderobe was on the second floor, down a dark, narrow hall near Simon's chamber. She supposed she would have to go there if she wanted privacy. So, she picked up a candle and reluctantly headed for the stairs.

I really really hate this place, Diane thought, certainly not for the first time, as she adjusted the clothing she'd worn for the last several days after she'd finished in the garderobe. She wondered why she'd taken her comfortable life at home for granted. Plumbing really was a big deal when you didn't have any. Toilet paper was the most important invention in the history of the universe. After that, came toothpaste. Toothpaste was as precious as gold. After she'd pantomimed brushing her teeth about a dozen times and Jacques finally figured out what she meant, he'd given her a piece of cloth to rub her teeth with and some bark to chew on. It worked, but it wasn't toothpaste.

And there was no use complaining about the situation when she was the only one who knew what was on her mind. If she ever got her voice back—*watch out for that day, Simon de Argent*, she thought as she pushed open the door of the garderobe with her free hand.

She was plunged into darkness a moment later as the candle was knocked from her hand. She was pushed roughly back against the wall as someone said, "Don't worry about her screaming."

Alys.

Fear raced through Diane. She struggled, but she wasn't being held by the other woman. She was shaken, then slapped hard across the face. Her senses reeled as the back of her head hit the wall. Then she was pulled forward and a mouth came down on hers in a hard, cruel kiss. She pushed ineffectually against the man's chest, but he only pulled away to laugh. He grabbed her by the hair and pushed her back against the wall again. He held her there with one hand pressed hard against her throat. Her lips hurt, her head hurt, she could hardly breathe. She struck out blindly, but was unable to touch either of the two figures that had her trapped in the dark corridor.

"Talk of the curse must be true, then," the man said. "Or she'd have made some noise by now."

Thierry.

"Take her to Simon's room," Alys said. "Have her on his bed, the way Berengar had Lady Genevieve."

"Remind the man of being a cuckold? Not I, sister. I said I'd help you. I didn't say I wanted to die."

"Then why don't you just kill the foreigner?"

Diane was pulled forward. Thierry twisted her arms behind her, holding her easily in a one-handed grip. He used his other hand to roughly caress her breasts. She kicked back at his shin, but he took no notice of her struggles.

"I'm not killing Jacques's pet for you," Thierry told his sister. "My plan's better. I'll have this one broken to my bed by the time your lover returns. He'll lose any interest he might have in her once he sees what an obedient and loving mistress she makes me."

Alys laughed. "You're right. Once he sees her with you, he'll recall that I'm as loyal and loving a woman as he's likely to find in this life."

"A short life, I pray."

"Amen," Alys answered him.

Diane kept trying to twist away, kept trying to kick the

bastard, but it did her no good. Thierry's hands didn't stop roving over her body the whole time he and Alys discussed her. She bit down on chain mail when she tried to bite his arm. He laughed at her.

Diane hoped someone would come along the corridor and find them. She prayed someone would help her. That someone would stop this. That she'd find a way to escape. But Thierry had a grip like steel. And, she remembered bleakly, he was in charge of the castle while Simon was gone.

Simon, she found herself praying. *Please, God, Simon where are you?*

"I want privacy," Thierry said. "A few hours alone with the bitch before I take her to my pallet in the hall."

"I told you to use Simon's room."

"I told you no."

"The solar, then. I'll keep the women in the hall until you're done."

"Good enough."

Thierry spun Diane around and hauled her over his shoulder. She shouted silently for Simon as Thierry carried her away.

Something felt wrong. Simon sensed it the moment he entered the great hall of Marbeau. He was the only one who seemed to notice. His men spread out across the room, to the fire and to the tables that hadn't yet been broken down from the evening meal, calling for meat and drink. The people in the hall lingered despite the hour, talking, playing games. They looked up at his entrance, the servants and pages bowed, but no one paid him any more mind than they usually did. Still, there was a kind of nervous tension in the air. He caught swiftly concealed looks of surprise on several faces. Of course, no one had expected the warriors to return so soon, either.

It was late, well past sunset. He was tired, stiff from many hours in the saddle. He wanted a hot meal, a cup of mulled wine and to strip off his armor and soak in a hot bath before he fell into his own bed. And perhaps a tale from Diane, he thought as he walked forward. He'd found her voice spinning stories in his head at the oddest moments while they'd hunted down the men who'd raided the abbey. He'd pictured her face while he'd sat around last night's campfire, imagined her movements, gone to sleep wondering how she fared.

He looked carefully around the hall as he approached the dais, but Diane was nowhere to be seen. Up in Jacques's room, he supposed. Which was where she belonged. Whatever his impulse, he would not send for her tonight. He would have his meal, and go to bed . . . as soon as he discovered just what it was that troubled him.

Alys came forward as he neared the high table. Her cheeks were flushed, her green eyes bright as a cat's in candlelight. "Well met, my lord," she called as she slid her arms around his neck. She pulled his head down and kissed him with the sort of swift passion he hadn't felt from her since their first night together. He opened his lips beneath the assault of her tongue, let the kiss go on for as long as she wanted, put his arms around her and drew her close. He felt nothing.

"I'm so happy you're home safely," she told him once she was done kissing him. Her voice was husky with desire.

"I'm hungry," he said.

She dipped her head and looked up at him through thick eyelashes. "For me?"

"For dinner first."

Instead of pouting, she laughed. "Of course." She took him by the hand and led him toward his chair. A trencher full of meat and a full goblet were set at his place before he reached it.

"The servants are more attentive than usual tonight," he commented as he reached his chair. Simon looked around once more. "Why is everyone up so late?"

"It's not all that late, my lord," Alys answered. "Rest yourself, eat. The pork is especially fine tonight."

The smell of the meat was tempting, but he couldn't bring himself to sit down and enjoy it just yet. "It is late. I expected to step over pallets spread out for the night, instead I find a crowd roistering as though it's a saint's day."

Alys laughed again. It sounded shrill this time.

Simon frowned at her. "What are the women doing here? Shouldn't you all be in the solar by now?"

The solar, he thought. *Diane*. The last time he'd seen Diane had been in the solar. He had a sudden impression that she was still there, in need of him.

"Where's Thierry?"

Alys put a hand on his arm. "Patrolling the bailey, I—"

"Damn!"

Simon shook off Alys's grasping hold, and ran for the solar.

10

The first thing he saw was Diane's overdress lying on the floor. The dark cloth looked like a congealed puddle of blood in the glow of the rushlights. Then he brought his gaze upward, slowly taking in the sight of a woman crouched on her side against a storage chest. Of the man who loomed over her, his arm raised.

Diane's hands were uplifted to ward off the next blow. She wore only a torn and bloodied shift, her back was bare and covered in livid welts. Thierry's breeches were pulled down around his knees, his cock hard and ready.

After that, Simon saw things tinged in shades of furious red. He didn't remember drawing his sword.

Thierry whirled around. He went pale. He dropped the thick leather belt from his hand. Lust faded out of his eyes. It was replaced with stark fear.

"My lord, I—"

He didn't have time to reach for a blade before Simon drove his broadsword deep into his bare belly.

A woman's scream rang out behind him, but Simon was more interested in the silent woman who cowered on the floor. He pulled his sword out and it dropped beside the dying man crumpled on the rushes. Simon took off his cloak as he went to Diane. He wrapped the girl in it, then helped her to stand. She flinched away from his touch. As she should rightly flinch away from any man's touch, he thought. She couldn't stand without his help so he didn't let her go though her eyes pleaded with him to. He tucked her close under his arm, where he could feel her silent, wracking sobs as he turned to face the crowd that had gathered behind them.

Alys knelt next to her brother, but her attention was on Simon. Her expression was full of the hate she'd always been so careful to hide before.

"Get out," he told her, before she could spew any poisonous words at him. "Take your brother's body and go back to my son."

"Denis will kill you for this!" she shouted back. "He'll have your vitals—"

"Denis may kill me." He pointed at Thierry. "But not over that. Or for bedding his supposedly cast-off lover. Don't you think I know that you stayed to spy for him when he rode away from Marbeau?" He threw back his head and laughed. It was the first time he'd felt like laughing in oh, so long, and there was no humor in it. When he looked at Alys again she was pale, and shaking with fury. "Get out," he told her again. "It'll be inconvenient no longer having you to feed false information to my rebellious son, but I'll manage."

"You were never any good at loveplay," she spat at him.

"You never gave me any reason to be. Get out. Pack your things and go, before I send you to hell with your brother. Joscelin."

The young knight stepped out of the knot of people crowded into the solar. "Yes, my lord?"

"See Lady Alys on her way. Escort her as far as Domiere. She's on her own from there."

Joscelin looked from him to Alys, his eyes as round as coins, but he answered promptly, "Yes, my lord."

Simon didn't wait to see Alys start her packing. He didn't care if she took the whole contents of the women's quarters with her. He gathered the shivering Diane up in his arms, and carried her from the room.

"She hasn't been raped, thank God."

Simon glared at the old man. "She might as well have been, Jacques."

Simon looked down at the girl who'd remained still on the bed in his room the whole time Jacques had examined her. He could tell that she was awake, because people generally didn't cry when they were unconscious, but she had remained limp, letting Jacques move her this way and that without any resistance. Even when he'd dressed her in a fresh shift she'd done no more than lift her arms when he asked her to.

Simon had watched in dark silence while Jacques ministered to Diane. He'd counted every bruise, every welt, every evidence of Thierry's lewd attentions that showed on her soft flesh. He'd counted, and found himself regretting that the man hadn't died harder.

Simon pulled the fur bedcovering up over her, then turned to find Jacques watching him steadily. "What?"

"Do you want me to take her to my chamber?"

Simon shook his head. "Leave her be. Let her rest where she is." The old man started to turn toward the door. Simon stopped him with a question. "Why did you let her out of your sight?"

Jacques's spread his hands. "It just happened. I was working."

"If she could speak she could have at least called for help."

Jacques put his hand on Simon's shoulder. "Don't worry so, Simon. She'll be fine. Get some rest yourself."

He wasn't worried. He was furious. She was a guest in

his house. He was responsible. He didn't want to be responsible for one more thing, but Jacques knew him too well. Knew he could not turn away.

"Damn you."

Jacques squeezed his shoulder. "I know. Go to sleep."

How? he wondered as he watched the wizard walk to the door. After the door had closed behind Jacques, Simon looked at the girl once more. She'd rolled over, her back to him, and to the light. He sighed. Then he stripped off his outer garments. The bed was meant for two, he was tired, and she was needy.

He felt her stiffen with new terror as he settled beside her. "Don't fear," he whispered as gently as he could. "You've nothing to fear." He adjusted the covers, and pulled the bedcurtains closed. Then, slowly, with infinite care, he put his arms around Diane and pulled her into his embrace.

He got claws raked across his shoulders for his trouble. He didn't try to pull away. He even let her bite his arm, and then his throat, but he didn't let her go. He kept his hold around her implacable, but as gentle as possible. He would have let her fight as long as she wanted, but she soon collapsed against him. He settled her head against his shoulder and felt her shuddering sobs deep in his own skin.

Eventually she fell into deep, troubled sleep. Simon stayed awake for a long time, thinking too much in the enveloping darkness. When he fell asleep he dreamed about his daughter Felice.

Despite the nightmares that troubled his rest, it was arousal that woke him. He held a woman in his arms. She was soft, warm, clinging. When he turned his head his cheek brushed against thick, heavy hair. The scent and silkiness of it sent a painful wave of desire through him.

For a few moments, all he knew was that he was with a woman in the intimate darkness of his bed, and that he wanted her. He hadn't really wanted anyone for a long time. Not since the day he learned of his wife's betrayal.

It was the memory of Genevieve's adultery that brought him back to the present, though it didn't kill the ache that centered more in his soul than his groin. The woman beside him was Diane. She would not want him. Him, or any man. Not for a long time. Maybe not ever. Who could blame her?

Slowly, careful not to disturb her, he slid away from her clutching embrace, out of the bed, away from the tactile comfort he'd unknowingly taken when he'd meant only to give. He rearranged the fur bedcovers over her, not just to keep the sleeping woman warm, but to obscure her tempting form from his sight.

He walked away from the bed and pulled back the thick tapestry that covered the room's one large window. Simon opened the shutters, letting in cold air as he looked down on the enclosed herb garden. It was barely dawn, the world was still full of shadows, with heavy clouds rushing by overhead. Simon didn't have to see the ground below to know every inch of what it looked like. The garden had been planted and tenderly cared for by Genevieve. It was still carefully tended, but he rarely opened the window to let in the sharp, sweet, heady scents that wafted up from the plants below.

To look out on the garden was to recall the sight of Genevieve kneeling among the flowers in her oldest dress, a wide straw hat covering her brown braids, her babies toddling up and down the raked stone pathways and wandering into trouble among the bushes. Genevieve's babies. His babies. Gone now. All of them were gone from him now. He even missed Genevieve, if only because the habit of their living together was still part of him. He'd tried to develop new habits, but wine, indifference and Alys had all proved less than effective in helping him forget a life where he had been, if not happy, at least content.

He stepped back, away from the hint of frost in the autumn air, away from the memories, his desires once more under control. He might wallow in self-pity occasionally, but he refused to live in the past. This morning, memory had driven out the remains of the lust that had woken him.

"Memory," he murmured as he went to dress, "has its uses."

Once dressed, he woke Yves, who slept outside his door, and sent the servant to fetch his breakfast. Jacques came in with Yves and the food a few minutes later. The old man didn't look like he'd slept any better than Simon. They sat down by the fireplace and shared the meal in silence.

After he'd drained a cup of morning ale, Jacques finally spoke, his voice a near whisper. "How is she?"

Simon answered as quietly, "Sleeping. But she can't sleep forever." He gestured toward the curtained bed. "She can't hide in there forever. Or in your room. Something has to be done about her."

Jacques put down his cup, then ran his fingers through his beard. "With Alys gone she'll be safe enough."

Simon gave his friend a hard look. "You expect me to make her my mistress, don't you?"

Jacques nodded. "That will give her the protection she needs."

"Being your guest should have protected her."

"I'm old," Jacques responded. "My vows will not let me perform magic that will do harm. People know they have nothing to fear from me. You, on the other hand, can rouse terror with the lift of an eyebrow. It's up to you to protect Diane."

"I didn't bring her here."

"But you care for her."

"I care for peace in my household. She's different,"

Simon went on angrily. "People fear the unknown. She's a beautiful, exotic stranger, an entertainer with no status, and under a curse besides. One man's already been tempted by that combination. Others will be, too."

"Not if you—"

"No."

"Ah, but you must."

Jacques sat back in his chair and folded his hands in his lap. Simon was warned by the calculatingly innocent look on the old man's face.

"What?"

"You want to do something to help the girl, don't you?"

"I want to keep peace in my household. All right, I want to help her," Simon conceded after a long, skeptical silence from Jacques. "But making her my lover isn't what she needs."

"It's exactly what she needs."

"She was nearly raped last night. She won't want a man."

Jacques shook his head. "Listen to my words, lad, not to your own notion of how the world should be. I said she needs you. She needs to love you."

Simon laughed. The sound echoed through the room, colder than the autumn wind that moaned outside. "I'm a dead man, Jacques. We both know it. The last thing anyone needs is to love me."

Jacques casually waved his words away. "You act as if you know exactly what the future will bring."

"I have a fairly good idea."

"You're far too much the pessimist."

"Realist," Simon countered. He knew it would do no good to continue the argument with Jacques. Jacques always saw the best in everyone and a ray of hope in the darkest situation. So he took a deep breath, kept his voice quiet, and asked, "Just how is it that Diane needs me?"

A bright smile broke over Jacques's features. "You mentioned it yourself last night."

Simon could remember no conversation from the night before. He remembered a rare, burning fury. He hadn't felt any emotion so intense since the day he'd learned his daughter had been abducted and there was nothing he could do about it. No, last night his anger had been even more intense, somehow more personal. At least there had been a way to save Diane, and that surely counted in part for the protectiveness he'd felt holding her in his arms.

"What did I say last night?"

"That if she had her voice back she could have called for help."

Would anyone have come to help her, he wondered, even if she could speak?

"Of course," Jacques answered the question he hadn't voiced. "But the point is, she needs to get her voice back."

"You laid the *geis* on her," Simon reminded the wizard. "You can break it."

Jacques shook his head. "You never have understood that magic has rules, and that those who use it have to abide by them."

"I've never understood magic," Simon agreed. "What was it you said would break the *geis*?"

Jacques's shaggy brows lowered in annoyance. "She has to fall in love. Have you forgotten?"

He had forgotten. Deliberately. Simon got up and built the fire without bothering to call a servant to do it. When he moved back to the waiting wizard, he said, "With me, specifically?"

Jacques tugged on his beard. "Yes."

He was lying. Jacques always pulled on his beard when he lied. Simon crossed his arms on his chest. He deliberately did not look toward the bed, though he thought he'd seen the curtains stir when he turned from the fire.

Whether she was awake or not, he didn't think Diane could have overheard their whispered conversation.

"The Second Coming might arrive first if we have to wait for someone to love me," Simon said.

"Bah. You're too modest. Why, I remember tales of you from Court. All you have to do is—ah, Diane! Good morning, child."

Simon found himself across the room at Diane's side, almost before he saw her. He'd scooped her up and deposited her in his own chair before she had a chance to flinch away from him. "You've had a bad beating and a worse fright," he told her as he set her down. "I'm not giving you a chance to faint on my floor as well the moment you're out of bed. Yves!"

Simon's deep, rich voice, full of faint amusement along with genuine concern, was the most comforting thing Diane had ever heard. She hated it. Hated the yearning to hear his voice that had made her brave the world outside the shelter of the curtained bed. She hated the comfort she'd craved, and gotten, from his momentary embrace. She'd woken up wanting him. Wanting him to hold her, to comfort her. To protect her.

She hated that longing. It made her feel weak and stupid and inadequate. She hated needing him. She hated the blind trust and faith in the power of Simon de Argent that had been born in her while she watched him kill a man. She should have been frightened of him. She was, but not because he was a murderous bastard with a long, bloody sword. She was frightened because she'd woken up wanting to run to him and hadn't been able to fight that longing for more than a few minutes.

What was wrong with her? She used to be strong, capable, independent. Now she had this deep feeling that she needed Simon to make everything all right. Just because he'd saved her. Just because he'd taken care of her. Just because. Now she watched him with hungry eyes while he ordered his servant about, and longed for him to turn a reassuring smile on her. He did finally, and she basked in the warmth his attention brought her.

Humiliation for her own weakness twisted inside her. She couldn't give in to the weakness. She had to fight Simon de Argent's hold on her emotions. She had to stay strong.

It took a great deal of effort for her to turn her gaze to the fire rather than continue to stare at him like he was the sun, or God, or somebody she could trust.

This place is hell, she reminded herself as the memories of what Thierry had done, and what he'd promised to do, forced their way to the surface. *They're all monsters. Even Simon's kindness is a trap. He can't hurt you if you don't care about him.*

She hated being weak and vulnerable. She hated herself, and she hated him because of how she felt. But hatred was good. If she could just hold onto it, she'd survive.

"I've ordered you a bath. It seems I'm always ordering you a bath." He laughed.

She drank in the sound, but she would not let herself turn back to look at him.

"I'll send a serving woman up to help you bathe and dress," he went on. "Come along, Jacques. Let's leave Diane some privacy."

She heard the old man get up. She heard the two of them move toward the door. She wanted to chase after them, after Simon, to tug on his sleeve like a child begging a grownup not to leave her alone.

She wasn't a child. She didn't move from where she sat but she did draw her knees up and shake with terror after he'd left. Fortunately, by the time the servants came in with the water she had managed to get herself under enough control to get in the tub and try to wash the memory of Thierry's touch off of her.

11

He'd seen the look on her face. He'd never wanted anyone to look at him like that. Fortunately, she seemed to be well aware of her actions, and didn't like them any better than he did.

Simon realized that it would be easy to make her love him.

It would be for her own good.

But dependence born out of gratitude had nothing to do with real love.

He couldn't do it.

Simon sighed with relief when the decision was made. He sat back in his chair on the dais and surveyed the doings of the hall, and tried to decide what he could do. The main room of the castle was distinctly quiet this morning. People were watching him furtively as they went about their business, trying to gauge his mood, no doubt. He wished someone would tell him if they decided just what it was, because he wasn't sure himself. A moment before he'd felt relieved, but now that the decision was made he was beginning to feel irritated. At least his usual sense of melancholy hadn't had any time to settle on him since his return to Marbeau.

"Futility, yes," he murmured as he stood and stretched. "Melancholy, no."

He went to stand by the great central hearth that heated the room. The constant fire burned low for the moment. He gestured to the boy whose job it was to tend it and watched the lad scurry forward with a supply of fresh logs. The trestle tables had been taken down after the morning meal, leaving plenty of space in the center of the room. As flames roared up, Simon stepped back from the stone rim that circled the firepit. He looked up as thin streams of smoke began to curl toward the louvered openings in the ceiling, then spread out like a mist across the upper air since the louvers were closed against a cold autumn rain.

The season was hurrying on too fast for Simon's taste. He used to enjoy fall. The turning of the leaves, the harvest, the feasting had all been a pleasant marker of his prosperous household's transition to the quieter winter life. Now, with no peace in his heart, and only one last battle to fight come spring, the prospect of the coming winter brought no sense of serenity.

All he had wanted was to get the season over with, to get through the interminable cold, dark days with the mindless round of habit. He'd thought to get by with the fixed winter occupations of church and chess, wine and hunting. He hadn't expected anything more between the first frost and the spring thaw.

Now he had Diane.

He wasn't even sure what that meant. He didn't want to think about it. Fortunately, he was spared from having his thoughts spin toward the darkly lovely, mysterious Diane, when a cold, damp wind alerted him to the opening of the hall's outer door. He turned to see Sir Joscelin coming toward him.

"You looked soaked to the skin," Simon observed as the young knight handed his cloak to a servant.

Joscelin joined him by the fire. After he tucked his gloves in his belt, he held his hands out toward the flames.

"The rain made the ride from Domiere a misery. I left Lady Alys in good hands at the abbey," he added. "The abbess will send word of just who comes to fetch her."

"Perhaps she'll take the veil," Simon suggested.

The knight gave him a shocked look, then smiled when he realized Simon was joking. "I have my own opinion, my lord." He looked around, as though wary of being overheard. "If you wish to hear it, that is," he added quietly.

Simon rubbed his thumb thoughtfully over the pommel of his dagger hilt. Now, here was a new thing. Joscelin had always seemed trustworthy, good-hearted as well, though Simon no longer had much faith in his own judgment in these matters. Was Joscelin thoughtful and observant, as well as loyal?

Simon cocked an eyebrow in question. "If you're about to tell me you don't think Alys spied only for my son, I would have to say I agree with you. She's a greedy child," Simon told him. "I'll miss her."

"But my lord—"

"She and her brother were informers I knew about. I'll have to ferret out whoever will replace them."

"Your people are true to you, my lord!" Joscelin protested.

"Except for those who revolted against me last summer."

Joscelin looked away, blushing. "Yes, but—"

Simon clamped a hand on the younger man's shoulder. "Even the king's sons revolted last summer. Perhaps it was something in the air. Or some new courtier's fashion for sons to repudiate their fathers. We at Marbeau have always followed court fashion." He heard the bitterness in his voice, and looked around quickly for another subject to share with the embarrassed young knight.

As he glanced up he saw Jacques coming down the stairs from the tower entrance. Diane trailed slowly behind him. A serving woman followed her, blocking any hasty retreat back up the narrow staircase that the reluctant Diane might wish to make. The old wizard was no doubt bringing the young woman to him for the sake of beginning this therapeutic romance.

Simon frowned hard at the old man, but his attention still focused on Diane as she drew near. His glance was drawn to her like a lodestone to iron. As hers seemed to be to his, for their gazes met and locked as if they could do nothing but look at each other and never get their fill of the sight. Stranger still, he found his heart racing at the sight of her. It took all his will not to cross the room and sweep her up in his arms once more. The woman was light as a feather, it would be no burden to carry her from place to place with her soft cheek resting against his heart.

That, he told himself, as Diane looked away first, was merely a surge of protectiveness—as if for a child. But the graceful form outlined by the tightly laced gown was that of a finely made woman. A woman he'd held close in the dark intimacy of his bed, and woke up wanting. He firmly ignored the heated rush of blood through his veins that gave the lie to his reaction being anything but a surge of lust. He was going to deny the girl love, and himself lust, and Jacques could stop handing Diane to him on a platter, the tempting old serpent.

For all that he was determined to avoid temptation, he still couldn't take his attention off Diane. He found it a wonder that she didn't wince with obvious pain at every step. Her long hair flowed loose like a maiden's about her shoulders, to help conceal a badly bruised cheek, he thought. Whatever the reason she wore her hair down, he took pleasure at the lustrous sight of it.

"That is the blackest black hair I have ever seen."

Simon had also had the thought, but the words came from Joscelin. Simon gave the man a sharp, annoyed look.

Sharp enough to send Joscelin backward a step or two, his expression full of alarm.

"My lord, I meant only that—"

Simon took an angry step toward Joscelin, his hand on his dagger. "She's beautiful, isn't she?" He growled the words, and thought he sounded more like an aroused guard dog than a man. He was shocked at his possessive reaction to Joscelin's harmless words.

Joscelin gave quick looks to the girl, and then the dagger. He gulped. "No. Not if you—"

Simon forced himself to be calm, detached, uninvolved. He spoke mildly to the alarmed young man. "Of course she's beautiful."

"Yes, my lord."

The knight looked at him desperately for direction. An idea occurred to him. Simon smiled, and recalled, "It was you who defended Diane when she refused to come to the hall."

"I did?"

Simon nodded. "Yes. Quite eloquently. You championed her."

"Did I?"

"Suggested she might be modest."

"Oh, yes. I recall that."

"And you do think she's attractive? Not some ugly foreign monster?"

Joscelin shook his head wildly. "Oh, no, my lord. She's lovely. And in need of protection. I would have challenged Thierry myself if you had not already—"

"In need of protection." Simon clapped a hand on Joscelin's shoulder. "You have the right of it, lad. Diane of Brittany requires a champion."

"But, my lord, you—"

"No, you."

Simon watched Joscelin look at Diane as she reached the hearth. She stood quietly between Jacques and the servant, head modestly down, hands tucked in the wide sleeves of her gown. She looked beautiful, and vulnerable, and exotic.

How could a romantic young fool like Joscelin fail to fall in love with her?

"As of this moment," Simon informed the handsome knight, "your duty is to guard this young lady's person. To be at her side at all times. To be her champion, and serve her in all ways gentle and just."

Joscelin's eyes went round, then a smile like the sun breaking through clouds lit his face. "Thank you, my lord!" he said.

Simon watched Joscelin hurry to Diane's side. He hid a smile behind his hand as the boy went down on one knee before her. She stared at Joscelin in surprise. Jacques looked at him in frustrated annoyance.

Simon walked away, satisfied that he had done his duty. Now all that needed to be accomplished was for Diane to fall in love with her knight errant. How difficult could that be?

12

"This is not going to work, you know."

Simon walked over to join Jacques by the window. The old man had been standing in the cold early-morning breeze watching the garden for nearly half an hour. "You're going to catch a chill," he told his friend.

"What are they doing out there?" Jacques wondered irritably.

Simon stepped between the wizard and the window. "It's called courtship. Or are you too old to remember?"

A reminiscent smile crossed Jacques's wrinkled face. "I remember courting my darling Anor very well indeed. And watching your father and Lady Gilberte. A pity both those dear ladies are gone now. A pity you never had a proper romance with Genevieve— or anyone else for that matter," he added. "You don't know what you're missing."

The man's tone was kindly, but Simon winced as though he'd been slapped. "Genevieve and I did well enough together."

"Until she went to court and discovered love."

Simon's voice was tight with anger as he answered, "I don't need to be reminded."

Jacques, of course, was not warned by Simon's tone.

He never was. "You've never been in love. You only understand duty. Genevieve found that she wanted more."

"So you told me when you persuaded me not to kill the adulteress. She died anyway."

"And you're still feeling guilty about it." Jacques shook his head sadly. "You sent her out in a storm and she caught a fever. She still went because she wanted to go."

Simon willed his bunched fists to remain at his side, for the temptation to strike the old man was very strong. "Don't do this to me."

"What? Remind you of your past? If you can't get over your past you'll never—"

"Am I cruel enough to bring up your mistakes? Do I reprove you for Vivienne's wickedness?" Damn! He'd struggled so hard not to strike the old man with his hands that he hadn't guarded his tongue enough, and had struck him with words instead. "I'm sorry," he said, as Jacques blinked back tears.

Jacques waved away his apology. "No need. I love my granddaughter despite her wicked ways. It's her turning her great gift to evil purposes that disappoints me. I don't regret teaching her magic. I regret her choice, but I don't blame myself for it."

Simon relaxed the tightly curled grip of his hands, and put them on Jacques's shoulder. "You've a great, forgiving spirit, my friend. You're a better man than I am."

Jacques shook his head. "No. Just older. Age doesn't bring wisdom, just a certain perspective. For those who don't drown in bitterness from the sorrows that befall them," he added. The tears were gone from his eyes. The speculative look was back.

Simon stepped away from him. He looked out the window, which was, of course, what Jacques had wanted him to do all along. Diane and Joscelin were in the garden. In the last three days, Joscelin had made an effort to show Diane every square inch of Marbeau. Or so Jacques had been at pains to tell Simon. She apparently made these excursions with the greatest of reluctance, but had taken a liking to the garden. Of course she liked the garden, Simon thought. It was privacy she sought, needed. He knew that instinctively. He knew that they were much alike.

Jacques was dissatisfied with Joscelin's efforts to win the fair lady's regard. Simon made himself deal calmly with the wizard's frequent reports. He never mentioned Diane's name, but he listened with more interest than he admitted. It was not his place to give Joscelin advice about the young woman. Besides, he didn't want to.

He carefully kept to his own chamber as the courtship proceeded. In fact, he'd spent three days fighting the urge to ask for Diane to join him to tell one of her stories. He would not ask. He would not order. He would wait. It was her choice to keep him company, or stay away. It was her choice to speak when she would. With any luck she would soon be in love and her voice would be free to say anything she wanted. In the meantime, he would not call her into his presence and demand the one thing that was hers to give.

This matter of choice was a new thing for him, and he didn't like it. It was a disturbing notion, and he didn't know how he had come to it. It wasn't natural to not be making the decisions for someone under his care. It went against the order of the world. It didn't feel right. The very notion of it, and not the longing to spend time with the absent young woman, kept him pacing his chamber like a caged cat while he allowed her the freedom of the castle. Or so he tried to tell himself.

Then there was the ridiculous matter of having to fight off the hollow ache that came from knowing she preferred to spend time with Joscelin instead of with him. It was an unexpected and thoroughly ridiculous reaction, and one he'd brought on himself.

"She's a great deal of trouble, isn't she?" Jacques asked from behind him.

Simon did not turn around to challenge this provocative statement. He didn't turn because his attention focused on the couple on the still frost-rimmed path below. Even from this distance he could make out the look of vaguely annoyed puzzlement on Diane's face.

When Joscelin put his hand on Diane's shoulder, and she immediately scurried backward, Simon shook his head in disgust. He ignored the jolt of jealousy that also passed through him as he said, "She's not ready to be touched yet, you young fool."

When Diane looked up and saw him watching her, he stepped back and closed the shutters, but not before intercepting a look from her that left him unreasonably shaken. He denied his soul's call to join her in the garden and made himself think about the duties he needed to perform.

There were parchments to be read on his work table. There were things to discuss with Jacques. There was All Saints' Day service to attend in less than an hour. He had more to occupy his mind and time than a pleading look from one large-eyed girl. But it was that swift glance and the unpleasant image of her with another man that he couldn't get out of his mind.

She didn't need to speak, Joscelin could talk enough for both of them. There was no getting away from him, either. He even slept outside Jacques's door. The problem was, she understood very little of what he meant. She understood the courtly words, but most of them were silly. Most of the time she just smiled vacantly while his utterances passed through her like white noise. His language was flowery, flamboyant, and apparently meant to impress her with his dedication to her chaste and comely person.

Or something.

His terminology was so convoluted it was kind of hard to tell what he meant sometimes. She missed Simon's plain, sarcastic, caustic way of speaking. She never had trouble understanding just what the master of Marbeau meant, sometimes without him having to say a thing.

Except that Joscelin wore chain mail instead of a plaid flannel shirt, he reminded her of her last boyfriend. Brad hadn't talked that much, but there'd been an air of puppy-like devotion Joscelin shared with him. An air that was probably as false. Brad was a supposed musician who'd wandered out of her life when he'd discovered her mother only worked with classical or jazz artists. Joscelin was hanging out with her because Simon told him to. She wondered if there was anyone who was interested in her for herself.

Simon had seemed to be the only one without an agenda. Her presence had been forced on him by Jacques. He'd done the best he could with the situations that had forced them to be together. Of course, now that he'd palmed her off on Joscelin he didn't have any interest in her either.

There was no reason for him to. She had no reason to be interested in him. It was just the gratitude she felt toward him, and the sense of security he gave her, that kept the gnawing longing to be near him from fading as the days passed.

It took a great deal of effort not to run away when Joscelin touched her. To give in to panic would be to let Thierry win, to let a dead man control her life. She was determined not to let that happen. Thierry wasn't going to have power over her.

She didn't run up to Simon's room when she saw him watching her from his window. She didn't acknowledge the heartache when he turned away. She made herself smile at Joscelin. She wasn't going to let Simon control her life, either.

Simon understood that, she knew he did. He understood that she needed to find her own way instead of hiding in his shadow. And in his usual autocratic way, he had set about detaching her from his person. It would have been nice if he'd given her the choice to walk away. A typically high-handed move from Simon de Argent, she thought as she backed away from Joscelin.

He followed her. She took a seat on a bench and proceeded to ignore him. It was a crisply cold morning, clear and refreshing but definitely a prelude to a winter sort of day. Several layers of clothing and a heavy wool cape kept her warm enough. Even her ears were warm, since the servant who'd been assigned to her had talked her into covering her hair with an embroidered veil. She looked the part, she supposed, of Joscelin's medieval fantasyland lady, except that her features were different and she still had no idea what part she was supposed to play. *Central Casting got it all wrong*, she thought.

Actually, she knew very well she'd been cast by Jacques to play Simon's savior from *ennui*. Or maybe it was despair. Lord knew the man sometimes looked like he could use a hug. Or, a shoulder to cry on. Or, at least someone to confide in. He had to get tired of being strong all the time. She had to admit that she didn't just long to be comforted by the man, she also had to combat the urge to comfort him in turn. To give in to it would be to let Jacques win. She wasn't going to let Jacques control her life, either.

Joscelin was still talking. It took some effort, but Diane managed to drag her thoughts away from Simon de Argent and focus on the handsome young knight.

" 'Tis a holy day," he said. "I haven't heard Mass for a few days." He held his hand out to her. "Will you come with me? We can say our prayers together, and take holy communion." When she stayed seated on the bench he went on, "Lord Simon said I should care for you, and surely the care of your soul is part of my duty."

Joscelin had showed her the small church that occupied one of the castle's several courtyards the day before. Except for a large stained glass window at one end of the building the place looked more like a prison than a house of worship. She found it curious that this fantasyland shared her own world's beliefs, but there was no one she could ask about it. She just had to assume that she'd landed in a parallel universe. She was glad that at least there were some customs and practices that she did understand, and could share.

"Please come," he said. He held out his hand again. "Everyone will be there."

She didn't want to go where there were people, but his look of entreaty was impossible to resist. She didn't take his hand, but she did nod and get to her feet. Maybe in church he'd be quiet. Maybe, if everyone was indeed there, she'd be able to slip away from him in the crowd. Maybe she'd find some time to herself.

Maybe Simon would be there.

13

"*No.*"

"But Father Andre—"

"It would be sacrilege."

The crowd of people was five-deep around the church door as Simon approached. Most of them were talking. The priest's voice was the loudest, but sounded the most uncertain. Tentative as usual, but still the cause of the trouble. Joscelin sounded polite as he argued with the priest. He was always polite, Simon thought. Which in this case was more of a character flaw than an advantage.

Simon shook his head and strode forward. The crowd parted at the sight of him, but there was continued muttering. There were many angry, nervous looks aimed at Diane, of course.

"You are a lot of trouble," he told her as he stepped to her side.

Far from responding with the pleading look he'd seen in the garden, she rounded on him with a glare.

Simon smiled. "I didn't say it was your fault. I said you're a lot of trouble."

She accepted this observation with a nod, then jerked her head in the priest's direction.

"What's the matter now?" Simon asked Father Andre.

The priest pointed at the blushing Joscelin. "He wants to bring the demon-spawned creature into the church."

Simon lowered his brows in annoyance. "The what?"

Father Andre sidled closer to the church door at Simon's low growl. He didn't meet Simon's gaze when he said, "Her."

"Her?"

"That one. The harlot who tempted Sir Thierry to his death."

Simon felt Diane go tense at the priest's words. Joscelin's hand went to his sword. Behind him, people began to murmur louder. Simon still couldn't resist responding, "Alys? Alys isn't here, man. Are you blind?"

Father Andre finally looked at him. "My lord, please. Don't let this—creature—enter the house of God. She would defile—"

"God can take care of his own house," Simon angrily cut the man off. "A demon would burst into flames if it entered a consecrated church. Would it not?"

Andre fluttered his hands before him. "I suppose. But she is—"

"Diane is no demon." He spoke loudly, wanting everyone to hear. Then he addressed the priest once more. "Would you deny any Christian soul entrance?" He leaned down and whispered in Diane's ear, "You are Christian, aren't you?"

Diane was almost too angry at the priest's vicious accusations to perceive how close Simon was to her. Almost. When his cheek brushed hers she noticed that he needed a better shave. She caught the scent of clove on his breath. She momentarily got lost in the sense of his nearness. He didn't touch her, but if he did she didn't think she'd run away. He had to repeat the question before she responded with a nod.

Simon turned his attention back to Father Andre. "Move aside, priest. I'm going to enter *my* church now."

He stepped forward, willing to push the other man aside if he had to. "Come along Diane, Joscelin."

Father Andre backed up as the three of them came forward. When they were across the threshold, he turned and fled toward the sanctuary of the altar. Simon watched him go with an annoyed shake of his head. Then he walked down the nave to take his usual spot at the front of the church. Diane and Joscelin flanked him. He tried hard not to look at the girl, though he was aware of her straight spine and the proud lift of her head.

He turned his attention to Joscelin as the people of Marbeau crowded into the church behind them. "What did you mean by bringing her here?" he demanded quietly of the young knight.

"My lord, I—"

"You should have talked Father Andre into bringing Diane to Mass instead of just surprising the man with it. Don't you know the fool can be made to believe anything is his idea?"

And why hadn't he thought to speak to Andre about Diane himself, Simon wondered. Having the priest champion her would considerably ease peoples' fears of her strange features. He hadn't thought of it, but Joscelin should have, if he was going to protect her. Jacques was right. The boy just wasn't up to it.

"And for another thing," he went on, fully prepared to spend the entire church service in the education of young Sir Joscelin.

Diane did not listen to the dressing down Simon gave Joscelin, though she was very aware of the deep rumble of his voice. She didn't look at him. She didn't look at anyone. She kept her gaze on the stained-glass window over the altar and held her fury at the spiteful ignorance of these people in check. Frankly, it felt better to be angry than to be frightened. She hadn't been frightened when the mob gathered behind the stupid priest. She had, in fact, been close to losing it and hitting the man before Simon showed up and handled the situation. She probably wouldn't have done it, but the urge had been there.

Simon had saved her again.

Oh, well, it was his job. He was the Lord of Marbeau. He was supposed to save the day. He didn't do it just because she was the one in trouble. He probably did the superhero to the rescue bit all the time. He certainly looked like a superhero, handsome and large and blond and broad shouldered. He wore a cape. She couldn't keep herself from finally glancing at him and smiling when she didn't think he'd be looking her way.

He was. He smiled back, just the faintest curving of his lips, then he turned his attention to the church service. Diane tried to do the same, but spent the rest of the long Mass being all too mindful of the tall man beside her. After a while, she decided that she didn't like this constant awareness of Simon.

She would have inched away from him, but his hand came out to grasp her sleeve when she tried to move. He touched the cloth, not her. She was grateful for that small, understanding gesture. Then anger at being grateful once again overwhelmed her and she jerked her sleeve away from his touch. She began to stomp off, but only got three steps. This time his hand grasped her elbow.

"You can't leave just yet," he whispered. "You'll still be accused of being a demon if you walk out before communion."

She looked toward the altar, and saw that Father Andre had begun to administer the host to a waiting line of worshippers. Simon was right, of course. If she left during this sacred rite she'd still be suspect.

"Come with me," he urged.

Since he still had a firm grip on her arm, she couldn't do anything else. So she sighed, and went to the altar rail with him. They knelt, and when Father Andre came to them, she opened her mouth to receive the small piece of bread he held out. The priest hesitated, but eventually responded to the frown Simon turned on him, and gave Diane communion.

The murmurs from the crowd were approving this time. A sense of relief permeated Diane as she followed Simon away from the altar rail. The people of Marbeau still weren't giving her any friendly looks, but the hostility that the priest had stirred up earlier had dissipated. For now, at least. She still didn't trust them not to turn on her. They probably didn't trust her not to turn into a flesh-eating dragon, either.

Truce, she thought.

"Truce," Simon said from behind her. "Peaceful coexistence is the best we can hope for right now."

She nearly jumped out of her skin as his words repeated her exact thoughts. This was too weird, and she wasn't going to put up with it.

Instead of returning to her place, she walked straight out of the church.

Simon came with her. She didn't turn around as she crossed the sunny courtyard between the church and the castle door, but she knew he was there. She told herself it was the sound of his footsteps behind her, but she knew she would have known he was there if it had been her hearing rather than her voice she'd lost. She didn't know why she had this connection to him. She did know she wasn't going to let it control her life. Somehow, she was going to get away from Simon de Argent.

Simon had no trouble keeping up with Diane when she quickened her pace. He just hoped she wouldn't start running. It would be most undignified to seem to be chasing a reluctant young woman across the inner bailey of his own castle.

"Do you want everyone to think I'm a randy old fool?" he asked her as they reached the steps of the keep. "You did very well back there," he added when she whirled around to face him. "If you go to Mass every morning people will accept your odd appearance better."

She slapped him.

He touched his cheek. "Perhaps odd was a bad choice of words." She gave a decisive nod. He tried another description. "Exotic?"

She hit him again. He'd expected it, and allowed it, just as he'd allowed her to strike him after Thierry's attack. He strongly suspected she was from a place where women were not as meek as they should be. Besides, after Alys's manipulative tantrums, Diane's honest anger was refreshing. A great deal about her was refreshing.

He took a step back. "If I call you foreign, will you still take offense?"

She crossed her arms angrily. Then she laughed. Even without sound, he found the transformation of her features delightful to watch.

She didn't know what was the matter with her. Except for the usual childhood fights with her siblings, she'd never struck anyone in her life until she met Simon. And for some reason, she'd hit him because she knew she could trust him. That didn't make any sense. Violence was stupid. Even violence brought on by the frustration of being voiceless and lost in a hostile place. And Simon had the power of life and death over everyone in Marbeau, including her. Maybe especially her. She was, after all, an odd, exotic foreigner. His *chattel*. The situation was terrifying.

She didn't know why she was laughing.

Except that he'd deliberately tried to charm her. It was nice to be entertained instead of being the entertainer. Joscelin had been trying to amuse her for three days. Simon managed it in a few seconds.

When he said, "Let's go in, shall we?" she nodded. But she didn't take his hand when he held it out to her. She wasn't ready for that yet.

* * *

"I sent a lad to do a man's work, I'll grant you that," Simon conceded to the smirking Jacques. He poured himself a beaker of wine and sat down on Jacques's bed. "Joscelin's not the sort a woman like Diane is going to fall in love with."

"He's far too nice," Jacques agreed.

Simon gave the old man a hard look. He sighed. He rolled the cup around in his hands. He looked about the room, at its curious collection of books and scrolls, its pots and shelves and cabinets and festoons of hanging dried herbs. The place was cavernous and crowded. An army could hide in here, he thought, and never be noticed. Jacques had invited him up for a little talk over wine after he'd spent most of the day at sword practice. The wine helped relax tired muscles, but the inevitable conversation was not so restful.

"About Diane?" Jacques questioned after a long silence.

Simon looked over to where the old man sat, in a chair that was said to have belonged to a Roman emperor. "She deserves better."

"You're the best she can hope for in this life."

Simon saw that Jacques sincerely believed what he'd said. Simon knew better. "There's very little I can offer her."

"You can give her her voice back. Why don't you concentrate on what she has to offer you?"

"I'm not going to fall in love with her, Jacques," Simon pointed out. "I can't. I won't. All I can give her is a little time, and some grief."

"Bah. All you ever see is the dark."

Jacques refused to understand. He always refused to understand. Simon got to his feet. He wanted more wine, but thought a clear head would be better, so he abstained. He carefully put the cup back down on the table. "There's nothing left but the night," he said. "Winter, then death."

Jacques stood, and dismissed Simon's melancholy with a wave of one gnarled hand. "You have the autumn, and winter nights can be long and pleasant. Don't try to predict what will come with the spring."

Simon already knew. Besides, arguing about his own future was tedious. "You're right, old man. I won't worry about it. Where's Diane?" he asked. "I'd better attend her if I have a seduction to get on with."

"A courtship," Jacques corrected.

"It'll work out to the same thing, won't it? I feel like an old fool," he added as he went to the door. "Where is she?"

Jacques combed his fingers through his beard. "In the solar, perhaps? I think I heard one of the women say something about asking her for a story after the morning meal."

"That was hours ago." Simon doubted she'd want to set foot in the solar after what had happened in there. Then again, she might have braved the place just to prove that she wasn't afraid. "I'll find her," he told Jacques. "Comb the castle in search of my lady love."

"You do that," Jacques said as Simon closed the door behind him. "I'm going to take a nap."

You know, Diane thought, caught between fury and amusement, *if that was a scene from a movie, the heroine would be charmed out of her undies by the hero's touching sincerity.*

This wasn't a movie, and she wasn't charmed. She was incredibly embarrassed. She hadn't meant to overhear the conversation. She hadn't known what to do other than stay where she was when the men came in. She and the slop bucket had been behind the tallest shelves in the darkest corner of Jacques's room in her continuing quest to go to the bathroom in privacy. Instead she'd overheard them once again making plans for her life.

The trouble was, it was hard to be angry with either man since she knew they meant well. Hard, but not impossible. Especially Simon.

So, he thought he could just *make* her fall in love with him, did he?

She wasn't going to be made to do anything. Even for the right reasons. Not that falling in love just to get her voice back was a right reason. Love just happened, it couldn't be forced. Not even by Simon de Argent.

Okay, she was grateful to him. She admired him. She thought he was handsome. Maybe she even worried about him, a little. That didn't mean she was fated to fall under the inevitable sway of his fatal charm.

The man had a few too many flaws for her to be swept away by the wonderfulness of his biceps and laconic smile. She loved listening to his rich deep voice, but that didn't mean she wanted him whispering sweet nothings— whatever they were—in her ear. Especially when she knew anything he said or did from now on would be a manipulative effort to save her from Jacques's stupid curse. She commended his effort, but she wasn't likely to fall for it.

Paternalistic was a very good description of Simon de Argent, she thought. High handed. A little bit too confident of his seductive abilities.

I wonder what he'll do? she thought as she waited for Jacques to begin snoring.

She wanted to wait until she was sure the old wizard was asleep before she sneaked out of the room. Usually, she wasn't that eager to join the rest of the household down in the hall.

I wonder what he'll say? I wonder what it would be like to be kissed by him?

Not that it would matter, of course. She had no intention of falling in love.

14

Diane was not in the solar, but Simon did encounter Joscelin as the young knight came in from the bathhouse after his own fighting practice. Simon commended him on his guardianship of the fair Diane, then sent him out on border patrol with a detachment of guards.

By the time he'd given Joscelin detailed orders, the hall was filling up with household members who gathered for the evening meal. Simon wove his way through the servants who were setting up the trestle tables and made his way to his own seat in the center of the dais. From there he observed the movements of his people while he thought about how best to proceed. It took him only a few minutes to come up with a plan of action. That done, Simon sent a servant to find the storyteller and deliver an invitation for Diane to sit beside him at dinner.

Diane was relieved when Simon asked her to join him at the high table. Actually, it wasn't a request. The words the servant repeated to her were flowery, but they were still an order. Which was better than an invitation, because it helped remind her of what he was really like. She could nurse a grudge about being ordered to her own first date with the Lord of Marbeau.

Also, it really wasn't a date. Dinner at the high table was the most public exposure possible at the castle. Everybody seated below the dais carefully watched everything that went on up among the favored few who got to share the table with his lordship. As much as she disliked the way people stared at her, tonight she preferred it to an intimate evening with the boss.

She got up off the landing outside Jacques's room where she'd been sitting, wondering what to do, when the servant found her. She adjusted her veil, smoothed the thick fabric of her overdress, and went down the stairs toward the hall with as slow and stately gate as she could manage in the heavy garments.

Simon actually felt Diane's gaze on him before he looked up and saw her at the foot of the stairs. She was standing beneath the glow of a rushlight, watching him. The first thing he noticed was that her cheek was still discolored with bruising. The second was that while her expression was quite serious, her dark eyes were full of amusement. He had no idea what it was about him that brought her pleasure, but he felt a rush of answering joy just to see her happy.

You are not going to fall in love with her, he reminded himself. Then he stood, and gestured elegantly for her to join him. When she reached his side, he made a show of sitting her in the place of honor on his right. Alys had been the one who used to appropriate this seat. He had been infuriated by her presumption, but had allowed it for the sake of his own plans. Now he freely gave a deserving lady her due, publicly acknowledging her exalted place in his house.

Diane thought the high-backed wooden chair looked uncomfortable. The seat was narrow, and the back was heavily carved. The design was beautiful, but not meant to be leaned back against. When she sat down, the room went dead quiet.

Until Simon turned to face his people and lifted his silver goblet high. "A toast to my lady," he called out.

His deep voice reached into even the furthest shadowed corners of the hall. There was a stunned interval before an answering roar of voices began. There followed a clatter of wooden and pottery mugs as the people of Marbeau joined him in drinking the toast. When he had taken a taste of wine, he carefully turned the jewel-studdeed goblet and handed it to Diane so that she could set her lips to the spot where he had drank.

Diane took the goblet, but she didn't know what he wanted her to do with it. From the eager way Simon, and everybody else, looked at her, something was clearly expected of her. It wasn't like she could offer a toast. She couldn't even talk. She was embarrassed enough by what Simon had just done that she didn't want to face the people at the other tables. So she held the goblet and concentrated on studying his exuberantly smiling face.

She liked the smile. It was such a rare thing to see that having him smile at her was like receiving a gift. She liked the way the faint lines around his eyes crinkled when he smiled. She liked the faint trace of dimples at the corners of his mouth. She liked the rounded, sensual curve of his lips. She liked the glow of pleasure in his amber-hazel eyes. She liked having him look at her. It made warmth spread through her even though she hadn't yet touched the wine.

She liked him, but she had no idea what the man wanted. She shrugged, and just stared at him helplessly.

Finally, the smile faded, and the room grew a little bit darker around her. He sat down, and explained, "You're supposed to salute me in turn." When she continued to stare at him, he took the goblet from her hands. "I see you're not yet ready for such an intimate avowal, my lady. I beg your pardon."

Apparently he wanted her to share his goblet. Why would sharing someone's glass, and germs, be considered an intimate avowal? And if it was so intimate why was it also presented as a public ceremony? This was definitely not her idea of romance. This was not what she'd expected as the first move of an attempt to make her love him.

He seemed irritated as the first course was served. Irritated and disappointed. Diane knew it was her fault, and almost gave in to guilt. She almost snatched up the goblet to take a good, stiff drink. She almost did it. For him. Because she—

Did not love him. She was just grateful. And his moodiness was a manipulative way of getting what he wanted. Or so she told herself. Simon de Argent was playing a game with her, she reminded herself. She did her best to keep that thought uppermost in her mind when he turned her way again after the server had moved on down the table.

He was smiling, but this time it didn't reach his eyes. His tone was pleasant, but it didn't sound sincere. "Share the meal with me, my lady."

She was not his lady, but she was hungry. She was also used to the idea that two people were supposed to share one plate. Well, one round of flat bread covered in yucky goop. She was used to the idea, but she still found the practice disgusting. That was why she always did her best to eat alone in Jacques's room instead of risking her life to the sanitary practices in the hall. Now, Simon wanted her to share his plate with him. Everybody in the room was still staring at them. Maybe the populace wouldn't be so interested if she just went along with the common custom this once.

She gave him a wan smile, and the faintest of agreeing nods. As she started to reach for the food, Simon put his hand over her wrist to stop her.

"Allow me, dearest Diane." Diane watched him

curiously as he picked up a piece of meat and held it out to her. He didn't release her hand so she could take it from him. He brought the meat close to her lips. "This dainty morsel is for you." His voice was a husky, sensual whisper.

The man was trying to feed her! Like a child. Like a pet.

Diane twisted her head away to avoid the food. She fought down a gag as she shot up out of the chair. She burned with humiliation as she backed away from the table. She ignored Simon's annoyance, ignored the hostile reaction of the watching crowd. She remembered how he had called her his chattel.

She wasn't his property. His trying to show the world that she was wasn't going to make her love him. But, of course, he really didn't want her to love him. He was just trying to placate Jacques. Simon didn't really care if she got her voice back. At the moment, she only cared about getting it back so she could tell him how sick she was of his and the wizard's spiteful games.

But since she couldn't talk, she turned and fled from the table.

Simon rose to his feet as Diane ran away. He could have had her stopped with a gesture to his guards, but he let her go. He had never been so insulted in his life. He nearly shook with rage at her insulting reaction to his gallantry. What was wrong with the woman?

He'd offered her the best his house had to offer. With his own hand. He, Baron Simon de Argent, Lord of Marbeau, had made it clear to the world how high his regard was for her. In front of the world, she had rejected him. She had forsaken his care, his patronage, looked as if she were sick to her stomach at the very thought of accepting his courtesy. How was he to court someone who treated him so? Why should he?

For her sake, Jacques might have said, had he been there. For duty's sake, his own conscience spoke up.

How? he wondered, when she'd insulted him so blatantly. Even Alys had never been so unkind. Even Genevieve had never rejected any honor he showed her. Who was this Diane to make a public show of her contempt?

Why? He couldn't help but wonder why. He looked around him for an explanation, but all he saw were the avidly curious and secretly contemptuous faces of his retainers. There was no explanation to be gotten from that crowd of carrion crows.

He would just have to get the reason from the source, he supposed. Rebuff him Diane might, escape him she could not. He would have an accounting from her whether she could speak or not. Still furious, he went after the woman he was supposed to make love him.

"Now you've made her cry." Jacques tried to block Simon's passage as he came through the doorway.

"Cry?" Simon pushed the old man aside. "Made her cry?"

"What have you done to that poor child?"

"Me? Ha!"

Simon went past the protesting wizard to get to the bed. Diane was curled up on it, shoulders shaking, face hidden by the heavy fall of her hair. Simon did not allow himself to feel a grain of compassion for her obviously upset condition. He was the offended party here.

"Come with me," he said, and grabbed her by the wrist. He hauled her from the room over Jacques's vehement protests. "We're going to discuss this in private," he called back to him. Then he dragged her down the stairs to his own chamber.

"Now, just what was that all about?" he demanded when the door had slammed behind them.

Diane pulled out of his grasp. She flung her hair from her face as she swiped away tears with the back of one hand. She took a proud stance and looked up at him. Her eyes were red-rimmed from crying, but her glare had the strength of a basilisk's deadly gaze.

He towered over her. "I should beat you," he told her. "Any sane man would beat a woman who used him so."

She lifted her stubbornly set chin, and pointed at herself.

"Yes, used me," he responded. "I've never been so insulted in my life."

The half-moon arcs of her eyebrows shot up in incredulity. She took a step back, pointed at him, and gave a silent laugh.

Simon crossed his arms. "I did nothing offensive."

Diane came forward again. She jabbed him in the chest with a sharp forefinger. Then she raised bent wrists to her chin, and panted.

It was his turn to be incredulous. "Treated you like a dog? What are you talking about? This makes no sense. It's you who treated me no better than a cur."

Her expression turned questioning.

He refused to believed this pretense. "I offered you my heart on a trencher and you—Don't look at me like that. I'm not lying to you." She gave another laugh, no less mocking for being soundless. He sighed. "All right. Perhaps I'm lying a little. A man's supposed to lie when he's courting a woman. I don't know why," he responded to her skeptical look. "It's part of the rules."

She tossed her head, and turned her back on him.

He found himself looking with great concentration at her still, slender form. Her proud gesture left him wanting to run his hands through the thick hair that fell halfway down her back. He found he suddenly wanted to put his arms around her. He found that he was no longer angry. He didn't know how she'd done it, but he'd gone from fury to a more tender, but equally strong, emotion within the blink of an eye.

He stepped closer to her. He took care not to touch her, for he well-remembered the wounds Thierry had made on her emotions. He did come close enough to inhale her scent, to feel the heat of her skin, and knew that she felt the heat of his. He closed his eyes. They stood that way for a long time. He waited until she was surrounded with the awareness of him, large and looming but unthreatening behind her, and then asked, "Why are we shouting at each other?"

She moved with reaction to his voice, just enough so that her back skimmed his chest. A faint shiver of laughter passed through her and he felt it ripple along his skin. Heat spread out from that subtle, delicate brush of her body against his. Still not touching her, his hands reached out and circled her slender waist. He wanted to draw her to him, enfold her in his arms, rest his head on her shoulder and breath in the scent of her night-dark hair. He did none of these things. He waited, breathless with arousal, afraid of rejection. He had never felt this tender need toward anyone before.

Diane didn't know what was the matter with her. One moment she was furious with the man. The next— well, she wasn't quite sure what exactly she was feeling at the moment. It was pleasant, strange, heady. She was warm and tingling, and it wasn't because she was standing too close to the roaring fire in the grate. It was because of the man who was so dangerously, deliciously close.

She could barely remember why she'd been angry. He'd made her laugh, and that made up for everything. It almost made up for Thierry. It would be so easy to move to face Simon, to put her arms around his neck, to turn her mouth up for his kiss. It was what would happen then that was frightening.

Simon had never felt this kind of vulnerability before. He knew what it was to feel helpless. It was an all too familiar sensation. This was just a new variety of the same old hated feeling. He knew every love song, every poem from the Courts of Love. He had even composed some of them himself, to flatter a queen. Now he understood all the allusions to the power women held over the men who desired them.

It was not right that a woman should have power over him. It was all very well to desire Diane. For what better way to make her love him but by worshipping her with his body? His emotions were already threatening to go past desire into a trackless realm. Had Genevieve felt like this, he wondered, when she met Berengar? As though she were about to step out of herself and be lost?

He made his hands drop to his sides. He took a step backward, and another. He put distance between himself and the thing he desired. Bitter cold seeped through him the moment he slipped away from Diane. It was a familiar feeling, one that had permeated him for a long time, but one he hadn't even noticed until it had begun to thaw.

"You should go," he told her.

When she turned to look at him, he almost went back to her. She blinked, and looked dazed. As though she was coming awake from a dream. She looked around her. Then at him. He was almost glad she couldn't speak. He moved further away from the fireplace, into the shadows so she could barely see him.

"I think you'd better go," he told her. "Let's just assume that neither of us meant to offend the other and get some rest."

Diane thought that if the man was trying to make her fall in love with him he was doing a poor job of it. Which was just as well. Or so her mind said. Her heart was saying something else, and her body was being totally rebellious about her determination not to get involved with this man. She was confused. So confused she didn't even remember what they'd been arguing about. It didn't matter. He wanted her to leave, and that hurt.

Leaving was for the best, she told herself. Her steps still dragged as she crossed the room. And she could feel his gaze on her even after she closed the door.

15

"Now, where were we?" Simon asked as she entered the room the next morning.

He looked up from his writing table with a smile Diane thought was as bright as the sunlight that filtered in the window behind him. Which was to say, it made the effort, but it was still November. It told her that he'd remembered his mission to make her fall in love with him for her own good. She'd been a little worried about Simon's intentions when he'd sent a guard for her after breakfast.

She smiled in response as he waved her forward, somehow pleased that the man was still making the effort despite his obvious distaste for the job. She'd left here the night before with her emotions in rags. She'd cried herself to sleep. She'd told herself she hated him, that she never wanted to see him again. Yet, here she was in the same room with him, and happy to be here. It made no logical sense. She could only conclude that logic had flown out the window the moment she arrived in Fantasyland.

Simon purposefully wanted the width of the heavy table between them since he wasn't sure he could deal with the possibility of physical contact just yet. He thought he was under control, but he wasn't going to test it until he could make love to Diane with the same indifference he'd felt toward Alys. The point was to give Diane pleasure, to rouse her tender emotions. He'd spent much of the night forcing his own emotions back under control. He'd also spent the time thinking, trying to decide the proper course to take with the exceptional, confused and confusing Diane.

He'd decided on honesty.

More or less.

He had been prepared for more tears, for more fury. He hadn't expected her to meekly settle into the chair opposite him and turn a knowing smile on him. She actually looked concerned for his welfare. He gave an inward sigh of pleasure. Trust Diane to make this easier than it should be. She would be easy to love. What a pity he couldn't. No, the real pity was that he was very hard to love indeed. Just ask every member of his family. Fortunately, for her sake and his, Diane was unable to.

"You take rejection better than most women would," he said as he leaned forward to rest his elbows on the table. "Were you, perhaps, a nun in your own time and place?"

I might as well have been, Diane thought as she recalled the circumscribed life she'd mapped out for herself back in Seattle in the two years since she'd graduated from college. She'd had her work, and that was it. She hadn't had a boyfriend in over a year, and hadn't wanted another one, either. She'd enjoyed watching other peoples' stories on a screen, so much so that she sometimes forgot there was a world outside the films she loved. Now that she was caught in her own melodrama she wasn't sure she was enjoying it, but she was aware that she'd been numbly moving through life instead of living it. She didn't want to think about which was better. She did know that meeting Simon was—

She shook her head in response to Simon's question.

He laced his fingers together and propped his chin on

them. She found the gesture artlessly charming. His gaze
on her was steady, assessing. She was fascinated by his
eyes, their sharp intelligence and feline-gold color. She
knew his device was a dragon, but to her Simon of
Marbeau was leonine, a big, dangerous, seductive cat.

After a moment she found it easier to look at his hands
than into his eyes. He had such long-fingered, elegant
hands, like a musician's. It was a pity they were marred by
the faint lines of old scars. Battle scars, she assumed. Or,
maybe Alys had scratched.

Diane hugged herself tightly. She was aware that the
sick wave of emotion going through her was jealousy. She
fought it, and looked away from Simon altogether. It
didn't help, because even though she concentrated on the
square of light coming in the window at his back, she was
all too aware of Simon's presence.

You're not in love with him, she told herself. *This is
just lust.* To prove the point, she tried her voice.

When her mouth worked but no sound came out,
Simon stood up and came around the table. "Not in love
yet, I see." He tried to make his words sound light, but the
joke fell flat for both of them. The look she turned on him
was anguished, as was the twist of pain around his heart.
"Perhaps I want someone to love me," he admitted.
"Though I didn't realize it until just now."

He was lying, of course, Diane told herself. Though she
had to acknowledge he looked and sounded good as he
mouthed the words meant to seduce her. She fought hard
to remember it was a deception as he took her hands in
his. Beautiful as those hands were, they were hard. The
man was all controlled strength, but his touch was gentle.

He stroked his thumbs across the back of her hands as
he said, "Sweet Diane, I fear we understand each other
not at all."

She looked up slowly as he spoke, up the long, hard-
muscled length of him. She was almost more aware of the

heat that rushed through her from his touch than of his voice. Almost, because his voice touched her as well. It brushed like heavy velvet along her sensitized nerves. He was the one who ought to be a storyteller since he could mesmerize her with a word.

He might as well have been naked, he thought. For his thick layers of clothing were no protection against the way she drew her gaze over him. He went hard just from the slow, intense scrutiny of Diane's fathomless dark eyes. Once again, this was going too fast. He had wanted her to want him, but had not expected it to happen so quickly. He was not prepared, no matter what his body told him.

He dropped her hands and turned away. He went back to his chair and slowly eased himself into the seat. "We need to talk." He folded his hands before him again. This time they were tightly clenched. "I need to explain some things to you," he corrected as she reacted with a sharp look to his ill-chosen words.

Simon tried to assume a lecturing tone. "Last night I tried to show my high regard for you in the most flattering way I know. You obviously did not understand my intent. We both came away feeling insulted. Let us now endeavor to come to an understanding of what is expected in our respective roles."

Comprehension gradually lit Diane's expression as he spoke. This awareness was followed by the skeptical arch of eyebrows that he found endearing. She leaned forward to rest her folded arms on her side of the wide table with casual, negligent grace.

He was not the one who was here to be charmed, he reminded himself sternly. But the fact that she was beautiful, and seemingly unaware of the effect of her beauty, was most distracting.

Diane had her emotions under control enough to be curious. She wanted to keep her mind working. She nodded for him to go on, and was determined to listen to what he said rather than just react to the sound of his voice. He was right, they were from different cultures. She'd gotten in enough trouble already from not knowing how this world worked. It was time she learned. He was offering to be her teacher.

Actually, he probably wasn't offering, he was making a pronouncement that he was going to teach her what she needed to know. That was all right. The reminder that he was autocratic, didactic, and lord of all he surveyed, was good for her.

Besides, one didn't fall in love with one's teachers, she reminded herself. At least, one shouldn't.

He picked up a roll of parchment. "Poems," he told her. "That speak of love and life and the rules of—"

Diane sneered. She hated poetry. She remembered English classes where she'd been forced to memorize crap written by sensitive, drugged-out, centuries-dead jerks in baggy shirts. Banal stuff like, "I arise from dreams of thee."

Simon leaned forward eagerly at her words. Her tone had been derisive, but at least she had spoken. "What say you, fair Diane? Have you fallen in love while neither of us were looking? Is this love that frees your voice?"

She shook her head, and recited,

"I arise from dreams of thee
In the first sweet sleep of night,
When the winds are breathing low,
And the stars are shining bright—"

Simon looked disappointed that she was still just parroting other peoples' words, but no more than she felt. Apparently, the poetry she'd recited passed for a story. She was determined not to tell any more stories. No more singing for her supper, even if it was the only chance she got to speak. So she shook her head rather than repeat the rest of it. Besides, it really sucked.

Simon sighed when she didn't go on, but he didn't ask her to finish. She appreciated that he didn't.

"I take it you do not admire poetry?"

You could say that, she thought. She gave a silent chuckle, amused rather than bitter that he could say anything he wanted.

"I used to enjoy poetry," he went on as he unrolled the parchment.

"But that was in another country," she said.

It wasn't from a poem, it was from a play, one that she'd helped videotape in college. It was also a comment.

He laughed with delight. "Yes, my dear, it was most certainly in another country. In Aquitaine." He realized what she'd done. "Clever girl."

It was a fluke, Diane thought, but she let herself bask in his approval for a few moments. She wondered if she could manage to dredge up enough appropriate comments to carry on actual conversations. No, she wasn't that clever, or quick-witted. In fact, all she could remember was the next line of the play. So she said it.

"Besides, the wench is dead."

The scroll dropped from Simon's fingers. His face went ashen. In place of his usually beautifully controlled voice, he spoke with a croak of pain. "Yes," he said. "She is."

Diane watched with a shriveling ache of conscience as Simon got up and walked away from his desk. With his back to her, he went and stared out the window.

"It was my fault," he added.

As she listened to Simon's pained words, she felt helpless and was hurting. She hadn't meant to do it, but she'd said something inappropriate again. She'd screwed up again. From this point on, she vowed, she was going to keep her mouth shut.

She was also going to stop being so reactive, so passive. She'd just hurt the man without meaning to. She needed to do something to make up for it. All that came to mind was to get up and go to him. She wasn't quite sure she had the courage to face the same sort of rejection she'd gotten from him the night before. She wasn't sure what she'd do once she reached him. Sure or not, she got up, and began to slowly walk forward.

Simon took several deep, ragged breaths. Though he'd had the window opening covered over for the winter with oiled hide, the cold air that leaked through was bracing. He was glad the translucent hide was too thick to give him a decent view of the dead garden and its ghosts. He had to live in the present, to live in the moment, but even with Diane, a child of the future, there was no escape from his mistakes and sins.

How odd, he thought, that the scars of memory did not ache so when anyone else reminded him of his past. Perhaps it was because he would rather keep the wrongs he'd done to himself. Or, more likely, he wanted this innocent young woman to think well of him. Of course, that could not be, not for long. Hadn't he decided that honesty was the way to her heart? If he used honesty correctly she'd end up feeling pity for him, and her compassion would trick her into love. It was simple. All he had to do was rip his soul open and present it to her on a platter.

With his purpose in mind, he took a deep breath and turned to face the object of his quest, only to find that she was standing just behind him. She had approached across the rushes on silent, softly shod feet. He had not heard her, nor had he expected to find her so close.

"If you were an enemy I'd be dead by now."

Her expression was full of concern, her dark eyes bright with unshed tears. Tears that were for him, he realized as he stepped forward and brushed a finger across her cheek. She was there for him. At his touch, one tear spilled over. The sight of it twisted his heart.

He would have wiped the tear away. He would have bent down to kiss the salty trail it left. He might have done many things, but the door crashed open before he had a chance to move closer to Diane.

Sir Joscelin hurried in, red-faced and breathing hard. The scent of horse, sweat, and fear trailed in with him.

"My lord!" he shouted as he hurried across the room toward Simon. "The raiders are massing to attack Marbeau!"

16

"Winter is no time to lay siege to a castle. Any fool knows that."

Sir Joscelin looked past him, and spoke to Diane. "Perhaps they are hungry samurai."

"What?" Simon had no time for riddles. And less patience for Joscelin making cow eyes at a woman. Especially this woman. Simon stepped in front of her. "What raiders? How many? From what direction do they approach?"

Jacques came in before Joscelin could answer. "Simon, my scrying glass has shown warriors massing—Ah, Joscelin's brought the warning before me, I see."

"So he has," Simon agreed. He looked from the old man to the young knight. Between Jacques's magic and Joscelin's early warning, the Lord of Marbeau hoped they'd bought enough time to plan the defense of his lands before they were attacked.

Simon turned to Diane. "Return to Jacques's chamber. I have work to do now." It was best to have her out of the way, where she wouldn't be a distraction for Joscelin, or himself. "You'll be safe there," he added with a reassuring smile when she didn't immediately obey.

Diane quivered with rage at Simon's easy dismissal of

her. He might as well have said, "*Go away, little girl. I'll take you out and play with you some more when I'm done with real man's work.*"

She wanted desperately to tell him that she was not Hong Kong Barbie, and didn't take kindly to being put back in the doll case. For the first time, she wished that she was in love with somebody—so she could yell at Simon de Argent.

She could accept the fact that the castle was in danger, and that it was his job to defend it. What she didn't appreciate was his automatic assumption that she had no part to play in the upcoming crisis.

Then again, she conceded with a hollow sigh, she supposed she didn't. She didn't belong here. She didn't know the rules. She hadn't done one sensible or useful thing since Jacques dragged her into this world. She didn't have to like it. She didn't have to appreciate Simon's throwing her out. She did have to obey him.

That didn't mean she didn't give Simon a venomous look as she passed him on her way to the door.

Her grandmother Teal had a saying, a saying she claimed she'd gotten from *her* grandmother. It went something like, "Make yourself useful as well as ornamental." Diane couldn't get it out of her head as she paced the length of Jacques's room over and over again. This wasn't the first time she'd been bothered by her tenuous position in this world, by her lack of purpose. She found this both odd and irritating, since she hadn't been particularly worried about a lack of purpose in her own world.

Maybe having so much taken away from her—her voice, her routine, her whole life—had left her wondering just what was left. She wasn't afraid to find out, but she was frustrated that no one would give her the chance.

And, why, she wondered as she abruptly stopped pacing, *am I waiting for permission to lead my own life?*

There were things going on out there. The woman who'd been assigned as her servant had told her that the castle was preparing for a siege. Surely there must be something she could do to help. She took a deep breath and went to the door.

She hesitated as she reached it. She knew that she'd face Simon's disapproval, and the hostility of the people of Marbeau if she stuck her nose in where she wasn't wanted. She'd been beaten, nearly raped, insulted, rejected, and just generally shown she wasn't wanted by almost everyone. Why should she try to help them?

Because not everybody was cruel and vicious, she reminded herself. Jacques, and Joscelin, Yves, and her own servant were actually rather nice people. More importantly, an image of Simon de Argent stuck in her head, looking like a grim, graying lion. The sad, determined, responsible, kinder-than-he-knew Lord of Marbeau needed as much help as he could get, and was too proud and stubborn to ask for any. Besides, it was Simon who had first told her to make the best of this bad situation. It was time she took some initiative.

She opened the door and took the winding staircase down to the hall. What exactly did one do when a castle was under attack? Run away, was the logical answer. Of course, running away probably resulted in people with swords chasing you down. She knew what happened after that, she'd seen *Braveheart* six times. Not to mention what she'd seen since arriving here, and here the blood wasn't fake.

Her stomach was twisted with nausea from the memories by the time she reached the hall. But her head was also full of scenes from some of the more realistic medieval movies she'd viewed. She reminded herself that she'd taken a few first aid classes back when she was a Girl Scout, as well. Surely, she had some bit of practical knowledge that she could put to use, she thought as she approached a group of women by the central hearth.

"I know I gave her holy communion with my own hands, my lord, but are you sure she's not a demon?"

Simon pulled off his helmet as a groom led his horse away. The sky couldn't decide whether to snow or rain, so it was doing both in fits and starts. The day was drawing to a close, though there hadn't been much light to begin with. His cloak was soaked through. His arms ached from sword and shield work, as did his back and thighs from sitting on a horse all day. The fighting outside the walls and in the bare woods had gone more his way than the invaders' in the last two days, but they hadn't been driven off. Tomorrow he would have to fight again. Simon wanted a cup of mulled wine, a joint of meat, and his bed. Of course he wasn't going to be so fortunate as to get what he wanted, not in this life.

First he took off his gloves, then he swiped sweat out of his eyes, then he turned to the anxiously waiting priest. "What?"

Father Andre hopped nervously from foot to foot as he answered, "The foreigner, my lord. She's in my church."

"What of it? We could all use to prayers for peace."

"She's not praying."

Simon was in no mood for guessing games. "What is she doing?"

"She's boiling water."

"Where? In the baptismal font? With what?"

He remembered the blaze that had been in the look she'd given him before she'd left his chamber. However, he refrained from suggesting to the priest that Diane could light fires with an angry glare.

"She brings the water from the bath house, but she does have braziers set up in the church," Father Andre told him indignantly. "She must be a demon, for she has the church as hot as the pit. She jumps around and points and grimaces at good folk until she gets her way. She's got the washerwomen laundering blankets and linen as well, as though it were spring cleaning time."

"What? Why?"

"First she swept out the rushes in the church. Those were fresh rushes."

"Why?"

"Somehow she managed to convince the women to use the church for nursing the wounded."

Simon nodded. "That makes sense."

"Does her washing the floor before letting anyone in make sense? And, she keeps scrubbing it, as though cleaned stones have anything to do with tending the sick."

"Perhaps where she comes from—"

"She won't let any wounds be cleansed except with her foolish boiled water. It's madness."

Simon rubbed his jaw. He could use a shave. Hot water sounded good to him. Perhaps he could get Diane to scrub him. "What does Jacques say?"

"To leave her be." Father Andre pointed a shaky finger at him. "You must do something."

"I'll have a look at the wounded," Simon agreed. The priest didn't look happy with Simon's words, but he turned and led the way to the church door.

There was more light in the church than Simon was used to, and more heat. The sensation was strange, but not unpleasant. He welcomed the warmth, and quickly shed his damp cloak. He tossed it over his arm, and stood for a moment with his eyes closed to let the warmth seep in. When he opened his eyes he saw Diane. For a moment he found himself simply studying her profile as she bent over one of the patients. She looked tired, and not quite so young as he recalled her being. Her expression also held something of the strength and serenity of a Madonna, as though she had no time for fragile emotions right now. He drank in the sight of her. It was as soothing as the mulled wine he'd craved a few moments before.

Apparently, he'd missed her even while his mind had been on nothing but the defense of Marbeau.

A half dozen or so of his soldiers and several injured villagers lay on pallets that took up the center of the nave. The place did not have the usual stench of a sickhouse. The wounded looked clean and well cared for. Simon gave an approving nod. He walked slowly to where Diane sat cross-legged next to a man propped up on pillows. She was patiently spoon feeding the man broth from a wooden bowl. Simon savored the sight of her even as he ran his gaze over each pallet he passed.

She looked up as he reached her. Her expression was wary and impertinent at once.

Simon smiled. "You think I'm going to send you back to your room, don't you?" He put his hands on his hips. "I should. This is no place for you. You're upsetting the priest," he added when her reply was a nonchalant shrug.

She lifted her chin haughtily, then went back to feeding the sick man with a feigned unconcern that plainly said she didn't see a large man in full chain mail armor looming over her. And wasn't about to put up with any criticism from him even if she did. He was more amused than annoyed by this act of defiance.

He knelt beside her, and turned his attention to the wounded man. This one had a deep sword slash across his chest, and another wound in his arm. Both were neatly bandaged with clean dressings. The man's color was better than Simon expected from someone so badly injured. His breath didn't come in sickening wheezes of the lung fever that often accompanied serious wounds.

Simon leaned forward, and his arm brushed Diane's. He patted the man on the shoulder. "How goes it, Philip? Have you any complaint of your nursing?"

Diane found the soft clink of Simon's armor as he moved incongruously musically and pleasant. She also found his closeness pleasant, though he stank of old sweat, horse, and blood. She didn't care how much he smelled. Maybe it was because she'd unconsciously been waiting to see him carried into her makeshift infirmary at any time during the last two days. She hadn't realized how much she hadn't let herself think about Simon until he was here beside her.

She darted one quick gaze at his raptor-sharp profile. He looked dangerous even while he made a compassionate gesture to one of his men. A ripple of excitement went through her, and she quickly looked away. Simon's proximity left her confused and shaken. Literally. She nearly dropped the bowl as the physical reaction overtook her. She closed her eyes for a moment, but that only made her more aware of Simon's presence. So she opened them, took a deep breath, and did her best to concentrate on her patient instead of the Lord of Marbeau.

"The foreigner's a good nurse, my lord," Philip answered before she could lift another spoonful of broth to his lips. "Best I ever had."

Simon nodded. "Good." He turned and took the bowl from Diane's hands. "You," he spoke to a woman nearby. The servant hurried to him. He handed her the bowl. "Finish feeding this man."

"Yes, my lord."

Simon hauled Diane to her feet, and, with his hand firmly on her arm, escorted her to the church door. "When did you last sleep?" he asked when they got there. "You're shaking from exhaustion."

Her shoulders shook, but with silent laughter. She covered her mouth with her palm to hide her amusement, but he saw the glint in her dark eyes even in the shadows of the church door.

"Are you going to share the joke, Diane?"

She looked up at him and shook her head.

Simon continued to frown. "If I drag you from here to get some rest, will you just come back?"

She nodded.

"I thought as much. I'm too tired to drag you very far, anyway." She reached up, and sympathetically patted his cheek. The warmth of her touch soothed him. He put his hand on her wrist and leaned into her cupped palm. "You take good care of my people," he told her. "Thank you for your concern."

Father Andre came through the doorway before he could say anymore. "What will you do about the foreigner, my lord?" he asked nervously.

Now, there was a very complicated question.

Simon released Diane's hand. He looked at the priest. "She is to have your cooperation in everything she does," he answered Andre.

"But—" the priest sputtered.

"If she wants to boil every bit of water in the well, you'll fetch it for her. The wounded are to be tended as she sees fit. Am I understood?"

Andre looked outraged, but Simon was more interested in the pleased expression on Diane's face. Not triumphant, but pleased. A bit of warmth curled around Simon's guarded heart at seeing that Diane was truly interested in caring for his household, and not simply trying to gain power over him with false kindness.

"Give my lady whatever she wants," he told the priest. "I'll give the same orders to the steward."

Andre knew when to give up. He bowed his head meekly, "Yes, my lord."

Simon turned his full attention back to Diane. "Come in to supper?" She looked tempted, then she gazed back at the sickroom. She sighed and shook her head. He sighed as well. "Well, I'm going to supper, and to take this armor off for a while." It was his turn to cup her cheek, and notice that he left a streak of mud on it when he took his hand away. "I'm filthy, and getting you that way. I'll get cleaned up and see you later."

He very nearly bent down to kiss the mud away before he left her. After he'd left her he didn't know why he hadn't.

Diane found Simon's cape next to Philip's pallet when she went back to check on the wounded man. Philip was asleep, propped up on a half-dozen pillows to help ward off pneumonia. The cape was damp. It smelled of wet wool and fur, and Simon, she thought when she surreptitiously rubbed her cheek against the soft, brown fur lining. In her own world, she was firmly against wearing animal fur, but this felt wonderful, she admitted. Wonderful or not, the weather was cold and Simon still needed it back. First she hung it up to dry on one of the clotheslines strung up near the charcoal-filled braziers. Then she spent several more hours moving among the patients. Oddly enough, seeing Simon, getting his approval for what she was going to do anyway, left her feeling happy and revitalized.

There wasn't much she could do, not really. Jacques had offered her a chest full of herbal medicines, but she didn't have the faintest idea how to use them. He'd also mentioned that Lady Genevieve had been the one who was good with herbs and plants. She hadn't really wanted to hear anything about the late Mrs. de Argent, so she'd set to work doing what she did know about.

It had not been pretty. She'd thrown up the first time she'd seen a sword wound up close and spurting blood. None of the other women who'd showed up to help tend the wounded had thrown up. So she'd told herself to get over it and get on with it. She'd gotten used to it.

She hadn't actually sewn up any of the wounds herself.

Several of the gentlewomen who spent most of their lives embroidering turned out to be skilled at the crudest kind of emergency surgery. Diane had made it her job to see that the wounds didn't get infected, or that other post-traumatic problems didn't set in. Keeping people warm and clean was the best she could do, and so far it seemed to be helping. Only two of the hacked-up soldiers that had been brought in had died so far.

The problem was, they kept bringing hacked-up people into the church, and burying more that didn't make it off the battlefield. Father Andre kept saying Masses for the dead while the women worked to save the living. It was a busy, noisy place, and Diane had made it her world for the last several days. She was afraid that if she left, she wouldn't have the courage to come back.

Once Simon's cloak was dry, she decided she should venture out, if only for a little while. She didn't want the Lord of Marbeau to freeze, after all.

She met Simon at the door as she was going out. He wore clean clothes instead of armor. His fair hair was combed back and glimmered in the moonlight that poured down from the indigo sky overhead. He carried a basket over one arm.

"The weather's cleared," he said. He held up the basket. "I've brought you bread and cheese."

He took her hand and drew her outside. The air was crisp, but not as cold as it had been earlier. Diane looked up and saw that the night sky was glorious, full of far more stars than she was used to. She took a deep breath. The air still smelled of mud and woodsmoke, but there was no taint of the sickness and sour sweat that filled the church. Just to breath in this different atmosphere was wonderful. She turned an appreciative smile on Simon.

He smiled back. "Let's sit on the hall steps and eat under the stars, shall we? I promise not to try to feed you this time," he added when she hesitated.

The night was beautiful. She was hungry. Besides, Simon was the only person in this world she really felt comfortable with. And he looked so anxious to please her. She didn't know why. She didn't think he was taking time out from fighting a war to romance her. Which was good, since she didn't have time to fend off being romanced. She nodded to his invitation, and they walked hand in hand to the hall steps.

Once there, she remembered his cloak, and handed it to him. "My thanks, lady," he said. He put down the basket and swirled the cape onto his shoulders. "Come, share this with me as well." He put his arm around her shoulder. When they sat she was pressed close to his side, sharing the warmth of his body as well as the cloak.

The moment Diane sat down all the work and stress nearly overwhelmed her. She was almost too tired to eat. She almost wished he would feed her and save her all the work that went in to picking up a piece of bread and bringing it to her mouth. She wished she could cuddle under Simon's arm, put her head on his shoulder and cry, or just sleep. She ate the food he'd brought instead.

It was easier to eat than to think. Easier to be with Simon than to crawl into a lonely, uncomfortable bed. He offered warmth and support and a companionable silence. Even if she could have spoken, she wouldn't have. It was restful just to be. After she'd finished eating, she put her head on his shoulder. She wasn't sure which of them gave the contented sigh. She didn't close her eyes, but looked up and started counting stars. Soon the world boiled down to the fiery points of light overhead and the soft breathing of the man beside her.

When she was nearly asleep, he said, "The fighting will be over tomorrow."

Diane wasn't sure how her left hand had crept up to rest over Simon's heart, but she snatched it away as she sat up straight. Still in the circle of his arm, she bent her head back to look at him. Despite the serenity of his expression she could see how tired he was. He was the one who should be sleeping and not feeding and comforting her.

"By sunset Marbeau will be safe," he went on. He touched the tip of her nose with one finger. "All will be well, little one." He gave a tired sigh. "Except for the granary that was burned, the livestock that was stolen and the dead and wounded the raiders leave behind. We'll have more of theirs to bury than of our own. That's what winning is, I suppose." He shook his head. "Never mind. I'm rambling."

She saw how tired he was, how worried. The man had all this responsibility and no one to help him shoulder it. That was the downside to being lord of all he surveyed. She wished there was something she could do to help.

The only thing that came to mind was to say, "Once upon a time, a war between many powers waged outside the fortress of Casablanca."

This time, finally, as they sat huddled close together beneath Simon's cloak, she was able to tell the story all the way through to the end.

Simon listened attentively, and gave a satisfied sigh when she was done. "Ilsa went with her husband, then, and Rick and Louis went to fight these Nazi barbarians together. Good. It was the honorable thing to do."

17

It was the male thing to do, Diane thought.

Perhaps the end of *Casablanca* was the right thing to do, maybe it was honorable, but nobody came out of it happy. They just did their duty, all brave, and noble, and long-suffering, and everybody in the audience cried. Well, it made a great story, maybe the best movie of all time, but it was just a movie. How would it really go in the real world? she wondered.

Not that she had to worry about the real world, not with all the troubles here in Fantasyland. She ought to get back to her patients. She hadn't noticed while she'd been talking, but the cold had managed to seep through even Simon's cloak and her layers of clothes. The only thing keeping her warm was their shared body heat. She yawned, and heard her jaw creak with the effort.

Simon brushed a hand across her cheek. "You're sleepy, and could use some wine to warm you, I'd wager." He stood, and brought her to her feet with him. When she would have started back for the church, he steered her toward the castle door. "We're both going to get a few hours comfortable rest," he told her. "Come along. There are others to see that the wounded are resting comfortably," he added when she tried to pull away. "You can supervise the sickroom again in the morning."

She supposed he was right. By this time of night the day's work was really done. Most people were asleep. She might as well catch a few hours rest while she could. So Diane nodded, and went with Simon into the hall.

Inside, the fires were banked, and the members of the household not manning the defenses were huddled together in warm, snoring clumps as close to the central hearth as they could get. He took her hand and led her tired steps through this human obstacle course. They went up the stairs. Yves was sleeping on the landing outside Simon's chamber. They stepped over him and went inside. It occurred to Diane as the heavy door closed behind her that she should go up to Jacques's room to go to bed.

"Why disturb the old man?" Simon asked, sensing her hesitation.

Why, indeed?

There were lots of good reasons to leave. She couldn't think of any as she looked into Simon's eyes. So she took off her cape, and followed him across the room to the big, curtained bed.

She drank down the cup of wine Simon poured for her from a silver flagon on a bedside table. It warmed her, as Simon had promised. Or maybe the heat that spread through her was at the sight of Simon's hard-muscled body as he stripped down to the linen breechcloth that passed for men's underwear in this place.

The breechcloth came off as well, but she turned away before she saw him completely naked. Her hands trembled a little as she put down the winecup. When she took her clothes off, she only managed to get as far as the linen shift she wore under all the layers of wool. She wasn't quite ready to face Simon de Argent with the vulnerability of being completely naked.

She was glad that the room was mostly dark as she

stood with her back to the bed. There was a lit hour candle on Simon's writing table in the corner by the window, the soft glow of the banked fire in the grate, and one lone candle next to the wine flagon. The carefully polished silver gleamed almost gold in the flicker of the candle flame.

Its curved surface mirrored Simon's movements as he came up behind her. She watched, almost as though she were dreaming, as his hands touched her shoulders. He slipped his fingers beneath the neckline of the shift and pushed it down over her arms. In a daze, she saw the reflection of her bared breasts, and felt the tension that radiated out from hardened nipples. Her head fell back against his matted chest as he lowered his lips to her throat.

The excitement that flamed through her as he kissed her wasn't from the wine.

He kissed her neck, her ear, her temple and jawline as his hands moved in small circles over her shoulders and arms. He turned her to face him and touched his lips to hers. The kiss was delicate at first, a whisper touch, an almost tentative trace of his tongue around the outline of her mouth. It was a suggestion, an asking for permission.

She replied by pressing herself against his naked body. She put her hand on the back of his head, tangled her fingers in his heavy hair and offered her open mouth to his exploration.

That the girl was willing, Simon had no doubt. That he wanted her, he had no doubt. His member was hard and his mind was eager to cloud with passion. He wanted to take her, to forget himself for a while between soft, womanly thighs. He tasted the eagerness in her kiss. Her tongue touched his, teased and ravaged his mouth with the knowledge and needs of a woman. He responded with a heady moan. This went faster than it should. This was not the way their first coupling should be. He was ready to go up in flames, and take Diane with him.

He relished the knowledge that she was no untried maiden. She was showing him vividly that the fear of a man's touch caused by Thierry had faded with the passing days. She might cry out when he entered her, but it would not be in terror. He should take her in his arms and place her beneath him on the bed.

"I should bed you," he said, voice rough and breathless. He pressed his hardness against the soft curve of her belly. "I want to bed you."

Who's trying to stop you? she thought. Her insides were curled with desire. The fierce tension of need was almost painful. She arched like a cat as Simon's hands stroked over her back and down her sides.

Simon made himself step away before his lust became too great to control. "No."

He retreated a step further, and snatched up his undertunic. He kept his gaze carefully away from her naked breasts. Once his arousal was covered he made himself look only at her face. His groin ached, his manhood demanded to have its way, but he refused to give in to his animal nature. He had a duty to treat this woman as an object of chivalrous devotion, not a common whore.

If she was to fall in love and get her voice back, he must practice restraint.

"I haven't the will to make proper love tonight. It would be a fierce coupling," he told her as she turned a confused look on him. "It's been too long. The fighting brings out the barbarian in me. It would be too wild, and hedonistic. Like the rutting of animals. Hard and fast and — "

He frowned at her eager grin.

"Wicked and sinful," he went on.

Sounds good to me, Diane thought. She took a step toward him.

He backed away. "Am I going to have to defend my virtue, woman?"

She nodded.

Then she stopped. If he didn't want to, he didn't want to. She remembered all those careful discussion on sexual ethics in dorm rooms and office meetings, on TV ads and in coffeehouse pamphlets. No was supposed to mean no, no matter what the gender of the person who said it.

Who'd have thought she'd need a lesson in political correctness from a guy who wore armor to work?

She turned her back to him and pulled her shift up from around her hips. If he didn't want to sleep with her, fine. She'd go to sleep. The last thing she expected was for Simon to crawl in beside her and pull up the covers a few minutes after she'd gotten into bed.

After Simon had watched Diane flounce across the room and settle herself on his thick, feather mattress he poured himself a full cup of wine. She turned her back to him, and he turned his to her. Desire still raged, but he drank it down. He forced it from his body, and to the back of his mind. He considered using his hand to relieve his immediate problem, but chose not to embarrass himself, or the girl, in that way. It took several deep drinks, and many deep breaths before he was able to calmly seek the place beside her still form. He trusted to very real exhaustion as much as the strong drink to help him to sleep.

When Simon didn't make any move toward her, Diane eventually relaxed. After a while she even stopped being angry at him. She even smiled into the darkness as his deep, steady breathing told her he was asleep. It took a few more minutes before she got over her embarrassment, and the sting of rejection, to see the incident as endearing. Simon de Argent was not a pig. An efficient, cold-blooded killer, maybe. A dictator, definitely. But he was not like any other man she'd ever known.

It was conceivable that she was beginning to care for him, a little. But she wasn't going to let herself fall in love. That would be letting another person determine her destiny—all those talks and meetings and ads and pamphlets had had plenty to say about that kind of codependent behavior, too.

Determination aside, she welcomed the closeness when he rolled over and into her embrace. She stroked hair off his cheek and cradled his head on her modestly covered breasts. He smelled good, he felt good, it felt reassuring to have someone beside her in the night. He obviously, if unconsciously, felt the same way. If a cuddle was what it took to get him through the night, she thought, then she was happy to oblige.

Simon woke to find Diane's hand very close to his erection. Her head rested on his chest. His arm was possessively twined around her shoulders. He didn't think she intended for her warm palm and slightly curled fingers to be so near his member, but the exciting sensation was more than pleasant. For a moment, the burning pressure in his groin distracted him from the knowledge that he had a hand cupped over one of her small breasts.

It seemed he'd woken up to the same situation he'd backed away from last night. He stared up at the tapestry canopy over the bed and considered his choices. He could wake Diane with languorous kisses, worship her body with his lips and hands, then make slow, passionate love to her. Or he could put on his mail and go out and kill people.

Duty dictated his decision. He got up and called for Yves to bring cold water. Lots of cold water.

"The men say they've never seen you fight so fiercely as you did today."

"I had my reasons," Simon replied.

He tried to ignore Joscelin as he looked around the interior of the church. The wounded were being well-tended, but Diane was not there. He turned around and strode back across the courtyard, with his helmet tucked under his arm. The young knight followed close on his heels.

"You were a lion of battle, my lord. Surely, the scattered survivors of that band of *routiers* will carry the tale throughout the land."

"That was why I let some of them live."

Joscelin gave a decisive nod as they entered the hall. "So no one would dare attack Marbeau again, though the landless mercenaries may be as hungry as wolves through the winter."

"Precisely."

Not here, either. Where was the woman? He took the stairs up to his chamber, annoyed that Joscelin still followed him. What was the young fool doing dogging his steps?

"I wonder where Diane's gotten to?" Joscelin questioned as they entered Simon's chamber. Simon watched in consternation as Joscelin boldly looked around *his* room. "Not here, my lord."

"Obviously." The relief in Joscelin's voice had been too evident. The jealousy in Simon's reply had been plain as well. To Simon at least. He handed Joscelin his helmet. "Go polish this."

The lad gave him an odd look, but he did leave. Simon went to his writing table, and sat down with a sigh. After a few moments, he called, "Yves!" When the servant appeared, Simon demanded, "Where's Diane?"

Before Yves could answer, Jacques came in. Diane followed him. She limped, and supported herself with Jacques's jeweled wizard's staff.

Simon was at her side instantly. "What the devil happened to you? Are you hurt?"

"Don't fuss like a hen with one chick," Jacques told him. "She fell over one of her patients and hurt her leg."

Diane pulled up her skirts as Jacques spoke. Simon

was so shocked by her immodest action that he didn't see the bruises and scrapes that marred her golden skin for a few moments. When he did, he scooped her up in his arms. The staff dropped from her hand with a mighty clatter.

Jacques hastened to snatch it up. "Careful! This is a family heirloom."

Simon gently deposited Diane in the chair he'd been using. He carefully adjusted her long skirts over her injured leg. A look sent Yves for food and drink. He looked back at the disgruntled wizard. "Ah, yes, the rod of power passed down from your illustrious ancestor. Mryddn, wasn't it?" he teased.

Jacques bristled. "Mryddn? That Cymri hedge wizard? Hardly. This rod was presented as a birth present by Dion of Epirus to his son, no matter what great-great-great Grandmother Morgause said about who fathered the babe."

Wizards were *so* touchy about their frequently incestuous and tangled family trees. There were so few born with magical gifts that they had to interbreed to keep the power. Sometimes that led to birthing monsters, such as Jacques's own granddaughter. Simon decided it would be better not to tease the old man about his ancestors if he didn't want to get into the subject of his descendants.

So, he asked, "If the staff's so precious, why let the girl use it as a cane?"

Jacques ran his hands lovingly over the carved and jeweled wood. "Damned old thing doesn't work anymore. Thought I'd put it to some practical use."

Simon looked down at the wide-eyed Diane. "How are you?"

"She's sore," Jacques answered for her.

"And how long will she be sore?"

"She'll be fine in five or six days."

"Damn!"

Simon realized he was glaring at the girl with unfair irritation. It was just that he'd had hopes, plans, fantasies, of taking Diane to his bed for long hours of passionate love. He was hardly going to carry out any of those erotic schemes when she'd be too uncomfortable to appreciate them.

Diane didn't know why Simon was annoyed with her, though she was certainly annoyed enough at herself. She knew she wouldn't have fallen at all if her attention hadn't been elsewhere. She'd spent the night in feverish, erotic dreams. She'd spent the night sleeping in the arms of the man those dreams were about. She'd woken to find him gone, and was stabbed with an unreasonable sense of grief at his absence. After a few moments, she decided that what she felt was worry, and went to work. She knew she was right to worry about Simon when reports of the fierce fighting outside the walls reached the infirmary—along with the wounded.

She hadn't actually fallen over one of the injured men. She'd actually tumbled hard onto the chain mail, helmet, and sword that the women had stripped off him and left in a pile Diane hadn't noticed as she hurried past with an armful of fresh bandages. She received a cut across her knee from the dulled edge of the sword, scraped her leg on the mail, bruised herself on the hard stone floor, and twisted her ankle as well. Jacques was right, she was sore, but she wasn't worried she was going to get an infection and die, or anything like that.

The whole incident was rather embarrassing. She almost didn't resent Simon being annoyed with her. Better annoyed than disgustingly solicitous, she told herself. His carrying her to the chair had been more embarrassing than the fall. Though there was a certain pleasant reassurance about being cradled against his strong, masculine chest, even though the tunic that covered it was soaked with mud and sweat. She was immensely relieved that he'd come out of the fighting filthy but unscathed. And just why was he annoyed with her, anyway?

When she gave him a questioning look, he put his fingers under her chin and tilted it up. "My apologies for my rude words, sweet Diane. It was tender concern for your well-being that caused my sharp words."

Simon smiled as Diane cocked an eyebrow sardonically at his flamboyant language.

"What?" he questioned. "Can I not speak to you with fair, flowery expressions?"

Diane drew her face from his grasp, and shook her head.

Simon spread his arms wide as he went down on one knee before Diane's chair. Chain mail clinked as he moved. "Then with what can I prove my true devotion, my—How about dinner?" he asked as Yves came in with a laden tray.

Simon got to his feet and went to change as Yves laid out the meal on the writing table. The servant took the mail away with him, to be cleaned and have broken rings mended in the armory. Simon gave himself a quick wash and dressed in a clean clothes before he joined Jacques and Diane once more.

Diane did not give in to the impulse to watch Simon as he got cleaned up. She still ached with longing from the last time she'd seen the man naked. She didn't want that ache to flare into desire again, so she looked around for anything else that could capture her attention. The food didn't do it. She would eat it, but didn't want to actually study it before she did. She didn't *want* to know what it was. Her modern American sensibilities didn't take to the menu here any more than they had to the truly alien, non-tourist cuisine she'd encountered on her one visit to Hong Kong.

Asia, at least, had McDonald's.

So she turned her attention to the pile of paper on the

desk. She supposed the stiff, yellowish stuff was actually parchment, but she wasn't sure what the difference was. Something to do with sheep, she thought. She picked up the parchment at the top of the pile. It was covered in spidery, splotched writing. Writing she couldn't read. She studied it hard, but the words didn't magically become clear as she looked at them.

She wondered why. She could understand what everyone said, they could understand her stories. She got Jacques's attention and ran her fingers over a line of words. Then she pointed to herself.

She had to do this several times before his eyes lit with comprehension. "You're wondering why you can't read?"

She nodded vigorously.

Simon's hand landed on her shoulder. "Can you read? In your own world?"

The excitement in his voice almost made Diane forget the electric jolt that ran through her from his touch. She looked up at him and repeated the nod.

"But not here?" Simon looked at Jacques. "Why not?"

"I was already starting to answer that." The wizard looked from one to the other, then he shrugged. "I have no idea."

"What?"

Simon shouted it, but Diane echoed the accusing word silently.

"What kind of wizard are you to—?"

"An old one," Jacques reminded Simon. He ran his fingers thoughtfully through his white beard. "No, perhaps I do have a notion of why Diane cannot read. It's only a conjecture, of course."

"A conjecture?" Simon frowned at the wizard. "Old man, I trust you and in your power, but your willingness to explore the limits of your imagination terrifies me sometimes."

The wizard lifted his head proudly. "What I can imagine, I can perform. Theoretically. Theory is the basis of what I do. Conjecture is what all magic spells are until they are proven with experimentation," Jacques explained. "Of course if it doesn't work, my subjects have this tendency to turn into frogs. There was one time—"

"I take your point," Simon interrupted. "What were you going to say about this notion you have about Diane?"

Simon's hand was still on her shoulder. His fingers made unconscious, comforting little circles on her skin while he and Jacques talked. Diane wanted to close her eyes and savor the sensation, but forced herself to concentrate on Jacques instead.

"Conservation of energy," Jacques said. "I'm old," he reminded them once more. "The spell that fetched Diane to Marbeau was looking for specific things, and gave specific things to the one it chose. So, Diane knows our language because she needs it to perform the requirements of the spell. She does not need to read our language to be a storyteller."

"So you gave her only what she needed?"

"The spell did." Jacques waved his hand dismissively. "Never mind, you can't understand the difference, nor do you need to."

"I don't want to know, either." Simon leaned forward eagerly. "But can she learn to read? We could communicate that way, could we not?" He squeezed her shoulder. "Why didn't you think of this?"

She looked up at him with a silent laugh. He saw the eagerness in her eyes, the same eagerness he was feeling. Love or not, perhaps they would soon be communicating with each other.

"Well?" Simon asked Jacques.

"Of course she can learn to read. She's an intelligent young woman, isn't she? Oh, before I forget." Jacques reached into a large pouch at his belt and brought out a folded piece of parchment. "Speaking of reading, this is why I helped Diane limp down here instead of sending her with a strong young serving woman. A messenger brought this while you were chasing off the last of the besiegers."

Simon took the parchment. After looking thoughtfully at the large wax seal for a few moments, he solemnly cracked it and read the contents of the message. Excitement drained out of him as he did so. His world came back into focus, and it had no eagerness or anticipation, or joy, in it.

Finally, he looked up at Jacques. "King Louis invites me to attend him in Paris."

Paris? Diane shot to her feet, then fell back into the chair with a sharp, silent wince. Beside her, Simon didn't pay her any notice. He stood rigid as a rock, the parchment crumpled in one tense fist.

Paris? she thought. Paris, France? Was she in France? What was she doing in France? When did France get wizards? And warriors? She'd thought she was in some sort of parallel fantasyland, but apparently her assumption was wrong. Apparently she was in France. Had she traveled through time? Not that that made any more sense than her traveling to another dimension. Maybe that was why Simon understood the line in *Casablanca* about "we'll always have Paris." Because he'd been there. He was going there now. She wondered why. And what year was this, anyway?

Before she could think of any way at all to phrase these urgent questions, Jacques asked, "Why would you go to Paris?"

Simon's voice was glacially cool when he replied. "Why, to get married, of course."

18

"You most certainly are going."

Diane shook her head one more time. She stomped her foot. The servants and soldiers waiting to leave with their lord and his luggage looked around nervously. Simon glared.

She refused to be impressed by his leonine glower. She wasn't going. The fact that Jacques stood at her back, blocking the entrance to the castle, and that Simon was looming down from his large stallion, kept her from stomping off.

She had spent the night coming to grips with the fact that this wasn't some alternate universe but that she had traveled back in time. She hated knowing that there were a lot of things that neither Simon nor Jacques had bothered to tell her. She'd forgiven them for their omissions. She didn't suppose it was all that important. For all intents and purposes, this ancient France was about as alternate a world as Oz.

She was over being angry about all that.

What she had no intention of doing was attending Simon's wedding.

It had nothing to do with how she felt about him. It wasn't love, it was pride. She wasn't letting any more strangers ogle and insult her. She was not going to be the entertainment at the reception. She wasn't going.

"You're going."

His household had spent the night preparing for the journey to Paris. No one had gotten very much sleep. The knights and foot soldiers who were to accompany him were still weary from days of fighting. They deserved a rest. He deserved a rest. Simon had little patience with the recalcitrant young woman he'd had to have fetched from Jacques's chamber.

"Your clothes are packed. Your serving woman is on the cart. Everything you need is here." He pointed at Diane. "You *are* getting up behind me on this horse and going to Paris. Today." He looked at the sky. It was just past dawn, clear and warm for the season. "It will be a pleasant journey."

Diane was not going to get up behind him. There was a sort of narrow seat with a footrest attached to Simon's saddle. It looked uncomfortable, dangerous and degrading. She pointed at it and shook her head.

"So you don't want to ride pillion, is that it?"

That wasn't it at all.

Before she could indicate any differently, Simon spoke to one of the waiting grooms. "Saddle a palfrey for my storyteller." He looked past her to Jacques. "It seems the woman can ride as well as write in her own tongue."

"She's clever," Jacques answered. "But she might make surly company if she doesn't want to attend you."

"Nonsense."

Diane pointed at her sore leg.

When she would have lifted her skirt to show off the bruises, Simon warned, "Don't." He cast a concerned glance at Jacques. "Can she ride with that leg?"

"She won't enjoy it, but she can ride." Diane turned a venomous look on the wizard as he asked, "Isn't it safer for her to stay here?"

Simon gave a cold bark of laughter. "I'm not leaving her alone again. Even the men she's nursed still call her foreigner and make the sign to ward off evil when her back's turned. Ah, you didn't know that, did you?" Simon asked when he saw Diane's indignant expression. "You'll be safe with me," he assured her. "You know that."

The deep rumble of his voice was seductively comforting. She hated the weakness of her reaction. She had to fight the longing to let him take care of her. Since it was the kind of relationship he automatically expected with a woman, Simon made it easy for her to slip into the role of dependent.

He was also right that she wasn't necessarily safe away from him. His people might be used to her by now, but many of them still didn't trust or like her.

"Are you coming?" he asked as a small, gray horse was led up to the castle steps.

Well, at least this time he didn't make it an order. Diane sighed, and arranged the plentiful material of her dress so that she could ride astride. She supposed that if Mel Gibson could ride in a skirt, so could she.

Diane found the saddle strange, but more comfortable than the Western style she was used to. She was delighted to finally find something more comfortable than she was used to at home. Her leg did hurt, but she tried to ignore it. She tried to ignore the man who rode beside her. It wasn't hard, at least for a while. She had a lot to occupy her thoughts for the first few hours of the trip.

She found it interesting that Simon hadn't just jumped on his horse and ridden off to Paris. When she thought about the primitive conditions of this place, it made sense. It was something of a shock to come to the realization that this *really* wasn't a place where you could get on a commuter plane and arrive somewhere thousands of miles away in a few hours. It sank in that you couldn't drive along the interstate and stop for a meal or at a motel anytime you wanted, either. Simon de Argent, Baron of Marbeau would not understand the concept of carry-on luggage.

Here, you took your food with you, and servants to prepare it, and soldiers to protect you, and tents and bedding. You had to bring fodder for the animals and fuel for the campfires, grooms for the horses, and people to forage for what you couldn't pack along with you. Simon had said something about hunting along the way. Which explained why there were sleek white hounds trotting along with the party, and a rider that carried a hooded falcon on one arm. The cavalcade was all very complicated, and rather grand. That was how rich folk traveled, or so it appeared from Simon of Marbeau's baggage train. She didn't want to think about how poor folk got around. On foot and hungry, if they traveled at all, she supposed.

The rich folk didn't travel very fast even though they didn't have to walk. She supposed the pace might get boring if they had very far to go, but with a sore leg and lots of new things to look at, she didn't mind for now. Diane's interested attention was taken up by the rolling countryside as the carts and riders slowly made their way further from Marbeau.

The world smelled better out in the open air, fresh and clean. She was used to blue-green forests and deep water. And wondrous mountains. At home she could look one way and see the Olympic Range, and looking the other way, she could see the snow-covered Cascades. She considered her home in the Pacific Northwest to be the most beautiful place on earth, give or take a lot of rain and that little problem with slugs in her bathroom.

This countryside was nice, the forest was pristine enough, but it didn't compare to home. The rutted track beneath the horse's dainty feet was not yellow brick, but Diane knew exactly how Dorothy felt about Oz.

Still, it was nice to play tourist for a while.

She hadn't been outside the castle walls since the night Simon had thrown her out then brought her back, bloody and scared out of her mind. She gave him a bitter look when she recalled the incident. He cocked an eyebrow in response, as if he knew exactly what she was thinking.

"You haven't seen my lands in daylight, have you?"

She sarcastically raised an eyebrow at him.

"Should I apologize for that unfortunate incident all over again? Didn't I apologize for it?" he asked when she glowered meaningfully at him. He waved one elegant, gloved hand. "Let's just put it behind us. We have a lot to discuss. Rather, there are some things you need to know."

When she thought about it, Diane couldn't recall anything she really *knew* about this place and its people. There were things she'd heard, things she'd surmised, but she didn't know fact from speculation. Simon had gotten her undivided attention, even though she'd been determined not to give it to him from Marbeau to Paris and back.

Now that Simon had actually offered to *tell* something, she couldn't help but give him 100 percent of her attention.

Simon liked the look of alert concentration on Diane's face. Though her eyes had a strange, intriguing almond shape, they were large and dominated her high-cheekboned face. His attention was often drawn to her eyes, because of the lively intelligence he found in her gaze, not just because they were a beautiful feature.

"Come, ride a little ahead with me," he told her. He touched spurs to his stallion. Diane had no trouble keeping up with him. He was pleased to discover that she was a good rider. He slowed the pace and drew up beside her once more when they were out of hearing distance of the rest of the party.

Simon automatically kept part of his mind on controlling his mount while he looked into her eyes, and spoke.

"I'm taking you to the court of a king, and that's a dangerous place to be. For anyone, not just a woman from a strange land and time." He chuckled at the sharp look she gave him. "Yes, I knew you were from the future. I assumed Jacques told you where you were. I forget that the old man often forgets to tell people things. He uses his age as an excuse, but he's just arrogant. And manipulative, but then we both know that."

Diane gave a firm nod.

"Always remember that he means well. If I didn't keep reminding myself of that, I would have throttled him years ago. But I was speaking of Paris," he went on. He sighed. "Where do I start? With the politics, I suppose. There are two great powers tugging at the loyalty and lands of the nobles who serve them as liege men. I have estates in France, Anjou, and Poitou, so I owe service to each of the rulers of these lands. Since most of my lands are in Poitou, my strongest loyalty *should* go to the Countess Eleanor, but it does not." He gave a hard, cold laugh. "I hate the woman's entrails, and curse her for the faithless bitch she is. Now," he continued calmly, "the countess is married to Henry, Count of Anjou—who is also the Duke of Normandy and the King of England."

He gave her time to absorb that this Henry was someone very powerful, with a lot of different lands and titles, but still the same person. Diane wished she knew something about history.

"I've sworn a great oath of loyalty to Henry. His wife and oldest sons are currently in revolt against him. In this family quarrel, many Poitevan nobles have joined with the rebels—more out of self-interest than sense. I have not sided with my liege lady, but with her husband. Henry is going to win." He sighed. "I would just as soon give up war altogether. But instead of tending to our own affairs, we barons have had to choose one camp over another, or be fallen on by all and sundry. Even though Henry will triumph, the fighting is hard on those who follow either faction. Many a fortress has already changed hands, more than once. Many more will fall come spring. Are you comprehending this, so far?"

Diane knew he was trying to keep his explanation as simple as he could for her. Even with the simplification, it was all very strange. It began to dawn on her that politics was very personal here. It wasn't so much nation against nation as family against family. It was rather daunting to be listening to someone who was intimately involved in the power plays and crises of the time. There didn't seem to be any end to the crises either. Just like home, but without the media coverage.

She almost laughed at a mental image of a CNN correspondent standing outside the castle gates and reporting on the recent siege.

"Diane?"

She shook her head, to clear it.

"You don't understand?"

Diane waved a hand to try to tell him that her reaction hadn't been to his question.

"You do understand?"

More or less, she supposed. She nodded.

"Good."

He was quiet for a while after that one decisive word. It was a grim, tight-jawed silence. They rode along, just barely able to be side by side on the narrow path. They were so close that sometimes their legs brushed against each other. Diane could tell that he did not look forward to any further explanations.

It had been fairly pleasant earlier in the day, but the wind was getting stronger and colder as morning moved into afternoon. They left the forest behind. Away from the trees, the road wound through dead winter fields.

After they splashed through a shallow stream that crossed the road, Simon turned to her again. "You've no doubt heard mention of Denis? And Vivienne?" She nodded. "Denis is my son."

She knew that as well. She nodded again.

"Denis and I have had a falling out over this rebellion. He sides with young Henry. That is to say, Denis serves King Henry's eldest son, who bears his father's name. Denis joined with the rebel faction for many reasons. So my son is now my enemy. He's seventeen, wild and full of himself, convinced he should have his inheritance before I'm ready to be laid in my tomb." After a short silence, he added. "Also, Denis and I have not been friendly since his mother died. So Vivienne convinced him to join in the rebellion. Vivienne is—not a particularly chaste or loyal young woman. She is a sorceress."

Diane sensed that there was a great deal Simon wanted to say about this Vivienne, and that none of it was pleasant. She tucked away the knowledge that Denis had a magician working for him while she tried to fathom the fact that Simon was at war with his seventeen-year-old son. That he was old enough to have a seventeen-year-old son was almost harder to comprehend. Simon looked to be in his early thirties, a little weathered, but youthful and strong. She had to suppose that people matured faster here than at home, and married earlier.

At home, a seventeen-year-old kid who gave his parents that kind of trouble might end up in therapy, or in a group home, or would run away. Here they also ran away, then joined the army, and brought it back to attack dad's castle.

Diane might have laughed, but there was nothing funny in this situation. So she looked questioningly at Simon.

"The King of France is no friend of the elder Henry. So he harbors the rebels and supports them. He is trying to influence those of us sworn to King Henry to join the rebels. The French king has been trying to bribe his vassals to fight against Henry. Hence the invitation to his winter court." Simon smirked. "He has made me an offer I can hardly refuse."

Diane gave Simon a sharp look. At the same time an intense emotion ripped through her that she refused to identify as jealousy. She had no reason to be jealous of Simon of Marbeau. None at all. Not a bit. Certainly not. Who the Baron of Marbeau married for diplomatic reasons even though he claimed to be loyal to this Henry person was nobody's business but the Baron of Marbeau's.

And he didn't know he was paraphrasing *The Godfather*—but now she was stuck with an image of the King of France looking like Marlon Brando with cotton stuffed in his cheeks. Not that she'd be seeing the king, or anything like that. She didn't suppose. Just because Simon had said he was taking her to court didn't mean she'd actually have anything to do with the movers and shakers of the time. Simon would probably leave his household at a hotel or something and go off to this king's palace for meetings, and receptions, and whatever, on his own. It wasn't likely that he was going to take her anywhere as his date, all things considered.

She did wonder if she'd get invited to the wedding. Wondered, and decided she didn't want to think about it. It was very frustrating not to be able to ask any questions. She had the feeling that Simon had really told her very little. He'd only disclosed some of the whats, but none of the whys of what was going on. She'd gone from being totally ignorant to having a vague notion of the shape of things. She was afraid that knowing a little bit could be more dangerous than being totally in the dark.

Simon leaned across his horse's neck and put his hand over hers. Though he wore heavy leather gloves, the warmth of his touch penetrated her numb senses. "Trust me, Diane." She turned her head to gaze into the intense expression in his amber-gold eyes. "No matter what you hear or see," he said. "Trust me."

Simon had no idea why it was so important to have her acknowledge this plea. Or why he had even asked this of her. What Diane thought of him should not matter. Perhaps it was because she was the one person who was completely innocent in all these machinations that made her goodwill seem important. Perhaps it was for reasons best not considered too closely. All he could do was hold his breath and wait while she silently considered his words.

He didn't know whether to be annoyed at her lapse of faith, or pleased that she took her time to think his words through. He did let his breath out in a gusty sigh of relief when she finally gave one faint nod of acquiescence.

He nodded back. "Good. I'm going to ride ahead," he told her. "To look for a campsite."

One of his steward's men had left the castle long before dawn to seek out a place to spend the night, but Diane would not know that he lied. He truly only wanted to be alone with his thoughts, but didn't know how to tell her so. He shouldn't have to tell her. He shouldn't feel the need to explain himself to anyone. He never had before. These days he made excuses and asked for promises from a young woman completely ignorant of all that was important and trivial in his world. A woman who had no importance, except to him. She was becoming too important to him.

Diane might be uninformed, but she wasn't stupid. Dumb but not blind. She learned quickly, and could comment correctly on a situation with the slightest change of expression or tilt of her head. Her mind worked very well indeed, and he found that what she thought of him was important. She was not like any woman he had ever known. He reacted to her as he had never done with any woman before. He wanted her. Her beautiful, delicate golden body fascinated him. Her unspoken thoughts intrigued him. Her company delighted him. She had seduced him without even trying.

Distracted him.

Made him feel alive again. More alive, in truth, than he had ever felt before.

Which made her the most dangerous woman in the world. More dangerous than Vivienne. More dangerous than the situation with his daughter, Felice. More dangerous than the offer of peace through marriage held out by the king.

She made him weak, vulnerable, almost hopeful that there could be more to his life than what duty and honor demanded. It was safer for Diane to have her by his side, but more dangerous for him. He had to keep his wits about him. He had to be careful.

He had to stop anticipating being alone in his tent with Diane tonight, and all the other nights of the journey. Although he had fantasized about an interlude with her away from the world when he insisted she accompany him, it could not be. It was only a fantasy. They would not become lovers on the road to Paris. He would keep to himself. He would keep in control. It would be for the best to wait to make her his mistress.

He would wait until her leg was healed, and he was no longer in immediate danger of losing his life. Perhaps not even then.

19

She'd been wrong about everything. Everything.

Her first misinterpretation of the situation had been a blow to her vanity. Maybe her pride. She had secretly thought that Simon wanted her to come with him because he wanted to seduce her. They'd spent five days on the road, and he hadn't made a single move. She felt like an idiot. She told herself that no other emotions could possibly be involved, that she wasn't hurt and feeling rejected. She should even be ashamed of herself. It would seem that Simon wasn't the sort of man who fooled around when he was engaged to someone else.

Good for him.

Her second error was in thinking that she would never see the palace, or the king, or the court. It turned out that noble visitors to Paris stayed at the palace. Actually, it looked more like a cross between a fortress, a monastery, and a flophouse than a king's residence, and Paris didn't look anything like she remembered from a trip there with her parents when she was fourteen.

She knew that she was on the Ile de la Cité because they'd crossed a bridge to an island in the middle of a river, not from any familiar landmark. They had passed a building under construction that might be on the site of

Notre Dame, but that was speculation on her part. She wanted something to look familiar just to make this world seem more real. Maybe it was better that it didn't. She was so confused by everything, from Simon's ignoring her through most of the trip to ending in the palace that she didn't know what she wanted.

She neither understood, nor liked, the communal way people lived in this time. When they had arrived at their lodgings in one of the palace's halls, the servants had claimed a section of floor space for the visitors from Marbeau. They then unpacked everything including screens for some small amount of privacy, bedding, clothes trunks, and cooking utensils, and settled down as if they were at home. The room was low-ceilinged, drafty, full of smoke from the open hearths, and dark. Diane found it creepy. The discomforts of Marbeau were luxurious by comparison.

Diane had been stared at by strangers from the moment they arrived, even though she kept her head down and her veil in front of her face as much as possible. She attracted unwanted attention, even in the gloom of the hall. It didn't help that Simon disappeared soon after their arrival. While strangers stared, pointed, and murmured, she stayed within the bounds of the household encampment. She got in the way, and was bored, since no one would let her help, but she felt safe enough.

That is, until Simon returned and said, "The king wishes to meet you. It seems news of your presence runs through the town like wildfire."

He glowered at her as though it were her fault. She noticed that he was wearing a long, belted, sapphire-blue tunic embroidered in silver thread. His gold mane was combed to a glistening shine and Yves had done an extra close job of shaving him. He never looked this elegant at Marbeau. Diane was rather stunned by the effect that this handsome man had on her.

"What are you smiling at?"

When she shrugged, his frowned deepened.

He took her firmly by the wrist and led her out of the building. They went across busy courtyards and along dark passages and through frostbitten gardens where people stopped strolling to gape at her, until they reached an ancient tower that dominated the riverside. Once guards at the wide doors let them into the tower, Simon took her up several flights of stairs and into a big room which had a fireplace and a window. She welcomed the light and warmth until she saw how crowded the place was, and realized that the man seated on a carved chair beneath a canopy of embroidered, blue velvet had to be the king.

He didn't look a thing like Don Corleone.

He did look old, and tired. He gazed at her from across the room with sharp curiosity. He beckoned them with an impatient gesture.

Simon stepped forward. She refused to move. He stopped with a jerk, and looked back at her. Annoyance blazed out of his amber eyes.

He said, "Be good," as he tightened his grip on her and tugged her forward.

It wasn't as though Simon hadn't expected this moment from the instant he'd decided to bring Diane with him. It was just that he had hoped it wouldn't happen so soon. Perhaps this was for the best, he supposed. Better to show the girl off and let her be a novelty for a few days, than to try to hide her and let rumors of her extraordinary appearance grow out of proportion.

Courtiers closed ranks behind him and Diane as they approached King Louis. They crowded close, these finely dressed men and women. Simon did not try to pick out individuals in the gaudily dressed aggregate, though he knew many of the nobles gathered here. He already knew the ones he sought were not in the audience chamber, so he ignored those who were. He could feel their emotions at his back: bored, jaded, malicious, eager for distraction. A murmur ran through the crowd like the buzz of angry flies.

Before them, on either side of the throne, were the king's clergy. These priests and monks in their rough homespun habits of black and brown and gray, with their tonsured heads and pious expressions, were the other side of the coin from the gaudy crowd behind them. Simon wondered which group represented dark, and which light, in the microcosm of the king's court. He trusted none of them.

"Don't be frightened," he whispered to Diane.

He wanted to tell her that he'd protect her, with his life if necessary, but this was hardly the place for such declarations. The sidelong look she gave him in answer told him that she had no idea what she should be frightened of.

Diane refused to let herself be impressed by the king. He was an old man, dressed in dull black, his hairy ears sticking out from beneath a round, woolen cap. She told herself that this man might rule a country, but it wasn't as if he'd had his picture on the cover of *Premiere* magazine or anything. This helped keep her from being scared spitless as she and Simon approached the throne.

She did remember to bob a respectful curtsy once she stood before the king, though.

"It seems the barbarian has learned some of our ways." It wasn't the king who spoke, but a tall, white-haired priest who stood next to the throne. He looked Diane over critically. "Do your people not usually grovel before their rulers and knock their heads against the floor to show homage?"

That'd really go over well at a business meeting, wouldn't it? she thought sarcastically. *My people shake hands.* Of course, her maternal ancestors, ancestors she'd been taught to respect, had showed deference to royalty that way.

"Do you not revere the king, who is God's representative?"

"Answer Father Raymond's question, girl," the king ordered. He looked suspiciously at Simon. "Did you bring a vainglorious infidel into my presence?"

Diane saw that they were trying to use her to get Simon into trouble. She didn't know why. Hadn't the king invited Simon here to make an alliance? Court politics, she supposed. Jockeying for position and points, playing power games. Maybe just sheer bloody-mindedness. Whatever was going on, she'd better do what she could to stop it. It was only a matter of swallowing a little pride. An obeisance wasn't too high a price to pay to help a man who'd saved her life more than once.

So, Diane gave Simon a swift, reassuring look, and dropped humbly to her knees. She tried to remember what she knew of the ancient custom. Let's see, was it nine knocks or twelve for the emperor? She settled for touching her forehead to the floor five times, because this old man certainly didn't deserve the same amount of respect as the Son of Heaven, whoever he might be at this point in time.

Simon watched in amazement as Diane humbled herself before the king. The court watched her actions in silence. Simon kept his gaze on her, but he could feel the scavenger eyes of all the others on him, felt the tension stretched taut through the room. A tender warmth spread through him as he realized her actions were for his benefit. She was a woman of great pride, but had the wisdom to disregard it when the situation warranted. He wished he had that same wisdom. For her sake, he would have to try.

He held out his hand to her when she was finished, and helped her rise gracefully to her feet. He wanted to bring her fingers to his lips, but knew the gesture would be dangerous for both of them in this place where any genuine show of emotion was a weakness. So, he calmly reached up and pulled off her veil, baring her blue-black hair and extraordinary features to the world. Diane gave him an annoyed look, then shook out her loosened hair. It settled in a shining black cloud around her shoulders.

The king squinted up at her while she stood passively before him. "This is not a Saracen face," he said. "I grew well acquainted with the looks of those infidels on crusade."

"She is from far Cathay, your grace," Father Raymond answered. "The land beyond the Silk Road where I traveled in my youth. Is that not so, girl?"

I'm from Seattle, Diane thought. Not that she could explain that, even if she'd had a voice to do it with. So she nodded.

Then she glanced at Simon, and almost laughed at the look of astonishment that crossed his face—crossed his face, and was quickly hidden by the cold, indifferent mask that she knew well from her first days at Marbeau.

"How did a female from such a strange land come to be in your household, Lord Simon?" Father Raymond asked suspiciously. "And for how long have you harbored this infidel among Christians?"

As if Father Andre hadn't already written Father Raymond to tell him all about her, Simon thought. He knew full well who spied for whom in his household.

"As you can see, I've brought her with me to exhibit before the king. Nor is she an infidel, your grace," he said to the pious king. "You need not fear for her soul, or that she taints the souls of those she dwells among." He gave a dismissive chuckle as he ignored Diane's hurt look. "Do you suspect me of negotiating with some far away kingdom because a lone foreigner resides in my hall?" He sneered at Diane. "A woman at that."

"But how came she to be with you?" Raymond demanded.

"Why does she not speak?" the king asked. "She obviously understands what we say. No one has heard her speak since your arrival. Is her silence a sign of insolence? Or of humility? I trust not the shrouded dagger subtlety of foreign ways."

"She can speak, your grace, but not just any words she might wish to utter," Simon explained. "Hers is the gift of storytelling, but no more. She talks only to entertain. She is a far-traveled troubadour under the influence of a *geis*, brought into my household by Jacques of—"

He was interrupted by a woman's laughter. Laughter that was as sharp-edged and dangerous as shattering glass. It was a sound Simon might have expected to hear again as he lay dying, but not before. Certainly not here. He was tempted to thrust Diane behind him for safety as he turned to face this enemy.

"Jacques," the woman said as she stepped out of the crowd. "That name explains all."

Diane had a feeling she knew who this woman was before the king said, "Know you of this, Lady Vivienne?"

"I know that my grandfather is a meddling old fool," the woman answered.

Grandfather? Diane took a close look at the woman as Vivienne stepped into a patch of watery sunlight let in by the window. Diane was immediately reminded more of the wicked witch in Disney's *Sleeping Beauty* than of the gentle old man who'd brought her to Marbeau. Vivienne was supermodel-thin and tall, with looks to match. Like the king's priests, she was dressed in layers of somber black and gray. On her, the colors looked elegantly stylish rather than unfashionably devout. Like she was the only person in Paris who actually dressed like she was in Paris.

Diane thought that Vivienne would be easy to hate. And suspected that every other woman in the room thought so as well.

Father Raymond certainly didn't look like he was

happy to have to share the stage with her. "Jacques may be old," the priest said, "but he is well-known to be an obedient child of the church. Tell us more of this woman, Lord Simon."

Simon made a curt gesture. "The woman's a mountebank, trained to tell stories and nothing more."

"But what of this *geis*? What quest must she pursue to break it? Will it bring harm to my lands or people?" the king asked.

"The *geis* will not be broken." Simon gave a mocking smirk. "Why should it be? It is more useful to keep her under the enchantment. It keeps her quiet when she's not wanted."

"So she is nothing more than an entertainer summoned by Jacques for your pleasure?" Father Raymond persisted. "Nothing more?"

"How like grandfather to give you a new toy when you've nothing else left to play with."

He ignored her mocking words, but felt Vivienne's gaze on him. It was like dagger points between his shoulder blades, but as hot and hating as ever. She would try to destroy Diane if he showed any trace of caring for the other woman.

"The foreigner is of no importance," he answered Raymond.

The king looked Diane over speculatively. "She's an ill-favored creature, flat-faced and yellow-skinned, but still a woman. Have you committed the sin of fornication with her, Lord Simon?"

It seemed to Simon that the king was far too worried about the state of other men's souls and the activity in their bedchambers. And blind, as well, to have called Diane ill-favored. The presumption of the king's question and insulting appraisal of a beautiful woman grated on him, but Simon was able to answer with the ease of truth.

"No, your grace. That is not the woman's function in

my household. I'll swear on all the holy relics of Notre Dame that I have not tupped her."

"Then you won't mind if someone else turns up her skirts?" a man called from the crowd.

The king glared down the ripple of laughter that spread through the court. Simon carefully kept his hand away from his weapon, but didn't bother to look around. He noticed Diane flinch. She looked devastated, but he could offer her none of the sympathy he felt. He didn't even have the luxury of taking the time to castigate himself for the horrible mistake he'd made in bringing her to Paris.

In the simmering quiet that followed the laughter, the king settled back in his chair and gave Diane an annoyed look as he spoke to Simon. "If you've brought her here as an entertainer, have her entertain. We'll have a story from her."

Diane stood very still. She couldn't look at Simon though he was all she was really aware of. She was too furious and hurt to turn to him. She didn't want to see the cold mask that might not be a mask at all. His words rolled over and over in her mind: mountebank, foreigner of no importance, trained, it keeps her quiet when she's not wanted. Not wanted. She was not going to cry. She could manage to be inscrutable enough not to cry just this once. She knew she wouldn't entertain Simon de Argent with her vulnerability this time.

She also knew that what he did in the next few moments determined whether she got out of this room alive or not. Maybe it determined if they both did. Her impulse was to turn and walk out. She was about three seconds away from obeying that impulse even though the room was full of people, hurtful hideous people, all of them armed with at least a dagger. The guards at the door wore swords. She didn't care.

This had happened so often that the ugly crowds almost didn't exist for her anymore. They were faceless extras on this horror-movie set. The only person who mattered was Simon. Only his reactions counted. She'd swallowed her pride once for him today. She wasn't prepared to do it again. She was prepared to attempt to walk out on the King of France if—

Simon's hand touched her arm. The pressure was gentle, reassuring. His voice in her ear was soft, devoid of any inflection. "Speak if you will. Tell one of your tales only if it is what you want to do."

For all her stubborn determination, she couldn't keep her gaze from flying to his. He calmly looked back at her, and for only a second, before he stepped away. The choice was clearly hers. Simon de Argent acknowledged that her will was her own, even if no one else in this world did.

There was only one thing she could do.

She told King Louis and his court all about *The Godfather, Parts I* and *II*.

20

Which didn't mean she wasn't still furious at Simon once she was dismissed from the king's presence. She walked through the parted crowd with all the dignity she could muster, then fled in tears down the tower stairs. It took her a long time to find her way back to the hall where they were staying. The cold of the short winter afternoon had seeped into her bones by the time she found her way indoors, but at least she'd stopped crying.

She was grateful to be among people she knew, and settled down to supper among Simon's household. The food was hot, and she had a seat near the fire, but she couldn't stop shivering. Nothing warmed her. Nor could she stop glancing toward the door. Time passed, food was cleared away, the fire was covered, people settled down to sleep, but Simon still hadn't returned.

She found her own pallet and settled down. Not to sleep. She turned her back to the doorway, but her senses were alert to any movement in the room. Even under a heavy blanket and a fur covering, she had trouble getting warm. She was cold on the inside, cold with fury, cold with fear. The fury was for Simon. So was the fear.

She hoped that he was watching his back, wherever he

was in this treacherous place, whatever he was doing. She wanted him safe, so she could have a turn at him herself.

Every thought she had was about him, every emotion centered on him. She didn't know what she thought. She refused to examine what she felt. She wanted to hit him. She wanted to hold him. She wanted to help him, and hurt him as well. She wanted to be with him and she wanted to run. She wanted him.

That was the most dangerous thing of all. This was not her time, not her place. She should look for a way to escape, some way home. She should forget the man, forget his problems, think about herself. She should get the hell out of here.

But she wanted him.

He needed her.

She didn't know which was worse.

At least he made her feel like he needed her. It wasn't true. It couldn't be. She was nothing. A mountebank. A foreigner he'd brought to Paris to entertain the king's court.

Bastard, she thought as she felt sleep finally overwhelming her. *Arrogant, lying, using ba—*

"Lord Simon?"

Simon recognized the priest on the ill-lit stairs as being one of Raymond of Chartres' subordinates. He gave the man a polite nod. "Father Paquin."

All Simon wanted was to find Diane. He'd spent hours attending court, chaffing inwardly to be gone while he talked, and feasted, and avoided seduction, and showed no discernible emotion all the while. Now that King Louis had retired for the night, he was finally free to go and he was in a hurry.

When Simon would have stepped around the priest, the man put his hand on his arm. "A few private words, my lord?"

Paquin was from Father Raymond. Raymond was not a friend of his, perhaps, but Raymond was certainly an enemy of Vivienne's. Simon gave a cold smile. "Of course."

Paquin nodded, and started down the stairs ahead of Simon. Simon waited until the man was nearly out of sight, then followed him all the way to a chapel on the riverbank. They did not enter together. The little church was dark but for candles before the altar. Simon kept his hand on his sword, just in case someone was waiting in the shadows. After Paquin had prayed before the altar for a while, Simon stepped forward and knelt by him, as though to make confession.

"Well?" he asked as he looked up into the man's face.

"Do you know why Lady Vivienne is at court?"

Simon hated to admit to ignorance, but he answered honestly. "I haven't the faintest idea."

"To negotiate your son's marriage to Marguerite deHauly."

Simon scratched his jaw. "How odd, I thought I was in Paris to negotiate *my* marriage to the deHauly heiress."

"And Lady Vivienne is trying to undermine that. She is doing her best to convince the girl's father that Denis de Argent is a better choice than his father. The witch can be very persuasive," the priest added with a sneer.

Simon knew that very well. He nodded, and got to his feet. "I thank you for this information, Father."

"I am happy to be of help, Lord Simon."

"Good," Simon said, and blocked the priest's way when the other man would have moved past him. Simon put a hand on Paquin's arm to stop him.

Father Paquin gave him an anxious look. "Yes?"

"I have a question." The man blinked nervously as Simon asked, "Are Gilbert Fitz-William and his—wife—" Simon very nearly choked on the words. His grip tightened on the priest's arm. "Are they in Paris?"

Paquin hesitated before he said, "Is murder on your mind in this house of God?"

Simon tilted his head sardonically to one side. "Possibly."

"Father Raymond said that that was what would interest you. That you didn't come to negotiate a marriage, but an assassination." Paquin shook his head sadly. "Is Gilbert's death what you truly seek? More than a marriage that will bring you peace and power?"

"I seek justice," Simon answered. "Is he in Paris? Is Felice with him?" The priest nodded reluctantly. "Where can I find them?"

This time, Father Paquin shook his head. Simon decided to let it go for now. He had the one answer he wanted. And a man who had influence with the king knew in what way he could be bought. Simon would let it go at that for now, though the thought of his daughter's having to spend even one more night in a forced marriage bed was hard to bear.

Even if she'd woken up screaming, no one could have heard her, Diane thought bitterly as she came out of the awful dream. Her breath frosted the air as she threw off the covers and sat up, but she was covered in sweat. It was sweat from fear that froze in the hall's frigid air. She was still half caught in the dream as she picked her way between the sleeping forms huddled on the floor. She moved through the darkness to the door, went past a guard who didn't seem to notice her, and moved, wraith-like, into the moon-frosted courtyard.

Nothing was familiar. She was nervously aware that this was not Marbeau, but a place where she was even more of an outcast stranger. Dangerous or not, she couldn't stop the urge to be outdoors. The shadows were dark black and threatening. The silver light was faint, alien. The stars overhead burned cold and far away. Diane turned slowly, around and around, searching for the threat she sensed watching her, just out of sight, the silent voice that called her. She spun, her cloak spreading out around her like dark wings, until she became dizzy. Until the dream images couldn't be fought off any longer and she fell. Not to the ground, but into her own memories.

She was back in the solar, alone with the man who'd dragged her in by her hair. Alone with the man who told her in vivid, disgusting detail how he planned to tame her, to keep her for himself, that she was his to do with as he pleased. He'd hit her while he gloated. He'd kissed her and fondled her. He'd forced her to touch him, told her how he wanted her to please him, what he was going to do with her. He kept hitting her, using a belt across her back to reinforce just who was in control of this situation. Of her.

The man in the dream was Simon de Argent.

What brought her out of the dream was that someone nearby was crying. The quiet sobbing was not her own, not a part of her nightmare. Someone else was in trouble. Diane responded to the need in the sound. The reality of someone else's pain was enough to help clear her head.

She found that she had fallen to her knees on the hard-packed frozen mud of the courtyard. Not Simon, she told herself as she got shakily to her feet. Not Simon, she wanted to scream to the presence she still felt lurking in the shadows. She had the odd sensation that something was trying to twist her memories. She fought that sensation, but it wasn't easy. She *knew* it was Simon who had saved her from Thierry, not the other way around. Still, she *felt* betrayed, and defiled, and helplessly angry at the Lord of Marbeau no matter what had really occurred that night.

She tried to hold onto the facts as she went looking for the person who was crying. But the dream had been so

vivid it was hard to keep the truth and the illusion sepa-
rated. What she found only a few feet away, hunched
among the gnarled roots of an ancient tree, was a skinny
girl. Even from a few feet away, and with only the moon
for lighting, Diane could tell that the marks on the girl's
pale face were not shadows. The bruise on the girl's cheek
looked new, but she'd had the black eye for a few days.

Anger on behalf of the abused girl drove out all of
Diane's confusion and self-pity. She couldn't ask the girl
any questions, or offer any words of comfort, but Diane
did drop to her knees and put a comforting hand on the
young stranger's shoulder.

She'd approached silently, and the girl was lost enough
in her own pain not to have noticed. The girl nearly
jumped out of her skin at Diane's touch. A frightened
gaze locked with Diane's. Even in the faint light, Diane
could make out that the stranger's eyes were amber. Her
loosely braided hair shone like spun gold even in the sil-
very moonlight.

Holy shit! Diane thought. *You're Felice!*

Simon hadn't told her about Felice, but Jacques had.
He'd told her that Felice was Simon's daughter, and that
she had been married over Simon's objections to a knight
that the king—Jacques hadn't said which king—approved
of. She suspected that Jacques hadn't told her anywhere
near enough.

Which was typical.

After a few moments, the girl blinked away her tears,
then ran the back of her hand across her cheek. "You're
the storyteller," she said. "My father's foreigner."

Diane frowned, but nodded.

Felice took a deep breath and sat up straight. Diane
had the feeling the young woman was going to pretend
she hadn't been hiding under a tree crying like a baby a
few seconds before. De Argent pride, no doubt. She
couldn't help but smile.

"I've heard about you," Felice said. "Vivienne says you're his mistress."

Diane got to her feet. She held out her hand and helped Felice up. She also shook her head vehemently as Felice watched her. They walked slowly into the center of the courtyard together.

Felice paused, then turned to face Diane. "Alys says you are my father's lover as well." Diane tried shaking her head again, but the girl ignored her as she went on. "That's why Alys came to Gilbert." Felice folded her arms defensively around her waist. "I'm glad she came to Gilbert for protection," she said, "instead of returning to Denis's bed. My brother deserves better than that whore."

Diane had no idea who Gilbert was, or why Felice was telling her these things. Maybe Simon's daughter wanted her father to know this information and couldn't get it to him herself. Well, if she expected Diane to act as a messenger she was out of luck. Diane wondered how she was going to tell Felice that she couldn't talk, so she didn't have much of a future in the courier business.

What Diane did think she needed to do was get Felice back to Simon. Somebody had beaten the girl up. Simon wasn't likely to let them get away with it.

Before Diane could think of any way to communicate with the girl, a noisy group of people entered the courtyard. These newcomers were brightly dressed courtiers, their jewels and fancy clothes illuminated by servants carrying torches. They had a pair of lute-strumming minstrels with them, and other servants with trays of food and wine moved briskly around, like waiters at a reception. It looked like a great party.

"I should go," the girl said as this moveable feast came closer.

She moved back into the shadows, but a woman's voice called out, "Felice! There you are! We've been looking for you."

Diane recognized the voice, and a moment later Vivienne had broken away from the group and was standing in front of her.

Vivienne beckoned to her friends. "Look, we have Simon's little friend too." A clawlike hand grabbed Diane under the chin. Diane's heart froze as Vivienne forced her to look in her eyes. "You're so pretty in the moonlight."

Diane forgot about Felice. She forgot about the party. She didn't know how she ended up back under the tree with Vivienne. "Let's have a few words in private, my pretty."

And your little dog, too, Diane thought, struck by the appropriateness of the witch's choice of words. *And you'll be the one doing the talking.*

Vivienne's smile was vivid. "Such bitterness I sense in you."

Vivienne stroked Diane's cheek. Diane wanted to jerk her head away, but couldn't rouse the strength to move, somehow.

"There's so much you need to know, pretty one. So much Simon and Grandfather haven't told you. You have so much to be bitter over. So much you need to make them pay for. You've been robbed, cheated, misused."

Yeah, Diane thought. *So?* Somehow she didn't think Vivienne was the caring type. *What's in it for you?* Diane wondered.

"Do you know why Denis hates his father?" Vivienne leaned close. Her voice was low and seductive. It spoke not just in Diane's ear, but her mind. "Simon killed Denis's mother. Killed her, and drove Denis from his lands when the boy objected to her wrongful death."

Diane shivered. She wanted to run. She didn't want to listen to this venom, but found that her back was pressed to the rough bark of the old tree. She was trapped. The world beyond where they stood was dark, empty, formless. Vivienne's hypnotic gaze bored into hers, and those eyes were the whole world. The power of the woman was inescapable. Vivienne was as seductive as hell.

"Denis has a right to kill his father. You have good reason to help him. Jacques stole your voice, took you from your own people for the pleasure of his master."

It was true. So true.

"I could give you your voice back, Diane Teal. Would you like that? To talk again?"

More than anything.

"Jacques can't do it. The old fool has lied to you. He hasn't got the power to give you your voice back. I have that power."

Diane believed her.

"You need me. I want to help you."

No, she didn't.

Vivienne's cold laughter echoed through Diane's mind. "Perhaps want is the wrong word. You know deception when you hear it."

Diane wasn't sure she did. Not from Vivienne. Not from Jacques. Not from Simon. Nothing was simple. Nothing was necessarily true. Not even what she felt for Simon. What was it she felt?

"It's true that Simon murdered his wife." Vivienne's harsh voice cut through her thoughts. "It's true that he's using you. True that Simon will toss you aside when he's done with you."

He's going to marry someone else.

"It's true that Jacques doesn't have the power to help you. I do. I'm willing to help you. I will help you."

Not for free. Nothing was for free.

"Nothing is for free. But help me and I will help you. All you have to do is help me."

Betray Simon, Diane thought.

"He deserves it. He's hurt you. He'll destroy you. You can have revenge. And your voice."

She desperately wanted to speak again. Vivienne was

right. He'd hurt her. Hurt her so bad. Taken everything from her. Treated her like dirt. Tried to rape her.

Simon had raped her.

She could see the details clearly, as though watching some grainy pornographic film of something that had happened to someone else.

He deserved whatever it was Vivienne wanted her to do.

Vivienne's fingers gently stroked her cheeks. "Don't cry, my sweet," that dark, seductive voice whispered. "I'll make it all better. You know I will."

21

Simon was on his way to find Diane when the laughter distracted him. Warned him, rather, for his hand went to his sword the instant the sound reached his ears. He saw lights in the distance, heard the faint strumming of lutes beneath the bright sounds of merriment.

Something felt wrong about the noise. No doubt it was nothing more than a group of young courtiers who'd adjourned to a spot far from the king's residence for a bit of revelry. That the spot they'd chosen was next to the hall where his household was lodged, disturbed Simon. He knew more than he wanted to about the revels of courtiers.

He knew that if he were young and randy, and reckless, he might be tempted to seek out the favors of a beautiful storyteller from far Cathay.

He, himself, was tempted, constantly tempted, even though he was no youth. The difference was that he fought hard to control his impulses. He knew the heedless young men of Louis's court would take what they wanted. Once more, he had brought Diane into deadly danger, and for a selfish whim at that. He should have left her sheltered at a nunnery, but had craved her company too much to really see to her safety. She had every right to hate him for exposing her to the court and its vicious games.

She had nearly broken before the king today, nearly let her pride lead her into a fatal mistake. So had he. He had given her a choice. He had let her decide her own fate, and his, before the king. He would have walked out with her if she had turned to go. He must have suffered a moment of madness! For an instant, she had been more important to him than his purpose in coming to Paris. He'd even been thinking of her while he talked to Father Paquin.

He would have to send her away, for both their sakes. She'd be happy to go. He had seen the look on her face when she left the audience chamber. He'd felt her anguish, and her fury.

She'd been through enough. Once he got her out of this predicament, he would find a way to make her truly safe from this world where she didn't belong.

He did not draw his sword, but he did move carefully forward, toward the revelers he saw in the torchlight up ahead.

She'd said something Vivienne didn't like, and now she was in trouble. Not literally spoken. Not out loud. Vivienne hadn't granted her that wish. Vivienne hadn't liked some of the things Diane had thought while the sorceress had been in her head, and had decided to let the Eurotrash loose on Diane. If indeed the odd conversation had taken place. Diane wasn't sure if she'd fantasized the whole thing or not. It had all been very weird and dreamlike.

No. She knew it wasn't a dream. It was just hard to accept the reality of the magic Jacques and Vivienne could wield, no matter how intimately involved she was in it. Even when they screwed around with her head and read her thoughts and messed with her perceptions.

Right now, she didn't have time to think about magic.

She didn't know where Vivienne had gotten to, and had her hands too full with Viv's friends to really care. There were three men, and Alys. And poor Felice as well. Simon's daughter stood inconspicuously behind the man who had his arm around Alys's waist. Felice was not one of Diane's problems, but Alys certainly was.

Alys wore a sneer, and a rather low-cut gown considering the winter weather. Her cloak was pushed back over her shoulders to reveal her décolletage. The men's gazes kept drifting to Alys's breasts. Diane's was on the dagger that Alys kept fingering.

"I want her dead," Alys said.   .

The men laughed. Diane hoped the sound didn't indicate their agreement with the redhaired woman. She was surrounded by the group. They'd slowly backed her against the stone wall of the building. They reminded her of a pack of hunting vampires from a gothic horror movie. Very glamorous, and decadent-looking, and full of glittering menace.

The servants and musicians didn't seem to notice she was in trouble. Her throat was dry, and she had a pounding headache. She almost wished one of the waiters would offer her a drink. She also thought that she was far too calm. Maybe she was so used to being threatened that the experience was getting a little boring.

Well, at least she'd learned that showing fear to these savages might cause them to attack.

"Dead," Alys repeated.

The one holding Alys said, "Don't be foolish."

"I hate her."

"I care not," he responded. "She's a pretty thing."

One of the men said, "Father Raymond told me her people perform hideous sexual perversions."

The men laughed again, and gave each other smirking looks. Diane couldn't help but roll her eyes. This reminded her of a couple of blond jocks she'd known in high school. They thought Asian girls knew more about sex than Anglo girls—like she'd been born knowing how to give head, or something.

"No wonder Lord Simon replaced you with her," one of the other men drawled.

Alys tried to lunge at the man who'd spoken, but her boyfriend kept a firm hold on her.

"Bastards!" she shrieked. "All of you."

"Fine talk from a whore," the boyfriend said. "My whore," he added, and roughly kissed her.

Diane noticed Felice's reaction as the girl stepped back to hide among the servants. It occurred to Diane that the man kissing Alys was the Gilbert that Felice had mentioned earlier. Her husband—who beat her, and fooled around with his mistress in front of her. The poor kid.

Did Simon know about this?

Gilbert let Alys go. One of the other men grabbed her, but she broke away. She pointed at Diane. "Take her!"

Diane looked around. She wondered if she could make a break for the hall door. She wondered if the guards keeping warm inside the building would help her.

"Don't fret, Alys, we'll have her," Gilbert said. "But we'll have a story first. Then, perhaps we'll watch while she teaches you some of her foreign perversions."

"Then we'll have you both," one of the others added.

"Perhaps even Felice could learn something from the heathen," Gilbert said. He patted Alys on the rear. "Then I could have both of you in my bed at once, the way the Saracens do it."

"Or all three of them," someone suggested.

The men roared with laughter, while Alys screamed in outrage. No one but Diane noticed Simon de Argent step out of the shadows.

"Gilbert."

He spoke quietly, but the deadly tone of his deep voice cut across the merriment more effectively than if he'd shouted. The courtyard was silent an instant after he spoke. The men whirled around. Alys moved behind Gilbert. Swords were drawn. The servants backed out of the way and the musicians scattered into the night. Felice lifted her head and took an eager step toward her father.

He halted the girl with a gesture. "Peace, child. We'll be going home soon."

Diane crossed her arms under her breasts. Simon was good at rescues. His timing was impeccable. She was too scared at knowing he was outnumbered to know if she was happy to see him or not. In fact, she wasn't even sure if he was here to rescue her. His attention was centered on Felice. As it should be, Diane told herself. Felice was his daughter, and she definitely looked like she could use rescuing.

Diane's heart twisted at the grim, implacable expression on Simon de Argent's handsome face. Who was there, she wondered, to rescue Simon?

Simon didn't care about the other two swordsmen. He kept his attention on Gilbert. "I'm going to kill you," he told the younger man.

Gilbert laughed at Simon's words. Simon understood Gilbert's attitude. The lad was tall, strong, younger, confident. Confident in the protection of the king as well as in his own abilities. Gilbert sneered as he stepped forward.

"We have no quarrel," Gilbert said, though he made no move to put up his sword. He put a hand over his heart. He sounded sincere as he said, "Call me son and we will be at peace with one another."

"You are no son of mine."

"Son-in-law," Gilbert answered. "The deed's accomplished. Let it be, Simon."

"I told you no when you came sniffing after Felice at Marbeau. She wanted none of you."

Gilbert's gaze flicked to Felice for a moment. "What does it matter what the girl wanted? The king wanted the match. It's a good alliance."

"The king does not decide where my children marry. I do. Felice did not want to marry. I agreed that she could enter a convent."

"That would have been a waste."

"Not to me," Felice spoke up. Her bruises shone dark and ugly in the moonlight. "I wanted to take the veil. It's all I ever wanted, to be a bride of Christ." Her voice was choked with anguish.

"Then that is what you will do," Simon told his daughter. He wanted to take her in his arms as he'd done when she was young. After nearly a year with Gilbert Fitz-William he doubted she was young anymore. This was no time for a fatherly embrace. He tried to reassure her by saying, "As soon as you are a widow you can take the veil."

"She's not going to be a nun," Gilbert said. "She belongs to me, my lord."

"I would have killed you sooner," Simon said to Gilbert, "if you hadn't hid in Paris behind Louis's throne. I might have waited to kill you in a challenge before the court. But —" He glanced briefly at Diane. He was glad he'd found Gilbert among the men tormenting Diane. It would make killing him doubly enjoyable. "This is more convenient," he said, instead of bothering to explain his reasoning to Gilbert and the curs with him. They'd pay as well, if any of them had touched Diane.

"I am under the king's protection," Gilbert pointed out. "We are both under the Peace of God while at court."

Simon shook his head. "You kidnapped my daughter on her journey to join the holy sisters at Fontrevault. It's time you paid for your sins."

"I wed the girl. The king sanctioned the marriage."

"I did not."

"I will be your heir after you've sent Denis to his grave. The king agrees that I should follow you as lord of Marbeau. It's a good match."

There was a note of desperation in Gilbert's voice, as though he'd just realized that Simon was not going to let him get away with abducting Felice. Simon wasn't going to let him get away with anything.

"Everyone thinks so," Simon agreed. "You fled to Paris, and the king denied my petition to return my child. The king sanctioned your marriage. Then he invited me here. Do you know why?"

Simon had spoken calmly, he hadn't raised his voice and his tone was reasonable, but Diane could tell, from her unnoticed spot by the wall, just how furious he was. Furious and determined. His cold resolve frightened her. She was looking into the face of a stone killer. She remembered the visions Vivienne had shown her. She was reminded of Vivienne's promise.

She wondered what she could do.

Simon watched as confusion crossed Gilbert's face. "The king brought you here to marry Marguerite deHauly." His face split in a wide grin. "I will gladly call her mother."

"Though she's no older than your own wife?" Simon questioned.

"Her motherly kiss will be all the warmer then."

Simon almost laughed. "By the saints, lad, I can see the lust for committing incest with my wife burning in you already." He did laugh when Alys moved from behind Gilbert. "Must you crave every woman of my household? Even the sluts and the ones I haven't married yet?"

Gilbert chose to treat his words as a jest, a shared attitude between sophisticated men of the world. He gestured over his shoulder, toward Diane. "Aye, my lord. I was just about to sample that member of your household when you arrived."

Simon wondered at the foolhardiness of the man's words. "Are you drunk? Mad?" he questioned as he gripped his sword tighter in his gloved hand. "Or merely too stupid to cherish life?"

"None of those things, my lord."

"Good. I'd hate to kill a drunken man. There's no sport in it."

"We are under the Peace of God," Gilbert reminded him again.

"Aye," Simon agreed. He decided to inform this pup who prided himself on his worldliness about the treachery and shifting needs of court politics. "Father Raymond of Chartres, the king's favorite priest, has offered me your life if I can take it, in exchange for my aiding the King of France against Henry Plantagenet. That's why I've come to Paris," Simon added. "Do you want me to kill him, Felice?" he asked his daughter as Gilbert moved closer to her.

He hoped the girl hadn't developed any fond feeling for the man, since Simon intended to kill Gilbert for Diane's sake, no matter what his daughter answered.

Felice crossed herself, and looked at her husband, head meekly bent. Gilbert began to smirk triumphantly. Then she said, "Kill him, father. I'll pray for his soul in the convent."

"As you wish, child."

As Simon threw off his cloak to free his movements Gilbert slapped Felice to the ground. This blow sealed the young fool's fate irrevocably.

Simon's movements were as graceful and deadly as a hunting cat's. Gilbert moved more like a snake, weaving and sinuous. Diane watched in fascination as the swordsmen met in the center of the courtyard. Torches and moonlight illuminated the clash of the heavy swords, making them seem to be almost magical weapons as the men engaged. One moment the flashing metal looked on fire, with the next thrust or parry the blades turned to ice. The men kept their gazes fixed on each other as they circled cautiously around the center of the courtyard. Diane watched the swords.

Errol Flynn hadn't fought like this.

There was no exchange of banter, just quickened breathing as swords met over and over. The sound the heavy weapons made as they struck each other defined the term "clash of weapons" for her. They didn't make a polite metallic clatter as they crossed. The noise was deeper than that, more serious, it had gravity and killing purpose.

The one sound she did recognize as absent was the tinkle of chain mail. The men were using big, chopping, slicing and dicing weapons, and neither was protected by any kind of armor. Simon was still in his blue and silver court garb, the torchlight illuminating the rich color and glitter of his finery. Finery that was no protection from Gilbert's sword. The men were exposing vulnerable flesh to sharp steel, and neither seemed to be frightened of the deadly consequences.

Diane was. Terribly frightened. More frightened as she watched this fight than she had been at any other time in the weeks she'd spent in the past. She wanted it to be over, but was afraid of how it would end. She wanted to close her eyes, turn away, run for the guards to put a stop to it. She knew there was no stopping this, and that to look away was impossible. She waited, rigid with tension, her nails digging into her tightly clenched palms.

Eventually, blood began to dim the reflection of fire and moonlight on the blades.

Simon knew his left arm was cut. It was inconvenient, but not serious. He wished he had his shield. He wished he was fighting from horseback. He wished he wasn't so aware that Gilbert's well-armed friends were waiting in the shadows. He didn't let any of his wishes matter as he moved in for one last attack.

Simon had gotten a good slice in across his opponent's upper left thigh, and a quick nick on his forehead. The lad was a fine warrior, faster than most Simon faced. But Gilbert had blood in his eyes, and a weakened leg. He didn't move fast enough when Simon feinted to the side, then brought a quick stab upward underneath Gilbert's raised sword arm and into his chest. Gilbert sank to the ground, dead before he hit it.

Felice gazed down at her dead husband with no expression on her face. Alys hissed furiously from the shadows. Simon could not see Diane from where he stood. He longed to turn to her, but the danger was not yet past.

Simon wanted to drop to his knees when Gilbert fell. He wanted to rest, to forget that he'd just killed a man. Duty wouldn't let him show tiredness now, or regret. Duty was all that kept him going. He had wanted Gilbert dead for good reasons. Now that it was done he didn't want to gloat, he just wanted to gather his child and his woman up and get them away from the scene of the carnage.

He had Gilbert's friends to deal with first. He looked around slowly, raking his gaze across each man. "Next?"

The larger of the pair stepped forward. Simon tensed, prepared to fight again. "I have no quarrel with you, Lord Simon."

"Nor I," the other one told him. "If Father Raymond thought your cause just, I'll not argue with him."

Simon didn't show his relief that these were courtiers who went with the winds of politics, not the loyalties of friendship.

"Wise of you," he said. He waved them away with his sword. "Begone, then."

They didn't hesitate to gather up their servants and head for the courtyard entrance. Simon kept his sword at the ready as he watched them go.

Simon didn't see the woman who rushed toward him. The long dagger in her hand was raised to strike his unprotected back. Diane saw. Her hand flew to her throat.

"Simon, look out!"

22

Take that, Viv, Diane thought triumphantly as she watched Simon snatch the dagger out of Alys's hand. *I can talk without any help from you, thank you very much.*

Diane was very glad she had told the sorceress to go to hell when she'd figured out how much Vivienne was messing with her mind.

"Wait a minute. I'm talking."

Simon pushed Alys away and looked over his shoulder at her. "Why, so you are."

The self-satisfied grin on his face would have been an insufferable smirk on anyone else. It was a smirk. It was just that on him it was—

Lovable.

Diane blinked. "This is a hell of a time to find out I'm in love," she muttered. Then she hurried forward to do something about Simon's bleeding arm.

She snatched up Simon's cloak and threw it around his shoulders as she reached him. "Hi," she said to the staring Felice, "I'm Diane. Let's— "

"Hush, woman." Simon pulled her into an embrace with his good arm, and kissed her.

The fiery touch of his lips drove words right out of her head. She had a great deal to think about, a million things to talk about, but time stopped, the cold winter night heated around her, and the heady glory of kissing Simon de Argent filled her world. She'd never been kissed like this before, and it didn't last long enough.

She wanted to cling to him, press herself against him and let the words spill out. She remembered the dead man on the ground and Felice who stood nearby. "Are you in really deep trouble?" she asked as she watched Simon look carefully around.

He tilted an eyebrow at her. "Possibly."

"Do we need to get out of town?"

"Definitely."

"Then what are we waiting for?"

"For the city gates to open at dawn."

"Oh." She searched the night sky. "How long is it until dawn?"

Diane remembered the guards she'd hoped would show up to stop the fight. Now she hoped they were sound asleep and hadn't heard anything. Why did things have to be so complicated? Why couldn't she just take this man to bed? She wanted to revel in having her voice back, and in being in love with Simon de Argent.

She did have him, didn't she? She wasn't the only one in love, was she? Should she ask? Should she have to? She might have her voice back, but the question froze in her throat. Maybe she didn't want to know. Maybe it would be better to concentrate on the problems of the moment and not dwell on all the ramifications of having taken Jacques's cure for the magic spell.

She watched in silence as Simon took Felice in his arms. "I am so happy to have you safe."

The girl clung to him. "I love you father. You've brought me peace."

Alys was on her knees at Simon's feet. Her face was tear-stained and full of hatred as she looked up at him. "What of me?" she demanded. "What have you brought me?"

Diane stepped angrily between Simon and Alys. "Oh, no, you don't," she told the woman. "Don't you dare blame your mistakes on him." The man took enough responsibility and guilt on his shoulders. Fierce protectiveness for Simon burned in her. She was prepared to fight off anyone who tried to hurt or use him.

"Get out of here before I call the police."

"The what?" Simon asked.

Diane ignored him. She was too intent on chasing off Alys to consider the cultural differences between them. "Attempted murder gets people in serious trouble," she told Alys. "Do you have any skills other than screwing around? Get a day job or something, okay? But get out of Simon's life."

Alys looked terrified of her, as though a toy had come to life before her eyes. The redhaired woman scrambled to her feet, grabbed her skirts in her hands, and ran.

Diane turned back to the watching father and daughter. She carefully did not look at Gilbert's body. "Now what?"

Simon marveled at the change in his enchanted storyteller. He found that he was the one who was now enchanted. By the sound of her voice, her confident attitude. He thought that the diffident, confused woman who needed him, and that he'd come to care for, was gone forever. He was both delighted, and terrified that when she had come to love him he had lost her forever.

Perhaps that would be for the best. For her sake, it would definitely be for the best.

He didn't point that out to her now, however. "Though I would love to stand here listening to you chatter for hours, we'd best go."

"Where?" Diane asked.

"To the convent of Sacré Coeur," Felice answered.

Simon held his daughter out at arms length. He studied her grave face in the pale moonlight for a long time. "Are you sure?" he asked at last. She nodded. He traced a finger along her bruised cheek. He understood her need, but his heart ached just the same. "Must I get you back to lose you so soon?"

"I've never wanted anything else, Father." Her voice was soft, but full of conviction.

He sighed. He'd done all he could for her. She was safe from Gilbert now. She'd be safe from the world at Sacré Coeur. Felice would be happy in the cloistered life, and out of the danger that loomed back at Marbeau. It was time to let her go.

"I'll miss you," he said. "But it is for the best. Wait here a moment."

He left Felice and Diane in the courtyard and went into the building. It took only a moment to pass the dozing guards, wake Yves, give his instructions then slip outside again. The women were speaking in whispers to each other. Whispers that broke off when he approached them. Talking about him, he guessed. He wasn't sure he wanted to know what advice his daughter had passed on to the woman he loved.

The woman he loved and should leave behind, as safe at Sacré Coeur as his daughter.

He gathered them up with a look. "Come along."

"No way."

"You'll like it here."

They were standing in the center of the cloister, on a raked, stone path lined with the dead, brown remains of last season's herb garden. The rocks made uncomfortable bumps under the thin soles of her leather shoes. She could hear the nuns singing their morning hymns in the nearby chapel as dawn bled pink into the pale white sky. Felice was with them. Her smile had been radiant when the abbess accepted her as a postulant. This was after Simon had woken the nuns up and explained his haste in bringing his widowed daughter to the convent.

Diane had managed to get hot water, an herbal salve and strips of fresh linen from the convent's infirmary. She'd tended to his wounds while Simon arranged Felice's generous admission dowry. It turned out he'd been setting up her staying at the convent too. At the same time, he'd been checking in Felice, he'd been making arrangements for her as well.

When Diane figured out what he was up to, they'd come out for a little talk while the good sisters went off for their morning prayers.

Simon loomed over her, his hair mussed, beard stubble beginning to show on his cheeks. His amber eyes were bright with the light of battle. He was trying to be autocratic again. She wasn't having any of it.

"I'm going back to Marbeau today, and you are staying here."

"Uh uh," she answered Simon.

He gestured around them, at the garden and the gracefully arched columns of the cloisters. "It's a comfortable life. A quiet one, full of prayer and contemplation."

"Don't like to pray. Don't like to meditate, either. I'm not even Catholic, I'm Anglican, similar but not the same. I'm not staying." Diane folded her arms and lifted her chin belligerently. "You can't make me."

Simon turned a mighty frown on her. "Of course I can make you."

"But you won't."

Simon found her sudden, teasing smile delightful. He was not happy about Diane's adamant refusal to see sense. He was enchanted by the way the morning light caressed her gold skin. He wanted to reach out and do the same. He jammed his thumbs into his belt instead and reminded her, "You've been beaten, nearly raped, threatened by the most powerful sorceress in the world."

"And fought her off, too," Diane said. She gave a proud toss of her head. "She tried to make me think you'd hurt me. Bad *film noir* stuff. No way did I let her get away with it. And there's no way I'm letting you out of my sight."

"I want you to stay here," he told her.

Her eyes narrowed suspiciously. "Why? Because you're marrying someone else and want me out of the way?"

"Of course not!"

He had answered her too quickly, too adamantly. The echo of his shout filled the quiet garden, and set a pair of startled doves on the roof to flight. His reaction to this accusation was so fierce that it frightened him. He wanted to grab her and shake her for daring to think he'd want anyone but her. He'd never *wanted* anyone but Diane, not really. He'd known lust, he'd known marital duty, he'd never known the need he felt for her before. He burned with wanting her, he knew he would fight the world for her, took delight in her pleasure and bled with her pain. Being with her was joy. To be away from her was an ordeal.

He supposed this must be what it felt like to be in love, and it came to him too late.

Knowing that he loved Diane, he had to do what he could to protect her. Even lie.

He forced his features into a mask of indifference, made his voice neutral. "Yes," he told her. "Because I am going to marry someone else."

Diane didn't want to believe him. But she was the one who'd brought the subject up. She'd spilled her insecurity out into the frosty morning air. It was her fault if he used it against her. She wished she'd kept her mouth shut.

No, she never wanted to do that again. She was never going to keep still, or quiet, or diplomatically silent about anything again. She wasn't going to find her voice and not revel in the power being able to communicate gave.

She had a great deal to say to Simon de Argent. Starting with, "I love you."

From his lack of reaction she might as well not have her voice back.

She hid disappointment as she waved a hand in front of his face. "Simon? Hello?"

He brushed her hand away. He took a step back. "I heard you." He turned away. "That's not important."

She stared at him, watched the corded muscles of his shoulder tense beneath the blue wool of his tunic. She didn't have to be silent anymore, but no words came to her as the seconds stretched out. The morning light grew stronger. The nuns began to sing a different song. This one was more somber, more like a dirge than a hymn of joyous praise. It suited the moment. It suited the situation.

Diane hated living her life to a soundtrack.

She turned and walked into the room off the garden where she'd cleaned up Simon's wound. She closed the door against the sound, against the sight of Simon. She didn't know why. She should have stood her ground instead of retreating at the first sign of indifference from him.

The room held a heavy table, two chairs, the walls and floor were stark gray stone. There was a plain cross on one wall. A small barred window let in a little light, and an hour candle burned on the table. The place was empty of life, sterile. Peaceful, maybe. Simple.

Felice had looked radiant at the idea of spending the rest of her life praying in this plain, peaceful, simple altogether dull and lifeless place. Diane wondered how long it would be before she started screaming with boredom with her newfound voice.

How long had she had her voice back? she wondered. Surely, she hadn't just fallen in love with Simon the moment she saw Alys try to kill him. It must have happened in little, step-by-step, small, imperceptible increments that snuck into her subconscious while she fought so hard not to let love happen. There was so much about him to love.

How was she going to fall out of love with him? She could tell from the pain in her heart, and her gut, and her head, that it wasn't going to happen in an instant. She couldn't turn off something that still felt wonderful despite the pain that laced through her. Not because of one knife thrust of indifference from him.

He had to do better than that.

She'd retreated, but she hadn't given up a fight that was barely started. Diane took a deep breath, and walked back out to the garden.

She was both surprised and immeasurably relieved to find that Simon was still there. She planted herself before him and put her hands on her hips. "I have a few things to say."

He folded his arms over his chest. "I'm sure you do."

Simon knew very well that he should have taken the opportunity to leave the convent. The arrangements for both the women he loved were taken care of. They needed time to settle into their new life, not a man fussing over them in this tranquil refuge of women. Instead, he'd lingered, and told himself that he was listening to the beautiful plain chant coming from the chapel. He told himself that he wanted to see his daughter one more time before he went about his business.

He'd stayed because he wasn't yet strong enough to say good-bye to Diane.

"You're a great deal of trouble," he told her.

She smiled. The warmth it sent into him was far superior to the winter sunlight. "So are you."

He should have bid her farewell, perhaps asked for one last, chaste kiss before making his way from the garden. Instead he asked, "If I trouble you, why do you want to talk to me?"

She gave him a shrewd look out of those dark, dark eyes. "Why did you hang around to listen?"

"Hang?" He touched his throat. "Only peasants get hanged." His life would no doubt end on a sword point. He didn't trouble her with that knowledge.

She didn't think he mistook her meaning at all. Words were a better shield to hide behind than silence. "You're the only person around here I can really talk to," she told him. "Besides, we have so much to talk about."

He tilted an eyebrow at her. "Such as?"

"Are you going to marry this heiress person?"

He had expected her to begin with an explanation of how she had come to love him. That she would want to discuss how Jacques had been right about how to break the *geis*. He wanted to tell her how happy he was that she had her voice back. He wanted to tell her so very much. But since she had chosen this topic of conversation, he answered her as directly as she had asked.

"Yes."

"Do you love her?"

"I've never met her."

"You can't marry someone you haven't even met."

"I've done it before. It's not as hard as you seem to think. You appear before the church door, make your vows, and live as best you can with the stranger you go home with."

"You didn't know Denis and Felice's mother before you married her?"

He might have laughed at the appalled look on her face, if the situation had been the least bit funny. "No. Why should we? Genevieve and I were fourteen and fifteen when our parents—"

"That's not even legal! Your ages," she added at his questioning look.

"I'm told the DeHauly girl is sixteen."

"You're kidding." Her eyes narrowed suspiciously. "How old are you?"

"Thirty-four."

"And you're marrying a teenager?"

"A what?"

"A sixteen-year-old."

He nodded.

"That's disgusting."

"Yes," he agreed. "But politics demands the poor girl end up with an old husband. I doubt she'll have to complain about her misfortune for long."

"She's sixteen!"

He didn't understand why Diane kept hammering at this point. "I doubt she's much younger than you."

Her mouth fell open. She pointed at herself. "How old do you think I am?"

He looked her over, head to toe, carefully memorizing each sweet detail of face and form and attitude to cherish after he'd left her. She blushed in the unintentional heat of his gaze.

He looked away as he answered, "Not yet twenty, I'd guess."

"Twenty-four. I'm twenty-four. And I'm not from China," she went on before he could register his admiration at how well-preserved she was for her years.

"Are you from the future?" he asked. "Jacques never lies, but I began to wonder if he'd made a mistake when Father Raymond said you were from Cathay." He reached out suddenly, putting his hands on her shoulders as an idea struck him. "If Jacques accidentally snatched you from a land at the other end of the Silk Road, you can make the journey back."

"No, I can't."

He glared at her, as if she was merely being difficult. "It's a long way, I know, but certainly possible. You can go home to Cathay."

Diane didn't like the way this conversation was spinning out of control. The original point was that she didn't want him to leave her at the convent, but their words had flown off in all directions instead of sticking to the subject. She supposed it was because they had stored away so many things to discuss during the time they'd been together. Now he was talking about sending her to China, which was as impossible as being left in a convent. She decided to settle this one point, then get back to the matter of most immediate importance.

"I am not from China, or Cathay, or whatever you want to call it. My mother was born in Hong Kong, my father in Glasgow. They both have British accents. They moved to America when they were married. I was born and raised in Seattle. I don't speak more than twenty words of Chinese, I own a wok but hardly ever use it, my math scores were terrible on the SATs, I think *The Joy Luck Club* was great, but I really don't identify with anybody in it. I'm half Chinese, half Scottish, damned proud of being both and you don't understand a word of what I'm saying, do you?"

Simon rubbed his thumb along his jawline. He looked thoughtful, and gave her one of those faint smiles that always melted her defensiveness. "What I think you mean, is that you want to be judged as a person and not as being from a certain people."

Which was exactly what she had meant, though she hadn't been able to articulate it herself. The man could understand her, whether she could speak or not. She nodded.

"But you still belong in a place," he persisted.

"Not in this convent," she told him. "Not in China." After a pause, she added. "Maybe not back in Seattle, even if I could get there." She had changed so much since meeting Simon. Her old life meant nothing to her.

The gentle understanding left his expression. The grip on her shoulders became hard. "You're going to try to tell me that you belong with me."

"I don't have to tell you. You already know we belong together."

He gave a sharp shake of his head. "You belong where you'll be safe."

"Where you won't feel responsible for my safety, you mean."

"Where no one can hurt you."

She saw his desperate determination to protect her. It infuriated her. "I'm responsible for myself. You let me make my own choice in front of the king."

"That was different," he said. "That was yesterday."

"What? I get one day a year to make my own choices, and you make them the other three hundred and sixty-four?"

"That sounds about right," he answered in his insufferably superior drawl.

"Everybody makes their own choices, every day." She didn't know when she'd come to believe that, but she knew it was true. She also knew it was a lesson Simon had taught her, maybe unintentionally, but it was a part of how he lived. She just didn't think he knew it.

"What an odd way you have of looking at things. Proper behavior is to subordinate one's will to God and those above you; peasant to vassal, vassal to liege. Woman to man," he added with a significant lift of his eyebrow.

"You don't live like that," she told him.

"Yes I do." He knew that he wouldn't be in such trouble if he wasn't intent on keeping his feudal vows to Henry Plantagenet. "I live by my word, by my honor."

"Which is a code you've *chosen* to live by."

Why was he talking philosophy? And with a woman at that. Diane constantly distracted him, even when she couldn't talk. Now that she could it would be too easy to get lost in knowing her, as a companion and a lover. It simply could not be.

"I choose to marry another woman," he told her. "I

choose for you to stay at Sacré Couer if you won't go back to Cathay. It is my will. That is the end of it."

Her reply to his adamant declaration was a loud, "Ha!"

The nuns were filing out of the chapel, two neatly ordered rows of black-garbed women. These were serene women, who knew their place. Many of them were elderly, having lived long, fruitful lives of prayer behind the sheltering walls of Sacré Coeur. Simon could give Diane nothing better than this, no matter how much it hurt him to leave her.

Simon took Diane firmly by the arm. He didn't answer when she protested. He took her to the abbess.

"Treat her well," he said as he pushed Diane toward the woman.

Without another word or look toward the woman he loved, he turned and walked from the convent, onto the streets of Paris.

23

"Coward!" Diane shouted after him.

She wondered if she imagined that he flinched as her accusation reached him. He didn't turn back.

He didn't want her. He was running away. She should have known it would come to this before she committed her heart to the man. She didn't belong in his world. So, he was leaving her exiled from his life as well.

"Damn him."

The black-veiled women gasped in unified shock.

They surrounded her like a murder of crows and she was hustled into the refectory by the crowd of women before she could decide what to do next. Her heart ached, depression began to swamp her. She'd slept little, eaten nothing, and the adrenaline that had kept her going was running out. She was a wreck, and nobody had even beaten her up recently.

Except Simon, who'd done it with words and the best of intentions.

"Idiot," she grumbled as she was led to a seat at one of the long refectory tables. "God save us from well-intentioned men."

"Amen."

Diane looked to her left, to find Felice seated next to

her. It was Simon's daughter who had spoken. "Are you agreeing with me? Or praying?"

"A bit of both," the girl whispered back. "You were calling on God's help. That's a prayer."

There was a bright twinkle in her amber eyes. Felice looked radiant in her white postulant's veil, despite the bruises on her face. Diane didn't understand it, but she guessed Felice was one of those people who really did have a religious calling.

"I should be working in the kitchen," Felice said as an old nun stopped behind them and put a dark slab of bread on the table in front of each of them. "But Mother Elizabeth thought I could better serve by helping you become reconciled to life in the cloister. Not all who enter these gates do so of their own will," she added sadly. "Just as not all women marry willingly." A haunted look crossed Felice's face.

Not all men marry willingly, either, Diane thought. She didn't think Simon had with his first marriage. She didn't think he was marrying willingly now. It wasn't fair to him. It wasn't fair to the girl. It sure as hell wasn't fair to her. Somebody ought to save that man from himself.

She ate most of the bread while she tried to get her confused thoughts together. She knew there was something she should be doing, but she was so tired, so emotionally drained. About all she had left was her sense of outrage, and it took a while before she could even work up enough of that to speak.

"What is wrong with you people?" she asked Felice after she'd had a bit of watery soup to go with the bread. "Why is your father doing what somebody else wants and marrying this heiress person?"

"To save Marbeau, I suppose," Felice answered. "It's a risky thing he's doing."

Fear knotted in Diane's stomach. It didn't sit well with her breakfast. "Why?"

Felice was very matter-of-fact when she replied. "If he takes a new wife and gets her with child, and then is killed in battle, both mother and babe will surely be put to the sword." She shook her head sadly. "Denis will have Marbeau, and no one is going to stop him. Not while Vivienne controls his actions."

Diane was too shocked to speak. She was used to not speaking, but not to having the words frozen in her throat out of sheer horror.

"Perhaps Father is marrying to beget a new heir in case Denis is the one who dies in battle," Felice went on. "The land must be passed on. The patrimony is all that matters."

No, Diane thought. *Simon is what matters.* She suddenly knew what it was that she'd forgotten to do.

"I have to go after him."

Felice looked utterly shocked. "You can't."

"Why not?"

"He told you to stay here."

"So?"

Felice considered the concept of defiance for a moment. She blinked, and licked her lips nervously. "You would go to him when he sent you away? When he put your safety and chastity above his male lust?"

"Yes," Diane answered firmly.

"You would offer yourself to him as his concubine though he has a new wife in his household?"

"No," Diane responded promptly.

"What would you do?"

"Keeping him from marrying anybody but me, of course."

Felice lowered her gaze. A tiny smile tugged at her lips. "I see." She looked back at Diane. "You would make him happy?"

Diane's heart flooded with hope, and determination. "Yes," she said. "I'll do my best to make him happy."

Felice's smile broadened into a grin. "Then why are you here?" she asked. "Go after the fool if you want him."

His household was waiting for him at the Grand Pont bridge. The crowded traffic of the city flowed around them on foot and horseback, in litters and on carts. But for one thing, Simon would be glad to leave the noise and crush of the city behind him. Every step away from Sacré Coeur had been torture, every moment more spent in Paris would be a temptation. The memory of Diane's face, her lovely voice pulled at him.

Her horse stood next to his, saddled, waiting. None of his people asked where Diane was, but he could feel the question in their glances. Simon ignored them as he approached his mount.

It was impossible to ignore Father Paquin when the priest stepped out from the shadow of the baggage cart. The clergyman planted himself squarely before Simon. "It looks as though you are leaving Paris, my son."

Simon nodded. "I've accomplished what I came for."

"Gilbert is dead." Paquin crossed himself. "I will say a Mass for his soul."

"Say several. Say one for me, while you're at it." Simon tried to step around the priest, but Paquin would not let him by. Simon sighed tiredly. "Father, I only want to go home."

"The king would not be pleased with your leaving." Paquin smiled. "You have not even sung for him yet."

"The king prefers hymns to love songs," Simon pointed out.

It occurred to Simon that he had never sung for Diane. She'd spent hours entertaining him and he had not thought to repay her in kind. He hadn't picked up his lute in many months. His heart had been dead to song, but suddenly it ached because he had never shared his one gift

with the only woman a love song would have been meant
for. Such music he could have given her—if only there
had been time.

"But the court so enjoys your talents," the priest said.
"You could serenade Lady Marguerite."

Simon rubbed his jaw. "I suppose I could."

Paquin smiled. "Then you will come back to the
palace?"

Simon gestured at his household. "I'm already prepared to take my leave of the city."

Paquin's eyes narrowed. "You killed a man last night,
broke the Peace of God."

Simon chose to ignore the faint threat in the other
man's voice. "Witnesses admitted my right to fight the
man."

"You got what you came for, my lord." Paquin leaned
forward, and whispered. "You cannot ride away without
paying for it. Father Raymond arranged for your meeting
with Gilbert. The price for that is an alliance with the
king, sealed with your marriage to DeHauly's daughter."

"Which would mean abandoning my vow to Henry
Plantagenet."

"You owe service to the King of France, as well."

Simon shook his head. "Not in war. I swore that I
would follow Henry and no other in war."

"Throw in your lot with France, I beg you. You will
have the king's support in all you do."

"Will that stop my son from attacking me?"

No matter what the priest answered, no matter the
king's promise, Simon knew Denis would ride against him
in the spring. Even if the king forbade it, Denis would be
persuaded to attack Marbeau. Simon knew his only choice
was whether to fight his son alone, or to accept the help of
troops provided by Marguerite DeHauly's father.

The bells of a nearby church began to ring. Closer,
Simon's stallion shook its head restlessly and snorted with

impatience. Simon longed to be off as well, to escape the island before he did something incredibly foolish just because it was what he wanted. Though he tried to keep his attention on the priest, he kept looking back the way he'd come. Back toward Sacré Coeur.

Paquin said, "You will defeat your whelp's mercenaries easily with DeHauly's aid."

Simon gave the priest an arrogant look. "You don't know how well I trained the boy."

"All the more reason to accept the alliance the king wishes."

"Perhaps I should stay," Simon agreed. "When I came here I thought I could. I tried to persuade myself that I could save my daughter, and my lands, and start over. I told myself that duty was all that really mattered. Not happiness, mine or anyone else's, just duty to my patrimony. I intended to betray my vows." His heart was ready to burst with the pain of knowing why he couldn't grasp this one last chance to save all he held dear. He said, "I can't do it, father. I would if I could, but I can not."

The priest did not look angry, but sad. "Why? Why stand alone when the king wants to be your friend?"

Because all he held dear was nothing compared to the woman he wanted.

He was a fool. He knew it. Not for abandoning his duty, but for abandoning the woman he loved. Even knowing that he had done it for her own good was no comfort.

She doesn't want to be safe, he thought. *She wants to be with me. She said so. I want to be with her. What more do either of us need?*

He had done what was best for her, but he had not done what was best for them. It was ridiculous to think that they could be together. Ridiculous, but the desire for Diane rose up and overwhelmed all reason.

"What am I doing here?"

When he would have turned away, Paquin grasped his arm. "It's not too late, my son."

"I hope not," Simon answered. "Perhaps she can find it in her heart to forgive me."

Paquin looked confused. "Lady Marguerite?"

Simon laughed. "I'm sure she's a fine girl, and will make Denis a wonderful wife."

"You're going to let DeHauly make an alliance with your son instead of you? You're denying the king's wishes?"

"There's nothing else I can do," Simon answered. Not and have the woman he wanted.

"Do you know what you're giving up?"

My life, he thought. *And gaining my soul.* "I know. Good-bye," he added. "I thank you and Father Raymond for at least trying to help."

He shook the priest off and went to his horse. He swung up on the animal's back and looked around. "I'll meet you on the road," he told his people. Then he turned the horse and rode into the traffic headed away from the bridge.

Diane had the hood of her cloak pulled down so far over her face that she could hardly see. The point was that she didn't want to draw any attention to herself, but she kept bumping into people and things, which wasn't doing her much good, either. The so-called street was narrow, full of churned-up half-frozen mud and things she could smell but didn't want to think about. This was definitely not the Paris she remembered from her adolescent trip.

Though she had followed Felice's detailed direction's to get to the main bridge over the Seine, she was worried that she was lost. She could hardly see the sky when she looked up because of the way the upper stories of the buildings leaned crazily out over the street. She was surrounded by people heading in the same direction she was. That reassured her that she was going the right way, and worried her because she didn't want to spook anybody and cause a riot because she looked different than they did.

She wanted to find the bridge and get out of town. Felice had given her a purse full of coins. Diane had them tied to her belt. The pouch jingled reassuringly against her thigh as she walked. Felice had said that these were her last worldly goods, saved to give to the poor but that financing her father's happiness was cause enough to give the coins to Diane. Diane planned to use the money to follow Simon back to Marbeau. She didn't know how she was going to go about getting there, but if that was where he was, that was where she was going to be.

It was silly, romantic, and foolhardy, but if she had to walk across France in the winter to get to him, she was prepared to do it.

And what would she do if she found him in bed with his new wife when she got there?

"I'll think about that tomorrow," she muttered as she continued on her way. It was the wrong movie for the situation, but it was about the best way to handle the situation—one day at a time.

"Maybe that's the best way to handle any situation," she grumbled, as she walked into the side of a horse.

There weren't that many riders on the street. Most people were on foot. There were a few ox-carts, there had been a monk on a donkey, and she'd noticed some people being carried by in box-shaped litters. The few riders she had seen had been sword-carrying males, in chain mail. She suspected that walking into a warrior could lead to big trouble. She hoped to get past this one without being noticed.

She started to back up, to try to disappear into the crowd. She'd barely moved before a hand reached down and twitched back her hood. Terror flashed through her.

The last thing she wanted was to have her face exposed. She felt naked as a disapproving silence emanated from the man on horse. Chilled with fear, she kept her gaze on the ground, and hoped the veil that covered her head was sufficient to hide her face from his examination. She would have turned and run, but the man had a firm grasp of her cloak.

"Look at me." The voice was a deep, rough growl.

Diane's head came up. She saw a frowning face framed in a gold mane, lowered brows over amber eyes, a full, sensuous mouth flattened in a disapproving line.

It took her a moment to realize that she'd walked into the man she'd been determined to pursue to the ends of the earth.

She was here, in front of him. Simon couldn't believe it for a moment. It was a miracle. It was surely meant to be. It was the sheerest folly. It was dangerous for her to be outside alone.

"What are you doing here?" they both questioned at once.

"Looking for you," they both answered.

For a moment Diane was too annoyed to feel relief, and then joy filled her. He'd come for her. He wanted her. He'd had no business leaving her in the first place, but he was back, and she instantly forgave him for acting like an idiot. A dear, caring, concerned idiot. She was tempted to hug the horse since she couldn't put her arms around Simon at the moment.

From his high perch, Simon looked around the crowd in irritation. People were staring. He saw a beggar cross himself and slink away into the shadows, and another make the sign against the evil eye as he gaped at Diane. Simon turned his frown on his beloved.

"Did you get your voice back just to lose your mind? Put your hood up, woman before someone sees you."

"Whoa! Wait a minute. You're the one who—"

Simon yanked hard on her cloak, and the next thing she knew she landed on her stomach across the neck of the horse. "Simon!"

He pulled her hood back over her head. "Hush."

Her indignant reply was muffled, but still loud. "Don't you tell me to—"

"We'll discuss your unseemly behavior in private," he told her as she squirmed around to look at him. "And we'll behave unseemly as well when I get you alone," he added. "It's a long ride back to Marbeau," he told her. "And we're going to enjoy every moment of it."

He held Diane securely around the waist as he kicked the horse in the side. For now, she was a squirming, wool-wrapped bundle imprisoned before him on the saddle. Soon he would make it up to her, he would unwrap her like a present, cherish her like the precious jewel she was. He would take her into his arms and show her all he felt. He would make this undignified exit up to her in a thousand pleasant, sensual ways.

But right now he had to get out of Paris before the gates of the city were closed against them.

24

"I have only my heart to offer."

Simon was on bended knee before her, his hands out-stretched in supplication. "Please take me, if only for a little while."

The vulnerability of his expression, the uncertainty in his rich voice tore at all Diane's defenses. She'd come into the tent prepared for a furious confrontation over who decided what was best for her. She'd fumed for hours. She'd spent the time in practiced silence, all through the ride, and even after she'd been eased down from the horse into the care of her own servant.

When they caught up with the Marbeau household deep in the woods west of Paris, night was falling, the tents were set up, dinner was roasting over a pair of camp-fires. Nobody looked surprised to see her. Or happy to see her, either.

Simon disappeared into his tent, and she accompanied her serving woman, after pausing to glare at his broad, retreating back for a moment. She bathed in a shallow tub, taking delight in the healing power of hot water, and the warmth of a tent heated by braziers. Then she put on layer after layer of the softest linen and silk, from milky white to midnight blue. She felt up for a proper argument when Yves came in and asked her to accompany him to Lord Simon's pavilion. Only to find the Lord of Marbeau kneeling to her in supplication.

How could she fight with someone who'd just offered her his heart? Why would she want to?

The tent was lit by many, many candles. It was as if he had brought the stars inside for her. They made the place mysterious and magical, redolent of beeswax, and honey, and cool blue smoke.

Their warm glow lent more gold to Simon's already bright hair and eyes. His black tunic was embroidered in wide bands of gold thread. It looked like they'd both dressed in the best they had for this meeting.

He stood as she stepped toward him, his hands still stretched out to her. She took them, and felt the hard calluses of his palms rub against the smooth skin of her hands. The contrast sent a shiver of desire through her.

She looked up, met a gaze that was filled with fire, a flame far more intense than the pale glow of the encircling candles. The expression in those eyes turned from entreating to commanding as he pulled her to him. She was drawn to his sudden imperiousness, and into his embrace. His touch filled her with inexorable need. The arrogant planes of his face reminded her of a hawk's as he swept down on her.

They came together in the center of the circle of fire. Their lips touched and clung hungrily. This was no time for tentative exploration, need drove them together.

"I've been waiting for you my whole life," he told her in a breathless moment between kisses.

"I know," she told him. And she did. "I arrived gift wrapped for you. And I'm glad."

"You shouldn't be." He traced his fingers over her lips.

"Jacques was right all along."

Simon laughed softly in her ear. "Let's not talk about Jacques right now."

"All right," she agreed, as her hands came up beneath his tunic.

He felt them splayed against the bare skin of his back, and quivered with desire as her fingers played down his ribs. "No Jacques. Just you and me. You're all I've ever needed. I was a fool not to see it sooner."

"I love you," she told him.

He'd heard her say the words before. Now he truly listened. He truly believed. He hadn't known how much he'd longed to hear the words until she spoke and they penetrated deep into his heart.

He kissed her throat. "You make me whole." Then his mouth claimed hers once more. "Newborn with loving you."

He touched her hair, it ran heavily through his fingers, pure black, shimmering and alive in the light. "So beautiful."

Diane had never felt beautiful before this moment. She was beautiful, for him. With him. She was alive with desire, near to drowning with the feelings he aroused in her. She closed her eyes and gave herself over to her other senses. He tasted and smelled and felt absolutely male, hard-muscled and powerful. She pressed herself to him, gave her hands free reign over his body, as he did hers. New, fiery pleasure blossomed wherever they touched.

It seemed only moments before their layered clothing lay piled beneath them on the tent floor. All that finery had just gotten in the way, but it made a comfortable enough mattress.

Simon lifted himself to his knees and looked down upon the splendor of Diane's unclothed body. Her skin was golden-pale, bathed in the gleam of candles, contrasted to the dark blues and blacks of their cast off garments. Her lips were lifted in an inviting smile, the peaks of her round breasts strained toward him. Her arms reached up to draw him to her. He shook with his own need, fought to stay restrained when he wanted to sink down upon her, into her. He had never felt so welcomed in his life, and he wanted to savor the moment.

He gestured toward the other side of the tent. "I had thought to use the bed."

"Don't need it." Her words came out in an eager pant.

"Are you well? Not stiff and sore from the ride?"

She threw her head back against the crumpled-up silk of her overdress. Her laughter rang out like the quavering of a bell. "I'm fine." She spread her legs welcomingly. "But I could be better."

Simon stroked her thighs, and the moist crevice that waited for him. She squirmed. He said, "I might not use you as tenderly as—"

"Now!" she interrupted. "Make love to me right now, Simon!" she demanded.

He responded instantly to her eagerness, and the demands of his own body. He filled her and made her his with one swift stroke. She moaned and called out his name as he came deep inside her, and he set a hard, fast rhythm that she rose eagerly to meet.

Simon knew he had never heard a more beautiful sound than that of her voice as their bodies melded. Nor had he felt anything so wonderful as the ecstasy that shattered all thought at the instant he spilled his seed into her.

Simon collapsed into her embrace. He had felt accepted in other women's beds, but he had never known this engulfing welcome. He knew without words that she wanted to be with no one else but him. That she would not turn away, not retreat into herself now that the deed was done. She was here with him as she had been with him, body and soul, in the act of love.

He could have wept on her breast, but Diane greeted him with soft laughter and a gentle kiss on the temple. She hugged him to herself and shared her happiness at what they had just done. He couldn't cry, not even with joy, he was too happy for tears.

Diane saw the hint of melancholy in the smile Simon gave her. She remembered that he'd had a wife, and at least one mistress. It occurred to her that neither of these women had given a damn about Simon de Argent. It twisted her heart, and angered her.

"Hasn't anyone ever loved you before?"

The question was out before she could stop it. Simon's eyes went dark with pain, his gaze shifted from hers.

"Talk to me," she pleaded. She touched his cheek, and he turned his head to kiss her palm. Sated though she was, desire fluttered through her again. It distracted her only a moment. "Is every woman in this century a fool?" she questioned. "Don't they know you're the most wonderful man in the world?"

"It only matters that one woman thinks so." He gave her a teasing look. He ran his fingers down her ribcage. It tickled, and he knew it. "That woman is you, I trust? Or must I go on a quest to find the woman who thinks I'm wonderful?"

"No quests needed," she answered. "No other woman need apply." She wagged a finger in his face. "Keep tickling me, however, and I'll bite."

Her hand slid down his chest, and then further down. The fingers that had been admonishing him a moment before closed around his member. Simon gasped. And began to rise.

"Do you think I can tup all night for your pleasure?" he questioned as her fingers played him with great skill. "I'm no young buck who can—"

"Of course you can." Her voice was sultry, her touch insistent. "For both our pleasure."

"Diane. I—Oh, that is sweet. Well, perhaps I'm not as tired as I—Ah!"

He wasn't quite sure how she managed to roll him onto

his back, but he landed there, with her on top of him. She leaned forward, offering her breasts to his eager touch. Her kiss was a long, scorching, delicious tease.

He was hard, pulsing with need, his blood burned, and he was ready to make love all night by the time she straddled him.

"These are a bit smaller than I remember."

Simon's hands were on her breasts. Diane opened her eyes. "What?"

They were on the bed, half covered in warm, soft furs. She wasn't sure how they'd gotten there, but she was glad Simon traveled with all the comforts of home. The candles were long since burned out and daylight filtered in through the white fabric of the tent walls. It was light enough to see the bemused look on his face.

He bent his head and ran his tongue around first one nipple, then the other, leaving them puckered and hard by the time he was done.

"You didn't have to stop," she told him as he went back to weighing her breasts in his palms.

"They are small things," he said.

"Thanks a lot."

"Beautiful," he went on. "Perfect. But I remember how they looked as they moved beneath the silk dress you wore when you first arrived." He planted a kiss on each breast. "I had never seen anything so arousing as the way you looked in that dress."

She propped herself up on her elbows. "Oh, yeah? You liked it?" It was nice to know that he'd noticed what she'd worn, even though it was months after the fact.

"Very much. And those flimsy, provocative—things—you wore underneath."

"Underwear. You liked my fancy underwear?" He nodded. "Good."

That flimsy bit of ivory lace had cost enough. And to think she'd only been wearing it for herself, not in hopes that the perfect man might offer to take it off of her. *I could do some serious damage for this man at Victoria's Secret*, she thought.

"If it hadn't gotten dragged through the mud I'd wear it for you again," she told him. "Silk dress, Wonderbra, and all."

Then she sat up laughing, knowing what he'd meant when he'd said her breasts looked bigger that night. Well, she wasn't going to explain the mechanics of padding them and pushing them up under her chin when he'd told her that her breasts were perfect when she wasn't wearing anything at all. She didn't want to talk. She wanted to make love again.

Yves, however, came into the tent before she could suggest it. Simon pulled the covers up over her and turned to his servant. "Are the horses saddled?" he asked. "What about the men, and provisions?"

"All is ready, my lord," Yves answered.

"Good."

Simon got out of bed. She noticed that he was already mostly dressed. Yves took a heavy woolen tunic out of a chest and handed it to Simon. He put it on, then accepted his swordbelt from the servant. Diane watched him dress with the depressing realization that they weren't going to have a leisurely morning to themselves.

Simon spoke to Yves. "Have Diane's woman bring her warmest clothes for the journey."

"Yes, my lord," Yves said, and went out again.

Diane threw back the covers, and was caught by a blast of cold air from Yves's departure. She scrambled out of bed and into the shift Simon tossed her from the pile on the floor.

"What's going on?" she asked as she found her discarded shoes. "Are you hungry?"

"Famished," he said. "We're leaving."

"Before breakfast?"

Simon smiled at the astonished, disgruntled look on Diane's face. "We'll eat on the road." He went to her, and pushed a strand of hair out of her face. He kissed her forehead. "We dallied late, and I let you sleep longer than I should just because I enjoyed watching you. Now we must ride hard to make up lost time."

"Do we have to go?"

"Yes."

She looked around the tent. "Couldn't we just take a few days off from the Middle Ages and be with each other?"

He put his hand on her shoulder. "We are going to be together, for as long as I can manage. I'm going to keep you as safe as possible. We're returning to Marbeau, my love. As quickly as we can. Though it grieves me to do without the amenities due my station you and I and a few men will ride ahead." He gestured at the contents of his private traveling quarters. "It won't be as comfortable as this, but it will be quicker." He grinned at her. "I have a big bed at Marbeau, you'll recall."

Diane shivered in the morning cold as her woman came in with her clothes. The woman looked disapproving, but made no comment as she helped Diane dress.

"And a fireplace," Diane said. "I have fond memories of being warm in your bedroom."

He smirked. "I'll keep you warm there. I promise."

"I bet."

Once she was finished he took her hand and led her outside. The horses were indeed saddled and waiting, along with a group of mounted soldiers and a pack horse. They were all just outside the tent. The tent where she and Simon had been making love. Where everyone *knew* they'd been making love. Diane blushed.

"There is absolutely no privacy in this world. I hate

that." Simon held her stirrup while she mounted, then he ran his hand up her calf—while everybody in the area avidly watched. "Don't do that!"

He laughed. "Last night you were the one who wasn't shy."

She shooed him away. "That was last night. In private."

He smirked, and swung up into the saddle of his stallion. "Privacy," he said. "Another reason to hurry home."

"Then what are we waiting for?" Diane asked, and urged her mount forward.

25

"Where did you learn to ride so well?"

Diane took her gaze off the threatening clouds that loomed above the bare tree branches, and looked at Simon. It seemed like the further they'd ridden during the day, the darker it had gotten. "I think it's going to snow."

He glanced up at the sky. "That's likely."

Diane didn't like the idea of being caught in a blizzard, but was a bit reassured by Simon's lack of concern. If a seasoned native didn't worry about the weather, she didn't suppose she should. "It's just that I'm used to a more controlled environment," she told him.

Simon had only the vaguest notion of what her words signified. "Your words have meaning, but no sense," he told her. "There's so much about you I do not know."

"I don't know much about you, either," she agreed.

"But more than I know about you. Where did you learn to ride so well?" he repeated his earlier question.

He was pleased that she had spent many hours in the saddle without complaint, and had no trouble managing her animal over rough forest terrain. She hadn't asked useless questions, either. She had done no more than give him a curious look when he'd directed the party off the road to ride across the countryside. If she was worried about danger she hid it well. Or, perhaps she trusted him to protect her. He hoped the trust was not misplaced.

Then, again, perhaps she simply did not comprehend that they were fleeing for their lives.

"I had a horse when I was a kid," she answered. "And years of lessons. All little girls love horses, right?"

"No," he replied. "I tried to teach Felice to ride. She hated it. So I left her to her prayers and needlework."

He wished now he had spent more time with his daughter. He cared for her more than most fathers did for girl children, certainly more than his father had for his sisters, but it didn't feel like it had been enough.

Diane reached over and touched his arm. It distracted him from his guilty musings. "She turned out just fine," Diane said. "Felice is one smart kid. Like her father."

"And how did you know I was thinking about my daughter? Are you a mind reader as well as storyteller?"

"I recognized the brooding look," she answered. "The source was easy to guess. And I'm not a storyteller."

"What are you, then? A noblewoman, certainly, if you owned a horse. What sort of life did Jacques snatch you from?"

Were you happy? he wondered. Did she miss it terribly? Was there another man there? One who had a right to her love and loyalty? Should he ask her these questions? He didn't know if he wanted to know the answers. It worried him when she was silent for a long time.

Diane wasn't sure how to explain how she'd lived in her own time. Simon's world had a simple hierarchy; people with swords— the ones with property and the ones who worked for them; people who prayed for a living; servants—lots of those; wizards and witches; ancillary womenfolk that were addressed as Lady this or Lady that. She wasn't quite sure what most of the noblewomen she'd encountered did for a living—needlework and sleeping with the guys with the swords, she guessed. Her place in this line-up was ambiguous at best, but probably easier to define than her role in her own time.

"I didn't really have a place in my own world," she said finally. "I hate to admit it, but I was totally useless. I had a job, but it didn't have any meaning. I never did anything that meant anything." She gave a derisive snort of laughter. "I wrote articles for a film magazine. I thought watching old movies was the most wonderful and significant thing anybody could do." She looked at Simon. "I was a complete slacker, and I didn't even realize it. Can you believe that?"

"I don't know," he replied. "What did you just say?"

She sighed. No, it wasn't possible to explain what she had done at home, since she hadn't done anything. "It's not important. What matters is that I'm here now, with you."

"Then Jacques did not take you from a life you cared for?"

She heard the hope in his voice, and it made her smile. But it was a sad smile. Maybe her life hadn't had any meaning before Simon came into it, but there were many things about it she missed. Not just the comforts, though she certainly longed for things like toothpaste and modern medicine.

"I miss my family," she admitted. "There's a lot of us, parents and a brother and two sisters. I've got two nieces and a nephew. My grandparents come to visit at least once a year—the ones from Hong Kong. I've only met the Scottish relatives a few times. They don't quite approve of Mom," she added with an annoyed frown. "Things haven't changed that much from your time, I guess."

Simon noticed that she had not mentioned a husband, or lover. He wanted to think that she was honorable enough not to have come to love him if there had been another man in her life. After all, not all women were faithless vixens.

"Your father," he asked, "is he a man of property? A warrior? How did he provide for his son and daughters? You weren't meant for a convent, I hope? Your talent for lovemaking would be wasted if you were," he added with a teasing smirk. Then he shook an admonishing finger at her. "And how did you learn such things as proper maidens should never know if you are not a traveling storyteller?"

"Sexist pig," she answered. "Why shouldn't a woman know as much about sex as a man? We like it."

He grinned. "I wasn't complaining."

She tossed her head haughtily. "You better not. Besides, I come from a place where men and women are equal." *Compared to here, that is*, she added to herself. "A woman is free to do whatever she wants in my world. I almost went into my father's profession."

Simon chose not to comment on such foolishness. "About your father?"

"He designs jewelry. He's famous for it."

Simon nodded. "An artisan. I see."

"And he owns a house on three acres on Vashon Island. So, yeah, I guess he fits your idea of a landowner."

This was indeed curious. "How can an artisan own land? That is against all—"

"And my mother works for a recording company," she interrupted.

"Your mother—?"

"You look like your brain is frying, dear. I think we better drop this conversation."

"I do not understand," he admitted.

"It doesn't matter."

Diane wished he'd never brought the subject up. Thinking about her family made the homesickness worse. She hadn't realized how much she'd kept it buried until Simon started asking her questions.

"What about your family?" she asked him. It was a

thoughtless, stupid question, considering what had happened in the last few days. "I'm sorry. The words just came—"

He put his hand up to silence here. "It is all right. There are some things you should know. You have but to ask."

The wind was growing colder, the day darker. She noticed a few flakes of snow in the air. She looked around, at the bare trees and withered undergrowth, at the other riders, anywhere but at Simon de Argent while she tried not to ask the question she wanted to.

"You will have heard," he said for her, "that I killed my wife."

Diane looked down at her gloved hands. She fiddled with the horse's reins. She let the nervous silence draw out a little too long before she said, "I heard, but I don't believe it."

Beside her, Simon gave a low, unamused laugh. "And why is that?"

"Because Vivienne told me," she answered. She looked at him. He was looking at his hands. Hands that were clenched in hard fists around his reins. Diane took a deep breath. "Vivienne told me you murdered your wife. She told me that's why Denis hates you. She tried to make me believe lots of things that aren't true."

"My wife is dead. My son hates me. You've seen me kill."

"Never without a good reason."

His expression was grim, his eyes full of old anger. "My wife betrayed me with another man. That's a good reason."

"I still don't believe what Vivienne told me."

"Why shouldn't you believe her? She doesn't always lie."

"But she knows how to twist the truth, I bet."

He nodded. "Better than anyone else I have ever

known. Vivienne can make you believe day's night, even while the sun is burning you raw. Denis believes everything she told him about what happened to Genevieve. And I'm not sure of the truth myself."

"What did happen?"

Simon swallowed hard. "It is a long, sad tale."

Diane thought they'd come too far in this conversation for him to try to worm out of an explanation now. "I've told you a few tales, my lord. Time you paid me back in kind."

He quirked a brow at her. "But you want a true tale."

"Fair's fair," she insisted.

"Very well. I took my wife to the countess's court in Poitiers. She found she liked the life there, soft, luxurious, full of song and dalliance. I played courtier games myself, flirted with the grand ladies, sang love songs to them. It was only a diversion for me. I meant nothing by it. I held my wedding vows sacred—like any other vow. I never took another woman into my bed until Genevieve was . . . dead."

"Oh," Diane said. It was a wholly inadequate word to use, but she didn't think he would accept any of the sympathy that flooded her. All she could hope was that talking about it would help purge him of the guilt she felt from him. "And?"

"He was my best friend at court. A man of great sophistication, of easy laughter and ready wit. Handsome."

"More handsome than you? Get real."

Her quick, indignant words made him smile, just a brief twist of his lips, that turned into a sneer as he said, "He had dark hair and flashing black eyes. Adultery was the fashion in Poitiers. Genevieve followed the fashion. I cursed the day we went to Countess Eleanor's court, vowed to do what I could to bring her decadent house down, and then I brought my wife home to Marbeau."

"Which is where she died?"

He shook his head. "No. Not at Marbeau. She died alone, in exile."

Diane could see that Simon was furious with himself over this. "Why?"

"I sent her away."

"After you brought her home. I don't understand? Did you lock her up in a convent, or something?" *Like you tried to do with me*, she thought, but this was no time to bring his high-handed treatment of her into this.

"No," he said. "I did my best to forgive her, for the children's sake, for the life I thought we had built together. I wanted us to go on as we had. How foolish that must sound to you."

Diane remembered the bruises on Felice's face. She remembered the nasty threats Thierry had made to her. She had a good idea how men normally treated women in this world. Simon had called her his chattel, but he had never treated her like his possession. She supposed he had that right in this time and place where men held absolute power over women. Simon, she thought, was an exceptional man in any time. He was a paragon of compassion and virtue in this one.

"You're a good man, Simon de Argent," she told him. "And nobody seems to have sense enough to realize it. All you were trying to do was save your marriage. That's not foolish. What went wrong?"

"Genevieve didn't want to stay. She wanted to be with her lover. She pointed out that we did not love each other, and it was true. She wanted more than contentment." Simon gave Diane a long look. "Now I know what she meant. I understand the sacrifices she was willing to make for love. Then I thought the life in Poitiers had driven her mad."

"What did you do?"

"I let her go. Only—" He choked on the word, then went on, voice rough. "It was winter, storming. I was furious. And I sent her out into the storm. She caught a fever during the journey, and died of it. So, you see, I had a hand in my wife's death though I didn't deliver the blow."

She would have answered something, she knew, but before any words came to her, Simon spurred his horse forward through the flying snow. He rode quickly past the guard riding point and was soon out of sight on the twisting path. Diane didn't try to follow. She was frozen, but not by the cold winter air. The burning cold that filled her was reaction to Simon's pain. She had never known that you could hurt more for someone else than you could for yourself.

She cursed herself for having made him talk about his wife. She worried that he wouldn't come back. She fussed and fretted in fretful silence as the short afternoon and the miles went by. Fortunately, the snow soon stopped.

They had made camp and she was helping to gather firewood when Simon at last came riding up. Her heart leapt painfully at the sight of him. She hurried forward.

He jumped down from his horse and took her in his arms, forcing her to drop the sticks she'd picked up. "Do you hate me?" he asked.

"Hell, no." It was not, perhaps, the most eloquent way of expressing herself, but the question had taken her by surprise. "I love you."

"I thought that after you knew about what I did to Genev— "

"Genevieve is responsible for her own mistakes!" Diane shouted. They were inches apart, Simon blinked and jerked his head back at her yell. She took his face between her hands. "Isn't she?" She suspected tough love would work better on this man than squishy sympathy.

"You sound like Jacques."

"He's very wise. Totally unethical," she amended. "But wise."

"Wizards live by their own rules."

"And take responsibility for their own actions?"

"Just as you think everyone should?" he questioned back. She gave a decisive nod. "I've thought a great deal since I left you," he went on. "I ended up thinking that perhaps I dreamed that you cared for me. I feared that no one could care for me."

"You're an idiot," she answered lovingly. "An over-imaginative idiot."

He gave her his most superior glare. "You don't have to be quite so blunt."

"And *you* can give the guilt a rest."

Simon believed he understood the thrust of what Diane said. Perhaps he had punished himself for too long. But how did he stop? How did he forgive himself? He'd spent the last hours asking himself that. The only answer that made sense was that he did it with Diane's help. That he accept her belief in his goodness and try to believe in it himself. Then his mind had wandered onto the possibility that she couldn't care for him and he'd rushed back to confront her.

"I am an over-imaginative idiot," he agreed with her. "A hungry one." He straightened, and took her hands in his. "What's for dinner?"

"Men," she complained, and led him toward the campfire.

26

Three days of sleeping on a bedroll on the ground, even wrapped in Simon's arms, were three days too many as far as Diane was concerned. She woke up more stiff and sore each morning, and more in need of a bath all the time. The cold permeated her bones, and that made her dream about long, hot baths as much as the dirt on her skin and clothes did.

Still, she enjoyed the waking up in Simon's arms part. She loved the closeness they shared when they lay down each night by the campfire, wrapped in their cloaks and a fur blanket. They shared body heat and whispered conversations in the dark. She would rest her head over his heart, or he would rest his head on her breasts and it would be so peaceful. Desire hummed between them constantly in the night, and their hands often roamed, though he had an easier time of it since she wasn't wearing a layer of iron rings under her outer clothes. They exchanged long, deep kisses, whispered endearments and confidences. She liked it when she made him laugh, loved the way the sound of his amusement rumbled in her ear.

She would have loved to be able to make love, but not in a camp full of his men. And not to a man who wouldn't take off his chain mail, even to sleep. Besides, it was still public, no matter how dark. Anyway, it was too cold to get naked, and she refused to get her clothes any more messed up than they already were. Simon said he didn't understand her reticence, but, not being a raw boy, he was able to contain his animal lust until he could get her alone in his bed.

"With any luck, that'll be sometime today," she said as she helped him roll up their bedding on the fourth day of the journey. "I thought you said we were taking a short-cut," she said when he gave her a curious look.

He handed the bedroll to one of his men, then gave her a hand up. "Did I say that?" He touched her cheek. "Don't fret, it's not far to Marbeau."

The horses were saddled and ready to go, her and Simon's bedding the last thing to be loaded onto the pack-horse. The fire was out, the ashes scattered. It was time to go. They always ate a breakfast of stale bread and dried fruit as they rode, and passed around a skin of watered wine. Simon helped her onto the horse and handed up her rations. Then he mounted his stallion and led the way out of the clearing where they'd spent the night.

Diane ate her bread as they rode along, and watched the men who surrounded her. They were silent, alert. Tense. She found it rather conspicuous that she was in the center of a protective circle of horsemen. Simon rode ahead. His bright hair was hidden by a chain mail coif. He always rode in full armor, all the men did. For some reason, this fact took on ominous significance for her this morning. This morning they looked like they expected trouble.

Diane tried to tell herself that she was just being para-noid. Except that after a while she heard the hoofbeats coming up behind them. They were being followed.

"Damn!" The vehement whisper burst out of her on a flash of terror.

Terror that turned to desperate anger a moment later

as Simon turned his head to meet her gaze. His look was full of reassurance, but she saw the worry deep in his eyes. Her anger was for him. The man deserved some peace, some rest. Why couldn't they leave him alone?

And who were *they* anyway?

She left the center of the pack and moved up beside Simon. He didn't look happy to have her company. "Does the whole world have a contract out on you?" she asked.

"What? The world is at war," he went on before she could explain.

"With you, specifically?"

"Unfortunately, yes."

She glanced behind her. "We're being followed."

"We've been followed the whole way."

"Why?"

He quirked a brow at her, though the sardonic gesture was impeded by the mail hood that covered his forehead.

"Stupid question," she agreed. "Why do these people intend to attack you?"

"I'm not sure."

"Why aren't you sure?"

"Because, I don't know which particular enemy is about to catch up with us."

"Oh." He was right, the world was at war with him.

One of Simon's men rode out of the trees ahead of them. He pointed to the way he'd come. "The ground opens up around those boulders yonder. A good place to make a stand."

Simon nodded, then he gave orders to his men. Diane remained silent while Simon organized the horsemen for a battle.

Another scout came up from the rear to report, "I counted no more than fifteen, my lord."

Diane's stomach clenched with tension. Fifteen. Simon had only six men with him. Seven against fifteen. She hated the odds. Simon seemed unconcerned. In fact, his expression was so cold and unreadable he might have been carved from marble.

He asked, "Whose colors do the horsemen wear?"

"France's, my lord."

"How flattering," he drawled. "It seems the king himself will be disappointed at our survival."

The men laughed at his bravado. Diane didn't see anything funny in the situation.

"Couldn't we just run for it?" she asked.

"That's exactly what you're going to do," Simon told her as they reached the clearing. He pointed to the left. "Marbeau is that way. You can be there by sunset."

"I'm not leaving you."

"You'll come to a road. Go west on it."

"I said I'm not going. I can help you."

"Can you use a sword?" His hard expression didn't change. She shook her head. "Can my lady wield a bow?"

"No. But—"

"We don't have time to argue, Diane. My men and I have a better chance of winning this fight if we don't have to worry about protecting a woman. You have a better chance of surviving if you're not here." He stroked two fingers across her cheek, and traced her lips. His soft touch belied the harsh look on his face. "I want you to survive, Diane."

How was she supposed to survive without him? She also had to agree with his logic. She would just get in the way if she stayed. She wanted to do whatever she could to improve Simon de Argent's chances.

"Damn it, Simon."

"I know," he said. He stroked her cheek again. She kissed his gloved palm. "It's hard to part with someone when you don't know if you'll see them again."

"Damn right, it's hard."

"Trust me. We won't be parted long."

She sighed. "Don't get dead."

"My lord!" one of his men called. "They're coming!"

"I won't," he promised. He pointed to her escape route. "Go."

She wheeled her horse and kicked it into a run. She didn't look back, not even when she heard the shouts and the clash of swords.

This was her fault, Diane thought as she put distance between herself and the fighting. She had gotten him into trouble with the King of France. The king had wanted Simon to marry, to make an alliance with France. Instead, Simon had chosen her. He'd chosen love over duty, and he was in trouble because of it.

"It's all my fault," Diane told the horse, and wiped tears off her face. She was very nearly blinded as the tears continued to fall. Her moistened cheeks burned painfully in the cold wind. "If Simon survives," she vowed, "I'll make it up to him somehow. I'll make him happy. I swear to God I'll make him happy. I'll never leave him. I won't let anyone hurt him. Somehow."

She found a dirt track and turned onto it, making a guess about which way was west. The temptation was to go back to Simon's side. She fought it and went on—only to ride straight into a group of warriors watering their horses as she reached a stream.

One of the men grabbed her horse's reins before she could turn and flee.

Another man planted himself in front of her on the narrow path. "Hold! Who are you?"

Diane nearly fainted with reaction as she recognized the man. Since she didn't have the time or luxury for fainting, she threw back her hood and shouted, "Joscelin, Simon's being attacked!"

The young knight peered at her out of narrowed eyes. "Diane?"

"Simon and his men are fighting in a clearing back that way. They're outnumbered two to one by—"

"You can speak?" Joscelin looked stunned, and not a little frightened. His men milled around her as he continued to stare at her.

"I can speak." She leaned forward over the neck of her horse, and spoke, slowly and carefully. "Get going. Your liege lord needs you, Joscelin. Right now."

"It's a miracle."

"Yes," she agreed. "We'll discuss it when you get back."

His face lit with a sudden smile. "You're back! You can speak!"

"Lord Simon," she replied, "needs your strong right arm, fair sir." Joscelin liked that sort of language.

"Of course," he said, with a decisive nod.

He quickly mounted his horse and ordered his men back along the way she'd come. He left one man to guide her to Marbeau. Diane counted eight horsemen, plus some foot soldiers as Joscelin's patrol hurried off.

She just hoped the reinforcements didn't come too late.

"I told you to trust me."

Diane rushed from the warmth of the hearth and into Simon's open arms. She'd been standing by the fire for hours. Not even Jacques had been able to get her to leave the great hall. She knew Simon would come there first when he came home. So, she waited for him there.

When his arms closed around her she was nearly crushed, and she didn't mind a bit. She was holding him as hard and tight as she could. People gathered curiously around them in the hall, but she paid them no mind.

"I'm never letting you out of my sight again," she told him. "Never, ever again." Then she remembered that he'd been in a battle and held him out at arm's length to look at him. "Are you hurt? Are you all right?"

His eyes glittered with merriment. "Do you have boiling water ready?"

"Of course. Where are you wounded?"

"I'm not."

"But you need boiling—"

"I just want a bath, darling."

Diane very nearly collapsed with relief. "Don't scare me like that!"

He drew her to him and put his arm around her shoulders. "Come and help me bathe."

She wanted nothing more than to get him alone, but hesitated and looked around as other men followed Simon into the hall. "The wounded?"

"The dead are in the chapel," he told her, and urged her toward the stairs. "There are no wounded."

"You won?"

"We lost fewer men," he answered. "We're within the protection of my stronghold."

She hated the fact that he was being equivocal. She hated thinking that he'd won one battle, but that he was still at war. She didn't want him to be harm's way ever again. She didn't know what she could do about it, so she relaxed against him and went with him up the stairs to his chamber.

Simon called for a bath as they went, and servants scurried ahead of them to prepare it. A warming blaze roared in the fireplace by the time they arrived. Candles illuminated the room, the bed was turned down, revealing fresh linens. Water soon steamed in the copper tub.

Simon swept Diane into a passionate kiss the moment the door closed behind the servants. Her lips were so sweet, pliant and demanding at once. Her mouth tasted of strong wine that brought him back to life. His weariness faded with the intoxication of her kiss. Her fingers combed through his tangled hair. When they caught in a snarl the slight pain brought him back to himself. He stepped back.

"How can you bear my stench?" he asked her. He unfastened his cloak and let it drop to the floor. His surcoat followed. "Help me with this." Diane assisted him in tugging off the heavy chain mail coat. It chinked and clattered as it joined his outer clothes on the rushes. Diane's fingers then worked nimbly at the ties of the padded shirt that came off next. Beneath that was his linen undertunic, and, finally, bare skin.

Diane didn't stop when she found his flesh. Her hands continued to roam over his chest and back and shoulders. She stroked him from his belly up to his throat and back down again. Her fingers trailed fire. Simon threw his head back and let them roam at will wherever they would. He wasn't quite sure how long it was before she had him completely naked, or how the operation was accomplished. He did know that he no longer craved a bath. All he wanted was her.

She still took him by the hand and led him to the tub. "I want you clean all over," she said with a smile that tantalized and promised all at once.

"Then I'll have you in here with me," he told her as he settled into the herb-scented, wondrously hot water.

She handed him a pot of soap and a washcloth. He used them without paying much attention to what he did while he watched her undress. He was sweating from more than just the near-scalding water by the time she stood unclothed before him. Her youthful flesh looked like it had been coated in honey. He longed to lick her all over, to have the honey-taste of her on his tongue.

Diane loved the way Simon looked at her when she was naked, with an admiration that was close to worship. Not to mention hot-eyed lust. No one had ever made her feel so female, so wanted, and so wanton. Wanton. What a wonderful, medieval word. She said it aloud.

"Wanton."

He held a hand out to her. "So you are. So am I. Come here."

The tub wasn't big. There wasn't really room for both of them. She didn't mind the intimate contact of his wet skin against hers at all as she slid into the water with him. His hard-muscled flesh was slippery with soap. She rubbed against him, then ran her hands over her body. His hands followed where she led.

She cupped water in her palms and spilled it over her breasts and his chest. The wetness and soft soap made their bodies slippery, smooth and slick where they rubbed together. The contact was electric. The tension delicious. The act of washing each other turned into a slow, sensual dance.

When they climbed unsteadily out of the tub, all Simon wanted was to carry Diane to the bed and have her. They dripped water onto the floor as they moved, cool now from their having spent too long at loveplay. Fortunately, warm air circulated in the room from the fireplace. Candlelight danced around them, reminding Simon of the night they'd spent in his tent. That had been a perfect night. This would be another.

"I want to give you beautiful nights," he told her. "To save up memories for when—"

Diane kissed him before he could finish, and he was glad. He had to wrap a cocoon of protection around her, to arrange their time together so that she would come away from it without regrets.

His only regret a few moments later was when Diane moved away from him. He put a hand out to stop her, but she avoided his touch, and went down on her knees before him.

"What's this?" he asked, breathless with his need for her. "Doing homage to your lord at such a time? Come to bed and do me service there. I'll—"

When her lips touched his erection he ran out of words.

A moment later he could manage no more sound than a strangled, "Ah—!"

This was homage indeed, given with her soft lips and flickering tongue. He had never felt anything like this before. He had heard of this erotic practice, but had never before experienced it.

He closed his eyes, and all the world was centered in his groin.

Then she took the entire length of him into her mouth.

"Holy Mother!"

His hips bucked and his hands tangled in her hair as sweet tension built and built in his groin.

Then she pulled away. He wanted to scream.

She yanked him down onto her instead, wrapped her legs around his waist and guided his throbbing member inside her. He roared as need drove him hard and fast, and brought him to a shattering climax. No woman had ever given herself so completely, so freely.

When he collapsed onto her, spent and weary, all he could do was tell her, "I love you," over and over, and then babble nonsense like a youth with his first maiden.

At some point, he thought he promised her the moon, the stars, and all he owned if she'd only stay with him forever and a day.

Much later, they got up, found the bed, and she taught him how to pleasure her in the same way she'd satisfied him.

27

"Christmas in January? You're kidding."

"Joking?" Jacques asked. "No, of course not."

Diane looked down at Simon from where she perched on the edge of his chair. "When did Christmas get to be in January?"

He took a sip of wine, and passed the goblet to her. "When did it get to be at any other time?"

Diane carefully turned the goblet so that she drank from where Simon's lips had touched. It was unsanitary, but she'd learned that this was a very romantic way of showing affection here. She remembered how offended she'd been the first time Simon had tried to share a cup with her. She chuckled at how oblivious she'd been to the flirting signals when he was trying to court her.

"Christmas," she said after she'd taken a sip of wine, "is on December twenty-fifth."

"January sixth," Simon promptly answered.

She touched his shoulder, then played with a shining lock of his hair. The glow from the fireplace made it look like pure gold. "If you say so."

"The question is," Jacques said, from his seat on the other side of the fireplace, "are the two of you going to come out of this room long enough to celebrate the holiday?"

Simon exchanged a look with Diane. She giggled, and he felt himself flush like a lad. "I have been making the occasional appearance in hall," he pointed out to the wizard. "And at fighting practice."

Jacques took a chunk of cheese from the tray Yves held out. He chewed thoughtfully, and all the while eyed them with a teasing glint in his eyes. "As little as possible in the last fifteen days," he said after he'd swallowed. He made a show of looking around. "I don't know what you find so interesting in here."

"It's something you placed in here yourself," Simon told the wizard. Jacques gave a satisfied nod. Simon touched Diane's hand, and they shared a warm smile. "Something so precious, I have to keep it close by and sheltered," he added.

He waved Yves away when the servant offered him the food. The servant turned deferentially to Diane.

"Thanks," she said, and placed slivers of cheese and meat between slices of bread she'd toasted over the fire.

It pleased Simon that Yves smiled at her when she spoke to him. Yves moved back into the shadows after Diane finished making what she called a sandwich. Simon always trusted Yves to be there, waiting to serve. He was a good man. Simon hoped he would be loyal to Diane in the future. For Simon was formulating a plan of setting her up in a small household of her own.

Not that he had mentioned this to Diane yet. He and Diane had talked of little, and much, as the deep days of winter passed. He had tuned his lute, and played and sang to her. She had told him stories. They learned about each other's lives, and he avoided speaking of the future. They had the warmth of the fire and the bed, and each other. They had made love endlessly, and every hour had been precious.

Even though he had invited Jacques to join them for dinner tonight, he resented the old man's intrusion on their idyll. "I suppose you want to have a Christmas feast?"

"Of course." Jacques rubbed his hands together eagerly. "I'm like a child, I know, but I do love parties."

"Me too," Diane declared as she swallowed the last bite of her sandwich. "I love the whole Christmas package— the tree, the presents, the lights and carols."

"What?" Simon and Jacques asked together.

Diane leaned back against the chair as she looked from one blank face to the other. "Okay." Not only was the holiday celebrated on a different date, the customs were obviously different. "I might as well get with the program," she said. "I'll just have to enjoy it however you observe it."

She wasn't sure how she felt about leaving Simon's chamber. She was aware that at least a couple of weeks had passed since they'd gotten back from Paris, but it hadn't seemed like any time at all. She felt safe here. Which was just the way Simon wanted her to feel, she knew. She supposed she should try to make a place for herself. She'd made that vow before, and then backslid into concentrating on loving Simon. His world was part of what he was. She belonged where he was, whether she was wanted by the rest of that world, or not. Time to get out and about again.

"What shall we do first?" she asked.

"A Christmas feast is customary," Simon said. "And visiting church to celebrate the holy days."

Jacques waved his hands with a flourish. "And, a bit of magic from the resident wizard, of course."

"You just like to show off," Simon told him.

"That I do, lad."

The exchange between Simon and the wizard reminded Diane of something that had been bothering her. "When I first came here," she said, "I thought I was in some sort of alternate universe, or something. Some Tolkienesque or Jim Henson sort of land where magic works."

"Of course magic works," Simon answered.

Jacques peered at her curiously. "Do you know the Hynsyns? They're a mighty clan of sorcerers."

"Uh, yeah." Diane decided not to pursue that line of inquiry. "What I'm trying to say, is that my world doesn't have magic. You tell me I'm from your future, but how can that be?"

Jacques stroked his beard. "You don't think your world has magic?"

"Of course not!"

"What makes you say that?"

She thought about it for a moment, while Simon and Jacques watched her. It annoyed her that they seemed amused at her puzzlement. "Listen," she told them. "I don't remember a whole lot of history from school, but I know I did not read accounts of wizard wars along with what kings did in those boring books I studied."

"Of course not," Jacques answered.

"Every great house has a wizard or sorceress allied with it," Simon said.

Diane twisted his hair around her fingers, and tugged. "Then why haven't I heard about it? Why isn't it in the history books? Why didn't I believe in magic until I arrived here?"

"Well, you didn't need to, did you?" Jacques asked.

She gave him a stern look. "That's not an answer."

He pointed a finger at her. "Ah, but it was. We magicians don't like to be talked about, you see. If someone really needs a magician in your time, I'm sure a magician will turn up."

"If you come from the right lineage," Simon added. "Magicians don't work for just anyone."

Jacques's eyes twinkled with merriment. "He's a noble, he would think that way," he said to Diane. Before Simon could comment, he went on, "You won't read about us in any mortal chronicles. We don't allow scribes to scribble down any of our doings."

"Wizards don't like publicity?"

"We like privacy."

"You mean you just magically make people forget about you?"

"About their deeds," Simon clarified.

"Precisely." The old man sat back and folded his hands over his stomach. He looked about as smug as a well-fed cat. Diane expected him to start purring at any moment.

"Speaking of your doings," Simon said, wishing his dinner guest gone, "don't you have a spell you need to be working on?"

"That's *not* a subtle hint, lad."

Simon laughed. "I'm not a subtle man." He gave Diane a meaningful look. "I have my own plans for after the meal."

"Which don't include me." Jacques laughed. "Well, I brought these lonely nights without your company on myself, I suppose."

"That you did," Simon replied. "Did I ever thank you for bringing Diane to me?"

"No."

"And I'm not going to now."

Diane laughed, but the men did not. In fact, a very serious look passed between them. A flash of anger appeared in Simon's eyes for a moment, then was quickly suppressed as he turned a warm smile on her.

"I'm thankful to have you," he said. "But it was still wrong of Jacques to bring you here."

"I'm glad he did," she said. She looked at Jacques. "I thank you. Not for the stupid *geis*, though."

"That was an accident," Jacques reminded her. He stroked his beard thoughtfully. "Or perhaps some interference from Vivienne in the harmless spell I thought I was using."

"She can do that?"

"We throw curses back and forth at each other all the

time. Some work, some don't, some alter the magic we're attempting to perform. It's all part of this wizards' war she and I are fighting."

Simon said, "Good night."

He said it so firmly that Diane knew what he meant was that he didn't want Jacques reminding her that there was trouble waiting outside this little paradise they'd created. Jacques bid them good night, but she didn't let Simon get his way once the wizard had left.

"What's Denis like?" she asked.

Simon stiffened, and pretended he hadn't heard the question. He put his hand around Diane's waist and pulled her down onto his lap. She settled with her breasts pressed against his chest, and put her arms around his neck. He drew her into a lingering kiss while he let his hands roam. Though he felt the peaks of her breasts turn hard with desire, she broke the kiss and looked him squarely in the eyes.

"What's Denis like?" she repeated. "Why do you have to fight him?"

To avoid answering one question, he answered the other. "Denis is like me," he said. "Taller, darker coloring, like his mother, but with features like mine. A fine warrior."

"He must be gorgeous."

"I suppose he'd be called handsome. But he's rash, reckless, and high-tempered. The women like him just the same. They say he has charm. He spreads that *charm* around far too much. I hope Marguerite can tame his randy ways."

Simon put his head back against the back of the chair. He gazed past Diane, into the fire. How odd, he hadn't known he had any thought about Denis's future and here the words spilled out without his knowing they were there.

Diane leaned her head to one side. Her dark eyes were

full of speculation. "Marguerite? Isn't that the kid you were supposed to marry?"

He nodded. He touched Diane's hair, then traced the line of her jaw. "I preferred to make my own choice of partners."

"She's going to be your daughter-in-law? How did this happen?"

Simon sighed, then explained about Vivienne conducting marriage negotiations for his son. "A task that should have been mine," he added bitterly.

"Why not let him make his own choices?"

"Duty comes before choice. It's his duty to make a proper marriage alliance."

"You made a choice," she pointed out. "Me over—what? Safety? Protection from the king?"

He had hoped that she hadn't noticed that his loving her had caused him to make a major diplomatic error. He took her face between his hands. "I would have turned down the king's offer, anyway," he said.

"So, you didn't choose me over Marguerite?"

"Of course I did!" he answered without thinking. She gave him a superior look. "Very well, I concede that point to you."

"Thank you."

"You are the only good thing I have ever known. I love you." He kissed her lips, her cheeks, her temples.

She let him kiss her for a while, then she sat up straight. "Why do you have to fight Denis?"

"Because he's going to fight me," Simon answered. The weight of all the pain he had ever felt was in those words. The loss from every betrayal, the regret of every mistake.

"Why?"

Anger flared at her foolish persistence. He was barely able to keep his voice patient. "I've explained this to you."

"Yeah, yeah, yeah. You're on one side, he's on the other. He's mad because his mother died. He's greedy for

Marbeau. It still doesn't explain why *you* have to fight *him*."

Simon stood abruptly, very nearly letting her drop to the floor in his annoyance. He steadied her before she fell, but turned away when she put her hand out to him. "I have to," he said. "That's all there is to it."

"Why?"

Simon whirled back to her. "Duty," he said. "Honor."

"The code of the West," Diane muttered under her breath. She planted herself between Simon de Argent and the door, just in case the Lord of Marbeau tried to flee from this argument. "Why?" she demanded again. "Do you think that I can't tell that it's tearing you up inside? You don't want to fight him."

His face became an arrogant mask, the expression in his eyes so cold and forbidding that she took a fearful step back. "What I do not want," he told her, each word chiseled out of ice, "is to discuss this further."

She almost let it go. She almost backed down. He was the Lord of Marbeau, master of all he surveyed. He was used to being obeyed. Just because he was used to it, didn't mean it was good for him to always get his own way. For that reason alone, she made herself take a deep breath and stiffen her spine.

"Why do you have to fight this war with your son?"

"I will not discuss it. No woman makes my policy."

"No," she snapped back. "Just a misplaced sense of duty and honor!"

He grabbed her by the shoulders. "Who are you to tell me about duty and honor? You are the one who is misplaced."

"I've noticed that!" she heard herself shout. Something dark and ugly fought to take possession of her. It was months of fear and frustration distilled into pure fury. She struggled out of his grasp. "I don't belong here! Nothing you do makes sense!"

He stepped angrily after her as she backed across the room. His features were transformed by an ugly sneer. "We make sense. You don't even try to understand!"

"I understand that you want to kill your own child," she spat at him. "What kind of savage kills his own child?"

He jabbed his thumb against his chest. "This kind of savage!"

A part of her mind was alarmed at having lost control of the conversation, of herself. A part of her was appalled at the hurtful words she hurled at Simon. The rest of her wanted to strike out as she never had before. All the anger she'd suppressed boiled furiously to the surface.

"You're all crazy!" she shouted at Simon. "Every last one of you! Barbarians! You fight each other because you love hurting people!" He reached out for her, but she batted his hands away. "Keep your hands off me!"

She whirled and ran for the bed, where she buried her face in the pillows and began to sob like the lost child she felt like.

Pain twisted Simon's heart at the sound of her crying. Pain and compassion. He had not seen her like this since her first days at Marbeau. Even her reaction then had not seemed so severe, so heartbroken. And heartbreaking. Of course, he had not been in love with that frightened, confused girl.

"I'm so sorry," he whispered.

Simon knew this was all his fault. He had lashed out at her. He couldn't blame her for striking back. He could tell that the blows had opened up a door to things she kept hidden deep inside herself. It was the closed door to her own world, he supposed. The wonder was that Diane hadn't broken down from reaction to what had been done to her before now. If he had been transported into her time, he thought he would have gone mad instead of adapting the way Diane had.

He was ashamed of himself for what he'd said. She was not at fault because she couldn't understand the principles he lived by. She was from another place, one so different that he barely understood a tenth of the things she told him about it. Besides, she was a woman. She couldn't possibly understand why a man must fight for his honor, even when all else was lost.

She turned on her side when he went to her. She sniffed and wiped away tears before she looked at him. "I'm an idiot."

Simon sat on the edge of the bed. He tentatively stroked her hair. "You are a wonder and delight to me," he told her as gently as he could. "And I am a boor and a fool."

She wiped the back of her hand across her cheek again. "I don't know why I lost it like that. I'm sorry." She sat up.

"You lost nothing but a few tears," he told her. "You'll not miss them. I was the one—"

"Oh, Simon."

He was terrified that she would reject him—because he truly was a barbarian, a savage. He had never felt more relieved in his life than at her loving tone. Except when her arms came around him.

Diane held him tight, and let him hold her. Crying had helped. Being within the circle of Simon's arms helped more. All she had to do to get over this hysterical spell of homesickness was remind herself that if Jacques hadn't brought her to Simon, they never would have met. She would rather live here, like this, than be with anyone else. Tonight they would make love, and rejoice in being together.

But that didn't mean she was giving up on the subject of Denis.

28

She was wearing a new dress. It was deep blue, embroidered all over with silver Chinese dragons. Simon had presented it to her as a Christmas present. Diane loved it, though it bothered her that he'd given an order to the castle women to copy the shawl that hung over the fireplace and work their fingers to the bone on a gift for her. She knew that was how things were done, but it seemed wrong. She was grateful for Simon's thoughtfulness, but she wished she'd done something nice for the women who'd performed the real work of putting the dress together. She wished she had presents for Simon, and Jacques and Joscelin and all the servants who took such good care of them.

She didn't have presents to give, but she'd helped Simon hand out gifts to his retainers at the chapel door before church. That at least made her feel like she was doing something for Christmas. The gifts had been of food and clothing. Simon had started with the lowliest pot scrubbers and midden cleaners and worked his way up the social hierarchy through Jacques, and then herself. She had been delighted with the dress, kissed him in front of a ribald, cheering crowd, and had been impatient for the service to be over with so she could change clothes for the feast.

The little church had been lit with more candles than usual, and the air was full of incense for the special occasion. Father Andre's robes were embroidered in gold, and he'd given a sermon. A long one. She and Simon had held hands throughout the Mass, and given each other fond glances. The priest kept glaring at them as he talked, as if he was afraid they were going to fall to the floor on top of each other in an excess of passion. His sermon had dwelled heavily on Mary's purity and her subservience to the Lord's command. Diane got the feeling that the priest wished she'd stayed holed up in Simon's chamber and the hell out of his church.

And even though he was seated next to her at the feast, Father Andre was doing a very good job of ignoring her.

Now, as Simon sat down on her other side, his chair placed exactly at the center of the high table, she made herself forget about the priest's continuing animosity. She smiled at the man she loved. It didn't matter what anyone else thought as long as she was with Simon.

"You look lovely," he told her.

"Thank you." She gave him a gracious nod. "And you are the handsomest man in the whole world. Great outfit," she added.

Diane was delighted that he wore a blue surcoat embroidered in dragons that matched her new dress. She assumed that there was some significance attached to their wearing the same clothing. She was learning that this was a place full of symbolic gestures and signs and was trying to learn how to read the unwritten cultural language. This time might be barbaric, but it was anything but simple.

Simon gave a self-deprecating smile at her words. He was hardly the most handsome man in the world, or even at Marbeau. Sir Joscelin easily took that honor from him, but he was happy to see Diane's belief in her words shining from her eyes. To her, he was handsome, virile, and strong. For Simon, her belief was enough. She made him feel so alive, so young. So loved.

He sat beside her and took her hand in his. He kissed her palm, and each fingertip. "You are the jewel of Marbeau," he told her. "A lady of amber and onyx and golden pearl."

She laughed. It was so wonderful to hear the sound of her voice.

"What amuses you, my jewel?"

"That," she answered. "You calling me a jewel."

"Why? You are."

"I'm flesh and blood, sweetheart, but my Chinese grandparents are jewel merchants, they deal in precious stones. And since my father is a jeweler, it's all so—symbolic."

Past Diane, Simon heard Father Andre grumble into his winecup, "So his mistress is not only a foreigner and a mountebank, but a merchant's daughter."

Diane blushed at the priest's words, but her hand tightened around his when Simon would have reacted to the rudeness. "Merry Christmas," she said. "Peace on earth. What's for dinner?"

Simon forced himself to sit back in his chair, but he had to feign being relaxed to hide his fury. He hoped the priest passed out from drink before he offered any more insult. Simon waved a wine server forward to keep Andre's cup well-filled. From his own trencher he picked up a piece of pork simmered in dried mushroom sauce.

"Shall I offer you the best of my dish for all to see?" he asked Diane.

She ran a hand lovingly across the embroidery decorating her clothing. "As long as you don't spill anything on my dress," she told him.

"I promise," he said, and held the morsel for her to taste.

He ignored those who looked on as he demonstrated the depth of his regard for his lady, but was aware that Diane was acutely embarrassed by the attention. So he refrained from offering her another bite and they shared the trencher instead, with their heads close together so they could talk quietly above the noise of the feast. A juggler and jongleur from a traveling troupe performed before the head table, but neither he nor Diane paid them any mind.

"Why dragons?" she asked after the first meat course was cleared away.

"Dragons?" he asked as eels in broth were set before them.

She touched her sleeve. "Dragons are your device, right?"

"Nine dragons," he explained. "It is said that the de Argent who built Marbeau had to slay the dragons who dwelt in the nine hills surrounding the fortress. It was a mighty battle that lasted nearly a year and left my ancestor grievously wounded. Poisoned, in fact, and in pain for the rest of his life. It was the price he had to pay to hold his land. Though Jacques tells the tale differently."

"What's Jacques's version?"

"That my ancestor fed them a magical potion. That they are but sleeping, and the poison was some of the potion that he drank accidentally."

"Jacques would go for the magical touch."

Simon nodded. "I suppose he would."

"And what was this ancestor's name?"

He had hoped she wouldn't ask that. "Some say it was Simon," he answered.

She saluted him with the wine goblet. Her eyes glittered brightly above the silver rim. "I thought it might be."

"But some say it was Denis," he added.

"I think I'd rather believe it was Simon. But speaking of Denis," she went on.

He frowned. "We were not speaking of Denis. We are not going to speak of Denis."

"You still haven't convinced me that you have to go to war with him," she relentlessly went on.

This was not the time or place to discuss Denis, war, or why he should need to convince her of anything no matter how much he loved her. He wondered if all women in the future were so persistently opinionated. Their men must not beat them enough, he concluded. Not that he ever thought beating a woman did anyone any good. The men who did it were cowards, and the cowed women found subtle, vicious ways to get revenge.

Perhaps it was better to let Diane speak her mind, but not now. Besides, he didn't want to hear what she had to say. Her words made him think. He'd been sleepless and haunted about things he couldn't change since their last confrontation. He didn't want to think about the future, about possibilities when his way was clearly set.

Simon held hard onto his annoyance and refused to comment on any of these subjects. "You look lovely," he told her. "The garb pleases you?"

Diane didn't want to let it go. She wanted Simon to stop his crazy plan to go to war with his own son. Honor and duty did not cut it. It was stupid. Wasteful. This was also a Christmas party. It was no time to get into a fight.

"It makes me feel downright imperial," she answered.

Or, like the emperor's favorite concubine, she thought as she remembered Father Andre's earlier comment.

Actually, she didn't blame a priest at being upset by her and Simon's relationship. Monitoring the moral rectitude of his flock was his job. The disapproving looks she got from other people at Marbeau did bother her. She was happy to be involved in an affair with Simon, but she couldn't help but notice what the rest of the household thought of her reputation. She hated this communal life, and being the center of attention because she was Simon's lover. Maybe she'd go back to hiding in Simon's room tomorrow. But for now, she concentrated on having the best Christmas she could by Simon's side.

* * *

"A word with you, Diane."

Diane smiled gratefully at the very serious looking Sir Joscelin. "Sure."

The meal was over, the tables had been cleared away below the dais and now the household was involved in a game. It involved an apple, scarves and a great deal of whirling around. Diane could not figure out the rules, though she'd initially enjoyed the whirling around parts. It had felt like dancing in Simon's arms. Simon, however, had moved on to a new partner, and she had been passed along the line to Joscelin. She welcomed the chance to quit the game before she did something stupid.

"In private?" When she hesitated he added, "Upon my honor, I mean no dalliance, dear one."

If Joscelin said he didn't plan to put any moves on her, she believed him. Like Simon, he was a man of honor. She appreciated the whole honor thing, up to a point.

"All right."

"The solar is free. If you can bear the sight of the place where you were so shamed by—"

"Fine." She waved him toward the solar door. "No problem."

His brows knitted with concern. "You're sure?"

If he was so concerned about her psychological well-being, why had he suggested the women's quarters in the first place? She led the way through the crowd. "I'm sure." He followed like a devoted puppy.

Only one rushlight burned near the door of the room when they entered. Joscelin used it to light a few candles while Diane stood in the center of the cold, dark room and tried not to think about Thierry. Once some of the shadows were lifted by the addition of candlelight the place, with its loom, baskets of colored, spun wool and stacks of bedding and cloth didn't seem so sinister to her. The bundles of drying herbs that hung from the ceiling beams even gave the place a comforting, homey aroma. She'd tried spending some time there not long after Simon had kicked Alys out. The women had given her a guarded acceptance, just as they had during the siege. If she was going to be spending her life there, she supposed she should make the effort to get to know them.

She smiled when Joscelin turned back to her. "It's nice here," she told him. "Not a bad place to spend the day, I guess."

He stepped up to her and took a piece of folded cloth from his belt pouch. "This is for you," he said as he held it out to her. "My device, a favor for you to wear when I am your champion," he explained when she unfolded the strip of cloth to find that it was embroidered in a green-and-yellow geometric design. "Normally, it is the lady who gives the man her favor, but I wanted some way to show my devotion to you."

"A Christmas present?"

"If you will have it."

She kissed his cheek. It was freshly shaved, and his skin smelled of oranges and cloves. "Thank you."

"A present, and a promise," he told her. "Lord Simon has asked me to be your protector and succor when he is gone," he explained when she looked at him curiously. "Your service is to him now, I know. I ask nothing for myself, and mean you no disrespect. But there are things that need to be said between us."

"There are?"

He nodded. "I knew not when we would be able to be alone again, since Lord Simon keeps you so close—and rightly so." He put a hand on his breast. "It is his right, and his joy to guard you and keep you closed in a tower while he consummates his autumn with your summer love."

"Right." She had no idea what the man was getting at. Considering his flowery speech pattern it might be weeks before she did figure out what Joscelin was talking about. She tried to speed up the process with a few pertinent questions. "You wanted to talk to me alone. Why?"

"It pleases my heart to know the sound of your voice at last," he went on. "Someday, if I am worthy, I hope to hear endearments spoken to me from your honeyed tongue."

"Honey? Did Yves tell you about what Simon and I did with the honey?"

"I know nothing of servants' gossip." She could tell by the way he blushed that he was lying. "It is just that I think your lips would taste of honey, and be as sweet as your words."

She backed away from him. "Uh huh. I thought you said you weren't going to try anything."

His eyes went round with shock. He held a hand out to her. "Please do not misunderstand me. While Lord Simon lives, you are his lady. I will worship from afar until my time is come."

There was something rather unpleasant about what he had just said. Diane struggled to interpret the words, and a chill ran down her spine. "What do you mean, *while* he is alive?"

"Fear not, you have many weeks yet."

"I do?"

"And all is taken care of for after."

"After what?"

Joscelin nodded thoughtfully. "I see I was right to ask to speak with you. Lord Simon loves you too much to prepare you, but it must be done. I will take the duty of this burden for him. And gladly, dear Diane, though it causes me pain to speak of what must be spoken."

Diane put her hands on her hips. Hands that were balled into fists. She wanted to tell him that it was going to cost him even more pain if he didn't say something that made sense pretty soon, but she restrained her terrified impatience.

She spoke to him gently instead. "Please, tell me, good knight, what both of us are loathe to hear." *Before I strangle you with my bare hands*, she added to herself.

He bent his head sadly. "Lord Simon is most valiant in war. But, alas, too many are ranged against him for him to prevail."

"The odds are against him?" she interpreted.

Joscelin nodded.

Diane's heart twisted with pain. Her voice was rough with nerves as she said, "You think he's going to lose."

That couldn't be true! She'd seen the man fight. He was good. Damn good. But if the odds were a hundred to one against—

"It is not what I think that matters, dear Diane, but what Lord Simon says will come to pass."

"Simon?"

"When the time comes, he has asked me to care for you." Joscelin raised his gaze to hers. The look in his eyes was fervent. "I will gladly be your champion, though it means I will not be at his side when he goes into his last battle. I will make you my wife, if you wish it. I would do so even if Lord Simon did not offer a dowry worthy of a royal lady for your hand."

Diane barely heard his last words. She concentrated on the most important thing Joscelin had said.

Simon was going to die. He was resigned to it. Prepared for it. Looking forward to it?

"I hope so," she muttered under her breath. "Because I'm going to kill him."

"What?"

The door opened and Simon stepped in before she could answer Joscelin. "What are you doing in here?" the Lord of Marbeau demanded suspiciously as he looked at both of them.

Diane ignored him for a moment. She was icy cold with fury as she turned to Joscelin. She tucked the strip of cloth into her belt. "Thank you for the Christmas present, Joscelin. And the information." He gave her a slight nod.

His eyes darted between her and Simon. "If I have given offense—"

"On the contrary, you've been most helpful. Could you leave us alone, please?"

"Of course." He sidled past Simon, and was gone.

Diane closed the door behind him. She turned to Simon. He looked anxious.

"Diane?"

She smiled. She felt like her face was going to crack, because it was a smile made out of absolute zero ice. She had heard the expression coldly angry, but now she understood it. Simon reached for her. She put up a hand to keep him away.

"You are going to be sorry," she told him as she took a step away from the door.

"Sorry about what, my love?"

"Sorry that I ever got my voice back, you using, manipulating, son-of-a-bitch!"

29

"What do you plan to do, throw the fight?"

Simon didn't know what her words meant, but he had his suspicions about what Joscelin had been telling her. There was only one subject he could think of that might make her use such an imprudent tone.

"Was he speaking of the future?"

"It's about time somebody did."

Simon considered throttling Joscelin, but he needed the well-meaning lad too much to do any such thing. "What did he say?"

"He told me about . . . your . . . "

He saw her struggle with words she didn't want to think about. He didn't want to think about them either, but she had brought the subject up. He supposed it was time it was out in the open.

"Death," he supplied for her. "Demise." He added brutally, "Did Joscelin describe to you how my lifeless body would be devoured by carrion fowl while my son marches triumphantly into my stronghold?" He shook his head. "No, he's too discreet to lay out the grisly reality of what is going to happen."

She had gone from pale with anger to sickeningly white with shock as he spoke. She put her hand to her mouth as though she were nauseated, then she recovered, and pointed out, "At least he was willing to tell me a cleaned-up version of the truth. You didn't want me to know anything, did you?"

"No," he agreed. "I did not. Not until you had to know."

She crossed her arms beneath her breasts and hugged herself tightly. "Why?"

His heart went out to her, but he kept his hands at his sides. "How could I tell you? You don't understand. You can't."

"Why?" she repeated.

"Why do you keep asking me why?"

Her voice was still dead cold, but she was crying. "Because I want to understand. If you're going to die, I need to know why."

"You keep asking me why. There is no why," he answered tiredly. "There is only honor."

"Bullshit."

Her crude dismissal of all he stood for made him furious. "You don't even want to understand."

"I understand that you're stubborn, and blind, and arrogant, and totally committed to acting like an idiot. You don't have to fight your son."

He didn't want to go over this ground again. He might have walked out if she hadn't been standing between him and the door. She looked as fragile as glass. He feared she might shatter if he tried to move her aside. Besides, he didn't really want to walk away. He feared that if he did, a silence much worse than a curse would descend between them.

He told her, "If wanting what is best for you is arrogant, then I am guilty of that sin."

"You *decided* what was best for me. You don't have that right."

"Yes, I do."

"Because you're Lord of Marbeau?"

"Yes."

"Because I'm your mistress? Your chattel? Just another piece of property to dispose of as you see fit? What did you do? Put me in your will?" she asked mockingly. "To Sir Joscelin," she continued in a high-pitched voice, "I leave my left-over girlfriend—to do with as he sees fit," she added in her normal voice, but bitter.

"You are my mistress, and my property," he said, though he knew she hated hearing the truth. "What is the matter with that? You are the most precious thing I possess."

"You do not possess me."

"I—" He ran his hands through his hair in frustration. "I do not understand your attitude."

She made a sharp gesture. "I don't care if Jacques gave me to you as a present. Nobody owns me."

"My son will own you if I don't provide for you." Simon hated revealing just what her future could hold. He hated the bruised look that came into her eyes as he spoke. "He, or all his men. You'll be passed around for their pleasure if you are here when they ride in to Marbeau. No one but I— or Joscelin—would ever think to ask you yay or nay about when or how you are bedded. Do you want my son to make you into a whore?"

"Isn't that what you've already done?" she fired back.

"You are my *leman*," he said. "My *midons*." Whatever language it was they shared, these terms didn't translate. He could tell that she did not understand. "Concubine," he tried. "My heart and soul. There is no dishonor for a woman to be kept by one who adores her."

"Whore," she repeated. "Slut. Property to be passed on." She turned away from him. "How did I let this happen?"

Diane remembered the looks, the comments, the animosity from everyone around her but Simon, and felt that she deserved them. The attitudes of Simon's people grated and ground into her conscience. She'd been a toy from the beginning, and she'd let herself become even more of one. Because she loved him, the position she was in now seemed inevitable. Looked at objectively, her actions were not necessarily praiseworthy. She was totally dependent on a man, and gave her body to him as the price of his protection. That was being a whore.

"Love should not make someone dependent," she said.

He came up behind her, and put his hands gently on her shoulders. "You are not dependent because you love me. Never think that."

It was hard to think when he was touching her. He didn't try to draw her back when she moved away.

She found herself standing by the loom, studying the half-woven pattern someone had left to work on her fancy dress. At Simon's command. Everything was at Simon's command.

He hadn't commanded her to love him.

All right, she loved him, and gave freely. She didn't want to be with anyone else, but that didn't change the truth that she needed Simon to love her. Not just for her safety, but for her soul's sake. She hadn't been whole until they'd met. Even if he didn't think that his loving her made them equals.

"I'm beginning to feel sorry for Alys," she said. "Or at least understand her place in this world." She turned back to Simon and asked mockingly. "Do I make an adequate replacement, my lord?"

His face had assumed the indifferent mask he protected himself with, which was how she knew she'd wounded him with her words. "You are not her replacement."

She hugged herself again. "I might as well be."

"I don't know why you would think so."

"Because I'm not a permanent part of your life," she told him. "Alys was a diversion. A dalliance, I think you'd say."

"That," he admitted, "is true. To my shame. A diversion and policy. Nothing more."

She looked at him for a long time before she spoke. She saw the pain and confusion in his eyes, though his hawk-sharp features were frighteningly unreadable. She knew how vulnerable this man really was. How loving and good, but he was also wrong. Maybe he wasn't, not in his world-view, but she wasn't up to adapting to that view. Diane only knew that the relationship they had, the love they felt was so good and right, was based on something terribly wrong.

"I'm nothing more to you than a diversion," she said.

He shook his head. "How can you say that? My heart was dead before I met you. You've given me everything to—"

"Live for?" she interrupted. "But you still plan to die." He turned his head sharply away, as though her words had struck him like a blow. "I don't think life, love, mean anything to you," she went on. "I'm just one last fling for Simon de Argent before he gets on his big black horse and rides off to one final, glorious, suicidal battle."

He took a long, tense breath. He sounded as though he were in pain. "Suicide is a sin."

"But that's what you have planned."

"Not exactly."

"You can't kill your son. You won't abandon your loyalty to King Henry. So you'll go to war with Denis, and you won't be coming home."

"You know me very well."

She wiped away tears. "All I know is that you won't be coming home to me."

"No," he said through gritted teeth. "I won't."

Diane couldn't take her gaze off his suddenly ravaged face. She saw his vulnerability, and wanted to hold him, comfort him, apologize for hurting him. She wanted to tell him that the truth had nothing to do with her continued anger, even though she was furious. She wanted to explain that the truth had to be confronted, not hidden. To tell him that she was as angry at herself for willfully not seeing the flaws, the futility, the impermanence of their love before, as she was at him. She was angry at him, but it was hard to be blindly antagonistic to a medieval man for having a medieval attitude. Hard, but not impossible.

What she said was, "You have no plans for forever with me." It sounded petty, and stupid, somehow, against his determination to make a noble sacrifice. She just didn't understand how this sacrifice was worth it. "I can see how some wars are worth fighting, but this is a family quarrel—between Henry and his kid, between you and yours. I can see why you won't kill your child. I love you because you love him so much."

"He doesn't think so."

"He's an idiot. Why don't you just beat the shit out of him and drag him home? He's only seventeen!"

"He is a belted knight, with a hired army, a mighty sorceress, the support of Prince Henry and King Louis. There is no way out of this battle, Diane."

"You could just refuse to fight!"

"And Marbeau will still be overrun by some army or another. If Denis defeats me, the land is his. If someone else does the job, the de Argent lands go to the man who plants his troops in my family's fortress. I will not let the Dragon banner of the de Argents fall into alien hands. The dragons wouldn't like it," he added with a twisted, wry smile.

"Good for the dragons," she grumbled.

"Whatever happens," he went on determinedly, "you will not be here. You will be safe and wellcared for."

"No! I'm going to be with you. Dead or alive, we face it together."

"No!"

"Yes! Forever."

He was at her side in an instant. His hands closed around her upper arms as he towered over her. "If I could give you forever—"

"You could, but you won't."

He shook her. "How can I?"

"Think of a way." She pushed at his chest. "Let me help you think of a way. We could build a life together."

"There is no way out of this, Diane!" He drew her to him and kissed her. It was a hard, demanding, possessive kiss. And she answered it in kind. She clung to him, and clawed at him, and tried to draw him so close that they blended into one being. She could feel his racing heart and the thunder of blood in his veins. It was all a part of her. She was a part of him. She knew he tasted her tears as they kissed, bittersweet on his tongue, just as they were on hers.

"I love you," he told her when he drew his lips from hers. "With all my being."

"I know," she answered, holding him, and being held. "I know. And with all mine."

"But—"

"Please, Simon."

He stepped away. Then Simon stepped close again. He looked so weary. He stroked her hair, and cupped her face in his big, competent, gentle, warrior's hands. "Let us make the most—the world—out of the time we have. Let us make history together, legend, memories sweeter than the rest of our lives. Let us be together now, and forget what was and what will be."

The words were beautiful. Sincere.

Ridiculous.

"We'll always have Paris," she said, with as much sarcasm as her devastated emotions could dredge up. "Is that it?"

His expression softened. "Paris? Yes, that is truly where it all began for us."

Diane freed herself from his gentle touch. "That wasn't what I was talking about."

He blinked thoughtfully. "Ah," he said after a moment. "The story of Rick and Ilsa and Casablanca."

"Yes."

"I think I see what you mean." He put his arms around her once more. "How our tale is like theirs. Perhaps that is why I am so fond of the story."

She rested her forehead wearily on his broad chest. She felt so protected in his embrace. It was a feeling she tried hard to fight, and lost. "We're not like them," she said. "They weren't real."

"But the tale holds many truths about the sanctity of duty and honor. Truth has nothing to do with whether the people in the story lived or died."

"But we're not people in a movie. The screen isn't going to fade to black on the audience when our story's done. We're just going to be dead." She sighed heavily. "I don't want to live my life as entertainment for the ages."

He stroked her hair, and massaged her aching temples with his thumbs. "Would you not rather be remembered by the ages?" he asked. "To have the troubadours sing of our love through all time?"

"No." The word came out as a childish whine. She didn't care.

"Nor I."

She looked up to see that his amber eyes held at least a glint of humor. It forced a tiny smile from her as well. "At least you're not a completely romantic idiot."

"We are like them, though," he went on once he had caught her gaze with his own.

"How?"

"We have had, are having, an interlude with each other that we will remember all our lives. We will always have Paris. And, right now. I will cherish every moment I have with you for as long as I live."

Which won't be very much longer, she thought. She said, "I don't want just an interlude."

He ignored her protest. "And, like Rick, I must make the decision about our parting. It's not the decision I want to make, but honor requires it."

She was filled with a fresh burst of anger. Fresh tears threatened as well, but she wasn't going to let him see them.

"Screw honor!" She pulled away from him. She stalked toward the door. She heard him behind her, but didn't turn. "Screw you," she snarled. "And screw me, too!"

She would have slammed the door in his face, but it was too heavy to slam. So she pulled it shut behind her and plunged into the crowd still celebrating in the great hall.

"This is one hell of a Christmas," she muttered as she made her way toward the tower stairs.

It didn't help that she was half-blinded by tears, though she was glad that the room was dim and smoky. She didn't want anyone to notice her. She didn't want to run into a solicitous Joscelin, or a jovial Jacques. She was afraid of what she might do if she encountered either of those well-meaning men.

Instead, she encountered the priest. Just as she got to the stairs, Father Andre stepped in front of her. His face was red from drink. He wove from side to side in front of her. He reminded her of a drunken cobra. Diane tried to step past him.

He held a silver goblet up before her. "Peace, my daughter." His words were slurred, and his smile was lopsided.

What amazed Diane was that he was smiling at her. She wasn't sure what to make of his sudden friendliness. "Merry Christmas," she told him, and tried once more to escape up the stairs, but he wouldn't let her by.

He put a sweaty hand on her arm. "I want there to be peace between us, my child."

"Good," she said. "I'm glad. Excuse me." She tried stepping to the left.

He blocked her way. "Drink a cup of peace with me. Please." He urged the goblet into her hands.

Diane looked from the dark wine that filled the goblet nearly to the rim, then at the bright-eyed, smiling priest. This man was a stranger to her, one that had shown her animosity since she was thrust into this world. It was Christmas, he was a man of God, he was making a symbolic gesture of peace in a place where symbolism was important. Diane thought it was time she made a place among these people. It might help her find some solution, some way to keep Simon from dying for Marbeau if she could get the people of the stronghold as her allies.

"A toast," she agreed. As he avidly watched her she lifted the goblet to her lips. "To peace."

He made a cross with his thumb on her forehead while she drank. "May your soul be at rest, my child."

The wine was scented with almonds, and tasted bitter, but she took a long, deep drink to prove her good faith. It took more fortitude not to gag as she handed the half-empty cup back to the priest. She glanced around, and saw the crowd parting behind her as Simon strode purposefully toward her.

"Diane," he called.

Her head hurt. She didn't want to talk any more. "Excuse me, Father." This time she was able to get around the priest. She lifted her skirts and started up the stairs.

The world blurred within a few steps. Not tears, but dizziness, blinded her. She stumbled and fell forward. The stone was slippery beneath her hands, the stench of the smoke gathered in the air choked her. Her stomach twisted in pain. She looked up as hands touched her, but it was too dark for her to make out the face or form she knew was beside her.

"Simon?" Her voice was a weak rasp. Pain engulfed

her. It hurt too much to scream. Arms came around her, lifted her.

"Jacques!"

Simon's desperate cry tore through her head. She heard him breathing heavily, and cursing fate, and priests, and plots, as they rose higher and higher. It felt like he was running up the stairs with her. She couldn't tell. She didn't care. She was in his arms as the world slowly shut down around her. Being in his arms was all that mattered, even if she was dying.

30

"This is all your fault, old man."

"Odd. I thought it was Andre who poisoned her."

One voice was full of fear and fury. The other was cool, concerned and amused all at once. They floated in the air above her, heard but unseen. The world around her was dark. She was suspended somewhere between life and death, she knew that much. Awake but also asleep. Aware but unable to respond. She was comfortable. She didn't want to respond. She was resting. Resting comfortably. Comforted, also, since one of the voices belonged to someone she loved. The other belonged to someone she trusted, though she wasn't quite sure why she trusted him.

"What was that fool priest thinking of, Simon?"

"I've had him asked. Unfortunately, he confessed all before Joscelin could beat it out of him. The lad was looking forward to torture, and so was I."

She gave a mental tsk at his wild words, though she rather liked it when he was bloodthirsty on her behalf. She should be ashamed of herself.

"Why did he do it?"

"Politics, of course. And pure hatred of anyone who looks the least bit different."

"Yes, but priests don't usually do their own killing."

"He did it with the Church's blessing, at the Church's command. He did it to save my soul from the pagan temptress."

"Pagans don't generally take communion."

"Andre cared nothing for proof. To him, she's never been more than a soulless animal. That made him a perfect tool. Father Raymond sent him the poison, along with a letter offering me the marriage alliance again." He gave a harsh laugh. "The letter was to be delivered once I'd come to my senses."

"They assumed that her death would have broken the spell binding you to her, I suppose."

"So Andre said."

"Fool. What have you done with him? He isn't dead, is he?"

"Locked up. He claims only the Church can try him."

"Unfortunate, but true."

"Not that I care. I told him I'd be happy to execute him without waiting for a trial."

"But you think you might have a use for him."

"Perhaps. Will she live?"

"Perhaps."

"Damn it, Jacques!"

"Probably. I'm working on it. I have to use deep magic for such strong poison."

"See that she lives."

"Or what? You'll execute me?"

"It is all your fault."

"So you've said."

"It's not your fault that I fell into your trap," Simon went on.

"I thought you fell in love."

"The worst trap of all, my friend."

Diane tried, and failed, to rouse herself at these words. Not because of what Simon said, but because he sounded so sad, so resigned, when he said them. It's not so bad, she thought, if only you'd let yourself hope.

"Hope," Simon said, as though he'd read her mind. "She's given me the one thing I can't afford to have. It's like a gift of gold to a man who's taken a vow of poverty. What the devil am I supposed to do with it?"

"Well," Jacques drawled lazily. She could imagine him stroking his beard. "The monk would give this gold to the poor. That's the thing about hope, you can do some good with it."

Simon's laugh was harsh and cutting. "How?"

"That's for you to work out, my boy."

"That's your problem, you set events in motion then sit back and wait. Wait for what this time? I was already caught in one trap, why did you have to set another one?"

"Why did you have to take the bait?"

Diane resented being referred to as bait, and made a note to talk to Jacques about it when—if—she woke up. She could hear Simon pacing from one side of the room to the other. He paused in his restless meandering only long enough to stroke her hair before moving on.

"I tried not to fall in love," Simon said from the other side of the room. "It happened so gradually that all my defenses slowly melted away. She makes me happy, Jacques. I've never been happy before."

"I know."

"I wish I'd never known what happiness feels like."

"Why?" Jacques asked the question, but Diane thought it as well.

"I was resigned to my fate. Not looking forward to it as you seemed to think. As Diane seems to think, as well. I knew that I had no future. Now I want one. I want a lifetime with the woman I love. I want her to have my children."

Me too, she thought.

"To grow old together."

Sounds good to me.

"I want more than the diversion you gave me for my last days. I feel my days running out like sand through a glass and I want them back. I want more than the life I've had. More than duty and responsibility. I would start over if there was a way."

"I want more for you, too, Simon," Jacques told him. "And for Diane. I wasn't using her casually when I brought her to you."

That's good to know, she thought.

"Oh?" Simon asked.

"I searched time for the one woman who could save you from yourself. The one woman who would love you enough to want to. Of course, in the end, I suppose only you can do that, but Diane can help."

"Not if she dies. Not if people keep trying to kill her. And they would, even if I abandoned Marbeau and ran off with her. There's no place for her in our world."

"She might be willing to try."

"For my sake."

"For the sake of what you have together," Jacques said for her.

Simon sighed. "I would slay dragons for her, if I could."

"But you aren't willing to change for her."

I don't want him to change. I like him fine as he is, but breathing.

"I can't!" Simon gave a deep, rumbling chuckle. "Though if I think of something I'll let you know."

"Now, there's a hopeful sign. You're actually thinking about thinking."

"And this thinking has gotten me to wondering about something, old man."

"I don't like that suspicious look in your eye, lad."

"Nor should you. Because what I'm wondering is why I never thought of what I'm considering at the moment before."

"And what is it you're considering?"

"Something obvious. Something I should have thought of long ago. The one practical way to protect Diane after I'm gone. The only way to protect her. The best thing for her. The simple solution."

"Yes?" Jacques questioned.

Diane listened eagerly. Just what was this simple solution?

"Send her home."

"Home?" Jacques asked. "I think he considers where you are to be home."

Yeah, she thought.

Simon touched her again. She felt him play with her hair. She wanted to reach up and put her hand over his, but she couldn't move. She just continued to float, aware but cut off. It was almost as bad as when she couldn't talk, except that the floating felt good. She wondered just what sort of magic Jacques was using to create this almost euphoric condition. And, she wished he'd stop it.

"And where she is is home to me," Simon said. "But where she belongs is far in the future. Surely, you can send her there."

"Can I?"

The false innocence in Jacques voice made her smile, at least to herself. *Can he?* she wondered.

"You brought her here. There must be a spell to send her back."

But she didn't want to go back!

"Do you think so?"

"What I think is that you prevented me from even considering the possibility. That you used magic to cloud my mind, to hide the thought from me."

Jacques cleared his throat. Guiltily, Diane thought. "If I did, it seems the spell has worn off."

"And not a moment too soon. Can you send her home?"

"Do you really want her to leave you?"

Simon didn't answer for a while. His voice was rough when he did. "Of course not. There's no other choice. Can you send her back to the future?"

A sigh. "Possibly."

"Possibly? You don't know?"

Jacques hesitated for a long time before he answered. "I haven't considered sending anyone back. You know I have to think about something a while before I can begin conjuring."

"Then start thinking about it."

"I can't."

There was pure steel in Simon's commanding voice. "The devil you can't."

"I wish you wouldn't mention the devil just now, Simon, not with all the magic loose in the room. You never know who might show up if you call on them fervently enough."

Simon gave a disgruntled snort. "Don't try to distract me with such nonsense. I want you to work on the spell to send Diane back to her own time."

"Dead or alive?" Jacques's tone was harsh, a touch angry.

"What?"

"I can do one thing at a time. Right now I'm trying to save her life. Even as we speak, I am conjuring. If you want me to change the spell into a time travel one right now, I suppose I could. But she'd still be dying from poison when she got there."

Oh, she thought. *In that case—*

"Do it later, then," Simon said.

Don't listen to him, Jacques, she thought. She didn't intend to go anywhere, except maybe to sleep. She was so weary. The dark was so comfortable.

"Go away, lad," Jacques continued, more calmly, as Diane's consciousness drifted slowly away from the conversation. "Get some rest. Let me work."

Rest, she thought. Yes. Wonderful, wonderful, rest. That would be lovely.

* * *

"I'm not going anywhere."

"Of course you're not," Simon said. He tucked the fur blanket close around Diane's chin. "You're too weak to go anywhere." He smiled. It was like the sun coming out from behind dark clouds. "Welcome back to the land of the living." He bent close and kissed her forehead. A strand of his gold hair tickled her cheek. "And glad I am to have you here."

She was lying on her back, her head propped up by lots of pillows, in the middle of his comfortable bed. She felt like she'd been asleep for ages. The only thing she remembered when she opened her eyes to find Simon carefully watching her was Jacques and Simon's conversation. She was certain she hadn't dreamed it. She just couldn't remember how she came to overhear it in the first place. She must have been ill, but the details escaped her. She wondered what day it was. She noticed that Simon had several days' growth of beard. He'd been clean-shaven for the Christmas feast when last she'd seen him.

"I won't go away," she said.

"You won't have to. Not for a while yet." He smiled reassuringly, and cupped her cheek in his palm.

She dragged her hand out from under the heavy covers and clasped Simon's wrist. "You don't understand."

Her voice sounded weak in her ears. She felt weak, too weak to throw the covers off and grab the man and shake him. She felt too weak to talk much, really, but after all the time she'd spent voiceless she wasn't going to let a little physical debilitation keep her from speaking. Besides, she felt the desperate rush of time passing. She had a feeling she'd been sick for quite a while. The light coming in through the oiled skin that covered the window seemed stronger, closer to spring sunlight.

Soon, she knew, it would be too late to talk to Simon anymore. "I'm not going anywhere," she repeated. "Not back to my own time. Not away somewhere with Joscelin. I'm staying with you."

Simon had heard her repeat these words over and over for the last five days while he sat by her bedside. She said them so many times, it was a litany that he'd almost come to believe himself. He was happy to hear her say them while she looked at him. He didn't even care that there was stern stubbornness in that look. He loved her in any mood she cared to show him, as long as she was alive, awake, and on the mend.

He'd been frantically worried. He'd spent much of that time on his knees, praying for her life. He'd spent all of the time hoping. He'd spent some of it thinking. Before Diane had confronted him on Christmas he hadn't thought there was anything left for him to think about. His plans were made. He was unhappy about his course, but certain of it.

Then, he watched her nearly die. Nearly lost her. Not for the first time, but this crisis had been different. There had been no instant response he could make, no threat to her that he could vanquish with a sword or a lordly command. Her illness had shaken him like nothing had before. Shaken him out of his complacency as he had to helplessly watch and wait and hope.

Hope was turning into a habit with him. As was thinking and planning. His thoughts kept racing off in ridiculous directions, trying out schemes and fantastical possibilities. He felt like he was a character in one of her heroic tales, one whose duty it was to save the heroine, retrieve the treasure, defeat the Nazis, and get out alive. He felt wonderful.

Or, at least he had when she'd opened her eyes and looked at him a few moments before. He'd been waiting for the reward of that instant for days. It was a look of love and trust that made him feel like he could do all those things as long as she was at his side.

Rational as he tried to be, the wonder wouldn't fade, it

lit his heart, warmed him like no hearthfire could ever manage. This was what it felt like to be truly alive! All because this woman had come into his world, and changed him forever.

He didn't think he dared to tell her it was too late for change, for hope, for taking chances. She'd probably shout at him, or try, since she was weak as a kitten and could barely speak above a whisper. Besides, there was some small chance that she was right.

Simon walked away from the bed and sat down at his desk. He set out quill, inkstone, and parchment as he said to Yves, "Have Father Andre brought to me." He felt Diane's curious gaze on him while he wrote. He knew it was a measure of how truly weak she still was when she didn't even try to get out of bed to see what he was about.

He was sanding the wet ink when Joscelin pushed the disheveled priest through the door ahead of him. Days spent locked away in the dark had left Andre filthy, gaunt, and pale. Simon was not unhappy to see him that way. Or to note that Andre quaked with fear when he was brought to stand before the table. Father Andre's gaze darted, once, toward Diane in her nest of pillows and furs, then he looked down as Simon rose to his feet.

"I've made up my mind what to do with you," Simon told the assassin as he came around the table.

Andre's voice shook when he spoke. "You dare not kill me. It is a great sin to kill a priest."

He grasped the man's chin, and forced Andre's head up. When they were looking eye to eye, he said, "You know a great deal about the sin of killing." He was very tempted to shift his hold and strangle the man for what he'd done to Diane. Unfortunately, he had a better use for him. He stepped back and held the message out to the priest. "Take this."

After a short hesitation, Andre snatched the folded parchment. He turned it over in his hands, and ran his fingers over the still warm wax seal. "What is this? What do I do with it?"

"What it is is no affair of yours. What I want you to do is deliver it."

The priest managed to look even more terrified. "To Father Raymond?"

Simon laughed. "You failed him. I don't think you want to experience the penance he'd demand for your failure."

Andre bent his head again. His shoulders slumped. "That is true." He glanced back up, furtively this time. "Where is it you want me to take this?"

"Somewhere where you'll be sure to find protection, a rat hole I can trust you to run to. That would be in the camp of my greatest enemy, of course. Somewhere where you'll be greeted as a trusted old friend. The message is for my son," Simon concluded.

The man's look went from furtive and fearful to speculative. "And what does this message say?"

Simon had no intention of answering any questions. "Take him away," he told Joscelin. "Fit him out for the journey, give him a good horse and set him on his way."

He had no intentions of answering Diane's questions once the men were gone, either. He had set a new thing in motion. He had a plan. He wasn't in the mood to discuss it. Especially not when he wasn't sure if it was going to work. He might have learned to hope, but he still wasn't certain of his luck. It had rarely been good before.

"I have to have a long talk with Jacques," he said. He hurried toward the door before Diane's imploring look could call him back.

It was going to be a long, detailed talk, then Simon was going to leave Jacques alone. The wizard was going to have a great deal of thinking to do to prepare the spell Simon wanted, and not much time to do it in.

31

"*So you actually talk to people* on the other side of the world using this fishing net?"

"Internet. It's a communication network that links computers together. It's really very simple. All you need's a modem and— Actually, it's very complicated, but if you have a user friendly front end program you can access the Web and—" She sighed, and stroked his face. "It doesn't make any sense to me either, darling, I just know how to log on and use it."

"Log? Web? Are there spiders and woodcutters involved with this fishing net?" Far from looking as confused as he sounded, there was a teasing light in Simon's eyes.

Diane chuckled, and snuggled closer beside him in the big bed. He had woken her up only a few minutes before, with first a kiss, then a question. The heavy curtains were drawn across the bed, the only light was from a thick tallow candle on a shelf over their heads. She had no idea what time it was, and didn't really care. Time wasn't important when she was with Simon— except that it was racing away. She tried not to think about that.

So she answered his question with one of her own. "Why do you want to know about computers anyway?"

He put an arm around her shoulder. She rested her

head on his heart and looked up at him through his fuzzy blond chest hair. The angle and the shadows highlighted the imperious arch of his nose and the delectable line of his lips. The contrast fascinated her.

"Because you said that they are important. Power comes from knowing what is important to others."

"I thought power came from having the biggest sword." She inched her hand up his thigh.

"Computers. Swords. Each can be used as a tool of power in the right place and time. Is that not true, my lady fair?"

"Remind me to introduce you to Bill Gates."

"I shall make a note of it. Get your hand off my sword, woman, I'm not ready to be distracted just yet."

"It's a nice, big, sword," she crooned.

He laughed, and moved her fingers away from his groin. "And will get larger soon, I assure you. Now, explain to me once again about credit cards."

"You're just trying to get me used to the idea of going home, aren't you?"

"And you are trying to seduce me into letting you stay."

There was a sulking pout on Diane's lips. Simon leaned down and kissed it away. "It is a long journey," he told her. "One should be prepared for what is at the end of it."

"Grasshopper," she muttered. When he narrowed his eyes questioningly, she said, "You've been talking like the old monk on *Kung-Fu* a lot lately. *Not* a popular show in my neighborhood," she added.

Which, of course, explained nothing.

Simon had constantly asked her questions for the last six days. Every time she told him she wasn't going back to the twentieth century, he came up with some other query about it. Though she knew her explanations frustrated more than enlightened him, he showed no inclination to give up. Despite knowing that these talks were in preparation for the trip she had no intention of taking, she enjoyed the conversations. At first, they'd helped her ignore how bad she felt, then they relieved the boredom as she recovered her strength.

She felt much better now. So much better that just sharing the bed with him wasn't enough any more. She wanted him.

"No more talk," she said as she draped her arms around his neck. "Kiss me."

He touched the tip of her nose. "Wanton woman," he said. And did.

Their tongues twined, and her nipples grew hard as he touched her breast. He turned her onto her back. She ran her bare foot up his hard-muscled calf.

Metal rings scraped loudly against the overhead pole as the bedcurtain was pushed aside. Daylight and cold air rushed in. Diane gasped in alarm. Simon sprang up, a dagger snatched from under a pillow grasped in his hand.

"Hold!" Jacques shouted as he jumped out of his naked friend's way. "You're a bit skittish this morning, aren't you?" he added as Simon grabbed hold of a bedpost to halt his aggressive leap from the bed.

Simon glared up at him. "You could have been gutted!"

Jacques folded his hands over his stomach. "Nonsense. I trust your reflexes." He quickly glanced over the naked, flushed pair. The very air between them crackled with desire. "I can certainly see why you might be a bit annoyed at the interruption."

Simon pulled on a robe from the end of the bed. His eyes glittered angrily at Jacques, like a hawk who'd been deprived of its prey. He did lean over and put the blade back in its hiding place, for which the wizard was relieved.

"Ever the master of understatement," Simon said as he stood.

Diane sat up, and pulled the covers up around her chin with a disgruntled air. "Your timing's terrible, Jacques."

"Let's hope not, my dear. For all our sakes," he answered, then ignored her puzzled look and turned his attention to Simon. Jacques took a folded square of vellum from his sleeve. "You said you wanted to see this the moment it arrived."

Simon looked at the message in Jacques's hand, but hesitated to take it. He was almost frozen by a combination of dread and excitement. Everything depended on the words written on that paper. He glanced at Diane. She looked back, dark eyes full of curiosity. He wanted to ask her for encouragement, but she had no notion of what he planned. He had no intention of telling her, either, though he knew his habit of command without question was a deep, sore spot with her. Some things he was too old to change.

But not others. He took a deep breath, and accepted the message from Jacques. He broke the familiar seal, and forced his features to assume a mask of calm as he read. He managed to hide his reaction, though it was hard to contain the growing excitement as details fell more into place with every word.

"What?" Diane asked when he handed the paper back to Jacques. "What's going on?" she wanted to know as Jacques read. She slipped out of bed and put on her chemise. She put her hand on his arm. "Simon?"

"Is everything prepared?" Simon asked the wizard.

Jacques tucked the vellum back into his sleeve. "As ready as I can manage. When do we leave for the Dragonstone?"

Simon moved back a step, stretched and rolled his shoulders. He was not looking forward to donning his chain mail. "Within the hour."

"May the gods, new and old, be with us, my friend," Jacques said, and hurried from the room.

"You're coming with us," Simon told Diane before she could ask any more questions. "Dress warmly."

She put her hands on her hips. "What is this all about? Where are we going?"

Home, or to hell, he thought.

He took her into his arms. She tried to push him away. "Are you going to explain—"

"No."

"But—"

"Come to me, Diane."

She resisted his embrace, but didn't deny him the kiss he needed. He stroked her body beneath its thin linen covering until his fingers found the hard tips of her sweet little breasts once more. Soon, as desire built between them, her arms came around him. He knew he should not take the time for this, but he carried her to the bed anyway. This might well be the last chance they had to make love. Her fingers found the knot on his belt. He pushed her chemise up around her thighs. Moments later they were locked in reckless, relentless, driving passion.

Diane felt like she'd been riding a hurricane when they were done, or ridden by one, and didn't mind it at all. What was disconcerting was that Simon wanted her to get up and dressed, while all she wanted was to lie around and enjoy the languid afterglow from making love. He had immediately gotten up afterward, pulled the curtain closed behind him, and called Yves and his squire. Despite annoyed curiosity, she'd stubbornly stayed put while she listened to the familiar sounds of his being dressed for battle.

She didn't like this. Not one little bit.

"Diane," he said impatiently as he drew the bedcurtain all the way open. He was dressed in a dark surcoat over his mail. His long hair was pulled back and fastened at the nape of his neck. This made his features look starkly dangerous. "They're gone. You have to get up now."

The bed was warm, his scent lingered on the sheets and on her skin. She didn't want to think or to move. She especially didn't want to go off somewhere mysterious with him and Jacques. Somewhere outside the castle. She remembered the wizard mentioning something about the Dragonstone.

"What's Dragonstone?"

"A place near here."

"What kind of place? Why are we going there."

"We don't have time for me to explain."

"You just want me for a sex toy," she complained as she rolled onto her side. She propped her head up on her elbow, but before she could say anything else, he dumped a pile of clothing onto her head.

"Yes," he said. "And a traveling companion. Come along."

"But not a confidant."

Simon paused as he strapped on his swordbelt. "I'll tell you when we get there," he promised.

She got up. "I need a bath."

"No time."

She drummed her fingers on the mattress, then decided that she might as well get dressed. "So," she said when she'd put on three layers of woolen dresses and fastened a veil over her quickly braided hair, "who are we meeting at this Dragonstone?"

She put on her cape as he crossed the room. With one fierce tug he pulled her silk scarf down from over the mantle. Her stomach knotted with dread as he strode purposefully back to her, the silver embroidered material held out before him. His expression was solemn, as though he were performing a holy rite.

He carefully wrapped her in his dragon banner, fastened it over her cloak with a silver pin. She waited, frozen in place while he performed this symbolic gesture. Whatever it meant, it terrified her, almost as much as his next words.

"My son," he answered, and swept her out the door before she could draw breath to ask another, astonished, question.

32

"*Why?*"

It was a question he had often heard from Diane
before. Now it filled the silence as the sound of the wind
and the horses' hooves on the frozen earth could not. The
word hung in the air between them, colder and more pen-
etrating than the frosty air. They were not alone on the
road up the hillside. There was Jacques, of course, on his
fine white mare. Joscelin also, and Yves, and a few others
he trusted—people who put their trust in him absolutely.
These were the witnesses, and the ones he absolutely
would not leave behind, the ones he had bargained for in
his letter to his son. Their safety was almost as important
to him as Diane's. He was sure they must be wondering
what was happening, while his beloved Diane was the
only one with the courage enough to ask him why. Which
was why he placed her beside him on the last road they
would take together in this life.

"You always go against the order of things with that
word, my love." He smiled across the distance between
them. "Never stop."

Diane was terrified. She was furious. "You're going to
meet him, aren't you? Right now?"

"Yes."

"You're going to fight a duel?"

He nodded. "I've issued a challenge of sorts, yes."

This was ridiculous! It was awful. It was her worst nightmare. He was going to fight his son, and make her watch. She couldn't bear it. "I thought you were going to wait for spring!"

"I've changed my mind."

"You never change your mind about anything!"

"I've learned to," he answered. "You helped me." He reached over and snatched the reins from her hand before she could turn the horse. "You can't run from this," he told her. "None of us can."

"How can you do this?" The words came out as a piteous cry. "To me? To yourself?"

"I'm doing this for you," he answered her, voice soft but intense. "For us. And for once in my life, I am doing something for me."

Diane was frantic. She hadn't resigned herself to losing him, not in the spring, certainly not now. She knew it meant something for her to be with him, that it was important to him, but the symbolism was going to turn into sweat and blood and pain in a few minutes. Somebody was going to end up dead. Simon wasn't going to kill his own child, not even for her. She didn't want him to. And, once again, she was powerless in this alien land.

"I'm not going to watch you commit suicide."

His expression grew implacable. "Turn your head if you must when the time comes," he told her, "but you will be there."

"If that's all I can do, then I will."

"Fine."

They entered a clearing at the summit of the hill before Diane could think of anything else to say. It was a dark, sunless day, full of ominous shadows. A howling wind whipped the clouds overhead and the stripped branches of the trees that surrounded the bare circle of ground. A great, flat-topped boulder stood on one side of the clearing. On the other side, under a lone oak, another group of people waited. Diane recognized Vivienne standing beside a white horse. With her was a young man who looked like a dark version of Simon.

"Denis?" she asked, unnecessarily.

Simon nodded, and led his people over to the boulder. He could feel Diane trembling as he helped her down from her mount, as much with anger as fear, he knew. He didn't blame her. He touched her cheek. She flinched away when he would have kissed her.

"Trust me," he whispered.

"Don't get dead," was her fiercely whispered answer.

Jacques came up beside them. The old man gave one critical glance toward Vivienne, snorted with disgust, then announced, "I'm ready when you are, Simon."

Simon put Diane's hand in the wizard's. "Take care of her." Then he turned his attention to his son. He squared his shoulders, threw off his cloak, put his hand on the pommel of his sword, and strode toward the center of the clearing. He watched with outward calm while Denis shot a swift, nervous glance at Vivienne, then came forward to meet him.

Simon would not let himself think about how much he had missed the boy. He would not let himself be angry at Denis's betrayal and ambition. He would not let himself make excuses for his son, either. Yes, Denis had made bad choices based on the influence and examples of others, but those choices had been his. Diane had finally convinced Simon that everyone made their own choices, their own mistakes, and their own successes.

Denis spoke first when they were face to face, a sword's distance apart. "You look too healthy for my taste, old man," he said. "Your foreign bitch must suit you."

Simon saw the anger in his son's eyes, eyes that were

the image of his own in shape, but the same color as Genevieve's. He would not let himself be angry at the young man's ugly words. Though he was tempted to cuff the lad on the ear for being so hot with emotion before a battle. Hadn't the boy remembered anything of what he'd taught him?

"My lady suits me well," he answered. Only to receive a low growl from Denis in reply. "Before you reproach me with your mother," Simon went on, "kindly remember that she is a long time dead, through no fault of mine."

"Vivienne says—"

"She lies. You'd better learn to control her, lad, or you'll spend your whole life in thrall to one who is vowed to serve you."

Denis drew himself up proudly. "I didn't come here to listen to your advice."

"No," Simon agreed. "You came here to kill me."

"It's all I've wanted since you let my mother die!"

Simon nodded. "I know." He chuckled, and tilted a brow wryly at his son. "Why?"

Denis glowered. "What?"

"No. Why? It's a question I've been forced to consider a great deal lately. I thought I'd try it out on someone else for variety's sake."

Denis fidgeted with his swordbelt. "I didn't come here to talk. You issued this challenge, old man. Let's fight."

Simon took a step closer as he glared into his son's eyes. Denis flinched back a pace before he managed to hold his ground. "I'm not an old man," Simon told the younger man. "If I want to kill you, you will die. Don't doubt it, lad."

Denis drew his sword and rushed forward with a word- less shout. Simon sidestepped and drew only his dagger. He thrust the pommel of it hard into an unprotected spot at the base of Denis's throat as his son's momentum car- ried him past. Denis toppled, and Simon kicked his sword out of his hand.

When Denis was on his knees, choking, and trying to gather air into his lungs, Simon said, "How many times have I told you to keep your head down?"

Simon kept his own shock that victory had come so easily to himself. He hadn't been certain of victory when he came here. He hadn't been sure what would happen, which was why he hadn't explained his plan to Diane. He came here with hope, a hope too fragile to share, for fear of making her disappointment worse if he failed.

He barely heard the gasps and shouts of the people who watched. He did hear a woman scream. Since it was a sound laced with fury, he assumed it was Vivienne, and that Jacques's magic was keeping hers at bay. He concentrated on his son. Denis had obviously spent too much time playing the courtier since he left home. And trusted too much in the powers of his sorceress for his own good. Simon shook his head in disgust while Denis managed to look up at him from the ground.

"You better spend more time at fighting practice if you expect to keep Marbeau," he told his son.

Denis dragged in a great gasp of air and managed to croak, "What?"

"The question is why," Simon responded. He placed the tip of his dagger just under his son's nose, and pressed ever so gently. With that threat between them their gazes met. "I'm giving you your life, and your birthright a bit early, and you really should be wondering why. The thing is," Simon went on when Denis didn't speak. "I don't want it any more."

"Don't want—" Denis coughed. "Want—what?"

"Marbeau. It's yours. And you're welcome to all the trouble as well as the responsibility. Serve my people well," he added, "not that I can assure that you will this way any more than I could from the grave."

Denis blinked in confusion, then narrowed his eyes

suspiciously. "Marbeau? Mine? You brought me here to give me Marbeau?" Simon nodded. "Why?"

Simon laughed. He felt light as a feather. "I want to be happy," he told his son. And he was. Truly happy. He wished he could share this buoyant joy with Denis. "It's foolish I suppose, to prefer love over power, but that's the way of it for me. I'm going away. A long way away. The concerns of this world are no longer my affair."

"You—you're entering a monastery?"

Simon laughed again. "Diane wouldn't like that. Good-bye, son." He sheathed his dagger. "I love you."

Simon sprinted back toward his people without waiting for Denis's reaction.

Diane had nearly fainted when Simon was attacked, then nearly cheered when Simon disarmed his son. She managed to keep quiet through all of it because Jacques had warned her not to distract Simon, or to draw Vivienne's attention.

But when Simon ran up to her and grabbed her by the wrist, she couldn't keep quiet any longer. "What's happening?" she demanded. "What's going on?"

"We're leaving," he answered as he pulled her over to the boulder where Jacques was standing. He glanced questioningly at Jacques, who nodded.

"Stand just there," the wizard said. "Put your hands here."

Simon placed her hands, palms down, on the stone, then covered them with his own from behind. The stone was surprisingly warm, as warm as his living touch over hers as he circled her in his protective embrace.

"This is the Dragonstone," Jacques explained when she gave him a questioning look. "We have to call on its magic for the journey."

She looked back at Simon. "Journey? Where are we going?"

His eyes sparkled with laughter. "Seattle."

"What?"

"Why," he countered.

"Hush," Jacques said. "I've got work to do. Close your eyes," he added.

"Wh— ?"

"Just do it."

"Because I love you," Simon said, and got an annoyed look from Jacques. "I'll be quiet now."

Diane closed her eyes and leaned back against Simon. Jacques began to speak in a low voice. She didn't understand anything and didn't care. Simon was holding her, they were together. Everything else was details.

Jacques's words almost seemed to have weight and texture. The language was unfamiliar, but the sound of it was vast and deep and full of power. It was something to be listened to with your whole being.

At first she thought it was her imagination that the rock beneath her hands was growing warmer. She thought that her senses were alive, tingling with awareness, because of Simon's nearness. After a while, or maybe only a moment, she realized that there was something more going on around them. Something magical.

She could almost taste the magic. She could definitely feel it, like electricity flowing up out of the rock, through her, into Simon and back again. A circuit. A circle.

A spinning circle.

She grew dizzy. Though her eyes were closed and the earth was solid beneath her feet, the world began to whirl. Time began to tug at her, twist her into its forward flow. It was smooth, sweet. She felt like cream being stirred into dark, rich coffee, like a twist of caramel in chocolate. If she was cream and caramel, Simon was the coffee and chocolate. The imagery sent a wave of understanding joy through her.

Joy that was destroyed by sudden, hideous pain.

"Vivienne! No!"

The whirlwind turned into lava. She could feel herself melting into its blood-red flow.

"Leave my father alone!"

Simon's hands were torn from hers. She heard his cry of agony. She tried to claw her way back to him. She tried to call his name. It was too late. She was already caught in the spell.

"Let them go!"

Diane was drawn down, forward, into a volcano's mouth, through a long, burning tunnel. There was no escape.

Time flowed. She ran with it. Blind. Grieving.

Alone.

33

"*Hello?*"

"Diane?"

"What?" Where was she?

"Are you all right?"

She knew that voice. It seemed like she hadn't heard it in centuries. "Yeah, fine. Hi, Mom."

"You sound so depressed."

Diane blinked. She looked around. She could hear the shower running in the bathroom. The image on the television was frozen. It was an old black-and-white film. She must have paused the tape. Her eyes still burned from the intense flash of light. Everything seemed weird. Wrong. Out of place. The room seemed too bright. Too empty.

Something awful had happened.

She remembered the thunder, then lightning. The whole process had happened in reverse, like time running backward. Then—

What was she doing here?

She'd been standing in a clearing on the top of a wooded hill. She remembered the long, cold ride from the— "Stand just there," someone had said, and had placed her hand on a flat-topped boulder. "And don't move."

Then the world was torn apart. She reached out. Her hands closed on nothing. Then—

Then the phone rang and—

All was lost. Everything was gone. There was nothing to hope for after all.

Loneliness welled up in her, a dark, soul-crushing emptiness filled her. It was a physical pain. A wave. Like drowning. How had she gotten here? Why was she so alone?

"Are you coming?"

She grabbed onto her mother's voice. There was music in the background, wherever her mother was. Diane could make out a faint rumble of people talking, laughing. People who weren't alone. People who didn't know how futile it all was—or at least pretended not to.

Where had this horribly depressed mood come from? This was ridiculous. *Lighten up, Teal*, she commanded herself.

"Come where? Oh, the party. I don't know, I . . . "

"There's someone I want you to meet."

The firmness in her mother's voice told Diane that there was no way she was going to get out of this if she wanted peace in her family. She didn't want to meet anyone new. There was already some . . . some sort of weird dream, or something.

"Diane?"

She sighed. "I'm not sure I want to meet someone who plays lute for a living, Mom."

"He's a jazz musician," her mother reminded her. "The folk music is just a side project. Something new he's gotten into."

"Right, of course." She didn't care.

"Are you coming?"

Diane looked down and was surprised to see the silk skirt and tunic she was wearing. It was clean and fresh, sensually soft against her skin. For some reason, she remembered the shimmering ivory material as a mud-soaked ruin. She didn't remember when she'd put on the silk shawl wrapped around her shoulders. Weird. The dress getting destroyed must be something she'd dreamed.

She didn't recall when she'd had the dream, but bits of strange details about it were keeping her confused and unhappy. She was going to have to shake it off. Being around people might help. And she was dressed for the party.

"Is Dad going to be there?"

"Of course. Otherwise I might consider running off with the manager. He's *so* charming."

Diane was not used to hearing this sort of effusiveness from her mother. The cheerfulness made her own unexplained depression worse. She refrained from commenting and stuck to the subject. "Good. I want to talk to Dad about something."

Like maybe becoming an apprentice in the jewelry-making craft. She didn't know where the idea came from, but it seemed right. She was suddenly tired of watching movies all the time, with criticizing rather than creating things. She needed to *do* something. She had some artistic talent. When her father had tried to talk her into this before she'd scoffed at the idea, she'd said she wanted to be an *auteur* someday, whatever that meant.

"Darling, I have something more important in mind for you than talking to your father."

Diane didn't try to argue, though she had every intention of avoiding any attempts at matchmaking. "Yes, Mom."

"So get a move on. And bring your roommate. There's this cute roadie I want her to meet."

"Right. Fine. We'll be there. Cafe Sophie, right?"

Somehow, going to a party being held at an ex-mortuary seemed like an appropriate way to spend the rest of the evening.

* * *

Diane wanted to leave the moment she walked into the party. If Ellie hadn't pushed her into the crowd, determined to find the food, she might have. Everyone was smiling. She hated that. She didn't know why she resented everyone being so happy, but she did.

There was an undercurrent in the air, invisible but powerful, like electric perfume. Something sexy and exciting scintillated through the room, and everyone seemed to feel the buzz but her. The crowd that milled around the buffet tables was so cheerful that she wanted to kick someone. Instead she left her roommate to forage and went in search of her parents. She wanted to talk to her dad, and go home.

"I've got a headache," she muttered to herself as she skirted a knot of laughing people.

A tall, blond man was at the center of attention in this merry group. All the excitement was centered in this one spot. Diane wasn't interested in excitement. She noticed broad shoulders in an expensively tailored black jacket as she slid past him. She didn't pay him any more attention after she made a quick check to see that neither of the people she was looking for was near him.

"I hate everyone," she grumbled as she went on her way. "I want to cry. I'm bored and restless and lonely and sick of everything, and I don't know why."

"We French have a word for that," a deep voice said from behind her.

Diane froze in her tracks. There was something painfully familiar about that voice. It wasn't just deep, it was rich, like coffee or chocolate. Delicious. She turned around, very slowly, as he continued to speak.

"It's called *ennui*," he went on as their gazes met. Then he gave her a slow, charming smile.

Diane forgot to breathe for a moment.

He was tall, blond, handsome as sin, and sexy as the

same. He was so poised and confident that she hated him instantly. Besides, his beautiful voice was very familiar, yet disconcerting coming from a stranger. The sight of him made her heart race. It did more than that, it stirred desire. And something it would be safer to keep hidden deep in her mind if she wanted to stay sane.

"Did I ask you for a definition?" she snarled, and began to turn away.

He put a hand out, not quite touching her, but stopping her just the same. She looked down at his hand where it very nearly brushed against her arm. There was a small scar across two of his knuckles. He'd told her he'd gotten it in his very first battle.

This was crazy.

She would have run, but his voice held her still when she wanted to bolt. "I heard you ask why. I'm afraid I can never keep from answering a beautiful young woman who asks me why."

"I didn't ask—"

"Didn't you?" He stopped smiling. He moved his hand. This time he touched her, running his fingers along her jawline. "We've met before." He spoke quietly, his voice like dark velvet, but velvet that sheathed steel.

She couldn't deny it. "Somewhere."

"Where? When?"

He tilted his head to one side. It changed the way light and shadow played over his features, emphasizing the aristocratic arch of his nose and a slight sternness to his mouth. If there was anyone else besides them in the room, it didn't matter. In the background, beneath the murmur of voices, music played, jazz. The singer's voice was a rich baritone. He sang in English, with a hint of French accent. He sounded just the way the man before her spoke.

"Simon de Argent," she said. He nodded. Diane couldn't stop her fingers from tracing the outline of those sensual lips. She was filled with wonder. "Why?"

"You always ask me that."

"You never answer."

He smiled, and it filled her world. "I'm learning."

She smiled back. Her whole being smiled. She had never felt so happy before. "Who the hell are you?"

"I haven't the faintest idea," he replied, with that wry lift of the eyebrow she knew so well, and had never seen before. "But I seem to be rather famous and rich."

"How convenient," she said.

"I thought it might be," Jacques said as he came up beside them.

Diane turned her head, and was more surprised to see her mother on Jacques's arm than she was to see the wizard. "Did you cut your beard?" she asked the old man.

"Do you know Monsieur Pelliel?" her surprised mother asked.

Jacques kissed her mother's hand before Diane could answer, and gazed deep into her eyes. "Excuse us, my dear, but we have to have a little talk in private." He turned to Simon and Diane and put a hand on each of their shoulders. "Come along, you two."

Simon took her hand, and Diane found herself moving through the crowd. A handsome young man held up a champagne glass and smiled at her as she passed. "Joscelin?"

"I'd rather be called Jos," he answered, and turned back to Ellie.

Diane looked back at the proudly smiling Jacques. "But—? Who —?"

"Yves is around here somewhere," Simon said.

"That's nice."

"You do know all of us, don't you? The way we know you? The way I know you." His last words were spoken with jealous possessiveness. He squeezed her hand. "You're mine, Diane Teal."

She knew these men, or remembered, or imagined she

remembered knowing them. She was certain that deep in her soul she loved the one holding her hand.

"Here we are," Jacques said as he whisked them out onto the wet sidewalk.

The rain had stopped, but the air was full of cool, fresh moisture. More memories stirred as she took a deep breath. Memories, not imagination. They stopped beneath the glow of a street lamp. She and Simon grinned at each other. She slipped her arms around his waist. He took her face between his hands and tilted it up to the light.

"Now you two can get reacquainted in peace."

Diane's gaze slid sideways, toward the smiling old man. She'd forgotten that Jacques was even there for a moment. "What the—?"

"Oh, I forgot." He took a deep breath, held his arms out to the night, and spoke a magic word.

Everything came back in a rush, in a whirl, in a blinding flash of multicolored light. Past memories blended with current reality. It all made sense. It had really happened. Everything had worked out, and they were together once more.

Simon and Diane held each other in a tight embrace and laughed and laughed with delight.

"Damn, I do good work," Jacques announced proudly. He patted them both on the shoulder. "Have fun, children. I have to get back to the party." Then he was gone, and they didn't care.

"What happened?" she asked after they'd kissed for a very long time. "Back at the Dragonstone?"

"Vivienne tried to stop the spell." Simon threw back his head and laughed. "Apparently her interference only had a minimal effect." He held Diane close, where he intended to hold her forever. "Thank God."

"Denis stopped her," Diane said. "I remember now. I heard him."

"Did he?"

She looked up at him. "Your son loves you, Simon."

"Loved," Simon answered. A faint shadow of regret crossed his features. "That was a long time ago."

"But that was in another country," she told him.

He gave a faint smile as he remembered her saying those words to him in his chamber, back when she could only speak to tell stories. Back in the Middle Ages, when he was Lord of Marbeau. Even with the layer of knowledge of the modern world, and with the new identity that was also his, that time, the things they had done, held more reality for him. Marbeau was home. He would take her there. As soon as the American tour was over.

"I still own Marbeau," he told her. "I bought the tumbled down old estate and rebuilt it with the proceeds from my first two platinum albums."

"How did you end up a musician? A famous one? My father owns all of your CDs. That's why my mother was so happy to get involved in this lute project."

"Jacques arranged it all, of course. He slipped us into the world, made a place for us where everyone thought we'd always been. The only thing he failed at was bringing you with us." Simon frowned angrily. "Vivienne's doing, I'm sure. Fortunately her interference didn't last long."

"Thanks to Denis," she said. "I think it was his gift to you."

"A fair trade for Marbeau. He kept the land," Simon went on. "I've researched it. My family were lords of Marbeau until the unpleasantness in 1789."

"You mean the French Revolution?"

"Yes," the French aristocrat answered disdainfully. "That."

"Do you know what happened to Vivienne? She isn't going to pop up and—"

"No need to worry, my love." He stroked her hair. It seems Denis did marry the gentle Lady Marguerite—who sensibly poisoned Vivienne and settled down to live happily with her new husband."

"Good for her," Diane replied.

"Denis got what he wanted, and I got what I wanted, which is a second chance with you by my side."

"So it all worked out." She gave him a puzzled look. "But why did you end up a musician?"

"Why not? I vaguely recall Jacques telling me it's the only thing I have talent for in this time if I really wanted to retire from fighting. It suits my temperamental arrogance, don't you think?" He shook his head, almost in disbelief. "All that really happened. And everything from this life, as well. Jacques is right," he concluded. "He's good."

He kissed her again. When they were both breathless with desire, he said, "But you're better. You're pure magic, Diane," he told her. "I remembered you the instant I saw you."

She giggled. "Yeah. Right."

"I'm being poetic. Appreciate it."

"Let's go somewhere," she answered, with a wicked gleam in her big, dark eyes, "and I'll show you just how much I appreciate you."

"Make love?" he suggested. She nodded. He touched her cheek. "I want nothing better than to make love to you tonight. And every night forever after. Then," he added with a teasing smile, "I want to watch a tape of *Casablanca*. I've always wanted to see that movie."

She leaned her forehead against his chest and laughed until she was weak. Weak with love, and desire, and happiness. His arms stayed around her, and she knew that was where they'd always be. "I think I can arrange that," she told him. "This is, after all, the beginning of a beautiful friendship."

They began to walk away from the streetlight, away from the crowded cafe. The street was quiet, empty but for them, several long semitrailer trucks and a bus parked along the curb.

Diane read the lettering on the door of one of the truck cabs, then she gave Simon an amused look. "Is all that stuff really yours?"

He nodded. "Equipment, lights, what have you. For the Nine Dragons tour."

Diane chuckled. "Well, hon," she said as they walked off arm and arm into the night, "you never could pack light."

Let HarperMonogram
Sweep You Away

❦

SIREN'S SONG by Constance O'Banyon
Over Seven Million Copies of Her Books Are in Print!
Beautiful Dominique Charbonneau is determined to free her
brother, even if it means becoming a stowaway aboard Judah
Gallant's pirate ship. But Gallant is not the rogue he appears,
and Dominique is torn between duty and a love she might
never know again.

THE AUTUMN LORD by Susan Sizemore
A Time Travel Romance
Truth is stranger than fiction when '90s woman Diane Teal is
transported back to medieval France and must rely on the
protection of Baron Simon de Argent. She finds herself unable
to communicate except when telling stories. Fortunately she
and Simone both speak the language of love.

GHOST OF MY DREAMS by Angie Ray
RITA and Golden Heart Award-winning Author
Miss Mary Goodwin refuses to believe her fiancé's warnings that
Helsbury House is haunted—until the deceased Earl appears.
Will the passion of two young lovers overcome the ghost, or is he
actually a bit of a romantic himself?

A ROYAL VISIT by Rebecca Baldwin
An affair of state becomes an affair of the heart when Prince
Theodoric of Batavia travels to England to find a bride. He
is looking for a titled lady, but a resourceful and charming
merchant's daughter shows him that love can be found where one
least expects it.

And in case you missed last month's selections...
KISS ME, KATIE by Robin Lee Hatcher
Bestselling Author
When high-spirited suffragette Katie Jones takes a job at a local
Idaho newspaper with her childhood friend, Benjamin Rafferty,
she never expects love to be the top story. A warm and touching
romance from one of the most beloved Americana writers.

TEMPTING MISS PRISSY by Sharon Ihle
Award-winning Author
For Priscilla Stillbottom, working as a saloon singer in a Colorado mining town is hardly a fairy-tale existence—until handsome saloon owner Payton Cobb becomes her very own Prince Charming.

BLACKSTONE'S BRIDE by Teresa Southwick
Jarrod Blackstone is stunned when Abby Miller appears on his doorstep with his sister's orphaned children. But even more surprising—and thrilling—are the sparks that ignite between the rugged bachelor and the independent woman.

STEALING MIDNIGHT by Sonia Simone
Disguised as a highwayman, Darius Lovejoy happens upon Zoe Sommerville, a beautiful woman he believes can lead him to his prey. He steals her jewels, but she threatens to capture his heart.

Special Holiday Treat
CHRISTMAS ANGELS: THREE HEAVENLY ROMANCES by Debbie Macomber
Over Twelve Million Copies of Her Books Are in Print!
The angelic antics of Shirley, Goodness, and Mercy are featured in this collection that promises plenty of romance and dreams that come true.

MAIL TO: **HarperCollins Publishers**
P.O. Box 588 Dunmore, PA 18512-0588

Harper Monogram

Yes, please send me the books I have checked:

☐ *Siren's Song* by Constance O'Banyon 108228-7 .... $5.99 U.S./$7.99 Can.
☐ *The Autumn Lord* by Susan Sizemore 108208-2 .... $5.50 U.S./$7.50 Can.
☐ *Ghost of My Dreams* by Angie Ray 108380-1 .... $4.99 U.S./$5.99 Can.
☐ *A Royal Visit* by Rebecca Baldwin 108365-8 .... $4.50 U.S./$5.50 Can.
☐ *Kiss Me, Katie* by Robin Lee Hatcher 108388-7 .... $5.99 U.S./$7.99 Can.
☐ *Tempting Miss Prissy* by Sharon Ihle 108400-X .... $5.50 U.S./$7.50 Can.
☐ *Blackstone's Bride* by Teresa Southwick 108371-2 .... $4.99 U.S./$5.99 Can.
☐ *Stealing Midnight* by Sonia Simone 108458-1 .... $4.99 U.S./$5.99 Can.
☐ *Christmas Angels: Three Heavenly Romances* by Debbie Macomber
108690-8 (Trade Paperback) .... $12.00 U.S./$16.75 Can.

SUBTOTAL .... $_____
POSTAGE & HANDLING .... $_____
SALES TAX (Add applicable sales tax) .... $_____
TOTAL .... $_____

Name _____
Address _____
City _____ State _____ Zip _____

Order 4 or more titles and postage & handling is **FREE!** For orders of fewer than 4 books, please include $2.00 postage & handling. Allow up to 6 weeks for delivery. Remit in U.S. funds. Do not send cash. Valid in U.S. & Canada. Prices subject to change.   http://www.harpercollins.com/paperbacks   M04411

Visa & MasterCard holders—call 1-800-331-3761

CAPTIVATING AND HUMOROUS
HISTORICAL ROMANCE FROM
SUSAN SIZEMORE

Winner of the Romance Writers of America Golden Heart Award

AFTER THE STORM
When a time travel experiment goes awry, Libby Wolfe finds herself in medieval England and at the mercy of the dashing Bastien of Bale. A master of seduction, the handsome outlaw unleashes a passion in Libby that she finds hauntingly familiar.

IN MY DREAMS
In ninth-century Ireland, a beautiful young druid inadvertently casts a spell that brings a rebel from twentieth-century Los Angeles roaring back through time on his Harley Davidson. Sammy Bergen is so handsome that at first Brianna mistakes him for a god—but he is all too real.

NOTHING ELSE MATTERS
In the splendor of medieval Scotland, a well bred maiden is to marry a boorish young warrior. When tragedy strikes, the warrior's quest for revenge nearly tears them apart—until the lovers realize that nothing else matters once you have found the love of a lifetime.

MAIL TO: **HarperCollins Publishers**
P.O. Box 588 Dunmore, PA 18512-0588

Yes, please send me the books I have checked:

☐ After the Storm 108205-8 . . . .$5.50 U.S./ $6.50 Can.
☐ In My Dreams 108134-5 . . . .$4.99 U.S./ $5.99 Can.
☐ Nothing Else Matters 108207-4 . . . .$4.99 U.S./ $5.99 Can.

SUBTOTAL . . . .$_____
POSTAGE & HANDLING . . . .$_____
SALES TAX (Add applicable sales tax) . . . .$_____
TOTAL . . . .$_____

Name _____
Address _____
City _____ State _____ Zip _____

Order 4 or more titles and postage & handling is **FREE!** For orders of fewer than 4 books, please include $2.00 postage & handling. Allow up to 6 weeks for delivery. Remit in U.S. funds. Do not send cash. Valid in U.S. & Canada. Prices subject to change.   http://www.harpercollins.com/paperbacks   M04611

Visa & MasterCard holders—call 1-800-331-3761